Cyber Wars –
The Black Chamber

Michael Crawshaw

First published by BroadPen Books, St Albans,
Hertfordshire, UK, 2017

1

Dear Mom and Declin,

I'm writing this letter because I couldn't say what I wanted to over the phone. Words got stuck. Easier to write. I want to say I love you both so much. You were both always there for me even when I was a jerk.

Anyhow. We are flushing out Ramadi (second time round!). Lot of red on red doing the job for us. But Hajis hit us with Chlorine bombs yesterday. This is a big battle. We already sustained 10 casualties and one KIA.

I don't want you to worry about me. I'm not afraid to die. We all gotta go sometime. Maybe this isn't the greatest war. We all know a lot of armchair experts back in Fort Living Room are saying we shouldn't be here at all. Sometimes I wonder as well. But hey – Shut up and Color.

But if I don't come home for any reason …

Declin Lehane stopped reading. As he always did at that point. In any case, he couldn't see any longer with his eyes all filled up. He slipped the letter back in the drawer, slammed it shut and jumped to his feet. Three quick steps carried him across the floor to where George Bush hung from the ceiling.

A heavy right knocked George sideways. As he swung back Declin stopped him with a left then let rip. Left, right, hard, relentless.

Finally spent, Declin collapsed to the floor and watched George swing, in ever decreasing arcs. By the time the punch bag was still, Declin's eyes had filled up again. You didn't come home Josh. For no good reason.

2

'What the ...?'

The fracking crew stopped. Something was rattling inside the drill's metal casing.

'Doesn't sound good,' someone muttered.

Rex's mouth turned dry. 'What pressure we got?'

'Eighteen hundred.'

'Too high.' He radioed the pump room. 'We're reading eighteen hundred psi.'

'We've gotten fifteen here. You sure you're reading it right?'

Rex stepped over to the gauge. His eyes popped. 'Nearly nineteen hundred! Pull back the pumping. Now!'

'Reducing pressure ... that is, I ... this is kind of weird ...' The voice in the control room trailed off. Rex looked up at the white helmets conferring.

'What the hell is going on up there?'

'We can't reduce the pump pressure.'

'Why the hell not?'

'Commands aren't working. You want us to shut her down altogether?'

Rex wiped a salty forehead. The last time that happened they'd lost a million dollars and he'd lost his bonus. He looked away at the desert rock spires and buttes and wished he could go hide out there and leave the decision to someone else.

But the giant, metal rattlesnake stirred again. Louder. Suddenly the platform jumped and Rex was knocked off his feet. He looked up to see something blow out the top of the well head, soar through the air and crash in the dust a hundred yards away.

The site alarm screamed. The control room emptied faster than a church after Christmas service.

'Run!' someone shouted.

'Get the hell back here you sissies!' Rex shouted.

'The well is compromised. We've gotta get out of here.'

'We've got to make the well safe. That's what we have to do.'

Rex imagined the anti-frackers having a field day if the

Colorado river was contaminated with fracking fluid. But when he remembered the coffins of the two men killed by the rig explosion in Penn State he realized he couldn't ask his crew to risk their lives.

'Okay. Out! Everyone! Out!'

Rex waved them away. At the muster point he checked the headcount twice and when he was satisfied nobody had been left behind he hit the speed dial on his phone to the boss.

'He's in an important meeting,' his secretary explained.

'We got a compromised well,' said Rex. 'He'll want to know about this.'

'He gave me clear instructions he was not to be disturbed.'

Rex was about to protest when he saw the first responders arriving. He jogged back to where the yellow helmets were shuffling between their fire trucks and the river as they readied water supplies.

'I'm the Rig Manager,' Rex announced. 'You need any help?'

'Just keep yourself and your men well back. We'll handle it.'

Reluctantly, Rex wandered back to his men and found some welcome shade under a Tamarisk.

He should be up there with the fire crew. It was his rig. But, as he wondered what he could do to help, a flash of light brighter than the midday sun and a blast of heat body-slammed him against the tree. A thunder-crack broke overhead.

The hot air filled with dust. As it slowly cleared Rex discerned a glowing, orange column of cloud rising into a rolling, purple mushroom. Below it the well was on fire, surrounded by broken storage tanks and twisted pipes. The fire trucks and crew lay scattered like discarded toys.

Rex had pulled out his phone, thought about trying to get past the boss's secretary again and remembered his twitter account. He might as well break the news first.

'Emergency. Explosion at Cane Creek. Think all riggers safe but some of the fire-crew paid the ultimate sacrifice. #Heroes.'

* * *

Five thousand miles away in a secure warehouse in Dulwich, London, the Quadra Fund's filters picked up the tweet. One of a million from around the world that it parsed every minute, searching for key words that would trigger algorithmic computations in the ten-thousand qubit quantum computer.

3

The guy hanging around in the sharp suit was clearly out of place in the bustle of the fruit and vegetable market. He spent his time either on the phone or dodging the fork-lift drivers who seemed to be deliberately making his life difficult.

From the occasional glance in his direction, Mickey realized the suit was waiting for him. The head-hunter who'd rung earlier. Mickey shook his head. Hadn't he told the geezer, plain and simple, in words of two syllables, that he wasn't interested in what he had to say? What he was interested in, after hearing about the Hammers' injury list, was getting to a bookie – fast. He'd also noticed good odds for a well-bred horse allotted a basement mark for its handicap debut. So a few minutes shy of four o'clock he cashed up his till, packed and stacked the unsold vegetables and hurried for the market exit.

As Mickey drew close, the suit stuck out a hand and said in a Welsh accent: 'Evan Joiner. We spoke earlier.'

'We spoke but you didn't listen.'

'Unfortunately my client won't take no for an answer,' said Evan with a full-beam grin.

'Your problem not mine.'

'You're right of course.' Evan smiled, disarmingly. 'How are you enjoying a life trading vegetables instead of shares?'

'Loving it,' Mickey lied. 'And like I told you on the phone. I'm not going back to the City.'

'My client's office is in Mayfair, not the City.'

'Same difference. I'm done with playing Monopoly. I'm settled down. God Forbids and all that.'

'You have children?'

'Missus has one in the oven.'

'Congratulations. I guess you'll need to start thinking about school fees.'

'State education worked for me,' said Mickey, omitting the detail that he'd been expelled for fighting and left without qualifications.

'Of course you'll need a bigger house.'

'I'm planning to buy a farmhouse in Hertfordshire.'

'A farm won't come cheap?'

'A farm *house*. Not a farm.'

'Still be a million plus.'

'I've got it covered.'

That wasn't strictly true. Mickey had blown the deposit money on some dodgy bets and worse investments. But he'd make it back. His luck would turn eventually.

'I thought you left the City without any money,' said Evan, who had obviously done his homework. 'Rumor has it you left a twenty million pound bonus on the table.'

'I was insulted it was so little,' Mickey said, making light of what was still a painful episode. He'd not taken that lock-in payment, the pay-off for all those years of hard work, because his brother had tricked him into sharing it. How many times had he relived that stupid decision?

'So how will you afford a country farmhouse selling vegetables?'

'I'll have to sell a lot of veg,' said Mickey. 'Look, I know what you're doing. You're trying to convince me I need the money. But I don't.'

'Well, as I'm here,' said Evan. 'Can I tell you about it anyway? Just so I can tell my client I tried my best.'

Mickey hesitated. He was curious. But a part of him was frightened he might like what he heard.

'Go on,' he said eventually.

'Have you heard about the Quadra Fund?'

'One of these high-tech, high-frequency trading outfits.'

'So you keep in touch.'

'They're all over the papers. Fastest growing hedge fund in the City. Why does an outfit like that want an old-school trader like me? I can barely work my mobile.'

'Come in and have a chat and find out.'

Mickey caught his own reflection in a glass panel. Flecks of grey on top and in the stubble, sagging shoulders and a paunch under his apron. Hardly the City high-flier anymore. 'Answer the question. Why do they want me on board?'

Evan smiled. 'You are the old school, as you say. But you're still a big name. It will be a coup to get you to join. You'd persuade some of the more traditional managers to move money into the fund.'

Mickey wasn't sure whether to be flattered or insulted. 'What is this job exactly?'

'Anything.'

'Anything?'

Evan nodded. 'Within reason. They just want your name. So you could probably cut a nice deal. Part-time or non-exec. You might even be able to keep your market stall.'

It was an attractive offer. Too good to be true, surely. But Helen would never buy it.

'Thanks me old China, but no thanks.'

'How about you just come in and talk? Check out Cindy.' Evan winked, creepily.

'I'm more a Barbie type.'

'Well just come and see how the fund works. The power of the trading. The volume of information they sift. You'll be amazed.'

'It's a 'no'. Keep in touch with yourself.'

Evan pressed a card into Mickey's hand. 'Call me when you come to your senses.'

4

Washington had been fighting fresh snow when Declin left Ronald Reagan airport. Four hours south and sixty degrees rotation of the earth later it was pushing seventy in Houston. Through the cab window Declin admired the puffs of creamy cloud mirrored in the glassy skyscrapers of 'Space-City'. He smiled as he remembered the phone call that had sent him there. It had come in person from none other than Director Connelly himself.

How about that? The Head of the FBI calling Declin Lehane, in preference to a thousand other cyber agents, to investigate the possible hacking of Ryan Oil. The same dyslexic, disinterested Declin Lehane that teachers, other authorities and his mom had once agreed would amount to nothing.

As the cab pulled up outside Ryan Oil's concrete monolith headquarters, he pushed his fringe off his face and hoped Connelly's faith in him was not misplaced. Climbing out the cab he noted the shine had left his shoes and dusted them on the back of his calves. He followed Vin, the world-weary agent from the local field office, up the steps to the entrance.

'We're here to see Jack Ryan,' said Declin, passing over his badge to a receptionist. 'We're from the FBI.'

She smiled with big eyes as she issued him a security pass, and tried to discern the whole from the little that was showing of Declin's neck tattoo.

'It's the tree of life,' he volunteered.

She rolled up her sleeve to reveal a tattoo covering her arm.

'Owl and Sugar skull,' said Declin. 'Cool.'

She showed them to the elevators, where another receptionist picked them up and took them to a meeting room on the fifty third floor with a view of the glass and steel forest closing in. Declin thanked a waiter in a white jacket for a cup of coffee and a donut. The door opened and a posse of expensive suits and good leather filed in, made introductions and settled around the table.

At its head sat Jack Ryan, a double-sized man, who cleared his throat as the minute hand rose to twelve: 'There's only one thing on the agenda today and if you don't know what that is you shouldn't be here.'

A guy with thick blue glasses gave a report on the Cane Creek and Penn State well explosions. Declin made notes of the new vocabulary to check out later: clean burns, frack fluids, re-cap, rig rates.

A technician gave an explanation as to how the wells came to blow. Declin tuned in.

'We know both incidents occurred because the SCADA systems malfunctioned. That's the Supervisory Control and Data

Acquisition system. In other words the software. This caused the fracking pressure to rise higher than safe operational levels and the wells blew.'

'What caused the SCADA malfunction?' asked Jack Ryan. 'That's what we need to know.'

'The accident investigator is leaning towards the possibility that the software was corrupted deliberately.'

'You mean sabotage, right?' Jack Ryan turned to Vin, who he seemed to think was in charge. Must have been the grey hairs. 'That's why we called in the FBI.'

'Who manufactures the SCADA?' asked Declin.

'The Koreans,' replied Blue Glasses. 'Taekwa.'

'Do all your wells use Taekwa control software?'

'Around thirty percent.'

Declin didn't really feel as if it was his place to comment on how they ran their business, he'd spent ten years almost exclusively in the cyber world, but he'd heard no mention of shutdowns in the previous briefing. 'Have you shut down all those wells?'

Blue Glasses frowned. 'We haven't found problems anywhere else.'

'Don't you think it would be advisable to shut them down until we know for sure what's going on here?'

Blue Glasses turned to Jack Ryan.

Jack nodded his head. 'Agent Lehane is right. We should shut down the rigs using this faulty SCADA until we're sure they're safe.'

'Actually,' said Declin, unable to stop himself saying what seemed patently obvious, 'you should really shut down all your wells.'

Jack laughed. 'That's just not possible.'

'If this is sabotage,' Declin pressed, 'we can't yet be sure how deep the penetration lies. If they've done this to two of your wells they could have done it to any and all of them.'

'We'll check them.'

'Do that of course. But shut them down first.'

Jack Ryan pursed his lips, looked at a couple of people around the table. 'How long would the checks take?'

'If you put enough manpower on it I guess you can get the whole thing done in a matter of days.'

Jack pointed a fat finger at Declin. 'You mean, if *you* put enough manpower on it *you* can get the whole thing done in a matter of days.'

'The FBI won't be putting any manpower into the software checks,' said Declin, politely, non-confrontational, just matter of fact. Connelly had made that point clear.

'Why not?'

'That's your job.'

'And what's yours?'

'To solve the crime,' said Declin. 'If there is one.'

5

Mickey returned home to find Helen painting in the living room.

'You're home late. Again.'

'I popped into The Crown for a quick one after the market shut.'

Helen glanced at her watch. 'I'm glad it wasn't a slow one.' She set down her paints, sat back on the low stool and eyeballed him as if waiting for him to confess something.

'Good day?' he asked.

'You tell me.' She motioned for him to examine her picture. It was a still life of a pumpkin and cabbage.

Mickey didn't get why anyone would want a picture of a pumpkin and a cabbage but he told her he liked it and rubbed her tum. 'Everything all right in there?'

'She was kicking this morning.'

'She?'

'Just a feeling. How was your day?'

'The usual. Sold some cabbage. No pumpkins on my stall though.'

'So all's well? I mean in your mind.'

Mickey laughed. 'Well that's been messed up since I figured out Father Christmas couldn't fit down the chimney.'

'You're happy?'

'What are you getting at?'

Her shoulders dropped. 'You're gambling again, aren't you?'

'Why do you say that?'

'These late nights. Quick ones after work. In fact you're down the betting shop, aren't you?'

Mickey scratched the back of his neck. 'Sometimes. A bit. Only a bit.'

'Did you go there today after work?'

Mickey wasn't going to lie. No point. Helen could always tell. 'I did pop in, but it's not like it used to be. I'm not gambling. More like investing when I see a safe bet.'

'How much did you *invest*?'

'I had a little punt on a horse. It was its first handicap race you see …'

'How much?'

'Just a couple of hundred.'

'Two hundred pounds!' she shouted.

'Keep a lid on it. The neighbors complained last time you had a go at me.'

'To hell with the neighbors.' Helen threw a paint brush in a jar and the muddy water splattered onto the table. 'I'm saving every penny I can so we can put down the deposit on the farmhouse and you throw away two hundred pounds on a horse.'

'Look don't worry. It's all under control. It's not like before.'

'Prove it.'

'How?'

'Stop.'

'There's nothing to stop.'

Helen shook her head, looked back down at her painting, dabbed a fresh brush in some blue paste and stroked the canvas. She had gone into one of her submarine dives, silent running, and Mickey knew she wouldn't be resurfacing for hours.

'Well, unless you need me for a spot of nude modelling I'll leave you to it.'

He waited for a smile, but Helen didn't look up from the painting.

6

As they approached the Houston bureau's futuristic headquarters Vin explained that the external skin was made from heavily fritted green glass and, being almost opaque, it shaded the structure from the searing Texan sun and cut the air-conditioning bill in half.

'Green in both senses,' noted Declin.

'Thought you'd like that. You kids get all worked up about the environment.'

Declin figured Vin didn't share the sentiment but he didn't want an argument so he let it drop. They passed through the main entrance and security stiles, on towards the elevator, and both grabbed a coffee on the way to the cyber task force. As they entered the room everyone looked up expectantly, and with a shock Declin remembered that he was in charge. He drew himself up to his full six foot two inches.

'Hi. I'm Declin Lehane.'

Smiles and hands rose in acknowledgement.

Declin suspected they were expecting some big picture motivational clap trap. But that wasn't his style so he just cut to the chase.

'First pass on these Ryan Oil explosions suggests someone hacked inside the control software and increased the frack pump pressure until the wells blew. Prime suspects are anti-fracking protesters. We have a whole bunch of green blogs and websites chatting about it. I'll get strategic to check them out. I'll also get the field offices in Phoenix and Philadelphia to do trace-backs to find the server. The rest of the show is run by you guys. Director Connelly is taking a personal interest in this investigation so this is your chance to impress him.' He paused and looked at Vin.

'You know how the office works here. Can you appoint the usual tasks?'

'Our usual may not be the same as your usual. What do you want specifically?'

Declin caught a couple of smiles out of the corner of his eye and realized they were testing out how green he was.

'We need to trace Ryan Oil phone records and email traffic.

Update security checks on staff and security clearances for recent visitors. Check for signs of unauthorized access to property and equipment …'

Declin went on to cover every angle the investigation needed to take. By the end of it he got the feeling he'd won over the doubters. Including himself.

7

Mickey's horse was a short head in front as it came to the final jump. It hit the fence heavily and by the time the jockey recovered the horse was placed third and, being a flat-track bully that could only run well from the front, it went backward through the final furlong and finished out of the money.

Mickey sighed, tore up his betting slip and dropped it in an empty pint glass. He was wondering about getting another drink when a blast from the past entered the gloom of the pub. Mickey waved him over and shook his hand.

'Well if it ain't DI Frank Brighouse. Yorkshire's very own Sherlock Holmes. What are you doing out 'ere?'

'I'm looking for you,' said Frank.

Mickey raised his hands in the air. 'I was down the boozer with a dozen witnesses.'

'Don't worry. I'm just after a little chat.'

Mickey held up his empty glass. 'Good timing.'

Frank fetched two pints and set them down on the unstable table.

Mickey raised his glass to eye level. 'Your health and my good fortune.'

'Cheers,' replied Frank. He carefully took a sip and mopped up the spill from his drink with a beer mat before folding and placing it under the short leg of the table to set it straight. 'How's life in the vegetable market?'

'It has its moments.'

'No regrets leaving the City?'

'Never look back. Ain't that what they say?' Mickey studied the card Frank had given him. 'City of London Police, Economic Crime Directorate. Get you! That's the fraud squad, in old money?'

Frank nodded and took another sip of his drink.

'So what do you want to see me about? I'm guessing this ain't a social.'

Frank glanced over both shoulders. 'What do you know about the Quadra Fund?'

Mickey wondered at the coincidence of two people in as many days approaching him about the same outfit.

'It's a high-frequency quant fund. Top quartile performance.'

'Are you surprised at how good the performance is?'

'I don't understand all this computer algorithms malarkey. In my day we just bought low and sold high. It's a lot more complicated than that now.'

'There's some think their performance is helped by insider trading.'

Mickey shrugged. 'Probably. Everyone's at it.'

'You think that's all right?'

'It's just getting information first. The inside track. Where's the harm?'

'It's illegal. And we've got dozens of suspicious trade reports on the Quadra Fund.'

'And you've checked them out and found nothing.'

'What makes you say that?'

'You wouldn't be here otherwise.'

Frank nodded. 'How well do you know the Quadra Fund owner, Crispin?'

'Not well. Keeps a low profile.'

'Very low,' said Frank. 'Never given an interview. He owns the copyright to every photo ever taken of him. The fund has no website and the office has no nameplate. It's structured out of the Cayman Islands so we don't know who invests in it. Why so secretive?'

'Crispin is a bit of an iron fender. Don't bother me but maybe he keeps out of the limelight because of that.' Mickey looked down at his empty beer glass and checked his watch. If he didn't get back home soon Helen would think he'd been out gambling. Which of course he had. But she didn't need to know.

'Why are you asking me all this anyway?'

'I want you to go work for the Quadra Fund.'

'What?'

'While you're there you can sniff around from the inside and see what they're up to.'

'You want me to be a grass!'

'If there is anything to grass on. If it's all legit, no harm done.'

'What makes you think they'd want me to work for them?'

'Your friend Evan.'

Mickey raised an eyebrow. 'Have you been following him?'

Frank didn't answer. 'So how about it?' he asked instead. 'Take up the job offer. Earn yourself a little money and do the public a service at the same time.'

Mickey scratched his chin. The money would come in handy and Helen might even allow it if he said he was working for the police. But he wasn't a narc.

'Sorry, but it's a 'no',' he said for the second time that day.

8

A sonic boom sailed for several minutes over deserted tundra before rattling roofs, windows and the inhabitants of Fairbanks from their small hours' slumber.

Akna sat bolt upright in bed and re-booted her brain. There had been some sort of explosion. In the grey dusk she shook her husband's shoulder. He grunted and rolled over, comatose with whiskey.

She slid out of bed, pulled up the blind and opened the window. There was no sign of distress in the empty streets. But from the distant pump station a siren cried. Her curiosity aroused, Akna dressed quickly, slipped into her HUGs and Parka, grabbed her camera and phone, and ventured out into the steady cool breeze blowing in from the Alaskan ice pack. She shuffled over to the Cherokee. The cold engine took three attempts to get started.

On CB channel nineteen there was silence for a few minutes and

Akna sat patiently watching the sunrise light up the grassy tundra. The stillness was eventually broken by a state trooper.

'Calling any early birds out there, we had some sort of explosion at zero five fifty hours. Anyone got anything to report on that?'

Various people offered up the unhelpful observation that they had heard something but had no idea what it could have been. That of course didn't stop them speculating: a bomb, an airplane crash, a rig explosion …

'This is Tommo in pipeline security,' a voice interrupted. 'I think it was The Snake.'

Akna knew he meant the Trans Alaskan pipeline that had been given the nickname because of the winding structure that allowed it to contract and retract with the large temperature changes experienced throughout the year in the Arctic Circle.

'Go ahead, Tommo,' said the trooper.

'We're recording a drop in pressure in the pipe. It dropped off right around zero-five-fifty hours. So we're probably looking at a leak. A major leak looking at the drop in pressure. Too much of a coincidence for them not to be connected.'

'Where's the leak at?'

'Somewhere between pump stations one and two. Can't say closer than that at this stage. We're checking now, but could sure do with help from anyone who spots anything.'

Akna slipped the Cherokee into drive and pulled away. As she started on down the highway she saw red flashing lights in her mirror and pulled over to let two fire trucks overtake. She raced after them, as fast as she dared push the jeep on the slippery gravel track. A helicopter shuddered overhead and raced after the fire trucks.

Suddenly she remembered that she would lose mobile signal a few miles from town. And although she wanted to get her facts straight for her blog, she knew it was more important to be the first to break the news. She pulled over and tweeted:

This is the Green Inuit: Hearing reports of a major explosion and spill in the far northern section of the Trans Alaskan pipeline. Right in the path of the migrating central

caribou herd. And President Topps wants us to let Ryan
Oil go into the Arctic Wildlife Reserve and do the same to
the porcupine herd? No way! #keepRyanOilout

* * *

The Quadra Fund's computers parsed the tweet and, nanoseconds
later, programming triggered orders to sell shares in Ryan Oil, a
basket of other oil transportation companies and the company
that insured the pipeline, and to buy oil price futures.

* * *

Akna drove quickly but carefully along the muddy red scar that
is the Dalton Highway. Running parallel was another scar on the
landscape; the shiny, metallic, twisting Snake. Both ran away to the
horizon and neither had been there when Akna's grandfather had
hunted on that wild tundra.

She sighed at memories of a better world. Her spirits lightened
at the sight of a golden eagle, a reminder that her native world
had not yet fully disappeared, even if the bird was looking for easy
road-kill instead of hunting new born caribou calves as nature had
designed.

Beyond the eagle and over the horizon she realized the darkening
sky was not the raincloud she had first thought but billowy smoke.

The chatter on the CB radio started again as the first crews began
arriving. Akna was forced to pull up short behind a hastily erected
road block. She grabbed her camera and phone and walked up to
the state trooper.

He raised a hand. 'You can't go any further.'

Akna knew there was no point in arguing. She set up her tripod,
focused the camera on the flaming orange source at the base of
the black cloud and snapped off some pictures. The pipeline had
exploded on one of the sections where it was laid underground so as
not to disturb migrating caribou. And the blast had created a crater
a hundred yards across. Akna was no expert but that suggested that
the force of the explosion must have been tremendous. The crater

was filling with oil and over one edge were the scattered remains of a caribou herd: cows, calves, yearlings and bulls, indiscriminately blown to pieces.

Others, that had either survived the blast or perhaps arrived after, wandered aimlessly around the flattened tundra, pestered by biting mosquitoes and oestrid flies. But they could not move on. Disorientated, they would now be unable to make the long trek south to paw at the ground lichens under the softer winter snow below the tree line. They would surely starve and the golden eagle would enjoy lazy pickings.

9

Declin had been instructed to take the call from Connelly on a secure line in a private room. It was the fourth call he'd taken from the Director of the FBI in forty-eight hours.

'These cyber attacks are on a higher level than anything we've seen before,' Connelly said, his quicker than usual Boston brogue betraying his anxiety. 'These are major attacks on our energy industry. Billions in damages. And multiple deaths. It doesn't matter who's behind this, it will be an institution that takes the bullet. Maybe Ryan Oil, maybe Homeland, maybe the Telcos, but we sure as hell need to make sure it isn't the Bureau.'

'I don't see how we can be blamed,' said Declin.

'Ryan Oil are already suggesting we're at fault.'

'How do they figure that out?'

'They say they called you in to solve the cyber attacks on the fracking wells and you let them get hit again on the pipeline.'

'I advised them to shut down their drilling wells. They were pretty reluctant to even do that. I wasn't to know the pipeline would be attacked.'

'They think you should have known. Why didn't you advise them to raise their cyber defences across the piece?'

Declin didn't want to get into a shouting match. He remembered his counselling and took a deep breath and counted to three. 'I advised Jack Ryan that cyber defence was his responsibility.'

'I want to see evidence of that. I need clear-cut evidence we advised them appropriately.'

'I'll get you it.'

'And you are confident you can crack this case, Declin?'

'Of course,' Declin replied with as much authority as he could muster.

'Well, it sure would be appreciated if you could get someone under arrest.'

Connelly cut the call and Declin walked quickly back to the operations room.

'What did our great leader want?' asked Vin.

Other heads lifted up from behind their screens.

'Just checking progress,' replied Declin.

'We must either be doing something very right or very wrong if Connelly is taking a personal interest.'

'I guess so,' said Declin evasively. He nodded towards the main screen, which was showing the news headlines.

Top of the bill was a report from the Alaskan pipeline. A news-woman buried in all-weather gear was indicating the mess of metal seeping oil over the snow. She explained that fears of further cyber attacks had led authorities to shut down all oil pipelines in the country. This coming on top of the fracking well shutdowns had sent US energy prices through the roof. The picture switched to queues forming outside gas stations.

'Can you believe this crap?' said Declin. 'We're trying to keep everyone calm but the news channels are panicking the country into a full blown energy crisis.'

'It's all over social media as well,' said Vin. 'The advice is to fill the car with gas and a jerry-can as well.'

Declin was beginning to understand Connelly's concern. The population at large was growing angry. When that happened, reason went out the window. They didn't always accept the simple explanation. Nine-eleven: not the work of Islamic crazies, it was a CIA intelligence failure. Columbine massacre: not the work of an unhinged low life, it was the failings of the National Rifle Association. New Orleans: not the hand of God, a failure of the environmental agencies.

He remembered Connelly's instructions and turned to Vin. 'I need you to write down your recollection of the advice we gave Ryan Oil on cyber defence. And get someone to gather all the generic cyber advice we gave the company over the years.'

'What's this about?'

'Connelly wants us to cover our backside,' explained Declin. 'In case Ryan Oil blame us for failing to protect them.'

'That's crazy.'

'That's what I said. But we need to do it. Dig out all industry communiqués, advisories, email traffic and whatever else you can find to show that the Bureau has, on multiple occasions, advised Ryan Oil to raise its cyber defences.'

Vin shuffled his weight from one foot to the other. 'I don't like the way this is heading.'

'Me neither,' said Declin.

10

Mickey paused in front of the unmarked doorway and checked his watch. Five minutes late because of the traffic, but nothing to be done about that now. He pressed the intercom.

'How can I help?' a voice crackled.

'Mickey Summer. I'm here to see Cindy.'

'Come through.'

The door buzzed. He pushed it in and walked through to a security desk. The guard scanned Mickey's driving licence, ran an electronic wand up and down his body and frisked him thoroughly.

He motioned Mickey into an elevator waiting with doors open. 'Someone will meet you on the fourth floor.'

Mickey straightened his tie as he rode the elevator up. It felt odd to be in a suit again. The door opened on a young woman with hazel skin and brown oval eyes. She seemed to be deliberately dressing down, with her dark hair pulled back, thick-rimmed spectacles and no war paint. He caught a whiff of cinnamon as she introduced herself as Cindy. They exchanged pleasantries and she led him to a meeting room.

'Thank you for coming in to see me,' she said, as soon as she had sat down. 'Let me tell you what we're doing here at Quadra. We've built a system that combines some of the smartest brains with one of the most powerful computing systems in Wall Street or the City.

'We look for major market events. Black Swans or Dragon Kings. We only invest once they've happened but we're so far ahead in our information gathering, our analysis and interpretation that we are able to fully invest before the market has time to react. This has delivered top quartile performance for seven quarters in a row. Year to date, the fund is up one hundred and fifty percent.'

'Wish you'd told me that on January first,' said Mickey.

She smiled, though only to the edge of her mouth. 'Would you like me to show you round?'

'Sure. Let's have a butcher's.'

Cindy started with a room full of computer analysts.

'The team here are constantly researching and writing new algorithms to predict the performance of relevant securities and instruments after a particular trigger event.'

'A trigger such as what?'

'Such as those explosions at Ryan Oil in the US.'

'You saw them coming?' asked Mickey.

'Accidents happen all the time in the energy industry. Our programmers model what happened in historic accidents such as the Gulf of Mexico disaster. We model the share price movement in the companies involved, their competitors, the operator of the rig or power station, the insurer that would be hit by claims, the oil price, spot rates for electricity and so on and so on.'

'And then you wait for something to blow,' said Mickey.

'We listen. We need to get the news first, before share prices have moved. In a legal and compliant fashion of course. We use publicly available sources. All the conventional news channels but also online newspapers, blogs and tweets. Even if we don't always get the news first we still have an advantage. Because of all the work we've already done we react first, before the market has thought about the impact. We've already done the thinking.'

Mickey was impressed. 'So how much money have you made off the back of the Ryan Oil accidents?'

Cindy hesitated before pulling up a computer terminal. She tapped a ditty on the keyboard. 'Around fifty million pounds. It's gone well for us.'

'Not so well for the guys who died on the rig.'

'No,' she said, her eyes narrowing.

'Isn't it a bit weird investing like that? Chasing ambulances.'

'We don't only react to accidents. We also pre-empt. So, for example, right now we're all over this crisis in the South China Sea.'

Mickey had read an article in the Financial Times about the Chinese squabbling with its neighbors over various uninhabited rocks. Although he didn't work in the markets any more, he still took an interest. But he couldn't see how it would make for an investable event.

'How do you mean, you're 'all over' it?'

'We're monitoring every news and data feed we can to see if we can get an edge. We've spotted that China has been stockpiling oil for its strategic petroleum reserve at a record pace and it's been boosting output of refined products such as jet fuel and diesel. What does that tell you?'

'That it's hoping its economy will recover?' suggested Mickey.

'That it's preparing for war,' said Cindy. 'This is why our fund is long of oil and gold. Pre-emptively.'

'So you target accidents and predict war,' said Mickey.

'And peace,' said Cindy. 'We're programmed and ready to invest in infrastructure companies just as soon as we get indications that the Islamic State is going to be defeated.'

'Don't hold your breath.'

'We're very patient. We take a long view. And we're only interested in major events. Most funds spend too much time and brain power worrying about small price movements and arbitrage.'

'Do the staff have skin in the game?' asked Mickey, who was getting the itch again. It certainly seemed more fun than selling vegetables. And he had been good at it.

'Every employee is invested in the fund,' she explained before taking him on a tour of the hardware. A room purring with rows of computers stacked up to the ceiling.

'That's more computing power than NASA,' suggested Mickey.

'This is only a fraction of what we have. The rest is in a warehouse in Dulwich.'

'Cheaper rent than the West End.'

'Precisely. And it serves as disaster recovery.'

Leading away from the computer stack was a thick pipe that Cindy explained housed the fibre optic cables carrying trading instructions to stock exchanges around the world. It was a far cry from the City Mickey had joined as a post boy, when information was carried at the speed of shoe leather.

With the tour finished, they returned to the meeting room.

'So what do you think of the set up?'

'Impressive.'

Cindy smiled. 'So might you like to come on board?'

'I still don't get what you need me for?'

'It's Crispin's idea,' she said, with a distance that suggested she didn't necessarily approve. 'He'd like you to sell the fund to parts of the investment community that we haven't been able to reach.'

'The old school?'

'If that's how you'd like to put it. You're still very well connected. And you have a reputation for integrity that would help our image.'

'Do you have an image problem?'

Cindy crossed her hands and set them firmly on the table. 'We have been losing investors because of an erroneous investigation by the police into insider dealing. It's utter nonsense. They've found nothing because there is nothing to find.' She turned her palms up to the ceiling as if to prove the point. 'But the damage was done. Some investors got nervous and withdrew funds. We need to win back money.'

'Are you talking about a full-time role?'

'Hours to suit.'

'And what are you paying?'

'Point one percent commission on new monies brought in.'

Mickey rattled through a few possible and probable investors.

22

With good luck and a following wind he might be able to pull in a few hundred million pounds, so his cut would be a few hundred thousand quid. That would go a long way towards the house. But what if he couldn't sell the fund? What with all the bad publicity. He decided he needed some insurance. 'I'd want a signing-on bonus as a gesture of goodwill.'

'What would you be looking for?'

'A hundred grand.'

'That's a lot of money.'

'It ain't worth getting out of bed for anything less.'

Cindy smiled. 'We don't mind if you sell from your bed.'

'Wouldn't be the first time.'

Cindy mulled something over in her mind. 'That won't be a problem. So, do we have a deal?'

Mickey realized the palms of his hands felt wet. He wiped them on his knees under the table. 'I'll give it some thought.'

11

Declin's team had made good progress. They had shown that the malware used in the cyber attack on the pipeline was a derivative of those used in the attacks on the rigs. All had a common source file and all three used the same Visual Studio packer, which, although not unusual, suggested they had been made by the same developer. Field offices in Phoenix and Philadelphia had trace-backed all three attacks to the same server in Ohio. And a whole string of incriminating communications pointed to a group called Earth Defence.

Declin rang the local sheriff.

'What do you know about this Earth Defence outfit?'

'Self-styled eco-warriors,' said the sheriff.

'Previous?'

'Did a year in prison for turning off a safety valve on the oil sands pipeline. Fined for blocking an oil train near Seattle. Plus various misdemeanors, infractions, traffic violations.'

'Any cyber?'

'Not that we know of,' said the sheriff. 'But the group is led by a Doctor Kesling who studied cyber at MIT.'

'Interesting,' agreed Declin, though of course, like the communications they'd intercepted, that was only circumstantial. 'Have you got them under surveillance?'

'Just got the authority.'

'Don't do anything until I get there.'

'You're coming up? We do know how to carry out surveillance.'

'What we're needing is cyber forensics more than human surveillance. So I'll be using a cyber team from the Bureau. You can reach me on my cell phone or in their offices on Ronald Reagan Street, Cincinnati.'

'I do know where the Bureau's offices are.'

'Great. Meet me there tomorrow.'

Declin set down the phone and picked his jacket off the back of the chair.

'Do you really think you need to go up to Ohio?' asked Vin.

'I do. And you're coming with me.'

* * *

The Special Agent in charge of the Cincinnati office seemed as aggrieved as the sheriff that the young kid from Washington wanted to call the shots. But Declin didn't have time for repairing nose joints.

'You either play hospitable and give me what I need or I call Director Connelly and get him to ball you out over the phone. Your call.'

Reluctantly, he gave Declin the resources he needed. And by the end of his first day in Cincinnati, Declin was satisfied that between the Bureau and the local sheriff's office they had eyes on everyone and were monitoring all communications going in and out of the Earth Defence compound. Now all they had to do was be patient and gather up the incriminating evidence that was sure to come.

It had been a long day and Declin had just decided to head back to the airport hotel when he was told he had a call from Connelly waiting for him in a private room.

24

'Why didn't you call?' asked Connelly.

'There hasn't really been anything to report, Sir.'

'Why not? What are you doing about Earth Defence?'

'We've got them under surveillance …'

'Under surveillance? How about getting them under arrest?'

'We're still gathering evidence.'

'You've got incriminating communications. Get in there and bust the place open.'

Declin hesitated. 'I like to play things long, Sir. Get eyes on everyone, find all accomplices, make sure every base is covered before moving in.'

'We don't have the luxury of time. Ryan Oil is threatening to sue. The press are accusing us of incompetence. And now I've got Asimov on my case.'

Karl Asimov, the Director of National Intelligence, was one of Connelly's reports, and it was no great surprise to Declin that he was putting pressure on Connelly to clear this mess up before it landed at his own feet. Asimov's nickname in the Bureau was 'black box', because no matter how bad the incident or scandal surrounding him, and there had been many, he could work Washington so well that his reputation always survived intact.

'What does Asimov suggest we do?' asked Declin.

'Get someone in cuffs,' replied Connelly. 'ASAP.'

'So you're ordering me to go in?'

'That is precisely what I am doing. And make sure you have plenty of press accompanying you.'

12

Frank was not looking forward to the afternoon meeting with the review panel. In theory, its four wise men and one woman were there to help with Frank's investigation; to help him see, from the lofty height of experience, the wood for the trees. But Frank knew full well they had the axe sharpened to chop the whole thing down. His investigation into the Quadra Fund was over budget, running high litigation risk and, even he had to admit, going nowhere.

But he had to go into the meeting with a positive frame of mind. So at lunchtime he took a middling run to sharpen up; a steady-paced eight miles in gentle rain, from Canary Wharf, through the Isle of Dogs, under the Thames to Greenwich and back again. After a quick shower he put on a clean shirt, conservative plain blue tie and walked the short distance to the glassy offices of the Financial Conduct Authority on North Colonnade, arriving a perfect five minutes early.

He read some promo literature in the hope it might throw up some useful insight that he could use in the meeting. It didn't. Bang on the hour the meeting room door opened and the Super's head appeared.

'We're ready for you, Frank.'

Frank stood up tall and followed the Super into the room. He took the empty seat facing the long bench behind which the panel sat, shuffling papers. The Super made the introductions. The Chair looked at Frank over the top of his half-moon specs and asked for an update on the investigation.

Frank read from his notes. Partly to make sure he said the right things, but also to avert his eyes from the Chair's unsympathetic gaze.

'Let me summarize what's been tried so far,' said the Chair, when Frank had finished. 'You started with a part one RIPA for non-intrusive surveillance, and you used that to check all employee phone records and email traffic without finding anything suspicious. Then ...'

'That's not right,' interrupted Frank. 'There were plenty of things that looked suspicious, just nothing that we could escalate.'

'You found nothing that could be used in a court. Next, after a rather dubious interpretation of the financial terrorism legislation, you obtained a warrant to search the premises. You found nothing untoward. You interviewed every employee and this also yielded nothing.'

'We found evidence that the fund makes financial gains by systematically trading on information ahead of other market participants.'

'But information that it had gleaned perfectly legally,' said the

Chair.

'Legal at present,' said Frank.

'We have to deal with present law, DI Brighouse. And present law says there is nothing wrong with what the Quadra Fund is doing. Am I correct?'

Frank conceded the point with a curt nod of his head.

'What about your plan to get a man on the inside?' asked the Super, throwing out a lifeline.

'I'm still working on that, Sir.'

'Is this an undercover officer?' asked the lady.

'Member of the public, ma'am.'

'Who has agreed to work for us?' she queried.

'He's considering it.'

The Chair blew out in exaggerated fashion and folded his hands. 'It's clear to me that since we last reviewed the case you haven't made progress on any front.'

'We're learning more all the time,' said Frank. 'In fact …'

'Meanwhile your enquiry,' he continued, 'which has at times been very visible, has damaged the image of the Quadra Fund and deterred investors. The Fund has threatened to sue.'

'We can't be put off by the threat of legal action.'

'We most certainly can,' snapped the Chair, looking around at the other members of the panel. 'Any further questions?'

Three heads shook from side to side. Frank's eyes pleaded with the Super. But eventually he also shook his head.

'Well,' said the Chair. 'I'm satisfied that the risk reward balance here is out of kilter.'

'Give me one more month,' Frank pleaded.

'You've wasted twelve already. This investigation is finished.'

13

Turning off Interstate Seventy and swapping tarmac for gravel, the convoy maintained a steady fifty as it wound through a forest of redbud and dogwood.

The panel screen in front of Declin showed a mile to the target.

He looked up at the Domestic Terrorism Unit in the open back of the SUV ahead. Decked in green fatigues, body armor and helmets, fingering the assault rifles standing between their legs. One said a prayer and Declin immediately thought of Josh.

Josh had not been a regular church-goer, but he was always praying for this and that. Didn't do him any good in Iraq. Declin shook himself back to the present and checked his own standard-issue Glock, again. Surveillance suggested there wouldn't be trouble. He hoped not, for the sake of Doctor Kesling and his friends, because there could be only one winning side.

Five-hundred yards to go and a squad car peeled off to set up a road block.

'Twenty seconds to target!' The commander called in Declin's earpiece.

The agents in front braced as a low building came into view. The lead vehicle shuddered to a dusty halt and a team piled out and ran up the front steps.

Three heavy knocks on the wooden door. 'Open up!'

An agent started up a chainsaw mounted underneath his rifle, waited perhaps a second and plunged it into the door. It screamed in protest but splintered readily. The assault team ran through the hole.

'Do not move!'

'Hands above your head!'

'Turn and face the wall!'

Other assault teams ran to check assorted outbuildings.

A helicopter buzzed over the solar-panelled roof.

Declin jumped at an explosion inside the main building. And a second.

'Stun grenades,' explained the driver.

A bloodhound sniffed up the steps and disappeared into the building. A further spell of screaming and shouting displaced men and women in various states of undress.

'Rack 'em and stack 'em!' shouted the commander.

The bloodhound reappeared and its handler announced that the main building was now secure. The commander waved Declin and the other non-assault agents inside.

'Nobody touch anything,' shouted Declin, as he located the router. The lights on it were static, indicating no network traffic, so he was comfortable pulling the telephone cable from the rear.

'Okay. Forensics, you're on. And don't forget to check computer cooling fans for dust and hairs.'

Declin supervised the take down. Every powered-off computer, laptop and cell phone was labelled and put in an anti-static bag. Those that were powered-on were left to run while agents took videos of the screen displays before switching them off and bagging them also. USB drives, games consoles and a Sat Nav were also labelled and removed together with notebooks, sticky labels and every scrap of paper that might contain a hidden password.

Declin took detailed photos and notes of all undertakings. Once he felt confident the crime scene was secure and evidence gathering under control, he studied the displays on the walls of the room: charts of global temperatures, sea-levels and carbon-dioxide concentrations, the ubiquitous poster of a polar bear on a tiny ice flow, newspaper clippings of green articles and freshly-pinned cuttings about the explosions at the fracking rigs and the Alaskan pipeline.

The commander came over to examine the wall with him. 'Dumbasses didn't make much of an attempt to hide their crime. This is a slam dunk.'

Declin said nothing. He had a worrying feeling it had all been a little too easy.

14

Mickey had three major reservations about the Quadra Fund. The police thought it was illegal, Cindy was as warm as a polar vortex and her boss was as visible as Elvis. But no job was perfect and ultimately he'd put pen to paper because of the easy money. Sticking his snout back in the trough for a hundred bags of sand before he had to actually do any work. He'd be crazy not to. Particularly with a little one on the way.

The first few days left Mickey feeling lost and confused. He hadn't worked on the buy side before and the City had changed so much in the few years he'd been out. He also felt awkward because he hadn't told Helen what he was up to. He hadn't lied. She just assumed he was working on the market. He'd tell her eventually if the job worked out but he was already thinking of staying only long enough to justify his signing on bonus, then doing a heave-ho. So no point in upsetting her.

But to justify a hundred grand he needed to pull in a hundred million of new money. That, he figured, was doable. The fund's figures spoke for themselves but needed to be able to explain what lay behind the stellar performance. Nobody trusted a black box. So over the days he closely examined the monthly data going back to the fund's conception.

It hadn't been plain sailing. The early years had been pretty poor. But more recent performance had been impressive. Despite the odd blip the fund managed to get several big calls right consistently enough to deliver solid, absolute gains irrespective of the underlying movements in markets. He looked at the detail of what had been bought and sold and read the investor reports to understand the rationale behind those decisions. It all made a lot of sense. He resolved to ring a few friendly clients after lunch, when they were less hassled and some of them nicely lubricated.

Perhaps Cindy had detected his growing enthusiasm, for she shocked him by inviting him out to an Italian Deli in a courtyard off Regent Street.

'Quick service and decent food,' she explained, as they took a table. 'How's your orientation going?'

'I'm impressed,' admitted Mickey. 'Performance has been consistently good. At least in the last few years. I guess there were teething problems before that.'

'Performance improved once I came on board,' she said, without false modesty.

'I thought Crispin made the big calls?'

'He does,' she agreed. 'But I put the processes in place. That's what made the difference.'

'I can see why the regulator is suspicious though,' said Mickey. 'You're so far ahead of the game it looks like you have inside information.'

'Precisely. Whereas all we are doing is acting on publicly available information that others have been too slow to evaluate.'

'Hats off to your computers,' said Mickey.

'Computers are just a tool,' said Cindy. 'It's the process. We don't just let the computers take random bets.'

'So what's the overall investment framework right now?'

'War and inflation,' said Cindy. 'Thanks to President Topps' infrastructure spending the US economy is heating up and now it's got these energy problems pushing up fuel prices as well. That's going to lead through to inflation. Global inflation. And with inflation you tend to get more conflict. Eastern Europe is tense, the Middle East and Africa are both a mess and now we have this escalating conflict in the South China Sea.'

'So buy gold?'

'Bingo.' Cindy smiled, and instantly looked a lot younger, and more attractive. She tried to settle the bill but Mickey insisted on going Dutch. They walked back to the office and Mickey wrapped his arms around his chest as a blustery wind blew around them.

'I might take a punt on gold myself,' he said.

'You can't. None of us can make individual trades. It's in your contract.'

'Where was that rule buried?'

'It's the same with most hedge funds, Mickey. What you can do is buy the fund. That's probably the smarter way to go in any case.'

'Is that what you do, Cindy?'

'Every penny I can save gets put in the fund,' she said. 'You should do the same with your signing-on bonus.'

Mickey tried to look accommodating. But he figured if he invested in the fund he'd probably only make a ten or twenty percent gain because the fund was diversified to lower risk. But if he just made a straight bet on gold futures … Well he could make out like a bandit.

Dr Kesling was tall and wiry, with long ginger hair and an overripe lower lip that seemed to sulk at the indignity of being under arrest. He folded himself into a chair and Declin did the interview formalities.

'So why don't we start by you telling us what you and Earth Defence have been doing in your camp,' suggested Declin.

'Saving your asses,' Kesling mumbled.

'From?' asked Declin.

'Frying to death.'

'Global warming?'

'You got it,' he said.

Declin sympathized with the ends but clearly not the means. He pulled three photos from a file and laid them out to face Kesling.

'Let me show you three people who fried to death already. These men were in the fire crew that responded to the explosion at the Cane Creek fracking rig. They won't be worrying about global warming now. Will they?'

'I guess not,' Kesling said.

'Their families won't be overly bothered about global warming either. Would you like to explain to them how you're saving their asses?'

Kesling folded his arms but said nothing.

'I've also got some photos of the dead fracking crew from the Penn State explosion. I'll spare you. Don't want to have to clean up when you are reunited with your last meal.'

Declin drum-rolled his fingers on the table while he waited for Kesling to regain eye contact.

'The first I knew about Penn State was when I saw it on the television.'

Declin shook his head. 'We traced the malware back to your computer.'

Kesling smiled. 'I know that is not true.'

'We know the attack came from your offices.'

'We have a lot of people pass through.'

Declin placed his hands flat on the table. 'You're a green

activist campaigning against oil companies and you have previous convictions. That gives you motive. You're a former MIT student of cyber techniques. That gives you means. We traced the malware back to your offices. That's method. You need to start working on a better defence than simple denial. Try full cooperation and I'll see if I can get you off with manslaughter.'

'I can't help you, kid. If you traced the malware back to our offices then, as I say, it must have been one of our many visitors. Or more likely we were hacked into ourselves and someone has used us as cover for their own attack.'

Declin prodded away at Kesling's defences for almost an hour without making headway. He decided to try a different tack. 'This was a zero-day malware. It certainly wasn't easy to write. I'd say it would need someone with your level of sophistication in computing, Dr Kesling.'

'Appreciate the compliment.'

'You're familiar with Stuxnet?'

Kesling shrugged nonchalantly.

Stupid question of course. The malware that the CIA had used to derail the Iranian nuclear enrichment program was infamous.

'So you know how Stuxnet can be manipulated for attacks such as these on the pressure in a rig or a pipeline.'

Kesling uncrossed his legs and sat forward in his chair. 'You'd switch the Siemens Win SCADA for whatever SCADA software is used in the rigs and pipeline.'

'Then what would you do?' asked Declin.

'Theoretically?'

'Theoretically.'

'Change the target from the programmable logic controllers the Iranians were using to the pumping valves in the rig or the pipeline. Steal some digital certificates and away you go.'

'Simple as that?'

'I wouldn't say it's simple.'

'But you admit you have the capability of writing this malware.'

'I'm getting tired of this.' Kesling turned to his attorney. 'I've answered the questions. Can I go now?'

'Are you going to charge my client?'

'Not just yet,' Declin admitted. 'We've only just started forensic work on all the equipment we seized from the compound. We'll find evidence. Then we'll bring charges.'

Declin showed Kesling and his attorney out and returned to the interview room.

Vin was head down making notes. 'Well there's no doubt he's our man.'

'I'm not so sure.'

'Are you crazy?' Vin stared at Declin. 'We know it's him.'

'Yes, he delivered the malware,' said Declin. 'But I'm not sure he wrote it.'

'He seemed pretty clued-up on all the technical stuff.'

'Timestamps in the malware suggest it was not written in American working hours.'

'So he worked the night shift.'

'Plus,' continued Declin. 'He didn't know about the root-kit module.'

'What root-kit module?'

'The worm had a sophisticated root-kit module to keep it hidden from firewalls. That was the clever part. He made no mention.'

'Perhaps he just forgot.'

'The type of people who write these worms don't just forget. He was happy to brag about his knowledge. Why miss that out?'

'Maybe he didn't want to incriminate himself fully.'

'Perhaps. But I also checked up his record at MIT. He didn't finish his doctorate. He's got as much right to call himself a doctor as George Clooney.'

16

'Wotcha!' Mickey called into the kitchen, as he pushed his shoes off his feet without undoing the laces and back-heeled them neatly into the shoe cupboard.

Helen didn't look up from the wok of garlic-smelling gunk she was stirring. Mickey hid his disappointment at the apparent lack of meat in the meal.

'Smells good,' he said.

Still she said nothing.

'Are you OK?' he asked.

Helen continued to stir the dish, silently.

Mickey ran through birthday and anniversary dates but judged he was in the clear. 'Something went wrong at work?'

'Where have you been today?' she asked, ignoring his question.

He knew better than to lie. 'I went into the City.'

'Why?

Mickey hesitated. 'I was checking out a hedge fund. Pretty good. I'm thinking of putting some money in it.'

'What money?'

'Some of the savings.'

'You mean the money we are setting aside for the house deposit? We do have a baby on the way. Do you remember that?'

'Course I do.'

'So act responsibly. Stop gambling away our savings.'

'I invested it.'

'In a high risk hedge fund?'

'Actually that's a misconception. Hedge funds get the name because they hedge the general market risk and …'

'Whatever.' She turned off the heat and set the wok on the light laminate work top. 'Is that all you did today? Just saw this 'safe' hedge fund?'

Mickey hesitated. He'd popped into the bookies to follow a lead he'd been given on a dog running at Harlow. But she couldn't know that. 'I drove into the City and back again. Couldn't face the Rubik's.'

'You didn't stop anywhere on the way?'

'Had to stop at red lights. Rude not to.'

She folded her arms. 'Did you go into a betting shop today?'

Mickey scratched his head and frowned. 'Come to think of it I did put a little bet on. I got the nod on a dog from big Phil. You remember, the guy …'

'You also made a bet on Monday, didn't you.'

Again Mickey hesitated. She couldn't know for sure. And if she did know he'd blown fifty big ones she wouldn't just be standing there with her arms folded. She reached down and opened a drawer. For a second Mickey wondered if she did know and was going to pull out a gun. But it was a newspaper. She tossed it over.

It was the Racing Post, opened on a page where Mickey had circled the tip about the five furlong at York. He laughed. 'That was just a one-off on account of ...'

'They can't all be one-offs!'

'It's not a problem. So, I like a little punt every now and again. It makes up for not being in the stock market anymore.'

'Maybe it would be better if you went back to the City?'

Mickey tried to hide a smile. 'Do you really think so?'

'No!' she shouted.

'Shhh!' Mickey pleaded. 'The neighbors.'

'Embarrassed are you? You should be.'

'I'm worried they'll complain about the noise again.'

'You should be more worried about gambling away our house deposit. That just doesn't seem to bother you.'

Too late for that, he thought. 'Don't worry. We'll get the house. Trust me.'

'I hope I can, Mickey.'

17

Declin and Connelly arrived ten minutes early for the appointment with Director Asimov. Technically Connelly didn't report into Asimov, but he was higher up the Intelligence Community pecking order and Connelly had impressed on Declin the need to keep him sweet. They sat on a metal bench to one side of the entrance to the LX2 building, while Connelly smoked and ran Declin through his lines.

There was really only one objective: to leave Asimov in no doubt that the Bureau was on top of the Cyber investigation. At this point Connelly didn't want to hear about Declin's reservations and he was adamant that he should not pass any hint of them on to Asimov.

With five minutes to go, Connelly stubbed out his cigarette, ran his fingers through his thinning blond hair and led them into the building. They were shown into a long meeting room with views out over the parking lot and the perimeter of conifers stretching to the Capital Beltway beyond.

Asimov arrived and greeted them with a clammy, skeletal handshake. The speckled brown hair was said to be a transplant but he had no such trouble around his large chin where he played with the beginning of a curl on an otherwise tight beard. He wore a disapproving frown that Declin at first thought was in reaction to his own punkish appearance but eventually realized was a permanent feature.

Asimov was surprisingly softly spoken as he made small talk with Connelly while coffee was served. Suddenly he checked his wrist watch and announced: 'I got a hard out in fifteen minutes so you got precisely five of them to get me up to speed on these green hacktivists.'

Asimov listened without interruption while Connelly delivered an edited version of the progress report that Declin had just delivered. He cracked his knuckles and sat forward in his seat. 'We need to know if this thing stops here.'

'We have the ringleader and known associates all under arrest,' Connelly said. 'Now it's simply a question of building a case for the prosecution.'

'So they didn't get outside help?'

'We don't think so.'

Asimov frowned as if he suspected Connelly was holding out on him. He fixed Declin a stare. 'What do you think, Special Agent Lehane?'

'What do I think about what?' asked Declin trying to buy time.

'Do these cyber attacks stop with the arrest of the Earth Defence?' asked Asimov patiently.

Declin glanced at Connelly. He couldn't lie but neither could he speak his mind.

'Declin does have some concerns,' said Connelly eventually.

'Let's hear them.'

'Well,' began Declin uncertainly, 'I'm not sure the Earth Defence have the technical knowledge to find the exploits and compose malware this sophisticated.'

'Just how sophisticated are we talking?'

'It was a triple zero-day sniper attack,' explained Declin. 'And the code didn't have a single bug in it. Also to find three exploits in different SCADA, well that requires a lot of luck or a lot of manpower.'

'What exactly are you saying? You've arrested the wrong guy?'

'The Earth Defence definitely carried out the attack. They blew up the rigs and the pipeline. But someone else might, just might, have found the exploits and devised the malwares. Then they passed them on to The Earth Defence.'

Asimov took a deep breath. 'Who?'

'It's just a possibility,' said Declin. 'Not probable, just possible.'

'Who?' repeated Asimov.

Declin shrugged. 'Best guess would be North Korea. The SCADA was manufactured by them. Plus the malware is a Stuxnet derivative. They use them a lot.'

'So if they devised this and passed it on or sold it to Kesling, it's possible they have devised others and passed them on to other eco-whackos.'

'Possible.'

Asimov turned back to Connelly. 'So we're not actually in a position to give the energy industry the all clear.'

'We've done our job,' said Connelly. 'We've got the perpetrators under arrest. We've developed patches for these malwares.'

'And now you need to turn your attention to stepping up the energy industry cyber defences.'

'The FBI doesn't have resource to build cyber defences for the private sector,' said Connelly.

'You just hired sixteen hundred new cyber agents.'

'They are to fight cyber crime.'

'Better to prevent it.'

'With respect,' interrupted Declin, surprising himself. 'Surely that's Homeland's job.'

Asimov stared at Declin. 'Homeland are full on making sure the dot gov domain is secure.'

Connelly fixed Asimov an unsympathetic stare. 'Permission to speak bluntly?'

'Please.'

'We've been telling the energy sector they are cyber vulnerable for years. But they didn't want our help. They were paranoid that our offer was cover for something sinister. So they went it alone. Now they are in trouble. It's their tough turkey.'

'It's ours too,' said Asimov. 'If the energy sector gets taken down it takes everything else with it. Transport, light, heating, computing. The whole country goes down!'

Connelly turned to Declin. 'Is it possible to cyber secure the energy sector?'

'Nothing can be totally secure.'

'But could you raise their defences to the level of dot mil or dot gov?' asked Asimov.

'We could do that. But it's a big ask.'

'I'm not asking,' said Asimov. 'I'm ordering you.'

'I'll give any orders that need to be given,' Connelly said pointedly.

Declin broke the silence. 'I'd need help.'

'Your people would oversee operations,' said Asimov, 'but I would instruct the private sector to do the leg work.'

Declin thought for a moment. 'The whole energy sector? Up-stream and downstream oil and gas, electricity power generation, transmission, transformers? '

Asimov nodded. 'You got it.'

'Sure.' Declin nodded. 'But it'll take weeks.'

'Then you better get started.'

18

The Amtrak driver had been waiting fifteen minutes when the guard radioed through.

'Lewis, you got anything I can tell people back here? This must be our tenth unscheduled stop and passengers are getting restless. 'Specially those cowboys that came on early morning.'

The driver raised his eyes to the cabin roof. 'We got a single track section ahead and a one-hundred ton freight train coming down it in our direction. Ask them if they want me to play chicken.'

'Well how much longer you reckon? I got to tell 'em something.'

'Tell them to sit back and enjoy the view. They might never see it again.'

The driver turned to look out the window. Whisked clouds licked craggy peaks that fell to a bleached desert cut in two by a single grey line. Coming down it, growing steadily thicker, was a double-stacker of maybe a hundred cars. Its driver sounded a long horn, probably just to relieve the boredom.

Driving a modern train was a non-job. GPS told the center the exact location and speed of the train. The center set the route and instructed the train as to the speed it should go for optimum fuel economy and other traffic priorities. Being a passenger line, Amtrak always got lower priority than the freight that was owned by the railroads.

And so they waited.

And waited.

Until a rising pitch gave way to shock waves rattling the windows. The other train screamed by. It took a full three minutes for the tail to pass. The signal changed from stop to proceed and the train trundled forward.

Hundreds of miles away in Omaha, Nebraska, the operator of the Union Pacific Railroad set down her half-eaten burger and gawped at the screens in front of her. The signal and point dispatching controls were sending out rapid and conflicting instructions. The returning confirmations made even less sense. On the video screens the tracker-ball cursors flicked from one route to another, setting priorities at random.

She pressed the direct line to her supervisor. 'Control is freaking out.'

'How do you mean: it's freaking out?'

'I mean it's freaking, freaking out. You'd better come see.'

19

Declin lost no time setting up a task force to raise cyber defences across the energy industry. The priority was to increase the air gaps between the industry software and the global internet. But nothing could be made totally secure and there was always the possibility of human access, and so malware filters were also boosted across the piece.

But he did not let this work distract from what he felt was the more important task of finding out whether Earth Defence had outside help. The team had checked every email, pulled apart every file, ripped open every hard drive, and yet, frustratingly, they found nothing.

'We rushed it,' Declin said. 'Because Asimov wanted something for the cameras we moved before we were ready. He's screwed the investigation and put the whole country in jeopardy.'

'It wouldn't be a great career move to blame the Director of National Intelligence,' said Vin.

'I don't care about climbing the greasy pole. I want to solve this crime.' Declin drew a deep breath and clapped his hands. 'So let's make the best of the situation. What do we know already?'

'We know the malware came from the Earth Defence camp,' said Vin.

'But they claim it was a visitor passing through,' replied Declin, playing devil's advocate.

'We have maps, press cuttings and a whole bunch of social media chatter demonstrating they were taking a full on interest in the fracking well and pipeline explosions.'

'No crime in taking an interest,' said Declin.

'You're right,' agreed Vin. 'Kesling will play for plausible deniability. We haven't really got anything on him.'

'Maybe we don't need to worry about Kesling,' Declin said. 'If it wasn't him who devised the exploits and wrote the malware we need to find out who did before we get hit again.'

'You still worried?'

'Of course,' replied Declin.

'But what about this cyber defence task force? You said you were happy with how it was shaping up.'

'It's not just energy we need to worry about,' said Declin. 'Plenty of other critical infrastructure is vulnerable to cyber attack.'

20

'Sweet mother of God!' the supervisor shouted as he entered the control room. 'What have you done?'

'I done nothing. I swear. CADS just started freaking out.'

The supervisor jumped to the controls and tried to re-set the computer-assisted dispatching system. But chaos reigned. Lights flashed across the screen.

The operator took a call from the hump yard.

'Our computer systems have all gone down.'

'Ours too.'

'Jesus. What do we do?'

'Switch to the back-up,' the supervisor yelled.

'Can't. We tried. The back-up is down too.'

'Try moving them manually?' He knew it was a stupid suggestion but he had problems of his own.

'You ever tried pushing a hundred ton carriage over a hump?'

'Look, we got bigger trouble up here. CADS is down and I've got a few thousand trains running blind so you'll have to sort out your own problems.'

The supervisor picked a train at random and re-entered its identity and priority to see if the CADS would update and modify its determinations based on the train's actual movements.

Still no change.

'We have to shut the rails down!' he shouted.

'How?'

'Radio.'

'Radio what?'

'Radio every single driver to stop. Call passenger and hazardous first. I'll call nine one one.'

* * *

The driver's sixth sense was tingling. He'd passed three consecutive 'Stop Then Proceed' signals in a row. Ordinarily he'd expect a clear signal all the way through on a single track section. He hated single track. Never sure whether it really was just you or whether something might be coming at you round the bend.

He knew of course that nothing would be coming at them. He'd spent time at control and knew the interlocking at junctions prevented the displaying of a clear signal for one route when clearance had already been given to a train on a conflicting route. Even then a parallel computer system examined the route-setting commands. And, for all he moaned about how computers had made the driver's job boring, at least they did away with human error.

There was a short delay between spotting the train ahead and his brain processing what it meant. He jerked back the brake stick. The screeching filled his head as he was thrown forward against the window. He could see sparks from the braking wheels of the train ahead and the radioactive hazard signs on the steel casing. Both trains were slowing. Neither quickly enough. The last things he saw were the wild eyes of the other driver.

21

The runaway train came down the track and she blew. Mickey couldn't get the old nursery-school song out of his head as he watched the news of the multiple train crashes across America. Twisted carriages and buckled railway lines in forests, fields and cities. The crash taking up most airtime involved a train carrying nuclear waste. Film crews had been prevented from reaching the site, so some enterprising journalist had fitted a camera to a drone and flown that over. Down below in the desert, fire crews looking like spacemen hosed down containers leaking radioactive waste.

What a mess. *The runaway train came down the track and she blew.*

But what to do about it?

Sell US railroads. That was a no-brainer. But they were already down big time.

He realized share prices in US electricity generators would also come off in case the companies were forced to suspend nuclear generation and use coal, which cost more. But when Mickey checked those share prices he saw they had also already moved. The high frequency trading cheetahs like the Quadra Fund had worked it all out quicker than Mickey's human brain.

The news turned to concerns that the accidents were no accident. There were fears it was terrorism. Fear turned investors to gold. He checked the gold price on his phone. It had risen a hundred dollars an ounce. That was more like it. His option money would have tripled.

He punched the air. 'Get in there!'

'What's happened?' asked Helen, looking up from her book.

Mickey had been so focused on the news he'd forgotten Helen was in the room.

She looked at the television. 'What is so exciting?'

Mickey decided a half truth was the best option. 'Remember that hedge fund I invested us in? Well it had a big bet on the gold price. And gold has just gone through the roof on account of some nuclear accident in the states.'

'Really? Oh my God!'

'It's up a hundred dollars an …'

'I mean has there really been a nuclear accident?'

'Two trains piled into each other. One was carrying nuclear waste. There's been a whole series of rail crashes across America.'

'Is it terrorists?'

'They don't really know.'

'Dear God. Has anyone been hurt?'

'Well, yes, some deaths, yes. Quite a few actually. Thirty at the last count.'

'And you made money out of this, Mickey?'

'The hedge fund did. But it didn't know this was going to happen. It's just luck. I mean not good luck of course it's …'

'It's awful. Making money out of a disaster.'

'It's not like that.'

'How is it not like that? It's just like that. You should give any money you made to the relatives.'

'It's an idea,' said Mickey quietly. Like fart pads and mop shoes, he thought. He turned off the television and settled back on his pillow.

'It's the moral thing to do,' she continued.

'Look, I didn't kill them.'

'I'm serious. You should give back the money.'

The rising tone in her voice told Mickey she would soon be shouting. He pulled the covers off the bed and jumped to his feet.

'Where are you going?'

'The spare room. I've had enough preaching for one night.'

22

'Apologies for running late.' Connelly scurried past Declin and waved for him to follow into his office. His face was even redder than usual as he hung his coat on the back of the door. 'My driver had to wait an hour in line for gas. And they would only let him take half a tank.'

'It's the same across the country.'

'It's one hell of a mess.' He motioned Declin to take a seat but stayed on his feet himself, his legs set wide apart as if he'd wet his pants. 'So, where are you at?'

'The software in the Union Pacific control center was taken out by a logic bomb,' explained Declin. 'We've identified it. We've got a patch for it. And Homeland are screening all other railway control systems for that malware or similar.'

'When do we get the trains running again?'

'They're running already using a back-up radio system.'

'So I heard,' scoffed Connelly. 'Might as well go back to signalmen with flags. When do we get it properly back up and running?'

'It'll be a week before every railway has had its SCADA checked for the malware and cleared.'

'A week of disruption to freight, with all the consequences for industry and commerce generally.'

'We're doing the best we can.'

'Shit, Declin. Doing your best is what you do at kindergarten.

This needs sorting now.'

'Okay! But what do you want me to prioritize? The railroads, energy, the rest of industry, the actual investigation so we might find out who's doing this?'

'All of it!''

'Well I've got field offices around the country working with Homeland to check the voluntary assessments on all critical infrastructure industries, and to check gateway filters for the latest malwares.'

'Okay. Good work.' Connelly sighed and finally took a seat. 'How about the attribution piece?'

'Forensics traced the Union Pacific hacker to an ISP in Waziristan.' Declin handed Connelly a print-out from the Echelon listening system, of an exchange of messages between a hacker and his handler.

'Waziristan,' repeated Connelly. 'Where the hell is Waziristan?'

'Pakistan,' said Declin.

'Anything to connect the Union Pacific and the Ryan Oil attacks?'

'Probably unrelated. Different type of malware entirely.'

Connelly passed back the print-out. 'This attack doesn't sound like eco-hacktivists.'

'Cyber jihadists?' Declin suggested. 'I was wondering whether maybe we should be passing this to Langley.'

'I don't care if it's Wisconsin or Waziristan,' snapped Connelly. 'This is a Bureau investigation until I tell you otherwise.'

23

The Sat Nav announced his arrival at Berkeley Square, the headquarters of the Quadra Fund. Frank reversed into a parking bay and stepped out to feed the meter. But when he saw it was a quid for ten minutes he climbed back in the car and kept the engine running. He'd move off if a warden came and never mind the Antarctic ice sheets. He turned on Classic FM and waited. Around eight o'clock, just as he was getting fed up of Beethoven, the door to the underground garage swung open and a limo with blacked-out windows rolled up the ramp.

Frank followed it round the square as it jostled with black cabs and red buses down Regent Street. He grabbed his mobile and, with one hand, took a picture of the limo's license plate to check up later. He followed it through Piccadilly Circus, up Shaftsbury Avenue and down a side street. It stopped at a security box while the guard checked ID before raising the barrier and allowing it to proceed down the ramp and into another underground car park.

Frank pulled up and flashed his own ID. 'OK if I take a look around?'

'Sorry. Private members club.'

'I understand,' said Frank. 'I'll be discreet.'

The guard shook his head. 'It's strictly members only.'

'Look mate. I'm a police officer. You don't want to get in bother for obstructing police enquiries.'

'Do you have a warrant?'

'I can get one if you like. I could come back with a van load of uniformed officers and raid the club. Or you could just let me come in and have a quiet look around. Which do you prefer?'

'I'd prefer you come back with a warrant,' the guard said.

'I might just do that,' said Frank. Though of course, even if the investigation hadn't been closed down, he'd never get a warrant. Frank backed up and drove away, wishing for a world where the privileged weren't able to live in their own bubble.

He really did need someone on the inside of that bubble.

24

With cyber jihadists now clearly involved in the Union Pacific hack, the investigation was upgraded to a National Security Cyber Intrusion. And despite Connelly's attempt to keep control in the Bureau, Langley insisted on taking the lead. Annoyed though he was at that, Connelly managed to press the right buttons so that Declin remained involved. He even got approval for Declin to fly out to Waziristan, something that Declin wasn't quite as excited about as Connelly.

'I thought you'd want to stay on the case,' Connelly said.

'It's not that,' replied Declin. 'It's the idea of working with Langley.'

'I know,' Connelly laughed. 'Ivy League, wine-drinking, pipe-smoking, international relations types. But you can't always choose your colleagues.'

'I feel like it would be going over to the enemy.'

'That's crazy. We're all on the same side. Mostly.'

'Tell that to my brother Josh and all those who died with him in Iraq.'

'Don't start on that again, Declin. You can't blame Langley for that.'

'They fabricated the case for war.'

Connelly shook his head. 'I'm not going down that one again. So are you going to fly out to Waziristan or not?'

'Of course I'll go. I'm the right man for the job.' But Declin knew that before he flew into a Taliban-infested war zone he had to tell his mother. He'd promised. And if there was one thing he'd learnt from his wayward father it was that if you have to break a promise you have to do it up front.

25

Mickey made sure he got out of the house without waking Helen. He had a choice of two tube stations to go to. Plaistow was a little nearer but the walk to West Ham gave him more exercise. And he passed a bookmakers. Although the bookies was shut, he took a picture on his phone of some interesting odds on the midweek football. It started to rain and he'd not brought a coat, so he jogged down the wet pavement towards the tube. He was surprised how quickly he got out of breath. He dropped back to a fast walk just as a Beemer pulled up on the kerb ahead.

The passenger window slid open and as Mickey came alongside he saw DI Brighouse behind the wheel.

Mickey winked. 'Looking for someone special?'

'I'm looking for you.'

'Well you can give me a lift to the tube,' said Mickey climbing into the car without asking. He wiped the sweat off his forehead with his sleeve.

'You're out of shape,' Frank said.

'Tell me about it.'

Frank glanced over his shoulder and pulled out into the traffic. 'I thought you didn't gamble anymore.'

'Who says I do?'

'I saw you snapping the odds in the bookies back there.'

'Are you doing a job share with my missus?'

'No need to get defensive. Talking of jobs. Have you found anything of interest to me yet?'

Mickey shook his head. 'I've had a good butchers, but it all looks kosher.'

'I see the fund made a tidy profit from those rail crashes in America.'

'They just got lucky on the gold price. The markets got worried about these cyber attacks and gold shot up.'

'You did well out of it too.'

Mickey wondered how Frank knew about his investment. 'It's about time I had a bit of good luck.'

'The train drivers and passengers didn't have a lot of luck,' said Frank.

'You really are job-sharing with the missus. She's all upset about them as well.'

'Glad someone in the family has a moral compass.'

Mickey frowned. 'Hang on a minute. You wanted me to take this job.'

'To help us find evidence. Not to make a killing.'

'I took a punt, Frank. It's not a crime.'

They continued in silence until Frank pulled up at the tube station. 'What do you make of Crispin?'

'Not met him yet.'

'Don't you think that's odd?'

'He's a loner. That's not a crime either.' Mickey shrugged and opened the door. 'Thanks for the lift.'

'You'll keep me informed.'

'If there is anything to report.' Mickey climbed out the car.

'I'll expect to hear from you soon then.'

Mickey cupped his hand to his ear. 'Can you hear that noise?'

'What noise?'

'Woof, woof, rustle, rustle."

'What?'

'That's you, barking up the wrong tree.'

26

'But you promised,' his mother said, as she set down her coffee on the arm of the garden bench and stared blankly into a backyard full of pot plants. 'You promised you wouldn't go to war.'

'I'm not going to war.'

'I thought when you joined the FBI that meant you would never go abroad. After what happened to your brother.'

'I miss Josh too,' Declin said. 'But it's just the way things have worked out.'

'I can't lose both my babies.'

He sandwiched her small hands between his. 'I'm just going to investigate. I'm not planning on getting into any fights. I probably shouldn't have told you.'

'I'm glad you did.' She drew herself upright with a sharp intake of breath and rose to her feet. 'We'll talk no more about it. I'm making your favorite for dinner.'

'Great,' said Declin, as convincingly as possible. He had politely told her on a number of occasions that he wasn't overly keen on lentil bake. But she'd made it for a girlfriend he'd brought home and she'd somehow been left with the impression that it was Declin's favorite. After dinner they sat together on the sofa, flicking between the evening's game shows, until his mother started to wilt.

'You going to pay your respects to Josh?'

'Of course.'

'You're a good boy, Declin. So was Josh.'

He kissed her goodnight and headed up the stairs. He hesitated outside Josh's bedroom, opened the door slowly and turned on the light, though he could have pictured it perfectly even in the dark. The ceiling plastered with stickers and pennants celebrating Josh's college and local sports teams. His high school diploma and school year photographs adorning the walls. The shelf stacked with football helmets, polished stone souvenirs, bubbleheads, toy racing cars and other assorted knickknacks. The American flag draped over his bed. The stuffed tiger and kangaroo laying on the pillows.

His mother had not moved a thing since the day Josh had left for Iraq, creating the unsettling illusion that at any moment he might return. She felt her job as a parent had been to protect Josh while he was alive. Now that he was dead her job was to protect his memory.

'Good night, Josh,' said Declin as he pulled the door shut.

27

The final leg of the flight to Islamabad was on a Boeing 777, infamous for the short pitch between rows. Declin had to cast his legs into the aisle and be alert to passing traffic. He managed thirty minutes sleep at most and was not in the best of moods to encounter thirty five degree heat and high humidity.

Heavily armed embassy officials met him at the airport and whisked him in a blacked out SUV to the diplomatic enclave. There he met CIA station chief JC McCaw, an intense man with a fiery face and sharp nose.

'I like your style,' JC said, shaking Declin's hand with a builder's grip.

'Thanks,' said Declin looking down uncertainly at his new hiking pants and walking shoes.

'Not your clothes,' JC said. 'Or your tats and freaky hair do either for that matter. I wouldn't allow that on my team, but I understand we have to cut you cyber guys a lot of slack to get you on board. I'm talking about you coming out here and getting your hands dirty.'

'I'll go wherever I need to in order to solve this crime.'

'Let me brief you. While you were en route we picked up chatter linking the Union Pacific attack to a Taliban cyber group run by Wafic Said. Name mean anything to you?'

Declin shook his head.

'It does to me. We've been after him for many years. He's behind a number of bombings in Pakistan and Afghanistan but recently he's been focusing on cyber. It's safer but can be even more disruptive, as we've seen.'

'What's his cyber previous?' asked Declin.

'A couple of small scale penetrations of Pakistani government.'

'Has he claimed responsibility for the rail attack?'

'Just chatter.'

'We'll need help from the Internet Service Provider in Waziristan to locate the computer used,' said Declin. 'We need access to their server and router records. Can we get that?'

'For sure we could get help from the ISP,' said JC. 'But by the time we clear all the necessary protocols the chances are there'd be a leak. Then Wafic and his team disappear, taking their capability with them, ready to start up again elsewhere.'

'So what are we going to do?'

'We're going to do things the old way. Humint.'

* * *

The quiet, sun-baked streets of Bannu had an edgy, frontier feel befitting the last major town before the lawless mountain wilderness of Waziristan. And although Declin was in a 'safe' house, he felt anything but. He remembered his promise to his mother that he wasn't going to war. He wasn't so sure about that now.

'How long are we going to wait for this asset of yours?' he asked JC.

'As long as it takes.'

Declin jumped at the trill of JC's phone.

JC's blue eyes flashed to the screen and back to Declin. 'Car. Now.'

Declin peered out through the crack in the window shutters.

A white Opel sedan trundled down the quiet street. The driver stopped, struggled out of the car with a stick and a limp and looked around as he was frisked by the Waziri bodyguard. He was waved on to the house and ushered inside.

Declin knew this was the moment of greatest risk. He understood it was a basic rule never to trust a foreign asset. The primary concern used to be they would give false information. Out here the worry was they would detonate in your face.

'Who's the Waziri?' the driver said, jerking a thumb over his shoulder.

'He works for ISI,' said JC, referring to the Pakistan Intelligence Service.

'He's working for them today but tomorrow he could be in the hills with the Taliban. You shouldn't have brought him.'

'He doesn't know who you are or what we're discussing.'

'He has seen my face. I'm not meeting again like this. If you don't trust me, forget it.'

'Of course I trust you. I'm sorry.' JC offered the man a seat and poured three cups of chai as he introduced Declin.

The driver said his name was Abid and once the tension had eased JC asked him what he knew about Wafic Said and the Taliban Cyber.

'They did the attack on the American railways.'

'We know that,' said JC. 'That's why we're here.'

'You only suspected,' countered Abid. 'I am confirming he did it. He is being helped by two men who used to work in ISI Cyber Command. I have seen them at work in a room full of computers.'

Abid showed them a photo on his phone of a concrete building bristling with antennae and solar panels.

'That's a lot of equipment,' said Declin. 'Why hasn't ISI spotted it before now?'

'The equipment is supposed to be for the school next door. It was donated by a Swedish charity so they could do internet teaching.'

'And that fooled you guys as well?' asked Declin, looking to JC.

'We can't go round checking every school that has a broadband connection.'

Declin grilled Abid on the number and scope of the computers, the wireless signal strength, the broadband width. Abid was sketchy on these and other technical details as he was about the hackers' backgrounds, abilities and connections with other hacking groups.

'Is there any chance you could get access to one of their computers?' asked Declin.

'Too dangerous,' replied Abid.

'We need to know if they're planning other attacks.' Declin held up a memory stick. 'All you'd have to do is to stick this in any of the computers and we'll do the rest.'

'I already know the answer. There will be more cyber attacks.'

'What are they planning?'

'I don't know that.'

'Okay. So what do you know?' asked Declin.

'Only that there are more cyber attacks planned. I don't know what. I don't know when.'

'But you could find out.'

'I can't.'

'These people are plotting to kill innocent civilians.'

'I told you already. It's too dangerous.'

'For fuck's sake!' Declin stepped closer until he towered over the seated figure. 'Whose side are you on?'

'My side.'

Declin felt the blood rising in his cheeks. A hand gripped his shoulder and JC pulled him away.

'Thanks for the information,' JC said. 'You'll be paid in the usual manner.'

Abid nodded silently. 'I don't like your friend. If we meet again do not bring him. Or the Waziri.'

'However you want to play it.'

'I have to go. I've been here too long already.' Abid used the table and his stick to push himself upright. He hurried away as quickly as his gammy leg would allow.

Declin felt a little guilty as he watched him climb back into his car, keeping his face turned from the Waziri. He drove out of town, towards the Hindu Kush.

'Whose side are *you* on?' asked JC. 'You just threatened my best asset in the region.'

'If he's your best asset it's no wonder we're losing the fight against the Taliban.'

'What would you know?'

'I know we need to get access to those computers.'

'We can't,' said JC. 'That compound is deep in T-man territory.'

'So we need to send in special forces.'

JC shook his head. 'Waziristan is a long way from anywhere the meat-eaters could launch an independent operation. So they'd need the approval of the Pakistanis.'

'So?'

'Wafic would be tipped off and they'd be raiding an empty compound.'

'Well can't we go in ourselves?'

'I don't do suicide.'

'So what do you suggest we do?'

'My instructions were to verify the target.'

'Target?' repeated Declin.

'Langley wants a drone strike.'

'A strike!' Declin couldn't believe what he was hearing. 'We'll lose vital evidence. Our best chance of preventing the next attack.'

'We can't afford the time to gather evidence.'

'We can't afford not to!' shouted Declin, pushing his face closer to JC's.

'Back off, Feebie. You're a big guy but don't push your luck.'

Declin took a step back.

'Can you at least give me a couple of days to see what information I can pick up, before you go blow everything to pieces?'

'We can't wait. Abid could be on his way to tell Wafic about us right now.'

'You mean you don't trust him?'

'Basics,' JC said. 'If your asset doesn't trust you, then you don't trust your asset.'

28

'Good morning, Mr. President.'

'Good morning,' President Topps replied to the steward who took his jacket and hung it on a wooden valet. The President took a seat at the dining table and ordered black coffee, two eggs sunny-side up and white toast. He had ten minutes before his guests arrived. Just enough time to catch up on the news. A selection of the mainstream press was neatly laid out on the table. He glanced at the headlines about the chaos in energy and railroads and turned to a split screen laptop on which he surfed through his social media preferences. Predictably commentators wondered why the technologically advanced America was so vulnerable to cyber attack, and speculation was rife as to what industry might be hit next.

As his eggs were served President Topps noted with satisfaction that his carefully choreographed press campaign had succeeded in laying some, unfortunately not all, of the blame for the chaos with the previous administration's under-investment in cyber.

The steward answered a knock at the door and showed in the President's three guests. Martha Stapleton, National Security Advisor, dressed a little too showy for the President's liking, given they would be giving a joint press conference later. Close behind was Lawson Ladyman, Deputy Director for Operations at the CIA, his bald head glistening in the light from the crystal chandelier. The President also believed there was a lot of bare and barren country behind each ear, but his third guest, who the President had appointed himself, vouched for his efficiency. Karl Asimov, Director of National Intelligence, was unusually small and unimposing for a retired four-star general, but he was presently the most senior intelligence officer in the country and the President regarded his opinions above all others in Washington.

'Morning people.' The President motioned them to take a seat. 'Coffee?'

'Not for me,' replied Martha.

Asimov declined with a smile and shake of the head to the steward.

'Black for me,' Lawson said. 'Actually just a little milk.'

'So, you want to move on the cyber terrorist who hit the railroads,' said the President, who had already read Martha's security briefing.

'Correct,' said Lawson. 'We have credible evidence that Wafic Said is planning another cyber attack on mainland America. We want to hit him first.'

'We have any idea what that attack is?'

'Unfortunately not. But we know it is imminent and we need proactive action to prevent it.'

'By proactive action you mean a drone strike, right?'

'Correct.'

'Why don't we capture and render him?' asked the President. 'We might learn something.'

'No chance. Extraction from Waziristan would be impossible, now that our relations with Pakistan are ...' Lawson hesitated, 'cooler.'

The President turned to Asimov. 'Karl?'

Asimov placed his finger tips together under his chin. 'I think a drone strike is the most appropriate response. It also sends a message out that we will counter cyber terrorism with lethal force.'

The President turned to Martha. 'What's your recommendation?'

Martha was incredibly smart but incapable of giving a simple answer. As he listened to her run through the pros and cons of eliminating Wafic Said, the President remembered his chiropractic's instructions and sat up straight.

'So what's your recommendation?' he repeated when she had finished without actually giving one.

'On balance, yes, I think we should strike.'

He took a sip from a glass of water. 'And I take it Wafic Said is already on the Disposition Matrix?'

'He is,' replied Ladyman.

The President turned again to the Oval office window and looked up at dark clouds threatening to cover the entire skyline. 'You have my authorization.'

29

The drone was flying at sixty-thousand feet when its monitor switched from electro-imaging to infra-red and Declin saw a grainy outline of a compound and the neighboring school.

'Are you sure that's it?' he asked.

'Affirmative,' replied the drone's intelligence analyst, thousands of miles away at Nellis Air Force base.

Declin could make out shapes moving around outside the building. 'There are a lot of people down there.'

'Affirmative.'

Declin turned to JC who was stood beside him. 'There's at least twenty people down there?'

'Uh huh,' grunted JC.

'Maybe more,' Declin persisted. 'What do you think?'

'I also think there's at least twenty people. Maybe more.'

'And we don't even know for sure that Wafic is among them.'

'Wafic is down there all right,' said JC calmly. 'ForOp has tracked him. They can tell where his next crap is going to be. He's down there.'

'What about the collateral?'

'It is what it is. Besides, this isn't just about Wafic. We want to whack anyone associating with him.'

'Control, are we still on mission?' the pilot asked.

'Affirmative,' replied JC. 'You zero in on the building with the antennae at the back of the compound.'

'Beside the school,' said Declin pointedly.

'The school is closed,' JC growled.

The pilot locked the missile onto the computer building and fired. 'Bird away.'

The main monitor view switched to the missile mounted camera and Declin watched the grainy image growing clearer as it raced to earth.

Suddenly he jumped in his seat and jabbed a finger at the screen. 'I see a kid down there, JC.'

'That's just some short-arsed jihadist.'

'No,' said Declin. 'It's a child. A boy, I think.'

'So maybe it's Wafic's son.'

'There are women down there as well.'

'Wafic's wives.'

'Women and children,' said Declin. 'You have to abort.'

'Anyone mixing with Wafic is a legitimate target,' said JC.

'There's still time,' the pilot called through. 'Shall I abort?'

'Yes,' called Declin.

'Negative,' shouted JC. 'I'm the mission controller. Stay on the target.'

30

Mickey had struggled to find any common ground with the super-serious Quadra analysts, for whom a good night was a lecture at the School of Economics to be discussed over coffee or a glass of sparkling water. But Mickey found one who shared his two passions.

Uli was a shy Viking who became amusingly animated about football after a few drinks. But it took two full bottles, with Mickey holding back and leaving most of them to Uli, before there was any noticeable effect on his behavior. When he started to sing along to the jukebox Mickey decided to pop the question.

'What investments are you looking at, Uli?'

'I'm looking at those investments,' he replied, leering at a girl who was spilling out of her dress.

'Come on, what are you egg-head analysts looking at now?'

'Can't say. Compliance rules.'

'Never was much good following rules,' said Mickey. 'Tell me and I'll tell you who the next manager of Man United is going to be?'

Uli swung back to Mickey. 'You know?'

'A banking pal is one of their non-execs.'

Uli grunted and squinted at the food menu. He grabbed a barman carrying away glasses and nearly tipped them out of his grasp.

'Do you have chips?'

'I'm afraid the restaurant is closed,' said the barman, regaining his balance.

'Come on mate,' said Mickey, pulling out a twenty and placing it on the table.

'The chef's gone home.'

Mickey put another twenty on the table. 'Do us a favor. Rustle up a portion of chips from somewhere.'

The barman glanced over his shoulders, swept up the cash and hurried away.

'Come on, Uli. What should I be buying now?'

Uli checked over both shoulders. 'Beef.'

Mickey frowned. 'I mean what financial investments should I buy, not what food.'

'Crispin has us all working out algorithms on US cattle futures.'

'Why's that then?' Mickey poured Uli another large glass of red.

'Some hunch about soft commodities. Could be an inflation hedge. I don't know.'

'Thanks.' Mickey didn't yet know what to make of it, but decided to look into it in the morning, when his head cleared.

'So who is going to be the next manager of Man United?' asked Uli.

'Sir Alex,' Mickey replied. 'Coming back out of retirement. You heard it here first.'

31

Declin and JC cleared the helicopter down draft and walked slowly towards the choking black dust that was settling over what was left of Wafic's compound. They scrambled over the rubble and passed through some unhinged wooden doors to the interior. Declin clasped his hand over his mouth. Shredded burqas smouldered among severed limbs. The anguished wailing of survivors trapped in the rubble spurred on rescuers pulling at hot bricks and burning timber with their bare hands.

Declin moved to help but JC pulled him back. 'They won't want your help.'

'They're getting it anyway.' Declin grabbed a first aid kit and walked inside.

Slipping on pools of blood he came across a man, or rather only half a man. Everything below the man's chest had vanished. He moved on to find a young woman covered in blood and soot. Also beyond help. He found a young boy stood frozen stiff, staring at him with wild eyes. Declin looked down and saw the boy's calf was split open like a burst sausage. He dressed the wound, picked up the boy and carried him outside where a distraught woman, he guessed the mother, snatched him up and carried him away.

Declin went back inside and found a man with a large gash in his thigh. He bandaged him up. The man pointed to a younger man lying silently on the rubble. Declin checked for a pulse he didn't find. He tried CPR chest compressions for a minute. Still nothing.

'Sorry,' he said, shaking his head.

The man started to wail and ripped off his own bandages. Declin moved back into the fresh air and sat down.

'You've done your best,' called JC, walking up and taking a swig of water from his canteen.

'If I'd done my best, I'd have busted your head in and called off the drone strike.'

Declin snatched back his canteen and walked back into the compound. He moved among the rubble, cleaning more wounded and offering water to those who could still drink.

Finally, when he had done all he could, he came back out to where JC was standing beside a Pakistani army officer.

'Sitrep please, Lieutenant.' JC asked the officer.

'You can see for yourself. It's a bloody mess.'

'I didn't ask for a description. I asked for a situation report.'

The lieutenant stood a little straighter and stared over JC's head as he spoke. 'Nine confirmed dead so far and another eight expectants in the hospital. Women and children among them. This was a family residence.'

'It was a terrorist base,' corrected JC. 'And we destroyed it.'

'Unfortunately,' said Declin who had already realized there

would be no evidence to salvage.

'What about Wafic?' JC asked the lieutenant.

'He's somewhere in there,' said the lieutenant jerking a thumb over his shoulder at the burning stew.

'Mission accomplished,' said JC.

The lieutenant shifted his weight to the other leg but said nothing. He turned and led the way to the school hall that had been turned into a hospital-cum-morgue. They walked passed a half-dozen bodies covered in sheets. Further along, two soldiers stood either side of a wounded man whose eyes were open.

Declin stared at the prisoner. 'How serious are his injuries?'

'Just burns and concussion.'

'He should come back with us,' Declin said to JC.

'I'll have to clear that with my superiors,' said the lieutenant.

'Consider it cleared,' said Declin. He took some cuffs from JC, secured the prisoner and pulled him onto his feet.

Outside, as his eyes adjusted to the bright sun, he heard a thump and whistle.

'Incoming!' JC shouted, pulling out his nine mil.

Declin pushed the prisoner into a drainage channel and readied to follow. But he realized JC was still hollering at people to take cover while standing in the open himself.

'Get down!' he yanked JC's arm and pulled him into the channel just as another mortar crumped nearby and a bright flash rose from the dust where JC had been standing.

'Thanks,' JC said. 'I owe you one.'

As Declin crouched in the muddy water with gunfire rattling overhead he thought of his mom. He couldn't die here. He couldn't put her through it again.

'What do we do now?' he shouted.

'You watch him.' JC crawled up to the top of the ditch and exchanged rapid hand signals with someone. Declin guessed it was the Pakistani lieutenant.

JC slid back into the channel, undid his belt and tied it round the prisoner's handcuffs. 'When I shout "Rapid fire", you two get out and run for the bird.'

Declin heard the shout. The air filled with gunfire. He climbed out, hauled the prisoner up behind and ran, the weight of his body armor suddenly forgotten. At first the prisoner dragged his heels, but when a machine-gun burst raked the ground beside them the prisoner overtook Declin and he struggled to keep up. His heart thudded crazily in his chest as his short rasping breaths failed to pump enough air into his lungs. He ran on empty for the last hundred yards and collapsed at the doorway to the helicopter.

Hands hauled him on board.

'What. About. JC?' he gasped.

But they either didn't understand his English or the question. There was no answer. Soon they were flying fast over the scorched brown desert. Declin felt he should be grateful to the crew for saving him, but that feeling was overwhelmed by guilt that, in a different war in a different time, nobody had been there to fly Josh to safety.

32

A stranger with short, rounded wings and a long, banded tail was paying a visit to the George Bush Center for Intelligence. As it settled into a high tree beyond the car park, Leon Calvara, Director of the CIA, lined up his telescope and noted the red eyes, black head, blue-gray upper parts and tail. The evidence suggested, beyond reasonable doubt, that it was a Cooper's Hawk. He made an entry in his log book, just as Lawson Ladyman came into the room.

'Asimov has been trying to get hold of you.'

'I've been busy.' Leon put the cover over the lens, and turned to his desk.

'He wants to discuss the drone hit on Wafic Said.'

'I know.' Leon stretched to pick up the briefing report. Second time of reading it was no more pleasant and, though Islamabad station were emphasizing the positive in taking out Wafic Said, they couldn't disguise the fact that women and children were among the dead.

'JC screwed up big time.'

'He's reported MIA.'

'Shit. Do the Taliban have him?'

'We don't think so.'

'Better off dead than a prisoner.'

'Islamabad have taken a prisoner of their own.'

'That's good,' said Leon. That was something he could throw back at Asimov when he eventually returned the call. 'I want to be kept in touch real time with that interrogation. Who's deputizing for JC in the interview?'

'The Special Agent from the Bureau.'

'Ah, yes!' Leon raised his eyes to the ceiling. 'Part of Asimov's great plan to promote interagency cooperation. Still, he is apparently the best cyber brain we have so he's probably the right choice under the circumstances.'

'There is one thing you probably should know about this guy.'

'Enlighten me.'

'His name is Declin Lehane.'

'I'm not enlightened.'

'He was caught hacking into Langley intranet some years back.'

'Looking for what?'

'Evidence of WMD in Iraq.'

'Did he find any?' asked Leon, unable to smother a smile.

'No, he didn't.'

'That was a joke, Lawson. You should know that better than anyone.' Leon smiled apologetically. Lawson had put a lot of hard miles in to recover from his involvement in that debacle. 'That's why our agency is now a political punch bag. That's why Cresta Patton has the President's ear on security while I report to a man whose idea of danger in the field is working from an internet cafe in East St Louis.' Leon suddenly remembered his blood pressure and took a deep breath. 'Anyway. How come Declin Lehane got a job with the Bureau if he has a criminal record?'

'He wasn't convicted. He was just a kid. People were so impressed with his hacking skills, he was offered a job here.'

Leon dropped his feet back to the floor and sat up in his chair. 'And?'

'He turned it down.'

'Reason?'

'He blamed us for fabricating the case for war in Iraq. His brother died out there.'

'A liberal conspiracy theorist,' Leon grunted. 'Let's keep a close eye on Special Agent Declin Lehane.'

33

'No sleeping!'

The Pakistani guard slapped the prisoner's face and his eyes slowly opened red. They shut again as the guard shone a floodlight into his face.

'You can sleep when you've told us everything you know.'

The prisoner's legs buckled under his forced position against the wall and the guard kicked him back into a squat.

This wasn't how things were done by the Fed rules, but Declin was increasingly clear this was not a Bureau show. He'd been appointed a bodyguard who left Declin in no doubt that even though circumstances had left him best placed to interrogate the prisoner, this was a CIA operation.

'Up,' said the guard. He pulled the prisoner to his feet, slipped a hood over his head and dragged him left, right, left, right around the room. Declin distracted himself by taking another look at the briefing report. This explained that the prisoner's *nom de guerre* was Rafique Kabul, but diagnostics were fairly certain that his face and his texting and email writing matched those of a Swedish convert, originally named Karl Ericson. He'd gone to Pakistan with a charity to set up internet in schools. He'd never returned.

After half an hour of zig-zags the prisoner collapsed and the guard hauled him back to his feet for another round. Left, right, left, right for another ten minutes until the guard was also exhausted. He let the prisoner drop to the floor.

'Can I talk to him?' asked Declin.

'Not yet,' replied the guard. He removed the hood, turned up the lights and turned on loud music.

Declin liked Green Day, but not at that volume, and the choice of American Idiot did seem ironic. He put on the ear muffs offered by the guard.

Half an hour later the music stopped. The guard dragged the prisoner to a neighboring room with a table and two chairs. One for Declin. One for Rafique. The guard and Declin's bodyguard stood on either side.

'Do you want to sleep?' Declin asked.

Rafique stared back in silence.

'You can go to sleep when you've given me the information I need. What can you tell me about the cyber attack you carried out.'

'Allah Akbar.'

'It was a clever attack from a cyber perspective. That was good work to find the exploit. What can you tell me about it?'

'Allah Akbar.'

Declin continued to probe unsuccessfully. He decided to try a different tack.

'Wafic is a computer genius isn't he?'

Rafique stifled a laugh.

The first crack in his defence.

'Wafic is the only person in the whole world who could have hacked into that railway control center.'

'Wafic didn't do it.'

'We know he did. We traced the attack back to his compound.'

'Wafic can't even program. He is just a show man.'

Declin smiled appreciatively. Rafique had taken a huge psychological step towards him. 'Your family miss you, Karl.'

Rafique's eyes glared at Declin, startled at the use of his real name or mention of family. Perhaps both. A mist of suspicion descended again and he turned away.

'Allah Akbar.'

'Your war is over now. It's time to start thinking of going home.'

'Allah Akbar.'

'If you don't help me, your home from now on will be Faisalabad,' said Declin, who knew that Pakistan's notorious central jail was feared by all. 'But if you help me out I can get you transferred to jail in Sweden. And with good behavior you might not be in for too long.'

'Allah Akbar.'

'You see,' explained Declin, 'I've got evidence the attack came from the compound. You are the sole survivor. You're a known terrorist. You're the man in the frame.'

Declin let Rafique come to terms with his predicament. The eyes faded. His jaw slackened. His shoulders sagged.

'If you tell me it was someone else who showed you the exploit and gave you the malware ... Well, then everything changes for you.'

Declin asked the guard to pour some tea and signalled for him to leave. Declin sipped his drink slowly. The CIA bodyguard declined. Rafique let Declin pour him a cup, but he left it on the table.

'You can trust me. And my American friend here,' said Declin, indicating the bodyguard. 'We're the only ones in the room now. I'll tell the Pakistanis you told me nothing. I'll take what you tell me back to America and nobody will know where it came from. And I'll let you go back to the cell and sleep. Sleep for as long as you want. Then I'll make sure you go home to Sweden. Would you like that?'

The prisoner's eyes started to close. Declin sensed he was finally coming to terms with his reality.

'So what can you tell me?'

The prisoner leant closer and whispered in Declin's ear. 'Allah Akbar.'

34

The Chief Scientist at the Plum Island Animal Disease Research Center froze a look of cool detachment. Look calm, she told herself as she removed her bio-hazard helmet and stepped out of her yellow hazmat suit. She moved into the first shower room, stripped off her thermals and dropped them in the disposal basket. She took a sharp intake of breath as she stepped under the hot, sterile water and scrubbed down harder than usual. In part because of the risk of a virus contamination. Mostly because she wanted to wash away her guilt.

She stepped through to the second shower and scrubbed down again. She stood drip-drying for a minute wondering what this meant for her career. But what was there to consider? She was in charge of Laboratory Research at the Center. The buck stopped with her.

She walked through to the vacuum room. After a short while she was dry, and some. Finally the UV light room. Some of her staff complained that they weren't allowed to use it for tanning. There'd be plenty of time for her to work on a tan if things panned out as she feared. She dressed slowly, took a deep breath and exited the air lock.

The Director of Security for the Center stood waiting, legs apart, hands on hips. 'Well?'

'Let's talk in my office.'

They walked in silence from the research labs to the administration center. She opened the door and showed him a seat.

'Now can you tell me what the hell is going on, Valerie?'

She hesitated while she tried to find a good way to put it. 'Our bio-security safeguards have been compromised.'

'You mean we have a leak?'

'Hopefully not.'

'So what exactly do you mean by compromised?'

'Some of the extractor filters in the lab appear to have lost their integrity.'

'Meaning?'

'There's a small chance a virus might have escaped outside.'

'Well that is just dandy.'

'The filters have a ninety-nine point-nine-nine percent HEPA rating,' she explained, although she could see he wasn't really listening any longer. 'Even if they are compromised they are still probably taking out ninety-nine percent of any viruses in the air, and any that do get through should get killed by the UV light.'

'When did you discover this?'

'We found that out a few days ago.'

'So why are you only just telling me now?'

She scratched the eczema on her hand. 'Today we also discovered a problem with negative air pressure.'

'A problem?'

'The pumps have stopped working, so the pressure in the lab is just normal atmospheric pressure. There is no negative air pressure.' She hesitated before deciding to tell the whole truth. 'Actually, with the high winds in recent weeks we've probably had a positive air pressure.'

'You mean we've been pumping air from inside the lab to the outside world.'

'Yes.'

'Air that contains viruses.'

'Correct.'

'Precisely what viruses are we talking about here?' asked the Director, his voice rising an octave. 'Ebola? Lyme disease? Smallpox …?'

'Hopefully not,' she interrupted. 'The Zoonotic pathogens are in a separate bio-containment. Which seems to be secure. We're checking that.'

'Oh my God. You're not sure?'

'At the moment all we know for sure is that we have an escape of the Foot-and-mouth virus.'

The Director paced the room, hands crossed behind his back. 'Let's back up a little here. Why did these filters stop working?'

'They should have been replaced, but the automatic monitors didn't pick up that they needed to be. We also do manual spot checks. It was one of these spotted they needed replacing.'

'Why did the automatic monitors fail?'

'A software glitch, according to the tech guys.'

'What caused the reversal of air pressure?'

'The pumps stopped working. Maintenance have fixed them now.'

'Why did they stop working?'

'Another software glitch, according to the techies.'

The Security Director walked over to the window. She stood to one side of him and followed his stare out over the open grassland to where a lone tree was bent almost double by the strong winds.

'Look at that tree,' he said. 'It's pointing at the mainland.'

'I know. I think we should quarantine Long Island.'

'Are you crazy?'

'Just as a precaution.'

'If we put New York on bio alert they close us down. Simple as that. In any case, think of the logistical nightmare of bio-scrubbing every vehicle going off the Island.'

'I think we need to react appropriately. At the very least we should probably kill all our livestock.'

'We'll never keep that quiet. Until we know whether or not we have got a leak we can't give the world the impression we have.'

'So what do you suggest we do?'

'Double scrub all employees leaving the Island. Don't explain why.'

'Is that all?'

The Security Director fixed her a stare. 'You religious?'

'Somewhat.'

'Then pray somewhat.'

* * *

Saybrook Enquirer Online: *'Employees of the Plum Island Animal Disease Center, landing at Saybrook Connecticut this evening have been talking of enhanced scrub downs on leaving the Island, amid rumors of a Foot-and-mouth outbreak. A spokesperson for the controversial bio-hazard research facility said this was purely precautionary and there has been no escape of disease or break of the quarantine.'*

35

Cindy had gone out to lunch leaving her computer on. Mickey knew it would automatically log out any moment but he passed casually by and looked at her monitor just as the Quadra's feeds were processing some obscure article about a rumored 'Foot-and-mouth outbreak' in America. He watched as trading algorithms automatically bought futures indices for US cattle and other cloven-hoof animals, while shares in insurance companies that had underwritten foot-and-mouth risk were sold short.

The fund was making its move, just as Uli had tipped him off that they would. He noted with alarm that the huge, leveraged bets the fund was making were not even hedged. That would give it more upside if things went right. But if they went the other way, the fund was exposed on the downside. He didn't know whether that was punchy or reckless, and he couldn't point it out because Cindy had made it perfectly clear that he was not supposed to know how they were invested. He hoped she knew what she was doing.

36

Dressed in full bio-suit, Valerie walked slowly into the field. On Tuesday the cows had seemed worryingly disinterested in their food. Wednesday morning the technicians had reported raised temperatures and a sudden drop in milk yield. Her heart sank at the sight of several cows walking tentatively, shaking a leg as if to dislodge a stone wedged in the hoof. Others were lying down away from the rest of the herd. White blisters bubbled on the bulbs of heels and clefts of hoofs. Lips quivered over frothy saliva.

As she drew close she could hear the smacking sound as the cows opened mouths, too painful to eat with. Calves tried in vain to feed from blistered teats.

'Round them all into the pens,' said Valerie. 'And fire up the incinerator.'

The technician nodded and called others to help. Valerie walked slowly back over the field, following the shadow of a cloud passing overhead on the way to the mainland. She passed through decontamination and returned to the administration building, where she went straight to the Security Director's office.

'It's out.'

'No. You have to stop it.'

'I can't.'

'You have to do something or we are totally screwed.'

'I'm preparing the incinerators,' said Valerie, unsympathetically.

'Will that contain it?'

'No. And now we need to impose a quarantine zone on Long Island.'

'The whole of Long Island, including New York?'

'Yes. We also need a fifty-mile restricted movement zone along the coast of Connecticut, and we should vaccinate every animal within that zone.'

'Oh shit. We really are totally screwed. But if we do all that we can contain it? Am I right?'

Valerie did not reply. Normally she was a glass-half-full sort of person. Right now the glass looked completely empty.

37

When Declin saw the prisoner Rafique again, he was strapped to a wooden table in the basement. Motionless, eyes closed. Declin wasn't sure whether he was still alive.

'He's sedated,' declared a medic in pressed white lab coat. 'Are you ready to talk to him?'

'Sure.'

She inserted a needle into a small bottle of violet liquid.

'What's that?' Declin asked.

'Something to wake him up.'

'Is that necessary?'

'Unless you want to talk while he's asleep.' She drew up the liquid, turned the needle to face the ceiling and released a few milliliters before searching for a vein near the prisoner's groin.

'What precisely is it?'

'It's a Benzodiazepine derivative,' she said. 'You'll find him more cooperative than he was in your last interview.'

As she inserted the needle the prisoner shuddered and screamed so loud Declin wondered whether the room's sound-proofing would hold. His mother had taken benzodiazepine for her anxiety after Josh's death. Declin was pretty sure whatever was in the syringe wasn't what his mother had had.

Unfazed by the screams the medic filled another needle, this time with a clear liquid.

'I'm not happy about this.' Declin placed a hand on her arm. 'You're clearly hurting him.'

'Squeamish are we, Special Agent Lehane?' She inserted the needle again. The prisoner groaned and started babbling in a foreign language. Declin guessed it was Swedish.

The medic studied an array of monitors. 'He's ready for you now.'

Declin was still uncomfortable but at least the prisoner no longer looked in pain. And he did have a whole bunch of questions for which he needed answers.

'What is your name?'

'Rafique Kabul.'

'What name were you born with?'

'Karl Ericson. But my name now is Rafique Kabul.'

Declin was impressed. The drug did appear to have made him more cooperative. 'What was your role in Wafic's organization?'

'To fight for Allah.'

'Do you fight with a computer? Are you a hacker?'

'Yes. I used to hack for Anonymous in Sweden.'

'How did you come to work with Wafic?'

'I came to Pakistan to install broadband in schools.'

'Did you write the malware for the railroad attacks?' asked Declin.

'No.'

'Did Wafic or someone else in your group write it?'

'No.'

'So who wrote the malware?'

'I don't know.'

Declin was about to ask again when the door burst open.

In walked JC, as if he had just returned from the washroom. 'Hi.'

'Are you okay?' Declin asked. 'Where have you been?'

'I took a little tour around the Hindu Kush,' said JC. 'Just got back. I understand our friend here has not been very forthcoming.'

'He's opening up now. He's told us the malware was not written by Wafic or his group.'

73

'He could just be denying it,' said JC.

'I don't think so.' Declin turned back to the prisoner. 'Who wrote the malware. Who found the exploit?'

'I do not know the name.'

The monitors blipped.

'That's not true,' said the medic.

'What was his name?' pressed Declin.

'I do not know the name,' repeated Rafique.

Again a blip on the monitor.

Declin felt sure he was holding back. 'The name.'

Rafique opened his eyes again. 'Nezzar. Something like this.'

Declin looked at the medic. 'Can we trust him?'

She pointed to the monitoring equipment. 'All his baselines match up.'

'It's just random noise,' said JC. 'He's not lying but he's talking nonsense.'

'What else do you know about this man Nezzar?' asked Declin. 'Can you describe him?'

'His face was hidden under his hood when he arrived and he only talked to Wafic.'

'What did they talk about?'

'Cyber attacks.'

'Was Wafic planning more cyber attacks?'

'Not Wafic. This other person.'

'This man Nezzar?' Declin glanced at JC and turned back to the prisoner. 'What is he planning to do?'

'I heard him say he had a plan to poison the very blood of the Great Satan.'

Again Declin exchanged glances with JC. 'What does that mean? To poison the blood of the Great Satan.'

38

The bulldozer slid its yellow fangs into the pile of rotting carcasses, triumphantly raised up three, carried them fifty yards and dropped them into the huge open fire.

The farmer looked away as the reporter shoved a microphone in his face. 'Tell us what the destruction of your herd means for your livelihood?'

'We've lost everything,' the farmer said. 'It took five generations of Winstons to breed this herd. Now it's all gone. We're left with nothing.'

'And who do you blame?' she goaded.

'The Government. They kept the disease alive in those laboratories on Plum Island. We've been saying for years that was madness.'

The bulldozer returned with a second offering for the pyre and now the reporter turned to the camera.

'What you're seeing now in the Winston farm in New Haven, Connecticut, is being played out on dozens of ranches across the county, as the United States Departments of Agriculture and Homeland Security try desperately to contain this outbreak of foot-and-mouth disease, which was allegedly started by a leak of the virus from the Plum Island Animal Disease Research Center.'

39

Mickey had seen enough burning cattle to get the picture. He hit mute on the TV and turned his attention to the prices on his Reuters screen. US cattle futures had gone through the roof and he reckoned he'd made a cool hundred thousand pounds already. He wondered whether to cash out, given claims by some US farming official that they had the situation under control. But he remembered similar false promises during the outbreak in the UK, and decided to keep the trade on.

He noticed that the general US stock market was off almost five percent. Some commentators were putting that down to the possible fifty-billion dollar hit to the US economy from a full blown foot-and-mouth outbreak. Others said it was more to do with worries over more cyber attacks. Sure enough the gold price, the classic panic buy of investors, was up a hundred dollars an ounce.

He looked through the glass windows into the analysts' room.

They were high-fiving and slapping backs. The fund had made big bets on both the cattle futures and the gold price. It had probably made a hundred-million pounds in a few hours. Hats off to the team. Whatever they were doing with their computers it was working.

He saw Uli disappearing outside, waited a discreet minute and followed him out into Berkeley Square. He found him smoking in his usual spot under the shelter of a plane tree.

'Maybe it's only a rumor, but apparently that's not good for you.'

'I only do it to be sociable,' said Uli.

He'd been on his own until Mickey arrived but didn't see the irony. 'You guys did a great job on this foot-and-mouth outbreak. Made out like bandits. What prompted it?'

'We can't talk shop.'

'Don't give me that. How did you manage it?'

'It's like fishing. If you lay out enough lines eventually something bites.'

'But you knew which line was going to bite. You told me to buy meat.'

Uli flicked the ash from his cigarette and flicked his eyes left to right. 'We didn't have that conversation, right?'

'Sure. But come on. How did you know?'

'We didn't have this conversation either.'

Mickey put his hands over his ears and shut his eyes.

'Crispin spotted tightening supply and demand.'

'How'd he spot that if nobody else did?'

'If I knew that I'd be the billionaire, not him.'

Fair enough. Mickey looked around the square. Despite the light drizzle it was relatively warm for winter and people were sitting on benches sipping coffees and snacking an early lunch. Most of them also hoped to strike it rich. But most would not. It was a myth that there were easy pickings to be had on City streets paved with gold. The gilded men like Crispin were few and far between.

'So what are you guys looking at next?' he asked.

'Leave me alone, Mickey. I've already told you too much.'

'Come on. Give your new best mate the heads up.'

Uli stamped out his cigarette on the ground, picked up the stub and threw it in a bin. 'I'm going back to work.'

Mickey walked back with him. 'Come on Uli. Give me a clue at least.'

Uli checked around him as they arrived back at the Quadra Fund entrance. 'All that glitters.'

'If you're talking about gold,' said Mickey, 'the word is glistens.'

'If you say so. But you didn't get that one from me.'

'But the gold price has already moved.'

'That's only the start. The Quadra is leaving its bet on.'

40

'How will they poison the blood of the Great Satan?' Declin asked the prisoner again.

Rafique struggled to talk. Or perhaps he was struggling not to talk. 'I don't know,' he whispered finally.

The polygraph spiked.

'He's holding out on us,' said JC. He stepped closer to the prisoner and shook him roughly. 'There will be more cyber attacks. Where will these attacks be?'

But Rafique slipped into unconsciousness.

'Can you wake him?' JC asked the medic.

'I can administer another dose of the serum,' she replied. 'But it's not without risk.'

'Do it,' said JC.

'Why take the risk?' asked Declin. 'Let's wait until tomorrow.'

'American lives are at stake. I want answers now.'

'But we may kill him.'

'He should be dead already.' JC looked back to the medic. 'Go ahead.'

'I'm having no part in this.' Declin stepped away.

The medic prepared another syringe and injected this into Rafique's groin, producing another piercing scream.

After a few moments Rafique began to mumble.

'Tell us what you know about the next cyber attack,' JC

demanded.

Rafique opened his mouth to answer but could only manage an escape of air and barely audible mutterings.

'What did he say?' asked JC.

'I couldn't make it out,' replied the medic.

'The next cyber attack,' JC pressed. 'What is it?'

But Rafique said no more. His eyes closed and his head fell sideways.

They watched as he slipped in and out of consciousness for a minute. The monitors flat-lined.

41

Frank paused outside DI Stone's office, uncertain why he had asked him to pay a visit. He knocked, entered and took the offered seat while Stone finished off a phone call.

Stone set his receiver down slowly and smiled. 'I've been looking into your pal Mickey Summer.'

'He's not my pal.'

'Interesting family background. Father went to prison for murder. Brother should have done.'

Frank shrugged his shoulders. 'Why were you looking into it?'

'We got a suspicious transaction report on him yesterday,' said Stone, setting his water down on the table.

'We've dropped the Quadra Fund investigation,' said Frank, feigning disinterest.

'This wasn't the Quadra Fund,' said Stone. 'Mickey dealt personal account from his broker.'

'Why did it generate suspicion?'

'He bought US cattle futures two days before anybody got wind of this foot-and-mouth outbreak.'

Frank hadn't picked up on the news. 'What outbreak?'

'In America. They've started burning cattle to contain it. Price of meat has gone through the roof.'

'So why are you interested in Mickey?'

'He has no history of investing in soft commodities. He must have got inside information from the Quadra Fund.'

'So did the Quadra Fund also buy cattle futures?'

'They bought just as the first rumors started coming out.'

Frank shook his head. 'Same old same old. They get all their ducks in a row. But they wait to deal until the very first bit of news so that they can explain it away as a quick reaction rather than insider trading.'

'Only Mickey didn't get all his ducks in a row, did he? Mickey bought too soon.'

'How's that any help to us? The review panel told us to close the Quadra Fund investigation.'

'We can investigate Mickey Summer on his own. We can pursue this without it looking as if it's the Quadra Fund.'

'Open a new investigation? The Super would see straight through that.'

'We don't tell him yet. Just routine checks at this stage. We've had a SARS report on Mickey Summer. You go and investigate it.'

'Mickey wouldn't trade on inside information,' snapped Frank, uncertain why he was so defensive.

'He has a gambling problem,' pressed Stone. 'And he's just blown the deposit on his house.'

'So?'

'So he turns to trading inside information to make good what he lost.'

'You suggesting we arrest him?'

'I'm suggesting you use the threat of arrest to get him working for you.'

Frank had to admit it might work. 'What's your part in this?'

'If it leads somewhere, we share the conviction.'

'If it doesn't?' asked Frank.

'Then you're on your own.'

42

Declin slept fitfully on the flight back state-side, troubled by the death of Rafique. Of course, it had been the icy medic who administered the drugs that eventually killed him, and JC who had pushed her to do it. But Declin should have tried harder to stop them. And what had they achieved? So they knew that more attacks were planned but they suspected that anyway and were none the wiser about what form those attacks would take. They knew someone with a name like Nezzar had helped Wafic but they had no idea who this person was. And with Rafique dead they had lost their only lead.

But when he landed at DCA and took his cell phone off flight mode he had more urgent things to worry about. The news was all about the foot-and-mouth outbreak. He had ten messages on his voicemail that he worked through as he waited in line for passport control. The most urgent was an instruction to report immediately to Director Calvara at Langley. He wasn't sure whether that was a good thing or bad but he couldn't turn up with sticky armpits and stubble. He hurried to a restroom, shaved too quickly and nicked his chin, washed his face, changed his shirt and ran for the taxi rank.

It was fifty deep. Murmuring apologies, he flashed his badge and jumped to the front. He told the driver to push the speed limits but stay legal.

He hurried through Langley main entrance security and walked quickly to Calvara's office. The Director was pacing the room, dictating into a voice recognition kit. He finished his memo and motioned for Declin to take a seat.

'You've heard about Plum Island?'

'Newswires full of nothing else,' said Declin. 'Was it another cyber intrusion?'

'That's the working assumption.'

Declin remembered the warning from Rafique Aziz. 'The prisoner I interrogated in Islamabad said the next attack would poison the very blood of the Great Satan. Do you think this is what he was talking about?'

'They sure poisoned our beef. But you tell me. We're establishing a full cyber task force to get on top of this.' Calvara dumped a file on the table. 'Welcome aboard.'

Declin opened the file and saw it was the paperwork needed to second Declin to the agency. Green sticky arrows pointed to where he needed to sign.

'Director Dominic Solo is task force chief,' said Calvara. 'You'll report to him.'

'Happy to join the task force. But I report to Director Connelly of the FBI.'

'This isn't a demotion. You'll be Solo's number two.'

'Happy to be number two. But I'm staying employed by the Bureau.'

'Why does it bother you?'

'I like working for the Bureau.'

'It's a temporary secondment. You're still employed by the Bureau. You're just joining a CIA task force for the duration.'

'I'm a Federal agent. I'm staying a Federal agent.'

'This has been cleared by Director Connelly and by Director Asimov.'

'I don't care if it's been cleared by the President.' Declin pushed the paperwork back over the desk.

'As you like. I'll fix a work around.' Calvara sat back down and put his feet on the desk. 'What have you got against this agency?'

'I don't like the way it operates.'

'Such as?'

'Well, mostly I wasn't impressed with the way you fabricated the case for war in Iraq.'

'Misinterpreted the intelligence is how we put it. But the case for war didn't need weapons of mass destruction anyway.'

'Some think it did. I'm one of them.'

Calvara studied Declin in silence. He looked to be about to say one thing but changed his mind. He asked for a debrief on Waziristan, even though Declin knew Calvara would have already seen a full written report from JC. He guessed it was some sort of test.

'We patched Nezzar into global communications,' Calvara said when Declin had finished. 'So far it has come up blank. Do you think the prisoner might have been misleading us?'

'I think Nezzar is as much as he knew of the real name. If JC hadn't pushed the prisoner so hard we might have found out more.'

'If he hadn't pushed so hard we might not even have the name,' countered Calvara. 'And at least we now know someone helped the Taliban cyber group. Could be the same people behind the attacks on Ryan Oil and Plum Island.'

'Any attribution leads yet?' asked Declin.

'Cheltenham picked up chatter pointing to the Syrian Electronic Army.'

'They're just a bunch of kids,' Declin said. 'Plum Island was a highly sophisticated attack. The Syrian Electronic Army aren't up to that. Someone gave them the malware and the exploit.'

'If you're right then you need to find out who, before they hit us again.'

'I might have already had the answer if JC hadn't killed my prisoner.'

'Rafique Aziz died from injuries sustained in the missile strike,' said Calvara. 'Remember that.'

'But I was there.'

'Get with the program.'

'I still think JC should've kept our only lead alive.'

Calvara tapped a large bony finger on the arm of his chair and fixed Declin a stare. 'I've heard only good things about your work for the Bureau. While you're on my team you make sure I continue to hear only good things. Understood?'

43

Mickey stopped as he turned the corner into Wigmore Street. He was about to pass the bookies. He looked at his phone and pulled up the message from Fat Jimmy about a neat accumulator. He shook his head clear, shoved the phone back in his pocket and crossed to the other side of the street. Head down as if battling a force-ten he marched on. But as he drew level with the bookies he caught its welcoming lights out of the corner of his eye and stopped again.

He'd made almost a hundred grand from the investments in gold and cattle futures so it made sense to keep going while he was on a winning streak. He stepped inside to make the bet before he could change his mind again. But he wasn't stupid. He only bet half his winnings. Kept the other fifty for the deposit on the farmhouse.

'The love of money is the root of all evil,' a voice said from behind, as he got back into the street. Mickey turned round to see DI Brighouse leaning against the shop window.

'Keep your opinions to yourself,' said Mickey, annoyed at being followed.

'It's not my opinion. That is Timothy, verse six, line ten.'

'Well, Timothy can keep his nose out of my life as well.'

'Jump in,' said Frank, pointing to a parked car.

Mickey hesitated. He realized Frank meant no harm and it was raining.

'I can take you home,' said Frank.

'All right then. I give in. But you can't stay the night.'

They climbed into the car. Frank pulled out into the light evening traffic. 'Which horse did you bet on?'

'So you were watching me.'

'I noticed you were looking at the horses. Which one did you go for?'

'A three-horse accumulator, if you must know.'

'You like betting on four-footed animals don't you.'

Mickey didn't get where Frank was coming from. 'I'm more into the football than the horses.'

'I'm not talking about horses.'

'Well I ain't bet on the dogs for a long time.'

'I'm not talking about dogs either.'

Mickey turned in his seat to face Frank. 'Well what the 'ell are you talking about?'

Frank dropped down a gear as he took a corner. 'You bought US cattle futures.'

Mickey didn't reply.

'Strange thing to do.' Frank looked straight ahead at the road.

'There's a first time for everything.'

Frank signalled as he took a wide berth around a bicycle. 'We got a suspicious transaction report from the broker you dealt with.'

'Why the hell are you stalking me?'

'We want to know where you got your inside information about the foot-and-mouth outbreak?'

'I didn't get any inside information.'

'So you just decided to buy cattle futures. Is that it?'

'There was a tightening in supply and demand,' said Mickey, winging it. 'Obviously I didn't know about the foot-and-mouth outbreak until everyone else did.'

'For the first time in your life you buy cattle futures. Just days before a hundred million cattle go up in flames.'

Mickey scratched the back of his hand. 'I had a hunch.'

'You heard it from someone at the Quadra Fund.'

Mickey realized there was no point denying it. 'How come you're still badgering after the Quadra Fund? I heard your enquiry got shut down.'

'I'm not investigating the Quadra Fund,' said Frank. 'It's you who's in trouble this time.'

'What!?'

'Insider dealing, Mickey. You might not think there's anything wrong with it, but the law does.'

'So I got a tip off at work.'

'From who?'

Mickey shuffled in his seat. He didn't want to land Uli in trouble. 'The quant guys.'

'So how did your quant boys know about the outbreak before it was made public?'

'You know how it works,' said Mickey. 'They've got hundreds of lines out waiting for a bite. They sift millions of tweets and blogs, they find out what's interesting and what's not. Then they write algorithms to take advantage of some event. But it may never happen and then they don't use it. This time it did.'

'Really?'

'Sure,' said Mickey. Did he really buy it? He didn't know.

Frank sniffed the air. 'There is a stink hanging over all this. And you're starting to smell of it.'

'I ain't done nothing wrong.'

'You've not done a lot right either.' Frank pulled up on the pavement outside Mickey's house. 'Always looking after number one. It's time you thought of someone other than Mickey Summer.'

Frank was starting to sound like Helen. The two of them were both so damn righteous. He got out the car, slammed the door shut and called through the open window. 'Thanks for the sermon. And love to Timothy.'

<h1 style="text-align:center">44</h1>

Hue Wing was growing impatient. The protest in Hong Kong's Victoria Park was losing energy. The pretty speaker in the yellow, pro-democracy dress was overly intellectual and losing her audience. The edges of the crowd began to fray as people drifted away down Causeway Bay and into the commercial district.

Hue slipped some black gloves over his badly bitten hands, checked his face was covered by the head scarf and sunglasses and climbed up onto Queen Victoria's stone base. He grabbed her bronze scepter with one hand and her crown with the other and pulled himself up to stand on her head. He politely but firmly demanded the microphone from the girl in the yellow dress. Disguising his voice in a fake Kunming accent to confuse State Security voice analysts, he shouted:

'Citizens of Hong Kong! What do you want?'

'Democracy! Democracy!' the crowd bellowed, waving the umbrellas that had become a symbol of the pro-democracy movement, as well as a handy defence against police tear gas showers.

'Why are you calling for democracy?' Hue asked. 'Democracy is only a system for selecting a government.'

Umbrellas wilted and the crowd fell silent, suspicious that Hue was a Communist Party provocateur about to plead for continued one-party rule.

'Democratic elections for a new government would be a good place to start,' Hue continued. 'Just as we did not choose Queen Victoria to rule over us, so we did not choose the Communist Party.

We must choose our own leaders. But democracy is only a means to an end. What is that end? What do we really want?'

Hue gazed at the puzzled eyes looking up at him.

'What we really want is freedom!' he shouted.

Now the crowd cheered again and the umbrellas sprang up like spring bamboo.

'Freedom from censorship. Freedom from corruption. Freedom from pollution. Freedom from persecution. Freedom from the arrogance of the Communist Party that believes it is the only party that can run our lives. The Party is just another dynasty like the Qing or Ming, holding court in Beijing, propped up by the suffering masses. The anti-establishment rebellion has brought change to America and Europe. In China the same change is long overdue. Remember the proverb: the best time to plant a tree is twenty five years ago. The next best time is now. We want freedom, now! Not just for Hong Kong. For all of China!'

The crowd cheered again and the other speakers standing on Victoria's base gestured for Hue to continue. But from his vantage point he could see olive green trucks approaching from the highway.

'Wujing!' he shouted before dropping the microphone into the upturned hand of Yellow Dress.

He climbed back down to Victoria's base as the trucks came to a halt at the edge of the park and spat the paramilitary police out of the back. They regrouped in lines. On command from a whistle the front row marched forward. Ten yards from the first of the demonstrators they turned into a blocking line behind plastic shields. The whistle blew again and they shuffled into a tortoise.

Yellow Dress shouted into the microphone: 'This is a peaceful demonstration! We have permission to demonstrate!'

But the tortoise advanced in quick step and tore into the outer edges of the crowd. A young boy escaping on a skateboard took a baton in the face and fell backwards off his board. Two policemen grabbed a foot each and dragged him into the back of a van. A group of young men broke paving slabs and hurled them at the advancing tortoise.

'Don't fight!' Yellow Dress called as a Molotov flew through the air and crashed off a shield. It landed on the road, burnt for a moment and died in a plume of white gas.

Another cocktail landed on the shield and rolled into the road. Now the police lines broke and the Wujing ran forward, batons swinging freely. Hue looked around for an escape route and saw a weakness in the police perimeter.

He swung down to ground level and was about to run when a cold hand grasped his.

'Help me,' said Yellow Dress. 'If they take me again they will kill me.'

'Go!' Hue pushed Yellow Dress towards the crane. She ran without turning back and Hue followed.He felt a blow on his back, turned and jump-kicked a Wujing in the throat. He swept out the legs of another, knocking him to the floor. He rose to punch the third in the solar plexus but he took a heavy blow to the head and his legs buckled.

45

In the Cyber Task Force room, hundreds of people were scurrying around while others sat at computers talking in headsets and frantically tapping at keyboards. Declin made his way over to the control team and introduced himself to Director Solo, a short guy with long brown hair.

'Pleased to have you on board,' said Solo. 'Strap in, get yourself up to speed and push whatever buttons you see fit. I'm not going to second guess you, Declin. Just keep me in the loop.'

It quickly became apparent that Director Solo had his hands full managing upstairs at Langley and outside to the press. That suited Declin fine. He set teams of investigators to re-establish means and methods of cyber infiltration, trace phone records and email traffic into and out of Plum Island and run fresh security checks on staff and security clearances for recent visitors.

He also assigned three teams to work on his favoured six-step threat/adversary model. One team analyzed capabilities and resources. Another looked at intent and motivation, while a third considered access and risk aversion. He gave them a couple of hours then gathered the team heads in an office for coffee and doughnuts.

'Let's share ideas and concerns,' said Declin, dunking a chocolate doughnut. 'First off, Access. What have you got?'

'Network forensics are pretty confident on all counts,' said the team leader. 'The Earth Defence and Taliban cyber got access through the open internet. With Plum Island the hackers managed to get into the intranet via Homeland's online job application portal.'

'Plum Island is a bio-safety level four facility,' said Declin. 'What's the point in going to that much trouble if you let cyber hackers in through your website! So, tell me about the why.'

'The why?'

'I get the Earth Defence blowing up the energy industry and the Taliban derailing the trains. But why release foot-and-mouth disease?'

'A fifty-billion dollar hit to the US economy,' she replied.

'If you've gone to the trouble of getting inside Plum Island, why not release a human pathogen?'

'Maybe they tried. But when they couldn't get that, they got the next best thing.'

'Capabilities next.' Declin drained the last of his coffee and tossed the cup into a bin. 'Dr Kesling could maybe devise the Earth Defence attacks. The Taliban cyber might have done the same. But The Syrian Electronic Army's last successful penetration was simple identity theft. Do we really think they are capable of the Plum Island attack? That's in a different league.'

'Maybe they got lucky,' said a team leader. 'They could have just stumbled across the exploit. And maybe that's why they went for foot-and-mouth and not a human pathogen.'

'Possible,' agreed Declin. 'But let's consider the possibility of outside help. Who do we suspect?

'The Syrian Electronic Army are based in Latakia. That is Syria state controlled territory. They could be backed by the regime.'

Declin shook his head. 'Assad has never had time to develop cyber capability.'

'The Russians?'

Everyone was well aware that relationships with the Russians had cooled to Cold War temperatures and they'd carried out plenty of previous cyber attacks on America. But Declin knew those had been mostly politically motivated. 'I don't see what the Russians have to gain from cyber attacks on our critical infrastructure.'

'More likely ISIS or Nusra Front.'

'But they don't have the cyber capabilities.'

'How about Iran?'

'They could do it,' agreed Declin.

'But they are Shia. Why would they be dealing with the Taliban?'

'They also have a long history of supporting Sunni terrorist groups,' Declin said. 'Anything to get at the Great Satan.'

The room fragmented into further discussion on attribution, but it was just so much guesswork. Declin called an end to the meeting and went for a walk to clear his head. Iran had any number of reasons for supporting cyber attacks on America: revenge for Stuxnet not least among them. Russia also had motive. The attacks weakened and distracted an old cold war enemy while strengthening Russia's new leadership position in the war on terror. Isis had even better motive. So too did rogue elements in Pakistan Cyber.

They could theorize all day but the truth was they didn't know and they didn't have time. Declin needed more facts. And there was only one place left to get them.

46

Kesling was sporting a new haircut, white shirt and blue tie. No doubt on the advice of his attorney.

'A lot has happened since we last spoke,' said Declin.

'Busy world,' replied Kesling.

'You saw the Union Pacific derailments and the nuclear spill?'

'You bet. The nuclear spill is, like, scary shit. Nevada is going to be a no-go zone for a thousand years.'

'What do you think about that?'

Kesling chewed it over for a moment. 'I think: why are we generating nuclear waste in the first place?'

'You think this leak might put a brake on nuclear power?'

'Let's hope so.'

Declin suppressed a smile. Kesling was walking right into his trap. 'And what did you think about the foot-and-mouth outbreak on Plum Island?'

Kesling shrugged. 'Plum Island was an accident waiting to happen.'

'It wasn't an accident.'

'You know what I mean.'

'But you're not bothered about all those cattle that are going to have to be culled.'

'The cattle were going to die anyway. And we consume way too much meat. Paul McCartney has a point.'

'So you sympathize with the cyber attacks on Plum Island?'

Kesling's eyes narrowed. 'Are you sure these are cyber attacks? Maybe Plum Island was their own mess and they're using a cyber attack to cover their backs. That was a top-security bio-hazard facility. That would take one hell of a hacker to get in there.'

'Someone like yourself?' asked Declin. 'You seem to know a lot about it.'

'Plum Island was nothing to do with me.'

'You could also have attacked the railroads,' Declin pressed.

'First I knew about that was when I saw it on the news.'

'We've found similar lines of code in the malware used in each attack. We think the same person is responsible for them all.'

Declin watched Kesling's face tense as he thought things through. He couldn't know that the railroad attack had been traced to Waziristan and Plum Island to Syria. Security protocol dictated they keep attribution under wraps as long as possible so that if Signal Intel picked up relevant chatter they would know it wasn't some idiot feeding off the news.

'We think that person is you,' Declin continued.

Kesling smiled. 'You have nothing on me.'

'You campaigned to have Plum Island closed.'

'I didn't,' replied Kesling, shuffling in his seat.

'You signed an online petition to have the facility closed.' Declin showed him a copy of the relevant document. 'And you have a conviction for criminal damage on an oil pipeline. Join the dots.'

'There's a big leap from one to the other.'

'That would be for a jury to decide.' Declin let the silence hang. 'Once we prove you attacked the fracking rigs and the pipeline – and you know that we will prove that – then it's a simple logical next step to show you're also guilty of similar eco-terrorist attacks on the nuclear waste train and on Plum Island. You'd be facing so many murder and terrorism charges we wouldn't know where to start.'

Kesling glanced at his attorney but said nothing.

'Shall I tell you something interesting?' Declin continued. 'The Union Pacific control room that was hacked into is in Nebraska but most of the fatalities on the trains happened in Nevada.'

Kesling's face screwed up. 'That's interesting?'

'It sure is, because Nebraska and Nevada have something in common.'

'Both start with 'N' and end in 'A'.'

'Something more relevant. They both have the death penalty. So wherever you get tried, that's what you'll get for murder.'

'Is that right?'

'Lethal injection.' Declin noticed Kesling's eyes widen. He decided it was time to throw out some rope. 'But if you give us someone else to put in the frame, you prove that you didn't write the malware, you tell us who did, and we'd be able to drop the murder charge in those states.'

'I had nothing to do with Plum Island or Union Pacific.'

'Let's recap,' said Declin. 'Our country has suffered a series of cyber eco-terrorism attacks. People have been murdered. We want to find those responsible. Right now you're all we've got. You're facing multiple charges. Even if you avoid the death penalty you'll be going to prison for such a long time that if you ever get out, there won't be a slab of ice left in Antarctica.'

'Could I have a word with my client in private?' asked the attorney.

Declin left the room and walked a little way down the corridor.

After a few minutes the interview room door opened and the attorney called him back in. Kesling sat forward in his chair with his elbows on the table. 'He went by the name of Putin.'

'First name?'

'Vladimir,' whispered Kesling.

'Vladimir Putin?'

Kesling's cheeks reddened. 'I guess it wasn't his real name.'

'I guess not,' said Declin. 'Can you describe him?'

'He contacted me first through the website. Then he asked to chat off-line.'

'What did he sound like? Any accent? Russian perhaps?'

'It was all done by text.'

'Do you still have the phone?'

'I destroyed it.'

'When was this?'

'Early December last year.'

'What happened next?'

'He sent me a memory stick in the post.'

'Where did he send it from?'

'New York postmark. I noted that.'

'Then what?'

'He texted me and explained there were two malwares on it. One to shut down a fracking well and one to shut down an oil pipeline.'

'Do you still have this stick?'

Kesling shook his head. 'Also destroyed.'

'Did this Vladimir Putin guy say why he wanted to do this?'

'He just said he wanted to save the planet.' Kesling shrugged. 'How was I to know any different?'

47

When Hue regained his senses he discovered that he was cuffed in the back of a moving van with perhaps twenty other pro-democracy protestors. He had no idea how long he'd been unconscious, but his head felt like it was gripped in a vice. They travelled in silence for several hours. When the truck finally came to a stop, the doors opened on a freshly-painted sign announcing The Ministry of Health and Welfare's Drug-Rehabilitation Center. The new name the Party had adopted for re-education camps.

They lined up beside a fence topped with razor wire. Beyond this a guard tower overlooked an exercise yard where prisoners stood with faces turned obediently to a huge screen running party propaganda. One older woman with a pale, anxious face crouched to one side of the yard. She had been forced to stand with knees bent and arms stretched behind her in the so-called jet plane position favoured in the Cultural Revolution. A hand-written sign hung from her neck: 'I will learn to love the Party'.

The message was not lost on the new arrivals as they filed inside a low building. Standing in the doorway an officer stared with contempt at each newcomer from under his peaked hat.

As he passed the officer Hue leant close and whispered under his breath: 'Five million Yuan.'

The officer's ears pricked, but he said nothing and Hue walked on through another door. On the other side he was offered a glass of water and a pill. He drank the water and pretended to take the sedative, holding it in his gum until he could spit it out without being seen. He waited his turn to be processed. Eventually he was led into an interview room, empty except for one plastic chair and table. Hue stood. The Mongolian officer entered the room, studying Hue's identity papers. He checked the photo against the face and dismissed the guard.

'You mentioned five million Yuan,' he said, tilting his head slightly to one side. 'That is what you are offering me to let you go?'

Hue shook his head. 'Five million Yuan is what you will pay me to stop me from telling my father about your mistake.'

The officer's smile vanished. He looked again at the ID and walked quickly out of the room. Hue stepped over to the door and put his ear to the open metal grate.

'Check this name and ID on Baidu,' the officer barked. 'Find out who is his father.'

A few moments later another man called out, 'Bloody hell!'

'Who is it?'

'His father is Min Hung.'

'Let me see.' More swearing. 'Bring me his phone.'

Hue smiled as he pictured the officer's worried eyes looking through the fake contacts list on the decoy phone.

'Check this number.'

The officer read out the number Hue had input under 'Baba'.

'Shall I dial it?'

'No! Check with the operator.'

The assistant asked the operator to identify the number.

'No problem,' he said after a short time. 'Thank you.'

'Well?'

'It is the office of Min Hung in Wuhan.'

Hue smiled as he sensed the fear in the other room. Min Hung, the Party Secretary for Hubei province, public face of the anti-corruption drive and next in line for promotion to the ruling Politburo Standing Committee. Min Hung was not someone to upset.

A few more expletives before footsteps returned. Hue stepped away from the door. A metal bolt slid open and the door swung in. The guard un-cuffed Hue and the officer handed back his ID and phone.

'You're free to go.'

Hue followed the officer outside where he instructed his driver to give Hue a lift back to Hong Kong.

Hue climbed into the passenger seat. The word had spread around the guards and a farewell committee of sorts gathered to catch a glimpse of the son of Min Hung.

Hue imagined how much more frightened they would be if they knew the identity of his real father.

48

As Declin waited for people to gather for the latest agency briefing, he saw a number of new faces; reps from various military forces and intelligence agencies and others from Homeland departments. Solo updated everyone with the very latest intelligence. This included Declin's own findings from his interview with Kesling. Solo had fed the name Vladimir Putin into the system with predictably non-usable results. But they had at least established now that the Earth Defence had outside help. They knew too that the Taliban Cyber had outside help from someone called Nezzar. Whether it was the same person, and whether he had also helped the Syrian Electronic Army they did not know, but it seemed unlikely to Declin that one individual could post a memory disk from New York, take tea with the Taliban in Waziristan and reappear in the war zone of Syria. He expected this would now become a major focus of the investigation.

But instead, Solo announced that the President had ordered a Special Forces strike on The Syrian Electronic Army.

'No way!' Declin shouted. 'A strike might destroy the best lead we have.'

'The mission objective is to recover equipment and evidence intact,' said Solo.

'We need to monitor these guys,' Declin pressed. 'We need to learn who they are and what they want.'

'And while we're watching, they could hit us with another cyber attack.'

'Watching them is the best way to prevent another attack, if you ask me.'

'The President didn't,' said Solo.

'So was this the President's idea or did someone recommend this action to him?'

'You don't need to know the wheres and whys of a presidential decision, Special Agent Lehane.'

'Do the Special Ops team even know what to look for?'

'We'll brief them thoroughly.'

'I'm going with them.'

'I can't sanction that.'

'I'm not asking you to,' said Declin. 'I don't work for this agency.'

49

Full credit to old Xian, the forger who had made Hue's fake ID. Without it Hue would be languishing in the re-education camp like the other poor souls. Xian came from a line of revered scribes that had lived in the old capital for centuries. This and the fact that his name was so obviously associated with the ruling classes had left him terribly persecuted during the cultural revolution, and now he enjoyed beating the establishment with his forgeries.

It was Xian who had discovered the likeness between Hue and the real son of Min Hung, the Party Secretary for Hubei province. Hue had thought it too dangerous to pretend to be the son of someone so famous and feared. But Xian had convinced him that small lies are easily spotted, while big, bold lies are believed.

Indeed that was why democracy protests in Beijing were cut more slack than those in Hong Kong or Shanghai. The Wujing were scared of arresting someone in case it was a little prince or princess who would make a phone call to Baba and they would be the ones in trouble.

Xian had been proven correct. Nevertheless, Hue could not quite believe his luck that the ruse had worked. A part of him worried that the officer had let him escape the camp so they could follow him back to Beijing and see who he was connected to.

So before he returned to Xian to ask for a new identity, he mingled in the Friday afternoon crush at the market, looking for evidence of surveillance: a ducking head, an averted eye, unnatural tension in the movement of people.

When he was reasonably confident he was not being followed he found a 'back-watcher' that he had used before and slipped him fifty Yuan. He continued meandering around the stalls. He bought some rice noodles and sauce for his mother. After thirty minutes he returned to the back-watcher and received a reassuring nod of the head.

He wandered to one of the few remaining internet cafes. This one was really only in business because of the premium rate service it provided. Some of its computers were connected to a series of relay servers that evaded monitoring by state security. Hue settled down at one of these with a green tea and surfed through news channels.

There was no mention of the crackdown in the Chinese State news of course, but he found some heavily censored comments on a message board. He posted a report about the violent crackdown and the removal of prisoners to detention camps. It was immediately countered by lies from an army of cyber mamas. It was pointless; nine cows, one hair, as his mother liked to say.

He arrived at the printing shop that Xian used for cover. With a broad smile, old Xian invited him into the back room. He lifted Hue's cap and nodded as he saw the gash on his head.

'You are a lucky, lucky boy, Hue Wing,' he said.

'I'm going to need a new ID,' Hue said, ignoring the old man's concern. 'The other may be compromised now.'

'A shame,' said Xian, crinkling up his already heavily wrinkled face. 'You are proving to be a very costly customer.'

'I paid you five hundred Yuan for the last ID.'

'Hah! I had to pay a thousand Yuan for the chip data, because the thief knew it was Min Hung's son. Remember that my service is designed for migrant workers needing papers. For that I have to pay the local police a small protection fee. But if they find me giving papers to a pro-democracy activist I will have to pay many thousands.'

'Freedom activist,' corrected Hue.

'You are playing a qin to a cow,' he replied. 'I am not interested in your politics. I am only helping you because of your mother.' He bowed his head slightly and added, 'And in memory of your sister.'

'I am grateful.' Hue handed over a thousand Yuan. 'Let me know if you need more money.'

Xian took the money and locked it in a drawer. 'The son of another big Party name, if I can find one that looks like you?'

'It worked well last time.'

'When do you need the papers?'

'As soon as possible. There are demonstrations planned again for next week.'

Xian shook his head. 'Is democracy really so important to

you?'

'Not democracy, freedom.'

'But why do you bother?'

'For the same reason as you help me. I do it for my mother and the memory of my sister.'

<h1 style="text-align:center">50</h1>

Mickey had seen nothing like it since the financial crash. US markets were collapsing, with equity markets and treasuries both in freefall. But Cindy had not seen it coming and was taking no evasive action, she just stared at the screens as the fund lost millions every second.

Mickey could contain himself no longer. He walked into her office. 'Are you just going to sit there and do nothing?'

She looked up, her face paler than usual. 'What do you expect me to do?'

'Take corrective action before the markets fall further and we lose even more.'

'We're making money on gold,' she said pulling up a fresh screen. 'It's up a hundred dollars on the day.'

'Chicken feed compared to what we're losing overall.'

She sat up straighter in her chair. 'The fund doesn't play general market movements in that way.'

'That's why you're getting burnt.'

She bit her bottom lip and looked at him a while. 'We do analysis here, Mickey. We don't try to second guess general market movements. Crispin thinks it is impossible.'

'In that case hedge that risk out.'

'Crispin also thinks hedging is a waste of money.'

'Maybe he's not as smart as everyone says. You can at least trade around and make up for some of the losses. In volatile markets like this there is easy money to be made.'

'Really. So what would you do?'

'Well, as you ask, I've noticed some Footsie six-month call options that are wrongly priced. I'd grab a few of those for starters.'

She laughed. 'Maybe you're not as smart as everyone says either. You just told me you thought markets would fall further.'

'I do. But that trade is already in the price. And I might be wrong. The smart trade is to bet on a rally. Even if it doesn't happen the call options should get re-priced and you'll make money anyway.' Mickey suddenly realized he didn't know what Cindy had done before she joined the Quadra Fund. 'Have you got a trading background at all?'

'We'll stay on course with our existing investment philosophy,' she replied, ducking the question. 'It's served us well to date.'

'That's the Edward Smith philosophy,' said Mickey. 'Steady as she goes.'

Cindy frowned. 'I don't know the name.'

'Captain of the Titanic.'

51

First light flickered on a grey South China Sea. At the Chinese airbase on Yongshu Reef a Super Frelon helicopter sucked up its cargo of marines, lifted off the runway and turned ninety degrees. It hovered uncertainly for almost a minute, tipped gently forward and moved up and away. Through the open door the commander watched the other helicopters lifting off and fanning out for their own destinations elsewhere in the archipelago. Take-off and flight speeds were set so that everyone would arrive at their targets at exactly 06:00.

With similarly perfect timing the Flankers support aircraft appeared overhead, having flown from their base on Hainan Island. From there too, strategic bombers had been sent to destroy enemy airfields: the Taiwanese at Taiping, the Philippines on Thitu and Malaysia on Danwan Jiao.

The commander's own target was the Vietnamese occupied reef of Hongxiu Dao. Its defenders had been on high alert for a fortnight and the commander knew they would put up stiff resistance. By way of confirmation a salvo of SAM missiles raced up as they neared. The pilot dropped his chaff cloud to confuse the missiles' sensors and banked sharply. Protected in his anti-G suit the pilot would be relatively comfortable, whereas the commander and his marines were thrown around like winnowed rice hulls.

The Frelon resumed course as the Chinese destroyer Haribung pounded the Vietnamese artillery positions. The marines landed under cover of smoke, deployed and held a defensive position while the shelling unfolded. As they advanced the Vietnamese returned light arms fire. But they were heavily outnumbered and the Chinese advanced steadily up the length of the small island. After an hour of fighting, the Vietnamese made a controlled retreat and escaped from the north end in coastal patrol boats.

The marines carefully checked over every square meter of the island. The commander retrieved a Chinese flag from the helicopter and attached it to the white watchtower.

'The Party and the Motherland!'

52

A deferential drop in the hubbub greeted President Topps's arrival at the situation room in the White House West Wing. The President had filled the room with his closest advisors and a selection of cheese and salmon sandwiches that lay untouched at either end of the long wooden table.

'Okay,' he said, as he took his seat. 'The big item is the Cyber Crisis. But before we get to that we need to look at the South China Sea situation. I'll be straight up and say my inclination is to do nothing.'

'We just can't do that,' said the Secretary of State, Hank Hoffmann, staring at the President with his bloodhound demeanor. 'We have defence treaty obligations. I already made a statement reminding the Chinese of that.'

'Unfortunately without checking with me,' said President Topps. He turned to the Director of the NSA, Cresta Patton. 'Let's say we do nothing and we let the Chinese keep these islands. What have they actually gained?'

Cresta perched on the edge of her chair, her head tilted to one side looking at the President out of the corner of her eyes. This, coupled with her large nose, thin face and quicksilver hair gave the appearance of a grey parrot.

'The archipelago consists of around seven hundred uninhabited islands and reefs. The value lies in the territorial claim the islands give to sections of the South China Sea and the fishing and mineral rights which come with that. But it's the geopolitical gain that's more important.'

'And that's what we have to push back on somehow,' said Hank. 'At least listen to the proposal for limited military action.'

'Okay,' the President nodded. 'Let's hear it.'

General Horn, Chairman of the Joint Chiefs of Staff coughed to clear his throat. He had an irritating way of writhing enthusiastically when he spoke, and President Topps had long ago regretted promoting him from Cyber Command to a position as the first 'desk-soldier Chair' not to come from proper combat forces.

'We have a task force comprising fifteen Pacific-rim nations already on exercise in the South Pacific. We propose switching location to the South China Sea. What better way of blowing apart the Chinese blockade and establishing the waters as international?'

'I was elected with a mandate not to lose American lives policing other peoples' problems in other parts of the world.'

'We can't sit back and do nothing,' said Hank. 'That would only encourage the Chinese to move on to their next adventure, whatever that might be.'

'I'm not advocating sitting back and doing nothing,' said President Topps. 'For now we condemn the use of military force in the strongest possible terms, we firmly rebut their claims to both the islands and the South China Sea and we make it clear that our military shipping will respond to any hindrance with overwhelming force.'

'But militarily we do nothing?' asked General Horn with a look of mild disbelief.

'We have a major crisis on our own soil to deal with. That's what we need to turn our attention to now.'

He nodded to Cresta Patton and she briefed the room on the latest in the Cyber crisis. When she had finished President Topps turned to Sandy Bernstein, the Treasury Secretary. 'What's the cost of all this, Sandy?'

Bernstein had a blond Caesar haircut and the gym-toned physique of a younger man. He liked an audience and gave a detailed explanation of the damage to the economy.

The President sat forward in his chair. 'Some outside agency is co-ordinating these attacks, right?'

Cresta nodded. 'Certainly the eco hactivists and the cyber jihadists in Pakistan both had outside help. We're hoping the Special Ops assault on the group in Syria might help us connect the dots.'

'Let's hear about that.'

General Horn cleared his throat. 'The terrorist cyber room is in a heavily militarized residential area in the north of the Syrian port town of Latakia.' He flashed up a map on the screen. 'Carrier strike Group Eleven is currently with the sixth fleet in the Mediterranean. It will drop a SEAL team five miles off shore. They will proceed by inflatable to one mile offshore, scuttle the boat and swim by fin the final mile. Once they have re-orientated they will signal for the extraction team to leave the USS Nimitz by helicopter. Sixteen minutes later the SEALS will have secured the area around the cyber room and the extraction team will land and remove what personnel and equipment they can.'

'This is the smartest way to find out who is behind the attacks, right?'

'Given the urgency of the situation.'

'Declin Lehane is going in with the extraction team,' Cresta announced. 'He volunteered to go in with the SEALs precisely because he wants to make sure we get the best possible information.'

'He is?' asked the President.

'He's a cyber agent with the FBI,' said Cresta. 'He's been front and center of this investigation all along.'

The President looked around to see if anyone else had spotted the irony. 'Is that supposed to instill me with confidence? He hasn't had any success so far.'

'He's good and he's brave,' Cresta replied. 'I can't imagine any other cyber geek going in on an active mission.'

The President gave her the benefit of the doubt. 'Okay, so I like the plan. Do we tell the Russians what we're doing?'

'Hell no,' said Leon Calvara, Director CIA.

The President turned to the Secretary of State. 'Is that going to cause us problems, Hank?'

'We'll deal with it.'

'When do you go?' he asked, turning back to Horn.

'The teams are on thirty-minutes notice. They'd like to go at 05:00 Eastern European time, which will be 22:00 Eastern Standard time. That's ninety minutes from now.'

The President knew he'd looked weak backing down from military action in the South China Sea. He was pleased to be able to take affirmative action now.

'These cyber terrorists are a real and present danger to our country. Let's show them, and anyone else contemplating cyber war on the United States, that we will track them down, wherever they're hiding ... and mete out justice.'

53

The Stars and Stripes flying over the steel battleship produced a rush of adrenalin that warmed Declin against the sharp Aegean wind. He turned to view a flight deck stacked with perhaps one hundred aircraft in various states of preparedness.

Of the numerous combatants in Syria the only force that could seriously trouble the *Nimitz* was the Russians. Although they were supposedly an ally in Syria, they were the main competitor in the geo-political game, and it was impossible to tell how they might react to an incursion of Syrian air space. With a Russian airbase close it was a comfort to know that the *Nimitz* was ready to defend itself. If needed.

Scattered on the deck like children's toys were the *Nimitz's* own Wolf Pack and Screamin' Indian helicopters, designed for sea combat and maritime strike. The Special Operations wing preferred to use the Air Force Pave helicopter because the crew of six, with its highly advance navigational system, could fly almost undetected and land on a dime. Or, more particularly in this instance, on the roof of the cyber-jihadist house that had been identified in the stone maze surrounding the port of Latakia.

Declin boarded the waiting Pave, the pitch of its blades rising before holding impatiently. When the helicopter was finally released into the air it screamed away from the flight deck and dropped sharply, levelling out to fly 'feet wet' over the moonlit-crested waves. As they raced towards the Syrian coast the cockpit display of the countdown dropped to fourteen minutes. The lights of Latakia rushed to meet them and soon they were racing over the rooftops.

T-minus-twenty seconds and a voice called through to the pilot: 'The LZ is active.'

Declin gripped his bench seat. The plan had been for the Landing Zone to have been cleared by the SEAL team before they arrived. Muzzle flash and tracers rose from a warehouse below. The starboard gunner returned fire with a sustained twenty second burst that blew the front off the first floor.

Declin's mouth went dry as the bird landed inelegantly on the roof. It spat open the back door. Declin followed the rest of the team down the ramp.

A SEAL slapped the top of his head. 'Down!'

Doubled-up, his chest pounding like a pulsar, Declin ran over the roof to an open hatch. Through this and down a narrow staircase into a windowless space. With a flashlight he surveyed a room stuffed full of equipment. It would take a day to clear it under domestic protocol. He'd been told he had five minutes. And that was before the fire-fight had started.

'Take anything that is running or on standby first,' Declin shouted to the rest of the extraction team. 'And don't forget to snap a screen shot.'

As the others began unplugging and carrying away equipment he took a dozen photos of the room from various angles, trying to blank out the exchanges of gunfire between the street and the helicopter. The team hurried through drawers and filing cabinets, stashing anything in print or hand written. They still had plenty of drawers to work through when a shout came down the hatch.

'Time to go.'

Clutching a suitcase in each hand Declin hurried up the stairs. On the rooftop he ran in a crouch up a ramp into the bird, three guns blazing, blades straining to go. He noted a prisoner cuffed between two SEALs.

As the last SEAL dived in another shouted: 'Good to go.'

The bird screamed into the air and banked hard over the rooftops. As they reached the sea a Russian fighter buzzed them, demanding identification.

'Tell them we're a medical EVAC,' said the pilot. 'Request they escort us to open sea.'

The communications officer relayed the message. 'They still want us to ID.'

'Say again: this is a medical EVAC.'

'Copy that.'

The helicopter raced like a demented Nazgul until it flew over international waters. They were met by two F-18s from the *Nimitz*. After a moment of nerve jangling brinkmanship the Russian fighter peeled off.

The bird pilot moderated his speed and, finally, smiles broke out all round. No casualties for the home team and they'd brought back a stash of hardware. And another prisoner. Declin resolved to keep this one alive.

54

Hue knocked gently. After a long silence, cautious, brown eyes appear at the crack in the door.

'It's me, Hue.'

The chain rattled, the door opened and his mother raised her arms. 'My little Hue. What a nice....,' she started but the blast of cold air triggered a racking cough.

'You should see the doctor.'

'I've had this cough for years.'

'Precisely.'

'It's nothing.'

She motioned for him to kiss her and he took her small head in his big hands and kissed her thinning grey hair.

'Come in,' she said. 'What a nice surprise.'

'I told you I would visit on Friday.'

'Yes, yes. Come in. What a nice surprise.'

He followed her slow shuffle over the concrete floor and turned the thermostat up as he passed. The kitchen was no warmer, the steam from the rice cooker passing its heat into the night as it condensed on the windows.

'When are they going to double-glaze the windows?' asked Hue.

'Pah,' she said, whistling hot air through the gap in her teeth like a boiling kettle.

'But the development committee will do the work for free. They've been ordered to do it by the environment regulator.'

'Perhaps they will do it for free, but Toon Fui says I must first pay him five hundred Yuan.'

'For what?'

'Administration!' she scoffed.

Hue stopped himself from offering to pay the corrupt local housing official, because she would never allow it. He quickly ran through the gamut of emotions that she must have run previously: anger at the corruption, resignation that the only way to get the work done was to acquiesce, and finally indignation. He would also have chosen to suffer the cold rather than pay Toon Fui.

'I've made dinner,' she said, chopping an onion and pepper and adding them to a Wok of ginger and bean shoots.

They stood in comfortable silence under the light of a single uncovered bulb while she cooked and then he helped her carry the food to a table set for one. She swept cracked sunflower seeds from the plastic surface into a bin, laid out another pair of chopsticks and a glass of water.

Over dinner she talked about life in the housing block. Recalling the horror of her neighbor who had been trapped in the elevator for seventeen hours without her epilepsy medication. Reflecting on how the family two doors along dared to keep and feed three cats when many in the block were hungry.

She also worried over the arguments that fell through the ceiling from the new Huinan immigrant family in the apartment above. She puzzled over the high price of rice which was surely no less a commodity than the water that ran freely from the rivers.

Hue loved her anecdotes of a simple yet full life in the apartment block. It was comfortingly disconnected from the apparently rich yet empty life outside that his mother observed with only casual interest through the looking glass of her television. A looking glass with a two inch vertical crack down the left hand side that seemed not to trouble her.

Even if it did, she would no more allow Hue to buy her a new television than pay for double glazing.

'Any special friend I should know about?'

He smothered a sigh. 'No, Mother.'

'You're not getting any younger.'

'I know.'

Here was another disconnect. She, more than anyone, knew why there were two men of Hue's age chasing every girl in Beijing.

'There is change in the air, Mother.'

'It has been getting cold ...'

'I don't mean the weather. The people are turning against the party. The party leaders are scared. Even General Wing.'

'He told you this? You've seen him?'

'He called me the other day. It was a surprise.'

'What did he want?'

Hue shrugged. 'He wants to take me for dinner.'

'I thought you had disowned him.'

'He is a powerful man. Someday I might be able to use that power to my advantage.'

They both turned to look at a the wedding photograph with his father, a young man in utilitarian grey Mao suit.

'Be careful,' she said. 'Do not trust him.'

55

Declin commandeered a secure communications room in the heart of the *Nimitz*. Here, together with the Fleet Cyber team, he took a first pass through the haul from Latakia.

'Special Agent Lehane!' a cyber analyst called out. 'Take a look at this.'

Declin hurried over. 'What do you have?'

'I've found the machine code malware for the Plum Island attack. It was just sitting there on the hard drive.'

'Have you tried a file recovery?'

The analyst restored a deleted program.

'Bingo,' she said. 'The java source code.' She skimmed through the inline comments and program statements. 'There's the code for the air-filtration unit.'

'And that's the assembly code,' said Declin. 'And there's the call to the function.'

'We underestimated these guys,' said the analyst. 'They did write it themselves.'

'Not necessarily. Let's check the log.' Declin ran an automated recovery and worked through the log. 'It looks as though the source code was downloaded from a drop box.'

'So they didn't actually write it,' said the analyst.

'We need to grind away at this code. Somewhere in it there could be a clue as to who did.'

'Well one thing we know is that they speak English.'

'I'm not so sure about that,' said Declin. 'There are subtle differences in the quality of the English. The variables, classes and methods all use perfect English.'

'They have to,' said the analyst. 'Or they won't work.'

'Precisely. But the comments, in-line strings, commit messages and indicators are written in poor English. So either the programmer was partly illiterate, which seems unlikely, or they were written in the programmer's native language and translated to try and fool us.'

The fleet cyber analyst studied the code again. 'So what do you think was the original language?'

'We'll let linguistics take a look and see if they can figure …' Declin stopped mid sentence and jabbed a finger at the screen. 'Look at that. The path to the source file: user/malware/two sixty nine.'

'What about it?' asked the analyst.

'The compiler flags in the other malwares also had numbers at the end of the file name.'

'So?'

'You normally give malware a name, not a number.'

The analyst shrugged. 'So this compiler used a number. It's just a quirk.'

'Quirks are useful,' said Declin. 'I'll get analytics to check out the numbers. You keep digging here.'

Declin stepped over to the team studying the data retrieved from the cell phone. 'Anything good to report?'

'How good do you want?'

'Plenty.'

'Well, we have a whole bunch of incriminating chatter about the Plum Island attack,' said the analyst.

'That's good,' said Declin. 'But it's not really anything new.'

'We also have a number of texts referencing a man who was clearly co-ordinating the timing of the attack.'

'Name?' asked Declin.

'Referred to sometimes as Nez and other times as Nebuch. Do you think he's connected to the man the Cyber Taliban called Nezzar.'

'It's one person,' said Declin, disappointed that he had not realized it sooner. 'Nez, Nezzar, Nebuch are all abbreviations of one name. Nebuchadnezzar.'

'You know him?'

'He was a Babylonian king,' Declin said. 'But various crazies over the years, including Saddam Hussein, have adopted the *nom de guerre*.'

'So you don't think it's his real name?'

'It doesn't matter,' Declin said. 'A name is a name. Let's see what our prisoner knows about it.'

* * *

Declin had made sure the prisoner was taken into custody by the Fleet and not left in the hands of the CIA agents, who had coveted him from the moment he had landed on the *Nimitz*. He was pleased to find him looking well, if sweaty and wild eyed.

'What did you do in Latakia?' Declin asked.

'I am a bodyguard.'

'For who?'

'For the computer warriors.'

'Are you a computer warrior as well?'

The prisoner shook his head. 'I don't understand computers.'

With a little more questioning it quickly became clear that the bodyguard knew nothing of cyber warfare and Declin changed tack.

'Who is Nez or Nezzar?'

The prisoner frowned. 'I don't know that name.'

'Do you know a man named Nebuch or Nebuchadnezzar?'

The brow furrowed deeper. 'We had nobody with us with a name like that.'

Declin couldn't tell if the prisoner was lying or telling the truth. But they had the phone records so it didn't really matter. 'Were your computer warriors planning another cyber attack?'

The prisoner hesitated. 'Yes.'

'What were they planning to do?'

Again the prisoner hesitated. 'I don't know what they plan to do. But I heard them talking about another attack.'

'What did they say about it?'

The prisoner smiled. 'They are planning something that will poison the very blood of the Great Satan.'

'They already did that,' Declin said. 'They released the foot-and-mouth virus and poisoned the cows.'

'No,' said the prisoner. 'It is something else. I don't know what it is, but I think it is much more dangerous.'

56

Mickey knew that sooner or later, Cindy, Helen, Brighouse or even Mickey himself, would call time on his work at the Quadra Fund and he'd be back selling vegetables, which, when he really thought about it, wasn't such a bad way to fill the daylight hours. So he decided to keep his hand in and spend a day working at the stall. A busy start quietened down by late morning, and his neighboring stall holder came up to have a word. 'Your missus came by yesterday.'

'I know,' said Mickey. 'Why did you tell 'er I'm hardly ever here?'

'She asked.'

'Next time switch on brain before opening mouth.'

Johnny shrugged, impervious to insult. 'What have you been getting up to anyway?'

'People to see, places to go,' said Mickey.

'Newmarket, Aintree, Doncaster …'

'Not the horses. And don't you joke about that to my missus.'

Mickey stepped back to his stall to serve an old dear a pound of spuds. He just finished when a familiar face appeared. 'Here's trouble.'

'Depends on your point of view,' replied Frank. 'A word in your plug hole when you get a moment.'

They moved out of earshot.

'So what do you want?' asked Mickey.

'Incriminating evidence against your colleagues at the Quanta Fund.'

'I ain't found anything.'

'Maybe you're not looking hard enough.'

'Maybe that's because there's nothing to find.'

'Give me a break, Mickey. They're on the wrong side of the law. You need to decide which side you're on.'

'I ain't found anything,' Mickey repeated.

'What about the Cattle Futures trade?'

'I can't find any evidence that was from insider trading.'

'Looks like we'll just have to prosecute you then. Shame.'

'Whoa!' Mickey held his hands up. 'If they did have inside information I didn't know it.'

'Don't take me for a fool, Mickey.'

'I'm on your side. I've sniffed around and I can't find anything.'

'Sniff harder. Or I mean it. You're going to jail.'

57

Declin entered the name Nebuchadnezzar into NSA's global search and surveillance engines. While Echelon, Prism, NarusInsight, DISHFIRE and Fairview roamed through cyberspace, Declin tasked teams of analysts back home to trawl through Middle Eastern emails and meta data from phone traffic. They also loaded hotel reservations, travel bookings, online purchases, anything that could be recorded into the analysis.

Once he had something to report he rang Calvara.

'We've tracked down another cyber group in Basra,' Declin said. 'And they appear to be expecting a visit from Nebuchadnezzar. They're operating from a warehouse near El Asma'ai market. Local operatives have put the building under secure quarantine and surveillance.'

'So I heard.'

Declin was surprised Calvara sounded so underwhelmed. 'That's pretty good progress to my mind.'

'Progress will have been made when the cyber threat is neutralized.'

'Now that I can watch a group real time I hope to …'

'We don't have time for watching,' Calvara said. 'The President has ordered a Special Forces strike.'

'Not again? What's his problem?'

'His problem is America is under attack. His solution is to be proactive. You want to tell him he's wrong.'

'Put him on the line,' Declin shouted. 'I will certainly tell him that. We need to monitor the cyber jihadists in Basra. We need more intel.'

'Your sit-and-see approach hasn't got us a long way up to date.'

'My approach!' Declin wanted to throw the phone at Calvara. 'I've been hassled into premature action all along. That's where we have been losing the investigation.'

'Things moving a little too quickly for you are they, Declin?'

He ignored the dig. He had to make the most of the hand he'd been dealt. 'I need to hitch another ride.'

58

Hue employed his trusted back-watcher for a full hour around the market before satisfying himself that he was not being followed. He walked casually but purposefully to the bus station, conscious that the surveillance cameras were programmed to recognise erratic walking patterns. And of course although he knew the cameras were omnipresent on lampposts and street signs, he did not dare even glance at them because direct eye contact set off alarms and attracted scrutiny that he did not want at the best of times. And certainly not today.

He caught the subway to the 798 Art District. The pedestrian streets were lined as always with incongruous gorillas, dinosaurs and other sculptures, but a mean wind from the Mongolian plains had swept the Saturday crowds inside the Bauhaus-style former factories.

Hue made his way to the third floor of the Galleria Continua and meandered among the paintings of industrial wastelands, affecting as much interest as he could manage. He found the petite journalist standing beside a painting of a disused mine elevator. They made small talk around the picture until they were satisfied nobody was listening and that they had built enough cover to break into a normal conversation.

'So have you been sent by your masters?' Hue asked. 'Or is this another unofficial visit?'

'Unofficial,' she replied apologetically.

'What are they waiting for?'

'Validation,' she said. 'I need something. A name?'

'No.'

'Your place of work?'

'I can't give you anything. Why do you need it? The information I've given you so far has been accurate, yes?'

She smoothed a non-existent crease in her coat. 'The assessment team need to know why you gave us the information.'

'I told you why. We need help to fight the Party propaganda machine.'

'But if they do not know your identity how do they know you are not working for the Party to distract them.'

Hue laughed at the irony. He removed his cap and pointed to his gash. 'A present from the Wujing in Hong Kong.'

She raised an eyebrow. 'So you were there. I heard rumors that a pro-democracy demonstration had been broken up.'

'So you're a journalist. Why don't you write about it?'

'It wouldn't get passed by the censors.'

'Maybe a hundred were rounded up,' said Hue. 'They were taken away to re-education camps without trial. And no mention of this in the media.'

'Everyone is talking only about the South China Sea.'

'Which is exactly what the Party want. That's what it's about. A popular fight to distract people from fighting for freedom. Do you understand?'

'I'm sure you are right.'

'Well tell your friends in Spook City. And tell them to trust me. And to help the Freedom Movement.'

59

Declin travelled up front of an armored vehicle through Basra's morning rush hour. Iraqi troops waved them through an outer perimeter that had been secured with the help of the El Asma police department. The street outside the warehouse emptied as the Abrams tanks rattled to a stop.

The assault team charged the warehouse, shouting in English and Arabic, hammering on doors. A deep, hollow boom blew the window into the street.

'Booby trap,' said Declin's driver.

'Shit. Is anyone hurt?'

But the driver didn't answer. As the smoke cleared the assault team ran inside. A couple of minutes later a sergeant re-appeared. 'All clear.'

Declin dropped down into a street covered in rubble and shards of glass. Black smoke billowed through the empty window frames. Inside the warehouse he ripped a carbon dioxide cylinder from a wall and ran to tackle the fire. On the blackened wall on the far side of the room, a jihadist flag had somehow survived intact. Underneath it lay a mash of broken computer parts; circuit boards, transistors, screens, keyboards.

'They must have known we were coming,' said Declin. 'Let's see what we can find anyway.'

He instructed the forensics team to check through the room using standard procedure, swabbing surfaces and the remaining equipment for DNA, and dusting for prints. He found a router behind a pillar. It had survived almost intact and might have passwords that in themselves could reveal something.

He found documents left in the bottom of a metal filing cabinet that had otherwise been emptied. He scanned and pushed them through an encryption program on a laptop before sending them in a series of short digital bursts via satellite to Langley.

'Something interesting here!' A technician called out, holding what looked like a delicately carved cigarette box.

'Take a look inside.'

Declin took the box, which was surprisingly heavy. In place of the cigars or cigarettes he had expected, the box contained a single round metal disc.

'What is that?' asked the technician.

'Fucking hell!' Declin slammed the box shut. He turned to the assault team commander. 'I need a Geiger counter.'

'A Geiger counter? I don't have one.'

'Get one!'

A few minutes later the commander returned with headphones that Declin placed on his head. He opened the box and quickly passed the wand over the disc. Clickety click as the needle on the

Geiger display flicked up a notch. Declin shut the lid and set the box down on the table.

'I'm guessing that is Uranium.'

'What are these cyber guys doing with Uranium?' asked the technician.

'That's what we have to find out.'

As Declin looked at the sabotaged equipment surrounding him, he had a horrible feeling that they were behind the curve yet again.

60

Mickey needed to look at the Quadra Fund's historic trading to better understand how it worked and, more particularly, whether it really was making money by illegitimate means. He'd asked to see that information when he first came on board. But Cindy had refused and, although Mickey thought it strange that she was so precious about it, he hadn't pushed.

He couldn't figure out how to get hold of it until he hit on the idea of using a friendly, prospective client. He got him to send in an email request to see the trading data. Mickey forwarded this to a junior in compliance who he hoped would give out the information without asking questions.

No such luck. The junior passed the request on to the Head of Compliance. And that happened to be Cindy. She called Mickey in to her office.

'Why does your client want this information?' she asked, waving a print out of the email.

'What does he want?' asked Mickey, playing dumb.

She turned the paper round and slid it over her desk. 'Full details of our past investments and performance.'

'Don't we have it?'

'Of course we do. But no other client has examined our past trades with this level of scrutiny.'

'He is a bit of a pedant.' Mickey shrugged. 'I'll tell him "computer says no" if you like. It was a long shot pulling in such a big hitter anyway.'

Cindy's eyes lit up. 'How big?'

'Runs nine billion sterling. It could be ten. What's a billion here or there?'

'How much might he invest with us?'

'Small beer,' said Mickey dismissively. 'A few hundred million at a guess.'

He could see Cindy struggling with the temptation. 'I'm just not happy giving out such detail.'

'I'll just tell him we can't do it.'

Mickey turned and went back to his desk. He guessed Cindy was watching him and he tried to look as casual as possible as he picked up the phone.

'Wait!' Cindy called over. 'He can have it.'

'Where do I get it from?' asked Mickey.

'Compliance will send it. You just make sure it's worthwhile. Bring in the money.'

61

At Central Command's forward base at Al Udeid, Qatar, a nuclear technician confirmed that the metal disk Declin had recovered from Basra comprised weapons grade uranium.

'Can you tell where it has come from?'

'This sample is ninety-point-five percent enriched,' replied the technician. 'So it's not from any known nuclear facility in the West, or the small amount available on the black market.'

'But they are clearly making a nuclear bomb,' Declin said, guessing now that this was what the jihadists had been planning when they spoke of poisoning the blood of the Great Satan.

'Jihadists wouldn't have the expertise or manufacturing capability to make a proper nuclear bomb,' she replied. 'But if they packed enough of this material round a conventional kinetic weapon they would still get a radioactive blast.'

'What's the difference?' asked Declin.

'One is a conventional explosion with some radiation to add to the panic but not really cause any more damage. Weapons of mass disruption, we call them. A real nuclear explosion would be a thousand times more powerful.'

'So how much of this material would they need to make a real, bona-fide nuclear bomb?'

'I told you, they don't have the technical ...'

'How much would they need?'

'Fifty kilograms to achieve critical mass,' she said. 'But they'd need the technical know-how to detonate it with a precisely calculated high-explosive blast. And these people just don't have that capability.'

'They weren't supposed to have the capability to attack US cyber space.'

62

Nebuchadnezzar slotted the last of the metal discs into the hollow, ornate elephant that Hafez had bought in the central bazaar. He filled the remainder of the empty space with sand and super-glued the feet back on. He took a drink of water and wandered over to the window where Hafez was supposed to be keeping watch but had his head in his phone.

'Here, Nezzar,' said Hafez as he approached. 'Look at this.'

Nebuchadnezzar looked over Hafez's shoulder as he held the screen up so they could watch the video together. A line of black-clad brothers stood over prisoners knelt before a shallow ditch. The film focused in on a man who, behind the mask, was probably repeating words of inspiration from the great prophet. But Hafez's speaker had not worked since he fell on his phone during combat training.

When the action resumed the man raised his arm. In turn the brothers raised their swords. The arm fell swiftly and the swords followed, splicing heads clean from shoulders. They rolled into the ditch, followed, after a helpful kick in the back, by their recently separated bodies.

The brothers cheered.

Hafez smiled.

Nebuchadnezzar said nothing. He'd seen such scenes so many times before it no longer produced a response. He suspected the kafirs felt the same way. That was why the cyber attacks were so brilliant. And the best was yet to come. He checked the time on his own phone.

'We must leave.'

They packed the elephant in a wooden crate and lifted this onto the back of a pick-up. They drove south on roads filled with refugees. At the border with Kuwait they waited to cross during rush hour when checks were less stringent. Besides, the guards were looking for weapons and people, not ornate elephants.

63

As the plane doors opened and passengers jumped to their feet, Declin took his phone off flight mode and called his mom. He got her voicemail.

'Hi, it's Declin. I'm back in Washington. Safe and sound. No problems. Speak to you soon.'

No problems! Declin thought to himself. Other than trying to stop a nuclear cyber attack. He hurried through the terminal building. At arrivals a man holding a name board for him shouted to get his attention.

'I'm with Director Connelly,' he explained. 'We have a car waiting.'

'Lead the way,' said Declin, appreciatively.

He was surprised to find Connelly waiting in the car.

'I guess you're not here to drive me home,' Declin said.

'You're coming with me to the White House,' Connelly explained.

'To see the President?' Declin wasn't even wearing a tie.

'We're attending a National Security Council meeting on the Cyber threat. President Topps isn't happy with the way things are going. He's pulled the Cyber investigation from Langley and given it to Cyber Command.'

'More changes,' sighed Declin.

'Don't worry about that. Worry about how to explain to the President that we still don't know who is behind all this.'

64

Helen had prepared a full-on, candlelit dinner for two. Her latest work had been accepted for an exhibition in the Whitworth Art Gallery in Manchester and she wanted to celebrate. Mickey was pleased for her, but he wasn't in the mood for celebrations.

'What's the matter?' she asked, taking his hand. 'I can see something is on your mind?'

'It's that copper. He's hassling me to do his dirty work for him.'

'DI Brighouse? He always seemed a fair man. What does he want you to do?'

Mickey couldn't tell her the whole story or they'd be there all night, but he could give her the gist of the problem. 'It's this fund that I've been looking at. The Quadra Fund. Brighouse thinks it's bent. And he wants me to find proof and give it to him.'

'Why not?'

Mickey thought of Cindy. She'd clearly worked so hard to build the fund and if Crispin was using inside information she wasn't to blame. But of course, he couldn't tell Helen about Cindy either. 'I'd feel like a sneak. A grass.'

'If they're criminals, what does it matter?'

'There's normal people work there. It don't seem right, me dropping them in it.'

'Well don't. It's not your job.'

'That's just it, though. Brighouse is threatening to charge me if I don't help him.'

'With what? Have you done something illegal?'

Mickey realized he'd said too much. 'Nah. It's all just bluff. It was annoying me. But I'm not going to worry about it anymore.'

He squeezed her hand and kissed her. Got the clear impression she wasn't interested in any hanky panky, but at least he'd distracted her. He did the washing up, while Helen got herself tucked up in bed with a book.

When all was quiet he sat down with his laptop and loaded the disk that he'd retrieved from the friendly client. He started with the trade in US cattle futures that had made the fund, and Mickey, so much money. A note explained that Crispin had spotted a tightening supply and demand balance in US cattle futures and instructed the analysts to write trading programs to exploit it. When the filters picked up an online article in the Saybrook Enquirer speculating a foot-and-mouth outbreak, this triggered the trades.

Very clever.

Then there was the shale-gas trade. Crispin had noted low inventories of US gas and instructed the analysts to write programs to exploit rising shale-gas prices. Here it seemed they just got lucky when prices did indeed go through the roof after all onshore drilling was suspended, following the fracking rig cyber attacks.

Mickey looked back through a couple of older trades. There was the image problem at Apple, when hackers posted hundreds of never-before-seen private photos of celebrities stolen from their iCloud accounts. The victims were mostly high-profile women such as Scarlett Johansson and Kim Kardashian. But the other victim had been Apple's share price. It had been whacked. Quadra had been on the right side. A note explained how Crispin had been worrying about the security of the cloud and the fund had sold Apple shares on the first news of the leaks.

Very clever.

Yet again.

Everything seemed to follow the same pattern: Crispin spotted a trend, the analysts wrote trading algorithms to exploit that trend and these were triggered by the very first flash of news, from the flimsiest of sources.

All very clever.

Perhaps too clever.

As Mickey looked back through the years of trades he couldn't find any major screw-ups. Where were the huge loss-making trades that had been triggered by a false tweet or a misinformed blogger? There were none. Every major trade was a sure-fire winner. Sure, the fund had made plenty of small trades that had lost money. But that was just the background noise. The big trades had all been clear winners.

And nobody, no trader in the world, computer or human, got it right every time. Not even Mickey at his best. The Quadra Fund performance was simply too good to be true.

65

Director Connelly's black limousine pulled up at the entrance to the White House. A valet opened the door for Declin and held up a black umbrella against the sleet rain, until he had made it round the car and safely to the white awning that extended to the kerb. Connelly was already passed the uniformed Secret Service guards and through the double doors into the building. Declin caught him halfway down the long hallway on the first floor of the West Wing. Further down, a Navy watch officer gestured to some steps, though it was clear Connelly already knew where he was going.

Down the steps, he took a right and stopped at a camera over a door beside a plaque with the words 'White House Situation Room. Restricted Access.' The door buzzed and Connelly pushed his way through.

The room was already full of top brass and politicians. As well as President Topps, Declin recognized Asimov, the Director of National Intelligence, Leon Calvara from Langley and Cresta Patton, Director of the National Security Agency. There were other faces he'd seen on television, but couldn't put a name to.

There was of course no place for a humble Special Agent at the oval table and Declin stood against the wall with the other advisors and assistants.

'First item,' announced the President. 'Will somebody kindly tell me what the hell we are doing to stop these cyber attacks on our critical infrastructure.'

'We're making good progress on cyber defence,' declared Cresta Patton. Declin figured she was remarkably young to be wearing the hats of both Director of the National Security Agency and Head of Cyber Command, but he had heard she was supremely good at her job.

'Good progress isn't good enough,' said the President. 'We need the job done and dusted.'

'Homeland's Einstein system has been installed at new locations where critical industries connected with Tier-one carriers. The vulnerabilities in US critical infrastructure are gradually being shored up. Individuals and organizations have scrubbed their computers and systems and updated their antivirus …'

'Don't give me this anti-virus crap,' interrupted the President. 'What about the airlines? Given the nuclear threat it's the airlines we need to secure from cyber attack.'

'The airlines are also in good shape,' said Cresta. 'Air Traffic Control has upgraded firewalls and tested various back-up systems. All airplanes that had been using the same computer for flight control as for interactive passenger entertainment have been forced to split the networks. And connections from ground support to aircrafts' computer networks have been cut back to the absolute bare essentials.'

'So in words of one syllable, can the cyber jihadists take control of an airplane by hacking?'

Cresta pushed her hair off her forehead and said firmly: 'No.'

'You better be right.' The President turned to face the rest of the room. 'So we're making progress on the cyber threat, but not yet there. Where are we on the nuclear threat?'

'Let me answer that,' said Calvara. On the screen at the end of the room he put up some drone footage shot before the Basra raid showing two men struggling to carry a relatively small but clearly heavy crate out of the warehouse in Basra and placing it in the trunk of a white Renault. CCTV footage from a gas station where the men filled up the Renault showed the car moving off towards the road.

Calvara froze the film. 'See how the car weighs down on the rear axle. Army Corps have tested the same make and age of car. They figure there's a weight of around 110 pounds in the trunk. Putting that together with the small size of the crate, suggests whatever is in that crate is very dense. Given that we found a uranium pellet in the house it doesn't take a genius to work out they must be carrying enriched uranium. Plenty enough for a dirty nuke.'

'Plenty enough for a full thermo-nuclear bomb,' Declin interrupted.

Calvara scowled and Declin suddenly realized that everyone was looking at him. What had he said?

'Apologies,' said Connelly. 'I didn't brief Special Agent Lehane here on the Situation Room protocols.'

'Forget protocol,' the President said, waving his hand in encouragement. 'What's this about a full thermo-nuclear bomb?'

'110 pounds is fifty kilograms,' said Declin. 'That's the mass of enriched Uranium required to achieve criticality for a full nuclear explosion.'

'We're not worried about that,' cut in Ladyman, also now breaking protocol and talking from the wall instead of the desk. 'We are certain the jihadists do not have the know-how or machinery to detonate the material in a conventional nuclear weapon.'

'Maybe they've thought of some unconventional way of detonating it,' Declin said.

'Maybe you're just making up a threat that doesn't exist.'

'I want to hear what he has to say,' said the President. 'What are you thinking? Speak up.'

'It's not my speciality,' Declin replied, a little worried that he was now out of his depth. 'But, just thinking aloud, maybe they drop the crate of uranium off the top of the Empire State building to get the impact to go critical.'

'They'd smash the sidewalk, is all,' answered Ladyman. 'Nowhere near enough compression.'

'Maybe they sit it on the front of a train and smash it into a station,' said Declin.

There was a short pause while Ladyman consulted with an aide beside him. 'Still not enough. For Uranium to go critical it needs to be hit by a super-massive bomb. The terrorists just don't have that capability.'

'Let's hope you're right,' Declin said.

'But they can still cause plenty of havoc with a dirty nuke,' the President said. 'If we assume they use cyber attacks in some way, how might they deliver it? I'm still thinking by plane.'

'Aircraft controls are now triple secure from hack attack,' Cresta said. 'I can't rule anything out. They keep surprising us. But I think it's real unlikely they can hack the controls of an airplane today.'

'How about a drone,' suggested Declin.

'No commercial drone has a payload anywhere near what is needed for a substantial bomb, and without a bomb all the terrorists could achieve would be a shower of uranium metal pellets.'

'Helicopter? Light aircraft?'

'Possible,' said Cresta. 'Homeland has stepped up security and background checks on all pilots.'

'So what I'm hearing is we have no real idea where, when or how the terrorists might explode this nuclear weapon,' said the President, looking around the table. 'Genius!'

'Our best line of defence,' said Secretary of Defence Pawel Syzmanski, 'is to stop the nuclear material getting into the country. We think it was moved out of Basra by car. We're trying to find out what happened to the Renault next.'

'It's coming by boat,' said Calvara confidently.

'Do you agree with that?' the President asked Pawel.

'We're certainly dealing with that threat,' said Pawel. 'We're screening every boat from the Gulf landing in America. It's a major task. It'll take a lot of resources. But we'll do our best.'

'Damn right you will,' said the President.

Pawel inhaled deeply. 'It's impossible to secure every port. The sheer volume of goods we bring in. I can't say whether it will be good enough.'

'So let's plan for the worst,' said Declin. 'Assume they do get through and detonate a dirty nuke. Are we ready to deal with it?'

'We've got contingency plans for a radioactive leak,' replied General Horn.

'Let's hear them in outline,' said the President.

'Response teams confirm the leak, establish a hot-zone, rescue trapped and injured, secure the radioactive source and provide decontamination to the victims.'

'Are you doing dry runs?' asked Declin.

'We don't want to cause alarm,' said Horn. 'We have one planned for LA. We could bring that forward.'

'I think agent Lehane is right. We should practice right now in all major cities. See how we cope.'

'It's going to be difficult doing that without creating a lot of panic.'

'People should panic,' the President said. 'We are at the highest nuclear alert since the Cuban missile crisis.'

<h1 style="text-align:center">66</h1>

Mickey waited until the last-but-one of the analysts had gone home. Antonio always worked late. It wasn't unheard of for him to work until the early hours and grab a nap on the waiting room sofa before waking to be first at his desk.

'Working late?' Mickey asked as he wandered into the room. 'Or does this count as an early start for you?'

'You're not allowed in here, Mickey.'

'I'm allowed in out of office hours.'

While Antonio wondered whether that was true, Mickey sauntered over to stand beside him.

Antonio turned off his screen.

'Something to hide?'

'You're not allowed to see what we're working on.'

'Why not?'

'Compliance.'

'Cobblers,' said Mickey. 'I was in this business before your egg hatched. There's no compliance reason why I can't know what you're working on. It's just a rule made up by Crispin.'

Antonio looked round the room as if he feared Crispin might be hiding behind a monitor.

'Divide and rule,' continued Mickey. 'It means nobody except Crispin has a full overview of the business. So nobody really understands what goes on.'

Antonio shrugged. 'It works. We've been the best performing hedge fund in London for the last three quarters.'

'Have you stopped to wonder why?'

'Better analysis of more timely information,' said Antonio, repeating a well-worn marketing line.

'You're 'aving a giraffe if you really believe that.'

Antonio said nothing.

'The fund just made fifty-million pounds on US cattle futures. What did Crispin know that everyone else missed?'

'Crispin is smarter than the rest.'

'I know all the players in this market, Antonio. Crispin's smarter than some. Not as smart as some others. Brain power hasn't got anything to do with it. There is only one reason he could take the risk and build up such a big position.' Mickey paused until he had fully captured Antonio's attention. 'He had inside information.'

'We sift millions of ...'

'I'm not talking about your fancy filters,' interrupted Mickey. 'The fund took such an aggressive position because it knew there was going to be a leak of the virus. It wasn't a calculated, hedged, investment position. It was a punt with inside information.'

'I don't believe that.'

'Well, don't you think it was a bit odd to suddenly start investing in cattle futures.'

'Crispin thought the supply-and-demand situation was tightening, so he wanted us to be prepared.'

'Except it weren't,' said Mickey. 'Go check yourself. Before the foot-and-mouth outbreak, US cattle futures were coming off on the back of oversupply. The only geezer in the world who thought it might tighten was Crispin.'

Antonio scratched his eyebrow and looked around the room for support that wasn't there. 'I don't know about all this, Mickey. I just do what I'm asked to do.'

'Same story with US gas prices,' pressed Mickey, realizing he had Antonio on the back foot. 'Whose idea was it to model for them rising?'

'Crispin of course.'

'And what reason did he give?'

'Tightening supply and demand.'

'Wrong again. There were fears of oversupply and inventories were being built. It wouldn't have made sense to expect US gas prices to rise unless you knew something the market didn't know.'

Antonio switched off his computer and stood up from his chair.

'I've got to go home.'

Mickey grabbed his arm. 'Tell me what you're working on now.'

'I can't.'

'The oil price, isn't it. I saw it on your screen before you closed it off. Are you expecting it to go up or down?'

'Up,' he whispered.

'Up?' asked Mickey surprised. 'Why would it go up? With the US economy tanking there's going to be a supply overhang. Why would the oil price go up?'

'Crispin says.'

'So what does he know this time?'

'I don't know.'

'Where does he get the information?'

'I don't know.'

'But you know something ain't right about this place, don't you?'

Antonio pulled his arm free of Mickey's grasp. 'I've got to go.'

67

At the port of Kuwait City, Nebuchadnezzar drove to dock sixteen where the *Amelia Riviera* was filling up with Liquid Petroleum Gas. They parked in an empty disabled parking spot and fetched the crate from the back. It was low tide and the gangway was steep as they struggled down with their heavy load.

A crew hand came up to help. 'What have you got in here?'

'Can you believe it is an elephant,' said Hafez, laughing.

'Really?'

'Of course it is not an elephant,' said Nebuchadnezzar, glaring at the stupid Hafez to be silent.

No further questions were asked as they carried the crate to the captain's private quarters. He told them to set it down in a corner and offered them coffee. After it was served he pulled the curtain over the peephole in the door.

'You have the money?'

'One hundred thousand dollars,' said Nebuchadnezzar handing over a large envelope. 'Count it.'

The captain opened it, glanced inside and nodded. 'I don't need to count it now. If it isn't all there, your elephant will not be delivered.'

'And another hundred thousand when you arrive.'

'I look forward to it,' said the captain.

Nebuchadnezzar smiled. 'This is a fine ship. You must be very proud to be captain of such a beautiful vessel.'

'I am. Let me show you around.' The captain led the two men around the ship. Starting with the huge engine room, through the crew quarters, round the deck and up to the bridge.

'It is all computer controlled,' said the captain proudly. 'The ship steers itself.'

'So I understand,' said Nebuchadnezzar. He signalled to Hafez that it was time.

Hafez contorted his face and made a violent gurgling sound as he dropped to the floor. There his body writhed and convulsed.

'Medic!' called the captain.

While Hafez continued his epileptic act, Nebuchadnezzar inserted a memory stick into the USB port on the navigation computer. Virus delivered.

68

General Wing's physician had insisted he incorporate some exercise into his daily routine. He had recommended Tai Chi, but they'd compromised on walking from his residence to his office each day. The morning air was sharp and the willows drooped over icy blue ponds. A green tea, another suggestion of the physician, was waiting for him at his desk, as were a small group of trusted Politburo members. Wing took a seat and sipped the tea slowly while the room settled. He set aside the tea, wiped his mouth with a napkin and handed it to his aide.

'Operation Nine Lines is a total success,' declared Wing. 'We are in full control of all the islands.'

'Is there any sign of a counter attack?' asked Lee Chung, the overly cautious Premier.

'Vietnam and The Philippines have flown their planes into hiding and moved all ships outside of the South China Sea,' said Wing. 'There will be no counter attack.'

'We've had angry protestations from the various ambassadors.'

'Of course.' Wing shrugged dismissively.

'And a statement from President Topps condemning the invasion and rejecting our claim to the South China Sea.'

'Mere words.' Wing was pleased that, as he had predicted, Topps appeared to be sticking to his election pledge not to be the world's policeman.

'Are you ready if there is a counter attack?' asked Lee.

'We have the Liaoning positioned to the west of the Islands. She has six fighters continuously in the air and Changhe early-warning helicopters. We are in full control.'

'There will be economic consequences,' announced Poo Yunshan, the Minister of Foreign Trade and Economic Cooperation.

Wing turned to face Poo. He was too interested in feathering his own nest when negotiating contracts with foreign multinationals. But because of their history together in the Youth League he was loyal to Wing and so he was tolerated. For now.

'Such as?'

'The Americans are lobbying for sanctions,' said Poo. 'The economy is already struggling. The currency has fallen again.'

'That is the irrational fear of capitalists,' said Wing. 'China is stronger today. China has shown itself to be the new superpower in Asia.'

Wing noticed Liu Gaoli vigorously scratching his eyebrow as he was prone to do when distressed. 'What are your thoughts, Liu?'

'I am concerned for political fallout.'

Liu wore many hats. He was first-ranked Secretary of the Secretariat, Chairman of the Commission for Building Spiritual Civilization, Leader of the Propaganda and Ideology Leading Group and President of the Central Party School. In general terms, Liu was the top official in charge of communist ideology. If Liu was concerned then Wing needed to be so also.

'But the people are very supportive. You said so yourself.'

'I am concerned about the Communist party in Vietnam.

They are facing growing calls to stand down because of losing the islands. Communism has fallen in Cuba. If communism now also falls in Vietnam, the pro-democracy movement here at home will be emboldened.'

'The Party is already under threat from the pro-democracy movement,' replied Wing. 'That is why we are taking positive action to win popular support. So that brings us to our next move.'

'I wonder about the timing.' Liu sucked in his cheeks. 'Operation Nine Lines has gone well but, perhaps we should let things settle. We can do more later.'

'We must act now,' said Wing. 'The Americans are distracted by their cyber problems. We must press ahead.'

'If we occupy the Diaoyu Islands, this will bring us into conflict with Japan. And America will be forced to defend them.'

'You under-estimate President Topps's self-interest,' said Wing. 'He will not defend the Japanese.'

69

Frank was in a good mood as he ran to the office. Feeling better for the knowledge that Mickey Summer was finally coming on side with the investigation. Mickey might be a big-mouthed gambler but he was a smart, big-mouthed gambler. He would come up with something.

Frank showered, took a huge drink of water to rehydrate, then arrived at his desk and poured a cup of coffee from his flask.

He saw one of the new kids smiling.

'How many coffee shops do you pass on your way into work, Frank?'

'Never counted.'

'Must be a dozen.'

'And?'

'They all serve perfectly good coffee.'

'Last time I checked they all charged for the privilege.'

'Well I hope when I make DI the pay's enough to afford a cup of coffee.'

'Plus I don't like skinny organic cappuccinos with de-homog-enized milk and vanilla flavouring.'

Frank made an exaggerated slurp and checked his to-do list and diary for the day. He noted a meeting had been put in first thing with the Superintendent. He hoped it was to tell him he'd been reassigned to another case team. But he feared it was something else. Meetings first thing were generally not good news. He put on his jacket and made his way down to the Superintendent's office. The door was open and Hillary from Human Resources was sitting to one side of the Superintendent. Not a good sign.

'Take a seat please.' The Superintendent motioned Frank to the empty chair on the opposite side of the desk, placed his hands flat on the table, cleared his throat and read from a script.

'On January tenth last year you were appointed as senior investigating officer to join the case team investigating suspected insider trading at a hedge fund called The Quadra. A case review panel recently decided to close that enquiry down and you were reassigned to other duties. We have reason to believe that you continued to investigate The Quadra after that point and that you carried out surveillance on the Managing Director of that Fund without receiving appropriate Regulatory and Investigative Powers.'

The Superintendent looked up from his notes and turned to Hillary.

'Would you like to say anything at this juncture?' she asked Frank.

He shook his head.

The Superintendent exchanged a glance with Hillary and turned back to Frank. 'Detective Inspector Brighouse, you are suspended from service, pending an investigation into the charge of gross misconduct.'

'There's no need for an investigation. I did it. And if doing my job is gross misconduct, then there's nothing more to be said.'

70

The Japanese coast guard Captain was alerted to a formation of planes over the East China Sea.

'Flying Leopard bombers.'

'Their course?' the Captain demanded.

'One hundred and twenty degrees. Heading for Yonaguni island.'

'The radar post.' The Captain looked out of the bridge and watched the planes flying low over the calm sea.

'Captain! You need to look at this.'

He ran over to see a navigation screen peppered with white flecks approaching from mainland China.

'A task force bearing for Senkaku,' announced the navigator. He overlaid satellite imaging to illustrate the full paraphernalia of ships. 'Will we intercept?'

Over the years the Captain had successfully challenged and seen off illegal encroachment on the Senkaku islands from Chinese fishing vessels and nationalist activists trying to land and claim them for China. However, he wasn't going to challenge a full task force led by China's latest nuclear battleship.

'Keep us at a distance of three miles. Radio base with a watching brief.'

He collected his high-powered binoculars and set them up on the deck. The task force settled off the main island. A party of several hundred Chinese marines ferried towards it. As the boats bumped ashore, an albatross took flight and a herd of sheep scampered from the rocky inlet. A marine disappeared into a ravine. He re-emerged on a narrow ridge leading to the top of the mountain and planted the Chinese flag.

71

Connelly was heading back to FBI headquarters so Declin took a cab from the White House. Looking out the dirty windows he saw black clouds threatening Washington with heavy snow. The city had only just dug its way out of the last snowstorm. Arriving at NSA headquarters in Fort Meade he felt jet-lagged and even more disorientated than usual by the towering box of copper-lined, black glass. He hurried inside and swiped through security in the lobby.

'Could you direct me to Cyber Command's operation room?'

'It's right here,' the receptionist said, drawing a circle on a map.

'Thanks.'

Declin headed off into the maze of corridors and grabbed a caffeine fix on the way. He was so focused on following the map and the signs that he did not at first notice the commotion at the airline ticket counter. It seemed the booking systems were down and frustration was mounting. Declin had no intention of flying again in a hurry, so he left them to it and continued on until he found the entrance to Cyber Command's operation room. The room was buzzing with hundreds working at neatly spaced workstations. It brought back bad memories of exams that Declin hadn't worked for.

'Special Agent Lehane!'

Declin recognized Cresta Patton from the Security Council meeting. 'Call me Declin.'

'Cresta.' She smiled warmly. 'Let me bring you right up to speed. We've had a couple of major breakthroughs with the information you sent us from the cell phone in Basra. Browser fingerprinting shows us the websites the phone visited.' She flicked quickly through jihadist news channels and chat-rooms, gaming sites and holiday destinations, but stopped at a Google Earth search.

'Where's that?' asked Declin.

'Kuwait City port. The phone's tracking records also revealed it had made a trip to the port.'

'So the uranium is coming by boat.'

'It would seem so.'

She brought up CCTV footage of the white Renault passing through the port's main entrance. 'That's as far as we've got. No further trace of the Renault. But we know it went into the port.'

'And you are searching the ships?'

'Every ship leaving the port bound for the United States is being thoroughly searched for radioactivity.'

'We can't let anything through.'

'We won't.'

There was no false bravado. She had an inner steel that impressed Declin. He was suddenly aware of a rise in the general hubbub across the room. Everyone was looking up at a news report on the giant screen that hung over the operations room.

'Behind me you see pandemonium,' said the reporter at JFK airport. 'Thousands of passengers stranded because of a catastrophic collapse in the reservation and operation systems of the major airlines.'

The camera panned left to a flight display board with almost every flight showing red 'CANCELLED'.

'The aircraft are working,' she continued. 'The cabin crew and ground crew are ready to work. But without the reservations database and the operational network the airlines have no way of organizing which passengers, crew or cargo go on which flight. And so they have resorted to cancelling every flight.'

'Shit,' said Cresta, turning on the speaker. 'OK, people. What have we got here?'

'It's a simple denial of service attack,' said one operator. 'We can re-route it on to the dummy server.'

'That's why we have it,' said Cresta. 'Let's do it.'

Frantic yelling down phones and hammering on keyboards and a shout from one end of the room. 'That's cleared it.'

'I doubt it,' Declin said.

'I'm through to American Airlines,' an operator called out. 'They tell me their operations are working again.'

'Same for Pacific,' called out another. 'No, wait, they tell me the systems have died again.'

'And American. They're back down.'

'And United.'

More yelling and hammering saw the second attack re-routed to another dummy server. But again this produced only temporary reprieve.

'This is a repeat slap-down,' said Declin.

'So we need repeat fixes,' replied Cresta. She gathered her bag and phone. 'I'm going to report up. You take control. Keep me closely informed.'

She left at a run. The room looked up at Declin. He turned on the speaker. 'Call your ISP response teams. Find out where this attack is coming from.'

A minute later an operator lifted one headphone off his ear and called out. 'It's AmerTelco. They've got a massive botnet.'

'Why have they only discovered it now?' yelled Declin. 'They're supposed to be on high alert and looking out for this.'

'They knew they had it and they've been notifying customers to clean up, but until now the botnet was being used for a low level financial spam. They didn't give it priority.'

'Idiots. Tell them to disconnect the infected computers.'

'It's not just computers. The botnet is using thousands of servers as well.'

'Shut them all down.'

The operator relayed this back to his counterpart. 'They're not happy with that idea.'

'I don't give a damn,' Declin replied.

'They say they have five million retail customers plus major commercial customers such as Amazon and eBay. They just don't want to cut it ...'

'I'm not asking their permission,' said Declin. 'I'm instructing them to disconnect the computers and servers connected to that botnet.'

The operator relayed Declin's order. 'They say you don't have the authority.'

'Is that what they think?' asked Declin.

'They say it would need to be a Presidential order.'

'Well get me the fucking President!'

72

Mickey met Frank in a cafe off Bond Street. He wasn't totally surprised to see him dressed in a tracksuit because he knew Frank liked his running. But he wouldn't have thought he'd wear that to work.

'Working from home today?'

'Something like that,' said Frank, irritation in his voice.

'What's up?'

'I'm suspended.'

'Clever.' Mickey waved a hand over Frank's head. 'No ropes either.'

'Only the one they're getting ready to hang me with.'

'You in trouble?'

'They closed the Quadra investigation, as you know, and they dismissed me for carrying on with it.'

'But that's bonkers,' said Mickey. 'You were right all along.'

Frank uncrossed his legs and shuffled a little closer. 'Really?'

'I had a good look through the past performance. Very clever the way they got all their ducks in a row to explain all the good trades they made. But where are the bad trades?'

'They do lose money on some trades. I've seen that.'

'Peanuts in comparison. All their really big bets come good.'

'When we pointed that out they explained that was because they cut their losses and run with their gains.'

Mickey laughed. 'It's a nice cliché, but it ain't so easy to do. Of course they've got lots of background noise trades going on every day. They win some and they lose some. But over the last two years they only ever made about six really big bets and they all turned out right. That's just too good to be true. They had to be acting on inside information.'

'But from where?' asked Frank.

'Crispin will have a network of sources built up over the years. He just waits until they come up with something dynamite and goes for it big time.'

'For example?'

'So maybe he has the Finance Director at Ryan Oil onside. He might have been cultivating him to tip him off ahead of a big announcement of a gas find. Only he rings and says they've got a well blown up and so Crispin shorts the shares instead. Or maybe he had a contact in the railroads to give him the inside track on railroad freight rates and traffic volumes as an indicator of economic activity. Only this time the contact calls to tell him about the rail crashes.'

'What about Plum Island?' asked Frank, who looked sceptical. 'Why have a contact there?'

'Maybe the contact was with the Department of Agriculture. That would be a useful source of information. You've got to remember that these hedge funds are massively well connected. They've got contacts everywhere.'

Frank pursed his lips. 'That's still all circumstantial evidence. Hearsay. I couldn't reopen the case with that.'

'Listen pal, I've gone right out on a limb here for you.'

'I need something concrete,' Frank explained. 'An email from one of these sources to Crispin, either with inside information or at least hinting at it.'

'I didn't see anything like that, but I'm not the only one who thinks it's dodgy. I talked to one of the analysts. A kid called Antonio.'

'What did he say?'

'He was careful not to say anything, but I could tell he thinks there's something fishy going on.'

'This is good, Mickey. I feel like we're finally making progress.'

'The thing is, Frank. This is where I get off. I've done what I can. I'm going to quit in the morning.'

'Not so fast,' said Frank. 'Have you forgotten about your misdemeanor?'

'You said you'd let that drop if I helped you out.'

'But you've given me nothing.'

'I said I'd sniff around. I agree it looks dodgy. What else can I do?'

'Check these out.' Frank passed him a piece of paper with some scribbled numbers. 'These are the sort codes and account numbers for some offshore accounts.'

'I get it,' said Mickey. 'You want me to pay you off with a bung.'

'We're not all motivated by money.'

'So what is this?'

'These are three of the biggest investors in the fund. So the ones with most to gain from insider trading. Privacy laws meant we couldn't find out who they are. Maybe you can do it from the inside.'

'What's the point of that?'

'We might find out that one of the accounts belongs to the Finance Director of Ryan Oil or someone at Plum Island. If we find a source then we're in business.'

Mickey sighed. 'I do this and then that's it, right. End of the line for Mickey Summer.'

73

'There is no choice, Mr President,' Declin repeated. 'We need to disconnect the infected computers and servers.'

'What does Cresta think?'

'She agrees with me.'

'People aren't going to like it,' replied the President.

'They know we are under cyber siege,' pressed Declin. 'They allowed their computers to become infected. They were told to get them scrubbed and they didn't.'

'I get that. But if we shut down Amazon and e-Bay we're basically shutting down e-commerce. That's another hit to the economy. And Joe Main Street isn't going to appreciate us stopping him shopping just so people can go flying again.'

'This is not just about the airlines,' Declin explained. 'This botnet could be switched to some other attack. It might even somehow be used with this jihadist nuke we're searching for.'

'Shut it down,' said the President.

'Thank you.'

'I don't need thanks. I just need you to stop these attacks. Just hours ago you guys assured me the airlines were secure. Now this.'

Declin didn't want to wimp out and remind him it was Cresta who had given the assurance. 'Apologies. We knew the flight decks were secure. We hadn't thought about check-in.'

'That's what worries me. Seems like the bad guys are one step ahead of us all the time.'

'We're catching up fast.'

'Let me ask you something. And I want a straight answer to this question.'

'Of course.'

'The army guys assure me our military machine is invulnerable to these cyber attacks. What do you think?'

'From what I've seen, I think the dot mil domain is secure.'

'You say that. Asimov assures me as well. But you guys used to tell me our critical industries were secure from cyber attack.'

'With respect Mr President, we always knew the public domain internet was vulnerable.'

'So why did we never do anything about it?'

'We had other priorities.'

'Such as?'

'Fighting terrorism. We needed the holes in the internet for our intelligence gathering on terrorism. We couldn't allow a secure, encrypted internet. We knew it left us vulnerable to cyber attack but it was the choice we had to take. That's why we are where we are.'

Declin faintly overheard someone telling Topps that the Japanese president was holding on another line. Declin had seen news that the Chinese had invaded the Senkaku islands. The President was clearly juggling balls.

'I got to go.'

'You concentrate on the Chinese, Mr President. We'll sort out the cyber threat.'

'You do that!'

74

Hue arrived at Diaoyutai State Guest Restaurant a good thirty minutes early and drank hot green tea while he waited for his father. The General had reserved a section of the restaurant for the two of them and Hue had to deflect inquisitive stares from the other diners, who were mostly the worst type of tuhao businessman; newly rich but ill-mannered and tasteless. When his father finally arrived with his entourage the stares disappeared. Nobody would risk eyes trespassing on General Wing's personal space.

Hue stood up and bowed deferentially. 'Father'.

The General nodded, took his seat and studied the menu. 'Are you well, Hue?'

'I am well. And you?'

'Triumphant,' said the General, without looking up from the menu.

He clicked a finger high in the air and the head waiter came scurrying over. 'There is no Xingjiang cuisine on the menu.'

'Ah, no, unfortunately not, General Wing.'

'This is still a Chinese restaurant?'

'Yes it is, General Wing.'

'And Xingjiang is still in China.'

'Let me talk to the Chef,' the waiter said, taking the menu. 'And for the young man?'

'I'll have the same,' said Hue.

'I am triumphant,' the General repeated. 'Everyone in the country is feeling triumphant after our glorious victories in the South and East China Seas. Am I right?'

'People are pleased you have reclaimed what had been lost to the Motherland.'

They made small talk as the junior waiters served the requested noodles, boiled in thick mutton soup and steamed twisted rolls. They left the room while the head waiter remained in attendance.

Hue was not especially hungry but picked at the noodles.

The General attacked his dinner noisily. Hue remembered his father eating like this when he was a child, much to the annoyance of his mother.

'How is your mother?' he asked, out of the blue.

Hue's heart missed a beat. Did he know he had visited her? Was his father having him followed? Did he know about the pro-democracy demonstrations? But he relaxed when he realized that it was an innocent question.

'She has a cough, but otherwise she is well.'

'I would look after her you know. But she refuses to accept any help from me.'

'I know.'

'Pah!' The General shook his head and threw down his chopsticks. 'The meat is too young.'

'Too young?' repeated the head waiter anxiously.

'The best quality meat is three years old.'

'Shall I ask the chef to prepare the meal again from an older animal?'

'No.' The General pushed the half-finished meal to one side. 'Leave us.'

The waiter bowed and walked quickly out of the room.

'I have never found anyone who can prepare this dish properly outside of Xingjiang.'

'Homesick?' asked Hue.

'Only for the food. Now,' he clapped his hands. 'Talk to me. What is the mood among the young people. They are happier now, yes?'

'The land recovery has been popular,' Hue said, choosing his words carefully. 'But the mood is cautious. The recession was already hurting. Economic sanctions will cause even more damage.'

The General shrugged. 'In the long run these moves will make the country stronger. There is much-needed oil and gas in the South China Sea.'

'The people do not care about the long term.'

'That is why the Party runs the country. The Party plans on fifty year cycles. We will need to develop the oil fields now to have the energy to power the economy in the second half of the century.'

'The Party is wise.' Hue picked up a pot of sauce and rolled it between his hands while he considered how far to go. 'Is it wise enough to accommodate the pro-democracy movement?'

'Accommodate?' The General took a sip of water.

'Economic growth and greater political freedom go hand in hand. Perhaps the Party should live with democracy.'

'Be careful.' The General threw his napkin on the table. 'I will crush the pro-democracy movement. Be sure to stay clear of it.'

75

Mickey wasn't sure how he could check out the bank account numbers without drawing attention to himself. And if Cindy found him digging around in private account details she'd give him the sack before you could say gross misconduct. He was relaxed about losing his job. He wanted out. But he needed to get Frank his information first to get him off his back.

He had noticed that a new kid in the back office was in the habit of working late. Like Antonio in research, she was probably under the mistaken impression that this would impress her new colleagues. In fact it demonstrated to Mickey that she couldn't get her work done in normal hours and she probably wasn't up to it. No matter, it did present him with an opportunity.

He fiddled around with imaginary tasks until the office emptied. He wrote the account details out on a fresh piece of paper in his own handwriting and took it downstairs. Sure enough the girl was the only person in.

'What did you say to upset everyone?' asked Mickey.

She looked up, confused.

'To make everyone leave,' he explained.

'They've all gone home,' she replied in a voice running on low battery.

'You should as well,' he said. 'Late nights can become a bad habit.'

'I'll be going in a minute.'

'Before you go, could you do me a big favor and print me out some investment reports? I'm seeing clients first thing and I need to work on it overnight.'

'What are the names?'

He handed her the offshore bank account details. 'You should be able to find them using these.'

'Can't you just give me the names?'

'They're all confidential. That's why they use offshore accounts. I never use the real names unless I absolutely have to.'

She sighed, tapped away on her keyboard for a while and pulled up the first account. 'What do you want printing?'

'Just the summary sheet,' said Mickey, disappointed to see that it was simply an offshore account for a large institutional investor he knew well.

'Try this one next will you?'

Again she tapped away, finishing with furrowed brow. 'This one is a restricted account. Only Crispin has access.'

'Ah, yes, I forget that,' said Mickey, glancing over her shoulder at the screen and making a note of the investor. 'Never mind. Try another.'

Again she tapped away. 'That's also only for Crispin.'

'One last go with this one.'

Slowly she tapped at another and shook her head. 'Also Crispin's.'

'Let me see?'

She turned off her screen but not before Mickey had managed to see the name.

Mickey shrugged. 'I don't know what's gone wrong here. Remember I'm a bit new to this place. Tell you what, let's leave it.'

He smiled and backed away to the door.

'You shouldn't have seen that information,' she said.

'I didn't. It was restricted so how could I?'

'I'll have to tell Cindy.'

Mickey grimaced. 'Hmm. I don't think that's wise. You'll probably lose your job and I'll be wrapped up in a ton of compliance red-tape. No harm done. Best just forget it.'

'I'm not sure.'

'I am. Go home. Get some rest.'

76

The President had convened another meeting in the situation room to discuss the cyber threat. The grey heads at the table were all convinced that the state power behind Nebuchadnezzar was Iran. They wanted it to be Iran. For them normal service had been resumed. An old enemy had reverted to type. The room was buzzing with anticipation of retribution.

Declin was not convinced.

Neither was the President. 'The Iranians deny any involvement in the cyber attacks,' he said.

'Of course they do,' replied Asimov.

'They say they don't have the capability to carry out these attacks.'

'But they do.'

The President ran his eyes around the room until he spotted Declin. 'Let's ask the new generation. Special Agent Lehane, do you believe Iran is behind these attacks?'

'I've seen no evidence that it's Iran, but I'm reasonably certain now that the malwares are all written on the same platform. There are clear similarities in coding, in packing, in the time zones they were written in, the computer language and, interestingly, the source malwares were all labelled using numbers rather than names.' Declin stopped. He realized he'd lost his audience.

'So you think they were written on the same platform,' the President said. 'The question is whether that is a state platform?'

'I think it has to be,' Declin replied. 'The attacks have been technically very sophisticated. Particularly this latest airline attack.'

'I thought that was a simple denial of service attack,' interrupted someone Declin didn't know.

'The D-DOS was just a distraction. While we were busy defending that they hit every airline with a dozen different phishing malwares. That's what's actually caused the damage. It's the most sophisticated attack we've yet seen. We traced it to an ISIS cyber group in Raqqa and we again found links to Nebuchadnezzar.'

The President nodded. 'Have you found anything that connects Nebuchadnezzar to Iran?'

'No.'

'Or Iran to any of the cyber attacks?'

'Nothing.'

'We have the nuclear material,' Asimov said. 'Let's not forget about that.'

'Have we found out the uranium came from Iran?' asked Declin. It was news to him if they had.

'It's a process of elimination,' Asimov said. 'The percentage enrichment showed the uranium was not from an old Soviet reactor or any other known nuclear facility. So most likely it came from a newly constructed enrichment facility in Iran.'

'But there is no newly constructed enrichment facility in Iran,' the President said. 'We have UN nuclear inspectors crawling all over the place.'

'They missed it. Mossad is convinced it's there.'

'Do the Israelis have intelligence we haven't heard?'

'For operational reasons they won't go into details. But they're convinced.'

'Can we trust them?' asked the President.

'Yes, we can trust the Israelis.'

Declin was beginning to understand President Topps and could sense he was not so sure about the Israelis, but perhaps couldn't reveal his misgivings in such company. The President rattled his fingers on the table while he thought.

'We've got the sixth fleet on standby in the Gulf,' declared General Horn. 'We can strike the Iranian nuclear facilities with thirty minutes notice.'

'Let's not get ahead of ourselves,' said the President. 'We found one pellet of enriched Uranium in Iraq. We can't bomb Iran's nuclear facilities on that basis. We need more certainty.'

'We might only get that once we're picking up pieces of metal from the dirty nuke they detonate in Manhattan,' said Asimov.

'Which is why our focus should be on stopping the dirty nuke.'

'Now we're stopping a dirty nuke,' continued Asimov. 'If we don't take out the Iranian manufacturing capability next time we're likely going to be facing down a fully functioning nuclear weapon.'

The President shook his head. 'That's not good enough. I'm not going to start a war on the basis of supposition and speculation.'

'Do we really need certain proof?' asked Asimov, looking around the table. 'Iran is a totalitarian state run by a regime with a poisonous ideology. We are as sure as we ever will be that the Iranians have produced enriched uranium in breach of the non-proliferation treaty they signed. We have all the justification we need to hit their nuclear generating capacity and fix a problem that an earlier administration created for us.'

The President shook his head. 'Our country is under cyber siege. We have a major situation developing with the Chinese that we are most likely going to have to face down soon. I am not going to set us against Iran on the basis of conjecture and speculation.'

'We don't have to do anything,' said Asimov. 'The Israelis will do it all for us. All you have to do, Mister President, is give them the green light.'

'Let's hear what the Israelis are planning,' President Topps said, though clearly reluctantly.

General Horn grimaced as he rose to his feet. Desk shrapnel, Declin had been told. 'This is the route of the Israeli mission,' said Horn pointing to a screen filled with a colored map of the Middle East. An orange line ran from Israel to the border of Iran. From there it fragmented into three arrows. 'Three sorties, each comprising two strategic bombers with fighter escort, would leave Israel simultaneously and fly up the Med, across Turkey and Iraq and into Iran, where they would break up to hit three separate targets.' He moved the image on to an aerial photograph of concrete buildings and roads dotted in the desert. 'The Natanz nuclear facility, Iran's main enrichment plant, housing more than three thousand underground centrifuges. This is of course the facility that Cyber Command did such a great job sabotaging with the Stuxnet malware.'

Next came a ground-based photograph of a huge domed building. 'The Esfahan plant where uranium ore is converted into gas. This facility is arguably only used for peaceful nuclear power generation. However, just as the Arak heavy water plant,' he flicked on to another white dome, 'which the Iranians have decommissioned, the Israelis take the view that they should take both these sites out as well, to be on the safe side.'

General Horn crossed his hands and placed them on the table. 'They are ready to go as soon as we give them the green light.'

'How will the Iranians respond?' asked the President.

General Horn put the regional map back up on the screen. 'They would certainly hit back at Israel. Their Shahab-3 missiles might even reach Tel Aviv. They would also try to hit Israel's Dimona nuclear reactor. And they would press Hizbollah in Lebanon and Hamas in Gaza to fire rockets into Israel.'

'What about collateral damage for us?'

'Even without actively supporting the Israelis, the Iranians will know we gave our blessing to the mission. They will have to respond. So we can expect Shia militias in Iraq to attack US assets and forces. They might well fire missiles at the US Fifth Fleet in the gulf and military bases in Qatar. And for sure they'll try and close the Strait of Hormuz.'

'If I might interject,' interrupted the Treasury Secretary. 'About twenty percent of world oil supply goes through that strait. If it gets disrupted the oil price will go through the roof and we'll be knocked into serious recession, if we're not already there right now.'

'I'm concerned about the economy,' said the President. 'I am even more concerned about letting all hell break loose again in the Middle East.'

'The Middle East is already hell,' said Asimov.

That was for sure, thought Declin.

President Topps sat in silence for a time.

'So, do the Israelis get a green light?' asked General Horn.

'No,' said Topps firmly.

'So we do nothing again,' said Horn.

'We don't bomb anyone until we have proof. That's the end of it.'

77

Senator Martin enjoyed his daily walks in the Capitol grounds. He tried momentarily to ignore his guest, his security detail and the crowds milling around on the broad, gently sloped limestone coping leading down to his hero, Lincoln. If only the present incumbent of the White House had half the foresight of the sixteenth President.

'Topps has frozen,' his guest announced. 'He won't give the green light to hit Iran.'

'So it seems,' said the senator.

'He just doesn't buy the case for Iran.'

'Well he's right, isn't he?'

'He doesn't know that. There is a good case for hitting Iran and most of the security council see it. But all Topps can think about is the next cyber attack.'

'That's understandable.' The senator shoved his hands deeper into his coat pockets. 'Given the nuclear threat level.'

'Topps is cracking up there as well. He's constantly reviewing his authentication code and letter of last resort. And he's changed his nuclear deputies again. That clown Martha Stapleton is fourth on the list to press the button for nuclear release.'

The senator shrugged his shoulders. 'If the situation has gotten to the stage where it needs the third deputy, we're all dead anyway.' He paused by the water's edge, took off his glasses and wiped off a fleck of dandruff. He took a sachet of bread from his pocket.

The guest glanced over at the sign prohibiting feeding the ducks. 'It says no feeding.'

'Sometimes we have to break the rules,' the senator replied. 'I don't feed them in the summer but they need it in the winter.'

As if to prove him right, the ducks rushed at the bread in a foaming squall of beaks and feathers.

'So shall we keep pushing Topps on Iran?'

'Iran was a side show,' the senator replied. 'I always felt it was stretching credibility. It's time to move on to the main event.'

78

Declin's screen flashed up with a ten-minute appointment reminder. He was due to meet some guy from the FBI's financial crime division who'd been chasing him for help on cyber defences for the financial system. He called his secretary. 'How did this financial crime appointment get in my diary? I haven't got time for that.'

'He was very persistent. He's waiting in meeting room sixteen. He said it should only take ten minutes of your time and he'd be really grateful.'

'I'll give it five.'

Declin put on his jacket. He'd heard the financial crime guys were a bit dressy. Wannabe bankers mostly. But when he got to room sixteen the guy sitting behind a cup of coffee was wearing jeans and a golf shirt. Declin took off his jacket and hung it over his chair.

The man introduced himself as Chuck. 'I understand you're the Special Agent in charge of the cyber attack investigations, right?'

Declin couldn't hold back a laugh. 'I was in charge a long time back when it looked like domestic terrorism by green hacktivists. Now that it's a full-scale terrorist cyber siege NSA, CIA and Cyber Command are all vying to run the show.'

'Understood,' Chuck nodded. 'But you're Bureau and you're riding point for us, right?'

'That's how Connelly puts it.'

'So.' Chuck lowered his voice. 'This goes no further?'

'Fine by me.'

'We've picked up credible evidence of a connection between the cyber attacks and a London-based hedge fund.'

'Connection?'

'The fund appears to have had advance knowledge of each cyber attack. The fracking and pipeline explosions, the railroads, the Plum Island leak, the airlines. They invested ahead of the curve on all of them.'

'How?'

'We don't know yet. But our systems spotted suspicious trades. So we started watching the fund. We've had Trojans on their computers, we've been monitoring emails and mobile calls. We don't know how they're getting tipped off, but we're fairly sure they are.'

Declin sat forward on his chair. 'Are you suggesting these attacks are just a way for someone to make money?'

'We're talking billions of dollars. It's possible the hedge fund is a front for the terrorists. Or one other idea we have is that the fund has an insider at NSA or GCHQ passing them early information on the cyber attacks before it becomes public.'

If it hadn't been another Bureau agent, Declin would have thought he was talking to a crazy. 'So if you're suspicious but you can't find evidence, why don't you just ride in there and bust the fund open?'

'Well here's where it gets complicated,' said Chuck. 'We got told to stand down the investigation.'

'Who by?'

'Connelly.'

'Connelly!?' repeated Declin. 'Did he give a reason?'

'Cited National Security.'

'I don't get it. National Security is the reason for cracking ahead.'

'That's all he'd say.'

'So what did you do?'

Chuck threw his hands in the air. 'I stood down.'

'So what do you expect me to do?'

'I stood down because I'm not going to disobey a direct order from Director Connelly. You may feel differently.'

'What makes you say that?'

'You have a reputation for being your own man.' Chuck smiled awkwardly. 'Something is badly wrong here. The Brits also had their own investigation into the fund and they were told to stand down.'

Declin frowned. 'So you want me to bypass Connelly?'

'You're working for Cyber Command now. Connelly wouldn't need to know.'

Declin agreed he could legitimately pull the investigation into his orbit. 'Who else knows we're having this conversation?'

'No-one.'

'Keep it that way.'

79

They'd arranged to meet in Hyde Park, but there was no sign of Frank when Mickey arrived, so he slumped on a bench and watched the pigeons fighting for scraps of bread thrown by an old bag woman. She was smiling, perhaps a little manically, but smiling nonetheless. She looked happy enough with her simple life, reminding Mickey that the sooner he got back to trading vegetables the better.

He reckoned he'd done enough now. He'd given Frank his considered opinion that the Quadra Fund was trading on inside information and he'd got him the names of three of the biggest investors in the fund who might turn out to be the source of insider information. Now Mickey was ready to ride off into the sunset.

Before he did that though, he needed to do what any right-minded person would do with the knowledge that the Quadra Fund was expecting an oil price hike. He rang his broker and put every penny he had into oil price futures.

Nothing wrong in that. He wasn't actually in possession of inside information. He suspected that Crispin had inside information but he didn't know if that was true. So he was innocent. Maybe not cross-my-heart-and-hope-to-die innocent. More the read-my-lips-no-new-taxes kind of innocent that politicians get away with all the time.

He looked up as Frank approached. 'Lost your watch?'

'Never had one.'

'Put one on your Christmas list.'

Frank sat down at the other end of the bench. 'So, I'm assuming you've got something to report?'

'Maybe I was just missing you.'

'Come on. What have you got for me?'

Mickey sat up straight and checked nobody was in earshot. He handed over a piece of paper.

Frank read the names aloud. 'Verity Investments. Investor Plan. Banque Cantonale.'

'Just three institutions,' said Mickey. 'They're all kosher.'

'So why have offshore accounts?'

'To pay less tax. And before you start, that isn't illegal.'

'Some say it should be. Anyhow, that's a bit disappointing. '

'Sorry.' Mickey raised his hands in the air. 'And that's me all done now.'

'Not now, Mickey. We're making headway.'

'Glad you appreciate what I've done so far. Over to you now.'

'You want to let them get away with it?'

'Not my job.'

'It's every citizen's duty to fight crime.'

'Insider dealing is just one money manager nicking off another. It's not murder.'

'It's not fair.'

Mickey shrugged. 'Neither is life.'

He thought of the lock-in money he'd left on the table at Royal Shire Bank because he'd let a mad moment of conscience get to him. He was done being the fool who worked pro-bono for the greater good.

'It may take a long time,' said Frank. 'But eventually I will bust the Quadra Fund. And I'll bust you as well.'

'There's gratitude for you. I did what you asked. I got inside the fund and looked around and I confirmed what you suspected. And I found out the names behind three of the bigger investors. Instead of thanking me you threaten to jail me.'

'I'm not stupid, Mickey. You've been happy to work for the fund to get your insider trades going. You've done very nicely out of it. You just placed a big bet on the oil price didn't you?'

Mickey opened his mouth to deny it, but realized Frank had to know. Fast work. He was impressed. 'I had a hunch.'

'A hunch that Crispin has got some fresh inside information that something is going to push the oil price up. It's seven years for insider trading.'

'I'll take my chances.'

'Your luck's not been too good over the years though, has it? Losing your dad and your brother. Leaving your RSB lock-in on the table. Gambling away the deposit on the house. Do you really want to trust to luck?'

Mickey sighed. 'So what's in it for me if I carry on helping?'

'I promise I'll do everything in my powers to get you off without a charge.'

'I'm not working for promises. You get me immunity from prosecution, nailed-on, in writing, including these past trades on cattle and gold and oil. Get me that and I'll keep going.'

'I'll have to think about that.'

'I also want immunity from prosecution by the Yanks. The Fed, the SEC, the whole lot of them.'

153

'I'll work on that as well.'

Mickey sat back and studied the rows of London plane trees in the park. Their leaves long since fallen and swept away. 'Do I keep the money I made on the trades if the Quadra Fund gets busted? Or are they classed as proceeds of crime?'

Frank opened his hands. 'If I get you immunity there is no prosecution. No prosecution means there is no crime.'

Like buds in spring, Mickey was starting to see new life in the game. 'Get me the paperwork and I'll think about it.'

80

Declin caught a red-eye to Heathrow and hired a red Fiesta. He enjoyed the challenge of driving on the left through London's busy streets, though why the Brits still had manual cars he didn't know. He'd thoroughly trashed the gearbox by the time he arrived at DI Frank Brighouse's cute terraced house in Greenwich. As Declin was parking the car a tall man in running gear appeared at the door, kissed his wife and hurtled off down the road.

Declin didn't have time to react before Frank had disappeared round the end of the road. He started the car, raced after him and saw him disappear down another road. By the time he caught up with him again, Frank had run into a park. Declin thought about sounding the horn but didn't want to draw attention to himself, so he raced round the streets and arrived at the other side of the park just as his elusive runner reappeared.

Declin jumped out the car and politely blocked his path. 'DI Frank Brighouse?'

'Who's. Asking?' he said between gasps for air.

Declin flashed his badge. 'Special Agent Declin Lehane of the FBI.'

'And?'

'I'd like to discuss certain financial matters in which we have a mutual interest.'

'Such as?'

'Not here.' Declin motioned towards the car.

Frank hesitated, but curiosity must have got the better of him and he followed Declin to the car and slid into the passenger seat.

Declin filled Frank in on his own background and his role in fighting the cyber siege currently underway in his homeland. He also explained how Chuck in Financial Crime had found suspicious trading patterns in the Quadra Fund, suggesting it had advance knowledge of the cyber attacks and that the Bureau had been following the fund for some time but had been told from on high to stand down the investigation.

'That's what happened to me,' said Frank. He told Declin everything he knew about the Quadra Fund and the implausibly good investment process that Mickey Summer had spotted.

'So where does Mickey Summer think the Quadra is getting its information?'

'From their network of sources,' Frank said.

'You think a hedge fund has better information than the entire Western intelligence apparatus?'

'Looks that way.'

It didn't ring true for Declin. 'I think more likely the insider is a bad apple inside NSA or Langley or British intelligence.'

'I don't see British Intelligence being involved. I can't speculate about the CIA. You'd know better than me.'

'Could come from any number of sources,' Declin said. 'That's why we're keeping this tight for now.'

'So you are not liaising with the CIA?'

'At the moment it's the Bureau investigating possible insider trading. We used a section seven-zero-two for the surveillance so far, but we haven't yet joined the dots to show that this is an intelligence matter. We'll let the CIA know just as soon as it's necessary. In the meantime we'd like you to keep this very tight. Who else knows what you've told me?'

'Just Mickey Summer. And he wants immunity from prosecution before he goes on.'

'What's he done?' asked Declin.

'He's been following the Quadra's leads.'

'Trading on inside information?'

'You could argue he didn't know for sure that he had inside

155

information.'

'Do we want to argue that?'

'If we want him onboard,' said Frank. 'We need to guarantee he won't get in trouble with the Fed or the SEC.'

Declin nodded agreement. He didn't have any qualms about letting the little fish go in order to catch the sharks.

'He'd also need protection from the UK regulators, and I'm not in a position to get that right now.'

'I'll fix it. But we'll want something in return.'

'I've told him we need hard evidence of insider trading.'

'More than that,' said Declin. 'We need Mickey Summer to find the source. This could be way more involved than insider trading.'

81

Nebuchadnezzar was starting to worry that his plan would never work. But just after Zuhr prayers, and undoubtedly inspired by Allah, Hafez had a breakthrough.

'Allah Akbar!' he shouted, blessing himself.

Nebuchadnezzar looked over at the screen displaying thin white lines criss-crossed over a green background.

'What are you looking at?'

'The navigation screen for the *Amelia Riviera*. I have access.'

'At last!'

'I can take control whenever I want. Just tell me when.'

'Not yet. I need to make preparations.'

Nebuchadnezzar picked up his gun and walked to the door.

'Where are you going?'

'I'll be back soon,' he said, ignoring the question. He hurried out to the pick-up. 'Take me somewhere busy. The market. Anywhere.'

The driver accelerated out the compound and sped down the cratered streets. This was the moment of greatest danger. If the Americans had tracked him down to the compound they would wait until he left before hitting him with a drone. He had been lucky to be tipped off in Waziristan and in Basra. But he couldn't trust his CIA handler. Someday his own usefulness would be over. Perhaps that moment had already arrived.

At the edge of the market the driver pulled up onto the pavement. Nebuchadnezzar took out the new mobile and entered the number for the broker in Dubai. He entered the code he had selected for this latest, most special of all the cyber attacks: 8.53.18.59.

82

At Hurlburt Air Base, Florida, a young sergeant in the US Air Force monitoring group was combing through social media posts from ISIS sympathizers. He came across a selfie from a man called Hafez Abdullah. His face was covered but it was the caption that interested the sergeant.

'Have given bay'ah to Nebuchadnezzar. He has a big kafir surprise on the way. May Allah accept me as mujahedin. Make dua.'

A reference to the elusive Nebuchadnezzar. He looked more closely at the photo and realized it showed a distinctive building behind Hafez Abdullah.

'We have an in!' he shouted, as he printed a screen shot. Within a minute the picture was circulated around the room and everyone set aside their other tasks to trawl through photos of buildings in Raqqa. It took just fifteen minutes before they had a match and the sergeant ran it over to the duty officer.

He immediately realized its significance. 'When did you get this?'

'About twenty minutes ago, Sir.'

The duty officer signalled for the sergeant to stand at ease while he read over the message. 'What is the big kafir surprise?'

'We don't know, Lieutenant.'

'And what do we know about Hafez Abdullah?'

'British Muslim. Saudi parents. Worked in computer forensics. Typical jihadist profile. A nobody who wanted to be a somebody. Went to Syria eighteen months ago as an aid worker. Joined ISIS early this year.'

'Bay'ah? Remind me.'

'To give an oath of allegiance,' explained the sergeant.

'And Hafez Abdullah has made one to Nebuchadnezzar.'

'Correct. We've positively ID'd the building as an ISIS command center. We've got co-ordinates. Air Combat Command could drop a couple of JDAMs and vaporize the building.'

'It might come to that sergeant, but for now let's get a monitoring drone on Abdullah and see if he gives us more clues about his kafir surprise or the whereabouts of Nebuchadnezzar.'

83

'Over the years the People's government has successfully reclaimed the lost territories of Tibet, Macau and Hong Kong. More recently we have recovered land in the East and South China Seas. All of these places are an inalienable part of the motherland. But there is one limb above all others that needs to be rejoined before we can truly feel whole again. The Motherland has been patient in waiting for this re-union. The people of the twenty third province have also been patient. We know that for seventy years they have waited for liberation from Imperialist rule. The time for that liberation is now.

'We call upon the citizens of the province to demand re-unification with their motherland. A reunited Taiwan will enjoy the same political freedoms and market liberalism that are enjoyed by Hong Kong and our other Economic Free Zones. We call upon the Taiwanese military to join the People's Liberation Army and retain the same rank as they possess now. We call upon the Political leaders in Taiwan to continue to govern the twenty third province just as the leaders in Hong Kong rule their province. We will preserve Taiwan's individual status as a member of international organizations. The government of China does not seek retribution for decisions taken by generals and leaders who are long dead. The Central People's government seeks only reunification. This time has come.'

Mickey clicked off the release from the Xinhua news agency

and pulled up the FTSE. Every stock was showing red, the market down ten percent.

'Scary.' Cindy nibbled her lower lip as she stared at the screens.

'The Chinese invading Taiwan or the stock market crashing?' asked Mickey.

'Both.'

'Well there's nothing you can do about the first and I told you before, you should either hedge out the market risk or trade your way out of trouble.'

'And I told you we don't invest like that. Where do you think this will lead?'

'Into trouble for sure,' Mickey said. 'The Chinese taking over some deserted islands was one thing. Invading Taiwan is a whole different shit show.'

'This could lead to nuclear war. If the Americans get involved.'

Mickey saw she was genuinely frightened for her life. 'I don't see President Topps going to war with China. He might be off his rocker but I don't think he's suicidal.'

'Let's hope you're right.'

84

Nebuchadnezzar waited in the car with his head covered under a blanket. The driver and two others ran into the compound. They disappeared inside the house and reappeared a moment later dragging Hafez along the ground by his arms.

'Salam, brothers,' Hafez called out. 'What is happening?'

'You betrayed us. Traitor.'

'Never. Not me. I did nothing. I swear.'

The driver smashed his gun butt against Hafez's head. 'You sent a picture.'

Hafez covered his head against more blows but stood his ground. 'I hid my face!'

'You showed the house in the background. The Americans know we are here.'

'Forgive me brother, I won't do it again.'

'That's right.' He pushed Hafez down into the dust and kicked him in the side. 'Kneel!'

'I am a faithful soldier.' Hafez began to cry. 'Show mercy.'

The gun pushed up into the back of his head. An ear-shattering crack and an intense roar echoed off surrounding buildings. Hafez fell forward into the dirt, his head blown open like a smashed melon.

'Let's go!' Nebuchadnezzar shouted, glancing up from under his blanket through the windscreen at the empty sky.

85

It was Mickey's first visit to the 'Ice Cube', the new American embassy in Wandsworth. He was impressed with the subtle high security. In place of the concrete barriers that had blighted the old embassy building, the new building's physical barriers were cleverly disguised as natural features such as grass berms, garden walls and a lake.

But there were also the machine gun posts and other traditional security to put off any unwelcome visitors.

As arranged, Frank was waiting for him at reception.

'What's this all about?' Mickey asked. Frank had refused to answer the question on the phone and Mickey was desperate to understand why the American embassy was suddenly involved.

'I'd like you to meet someone.'

Frank led the way to an FBI operation room and introduced him to Special Agent Declin Lehane, a strange-looking kid with tattoos and a punk haircut and more metal in his face than Ironman.

'I'm leading the investigation into the cyber attacks on America,' he said.

Mickey laughed. 'Couldn't they find any grown-ups?'

'I've got grown-ups among my thousand-strong task force.'

'Fairy snuff. But anyhow, what's all this cyber malarkey got to do with me?'

'We've reason to believe that the Quadra Fund is getting advance notice of the cyber attacks and trading on that inside information.

We'd like you to help us find out how. I would be able to arrange some financial reward.'

'I'm looking in any case and I ain't bothered about the money,' Mickey said, surprising himself. 'Although I am bothered about this immunity from prosecution you promised me, Frank.'

'Sorted. You're covered both here and in the States.'

Frank handed Mickey a brown envelope. Inside was a stack of papers.

Mickey glanced at one granting him immunity from prosecution in the UK and another in America.

'So do we have a deal?' asked Declin.

Something didn't fit for Mickey. 'I'm with you that Crispin is probably pulling a fast buck. He was an average fund manager when I knew him and the rest of the team haven't got a clue about trading. They just make these big insider bets. But, whatever, Crispin isn't a terrorist.'

'We don't know what his motive is at this stage. He could be three steps removed from the cyber attacks. Just turning a blind eye to them. But he knows something.'

Mickey was still unsure. 'If this involves the security services, cyber terrorism and all that, why do you need me?'

'You understand finance. And you're in situ. Our financial crime people have been watching for some time now. All communications have been monitored and recorded. They added print/copy integrity software on the network. They've had every conversation tracked. Every byte of information going in and out of that building has been checked. They couldn't find anything.'

'So Crispin must be meeting up in person.'

'We've also been watching. And listening to his conversations. Nothing.'

'Good old-fashioned letter in the post?' suggested Mickey.

'All mail has been intercepted at source and checked. Nothing. But one way or another, they're getting the information. I need you to find out how.'

86

Nebuchadnezzar had moved the team to a new safe house in an area still effectively controlled by Islamic State. It was the former residence of a senior Syrian government minister. As well as having high walls that had survived the fighting relatively intact, it had its own air-raid bunker, air-conditioning and expensive furniture. It also had a garden which, although untended, retained enough of its former glories for Nebuchadnezzar to enjoy a walk around it. Yet he could not completely relax.

Hafez Abdullah's moronic tweet meant the Americans would know for sure that Nebuchadnezzar was in Raqqa. Their drones would be watching. And with the ten-million-dollar bounty they had placed on his head, there were also plenty of brothers and sisters who would give him away.

So Nebuchadnezzar was alert to the slightest noise that might betray an American attack; the rattle of a window, the bark of dog, the Doppler of a fast approaching car, the whump of blades from an approaching helicopter. Although it was more likely they would get him with a missile that he would never hear.

His reflections were interrupted by a shout from inside the house and he returned to the operations room hoping that the team had rediscovered Hafez Abdullah's route into the *Amelia Riviera* control room. But it was a different group who had smiles on their faces. The team working on the energy attack.

'We have it,' announced Abu Obeida.

'Show me.'

Abu rattled his keyboard and clicked his mouse until he was, in a virtual sense, inside the control room for Enthalpy.

'Be careful not to alert their operators,' said Nebuchadnezzar.

Abu slowly lowered the rotation speed of a generator from fifty megahertz to forty nine.

'See?'

'Enough. Set it back to fifty.'

To Enthalpy's operators the change would have looked like just a random blip. But Nebuchadnezzar knew now that they could disrupt the electricity generating capacity for half of the United

States. This was excellent, though not the attack he had planned and not the attack the fund was expecting. He needed to alert the broker in Dubai, but it was too dangerous to travel outside the residence. At the risk of being intercepted, he sent the code for this attack from where he sat: 2.17.

87

Mickey put up his umbrella against the heavy, cold rain. Wished he'd ordered a taxi. Too late now, he'd just have to hurry along. His trousers got soaked in no time as he shuffled along the pavement. At the entrance to the alley a large puddle had formed. Too wide to jump. He tip-toed through and the water seeped in through his laces. He cleared the water hazard and hurried on again, suddenly aware of someone following him. Damn. The light in the alley was out. Still, just keep walking straight.

Half way down, just at the point he could barely see his hand in front of him, he heard footsteps approaching quickly. He looked over his shoulder and could see the black outline of two men running.

Shit. He took off for the light on the street at the end of the alley, but he was out of shape and they soon caught him. He turned to face them. They wore ski masks.

'I need a bigger head start than that, guys.'

The tallest of them swung a leather truncheon. Mickey put an arm up to block it but the man punched with his left and Mickey caught it full in his face. He lost his legs and collapsed to the floor. Someone grabbed a hand, pulled his arm round his back and pressed his knees into the small of his back. Mickey's face was pushed into the wet pavement.

'If it's money you're after,' said Mickey. 'There's two hundred cash in my wallet. Take it.'

'I don't want your cash,' the man replied.

'Will you take a cheque?'

Mickey groaned as his arm was forced further up his back.

'We're here because we hate grasses.'

'Hay fever?'

The attacker pushed a gun in front of Mickey's eyes. 'Don't talk to the police again. Or you'll never see your lady again.'

'Leave her out of it.'

'You leave her out of it by keeping quiet.'

'Okay,' said Mickey, desperate to smack him hard in the face but knowing he couldn't take two of them and he'd probably just be putting Helen in danger.

'Very sensible. I'm going to leave you now. You're going to lie face down on the ground for a few minutes.'

The man let go his grip. Mickey's arm dropped back beside his body and he took a deep breath with the weight off his ribs. He heard footsteps retreating down the alley and resisted the temptation to look. He gave it a minute, took out his mobile and dialled the house phone. He started walking back home. Through the puddle without tip-toeing. The phone rang with no answer.

He cut the call and dialled her mobile, walking faster as it rang.

No answer there either. He dialled the house phone again.

And ran.

88

Abu offered up a quick prayer and set to work. He retraced his steps through the trapdoor from the Entergy public internet to the company intranet and over the bridge into the control network. There he released the worm to corrupt the grid controls. Next he moved to the program that set rotation speeds for the turbines. As instructed by Nebuchadnezzar, he selected the Indian Point nuclear power station and lowered the rotation speed to thirty mega hertz. He worked his way back out of the system and closed his computer.

'All done,' he said, packing his computer into a bag. 'That was easier than I thought.'

'Come,' said Nebuchadnezzar, hurrying to the waiting car. 'We must sleep in the tunnels tonight. The Americans will be looking for us.'

89

Mickey turned the key and pushed the door until it jammed on the chain. Helen was surely in then. He stared through the frosted glass in the door and rang the bell. Nothing. He hoped for a crack appearing in the lounge curtain, but nothing moved. He rang the door bell again. Dialled her phone number but it went straight to voice mail.

'Helen!' He banged on the window, desperately hoping she'd just fallen asleep.

'You all right?' asked a neighbor.

'No,' said Mickey. He took two steps back and launched himself at the door. The chain snapped. He hurried into the house. 'Helen!'

Lounge, dining-room, kitchen. Upstairs. Bedroom. Spare room. Bathroom. Back downstairs two at a time. Dining-room again. Through the patio door to the garden.

'Helen!'

He dialled her number again. Through to voicemail again. He dialled Frank. His heart pounding with the dial tone.

'Frank. They've taken Helen.'

'Who's taken her? Where?'

'Two blokes jumped me down an alley. Said I'd never see Helen again if I spoke to the police. I've got home and she isn't here. Her phone is switched off. The bastards have taken her.'

'I'm on my way.'

'Why are you coming here?'

'We'll have to search the house …'

'She's not bloody here!'

'We need to search for clues; fingerprints, footprints, signs of forced entry …'

'Bloody hell, Frank. You don't need to be a detective to know who's done this. It's Crispin, ain't it. Or at least he hired the geezers that have done it.'

'We don't know that.'

'But you're going to arrest him?'

'If we find evidence linking him. I'll call a forensics unit and I'll be straight round.'

'Door's open,' said Mickey. 'I'll fix this my way.'

90

'Holy mother!' shouted the controller, as a red light flashed on the screen in front of him. 'Massive power surge into Indian Point.'

'Where the hell has that come from?'

'Indian Point is calling it in,' he said, shaking his head. 'But why?'

'They're running at thirty Megahertz! That's why.'

He hit an emergency line to the plant. 'Indian Point, you're running at thirty Megahertz. Correct back up to fifty immediately.'

'Negative.'

'What do you mean, negative? Do it. Now!'

'We can't. Our controls don't work. We can't change the setting.'

The controller checked the state estimator. Power from all the other generators on the grid was flowing into the slow spinning Indian Point. If they couldn't stop it, the finely-balanced rotors in the turbine would be critically compromised.

'Indian Point? You need to regain control of your settings immediately. You need to correct.'

'I'm telling you we can't do a thing …'

'I'm cutting you off the grid.' He hit the command to take Indian Point off the network. Prayed he hadn't left it too late.

Cracking and banging erupted from the open microphone. An alarm sounded and more red lights flashed on the control board.

'Indian Point? Are you okay?'

'Something just blew up big time.'

The controller pictured metal parts breaking from the turbines and being hurled from the machine, colliding into each other at incredible kinetic energies.

'What exactly?'

'Unit two has blown.'

'Call emergency response.'

'Will do. I'm going to evacuate.'

'Negative. Wait for the fire crews. You have to direct them.'

'What's to direct? There's flames all over unit two.'

'Forget the fire in the turbine. Let it run. You have to stop the fire spreading to the nuclear generator.'

'I don't want to be a hero.'

'You have to safeguard the nuclear generator and the spent fuel storage. If they go up you'll release radioactive waste into the air and into the Hudson.'

'Okay. Okay. I got you. Should we evacuate the neighborhood?'

The controller glanced at a map. Indian point was surrounded by towns and Manhattan was just thirty miles downriver. 'Yes. But the main priority is to stop that fire spreading.'

91

Mickey approached the white van parked at a meter on Berkeley Square. He recognized the pumped-up body of Dave Casey in the driver's seat. Beside him sat Winston, the huge black guy he remembered from Casey's gym. Mickey opened the front passenger door and climbed up into the seat.

'Your face is all messed up,' said Casey, sticking out a hand and crushing Mickey's. 'What happened to you?'

'I got jumped by a couple of blokes.'

'Who?'

'They didn't leave a business card.'

'What's this all about, then?'

'Someone has kidnapped my missus.'

'Kidnap?' Casey's grin disappeared. 'Why?'

'Stop me talking to the Old Bill.'

'Hold on. You said you wanted us to put the frighteners on some money man. Are you saying he kidnapped your wife?'

'I want to find out what he knows about it.'

Casey fixed Mickey a cold stare. 'You sure this is a good idea? What are the Old Bill doing about the kidnapping?'

'Looking for evidence. Building a bloody case for the prosecution. I told them to just arrest Crispin and shake him down, but they said they couldn't do that without proof.'

'But you're sure he's involved?'

'Certain,' Mickey said. 'And I haven't got time to wait for the police.'

Casey cracked his knuckles and smiled through his crooked teeth. 'Okay. But it's going to cost you double, now that I know about the kidnapping.'

'I don't work in the City now,' Mickey protested. 'I haven't got that sort of money.'

'My heart bleeds for you. It's ten grand or you're on your own.'

Mickey turned to look at Winston. 'Is it just the two of you?'

Casey feigned injury. 'He reckons you and me can't scare his banker friend on our own, Winston.'

'I was just wondering, that's all,' said Mickey. He spotted Crispin's PA going out for lunch. 'Ten grand it is then. Let's go.'

They jogged down the pavement. Mickey signed in Casey and Winston at the security desk as prospective clients. Casey made a surprisingly good impersonation of one, talking about prospective returns in a low-inflation environment.

'Did you actually understand that rubbish you were talking?' Mickey asked him in the elevator.

'I ain't got a clue. But neither did your security guard.'

Leaving the elevator, Mickey led them quickly across the floor and along the corridor to Crispin's office. He opened the door without knocking and looked quickly around the sparsely furnished room.

Crispin was retrieving a fax from the machine. He looked up and arched a bushy grey eyebrow.

'A word in your plug hole,' Mickey said.

'Your line of communication to me is through Cindy.'

'Funnily enough,' said Mickey, closing the door behind Casey and Winston. 'It is lines of communication I want to speak about.'

'And who are your friends?'

'I'll come on to that.'

Crispin set down the fax and checked the time on his watch. 'I'll give you one minute.'

'My wife has been kidnapped.'

'Kidnapped?' Crispin sat forward in his chair. 'Are you sure?'

'Course I'm bloody sure.'

'I'm sorry. Right. You've called the police I presume.'

'Give over with the innocent nun act, Crispin. You know all about it.'

'I can assure you I don't.' Crispin glanced at Casey and Winston but couldn't look either of them in the eye. He walked over to his desk and sat down. 'Look, what exactly is going on here?'

'I've taken out a contract with these men here. It's like a futures contract. Anything bad happens to my wife and they pay you a visit and make sure the same happens to you.'

'I have no idea what you're talking about. I'm sorry to hear about your wife's disappearance, but I know nothing about it. And if you don't leave immediately I will call the police.'

'No need,' Mickey said, suddenly unsure of his ground. 'We're on our way.'

Mickey led the way back out the office, ignoring the stares, wondering if he'd called it all wrong.

'What's going on?' Cindy asked, running up to him. 'What was all that shouting about?'

He hesitated, but realized she might as well know what she had got herself into. 'Someone has kidnapped my wife. To stop me talking to the police.'

'That's terrible.'

'Does anyone know anything about it?' he glowered at the wide eyes around the room.

'Of course not,' Cindy said. 'What are you going to do?'

'I'm going to find her.'

They left Cindy and the analysts in stunned silence and took the elevator to the ground floor.

'Thanks guys,' Mickey said, as they walked out into the square. 'I think Crispin got the message.'

'He ain't your man,' said Casey.

'Why do you say that?'

'He didn't know what you were talking about.'

'Maybe he was just playing cool.'

169

'You don't play cool when you're shitting your pants,' said Casey. 'Didn't you smell it?'

Mickey hadn't, but he had been so pumped up that he wouldn't have noticed anyway. 'So you think he's innocent.'

'He's guilty of being a banker. But he's got nothing to do with kidnapping your wife.' Casey took a parking ticket off his windscreen and handed it to Mickey. 'Nice doing business with you.'

92

'We need to replace the Indian Point generating capacity,' Control shouted.

'We're bringing on the hydro storage. But that won't be enough.'

'Purchase the rest on the spot market.'

'Got it. We're covered. All good now.'

An alarm sounded.

'Holy shit! Look at the Star-South Canton.'

The Control's eyes flashed over the readouts showing a massive power surge down the transmission line. How the hell was that happening? He realized that across Ohio surge protectors would be overwhelmed and computers, televisions, music players, microwaves, fridges and recharging phones would be getting fried.

Another alarm went off.

'Now we got problems on one thirty eights. All hell's breaking loose here.'

'We need to shed some load in Ohio,' Control shouted.

'Or we could gain some from Michigan.'

'Too late. The circuit breaker has kicked in. The Wawa line has disconnected.'

'Shit. Now we've lost connections with Canada.'

Control couldn't believe what was happening. A massive power outage and a nuclear emergency at Indian Point. He wanted someone to tell him it was just an emergency drill. But it wasn't.

'We're going to lose the entire Eastern grid.'

93

Frank persuaded Mickey to come along to a meeting at Snow Hill police station that he'd fixed with a DS Peterson, the detective in charge of the search for Helen.

Mickey wasn't overly impressed when Peterson sauntered into the meeting room fifteen minutes late, without apology. They made introductions and then Peterson asked: 'How can I help?'

'How can you help?' asked Mickey. 'Are you for real? Fucking well find my wife.'

'There's no need for bad language.'

'That's just for starters …'

Frank put a hand on Mickey's arm then turned to Peterson. 'So where have you got to?'

'Has anybody contacted you?' Peterson asked Mickey. 'Or tried to make contact?'

'No.' Mickey checked his phone. 'Nothing.'

'Any ransom note or email? Anything like that?'

'No.'

DS Peterson nodded and made a note in the pad.

'So what? Is that a bad sign?' Mickey looked at Peterson and then Frank. 'Should I be expecting a ransom note or something?'

'Typically,' said Peterson.

'Not in this case,' Frank said. 'There isn't a ransom. The kidnapping is to keep Mickey from talking to the police.'

'Perhaps.'

'Did forensics turn up anything at the house?' asked Frank.

'Nothing that would suggest a kidnapping.'

'Have you checked for film footage for motorists and cyclists?'

'Yes, we put an appeal in the Standard. Nothing has come up so far.'

'There must be something to go on.'

'I'm afraid not.' DS Peterson crossed his arms and sat back in his chair. 'We found no sign of any struggle at the property. Neither was there any sign of forced entry, other than the front door which you tell us you broke in, Mr Summer. '

'Did you check out the alley where Mickey was attacked?'

'Nothing there either.'

'Did you check properly?' asked Mickey.

'I know how to do my job, Mr Summer. We have nothing to suggest your wife has been kidnapped other than your say so.'

'Mickey isn't making this up,' said Frank. 'Look at his bruises.'

DS Peterson looked at Mickey but said nothing.

'Why would he make it up?' asked Frank.

DS Peterson turned to Mickey. 'How would you describe the relationship with your wife at present?'

'At present I ain't got a relationship because someone has kidnapped her.'

'Have you been getting along well recently?'

'Sure.'

'Your neighbors say there have been a lot of arguments. I understand she was getting fed up with your gambling. Is that right?'

Mickey glanced at Frank then back to DS Peterson. 'What's that got to do with anything?'

'I'm wondering whether she might simply have left you.'

Mickey wanted to laugh. 'What about these guys who jumped me then. What was all that about?'

'You tell me? You withdrew ten thousand pounds in cash yesterday. What was that for?'

'I don't know. You seem to be the one with all the answers. What are you thinking?'

'Do you owe anyone money?'

'This is ridiculous,' Frank interrupted. 'Helen Summer has been kidnapped. You need to take this seriously.'

'Now you're telling me how to do my job.'

'And I think I'll get your Superintendent to tell you next.'

'He's not going to take a call from a suspended officer, so I wouldn't waste your time. And I'm not wasting anymore of mine. We have reported her missing. That's all I can do for now.'

94

President Topps squeezed a baseball in his hand as he watched the news report of power cuts across the Eastern Seaboard. People complaining about the lack of heating, the lost freezer food, the computer damage. Worryingly, the reporter said there was little prospect of the power coming on again anytime soon.

'They have to get this fixed by nightfall,' the President said to Martha.

'I heard it's going to take longer than that.'

'How about Indian Point?'

'They managed to contain the fire before it reached the nuclear generator.'

'Good. But the fire is not out?'

'That's right.'

'And is this connected somehow to this dirty nuke plot?'

'We don't know.'

'Or maybe this is the plot to poison the very blood of the Great Satan. Send radioactive cloud over Manhattan. Is that it?'

'We don't know that either.'

'We don't seem to know very much at all.' The President bounced the baseball off the wall and caught it. 'What the hell is Cresta Patton doing over at Cyber Command?'

'I'm sure she's doing her best.'

'If she doesn't fix this mess I'll be the one who gets the blame. Cresta isn't standing for re-election. I am.'

'There is also the problem in China for you to consider.'

'Not my problem.'

'I'm afraid it is. There have been more critics railing against your inaction over Taiwan.'

'Not my problem,' he repeated.

'The Taiwanese claim you are breaking a long-standing defence treaty if you don't come to help them.'

'We've been over this so many times!' The President hit a direct dial to the Attorney General. 'Martin, could you clarify the legal position on Taiwan for me one last time.'

The President detected a slight gathering of breath on the other end of the line.

'If China invades Taiwan it will be illegal under International law and we would be entitled to defend Taiwan, but not obligated.'

'Entitled but not obligated,' repeated the President, looking at Martha. 'Remind me, Martin, one last time just what we are obligated to do.'

'We do not have a treaty obligation to come to the defence of Taiwan,' said Martin. 'What we have is the 1979 Taiwan Relations Act that commits the United States to help Taiwan defend itself.'

'This is the problem,' said the President. 'To most people it sounds like the same thing.'

'It isn't. Help to defend a country is a whole lot different from an obligation to come to its defence. We might limit our help to supplying arms and advice but it doesn't need to include US military engagement with China. On the other hand it might and it could.'

'What kind of fuzzy-headed agreement is that?' the President asked.

'It's all part of our policy of strategic ambiguity. It's designed to discourage China from attacking without encouraging Taiwan to be too bold in its own statements towards declaring independence, a move that China has always said would prompt an armed response.'

'So we are not obligated to come to a direct rescue.'

'Correct.'

'Thank you.' The President cut the call and turned back to Martha. 'We are not going to defend Taiwan. This is unfinished business between China and Taiwan. Not our problem.'

'Do we declare that as our position?'

'We'll keep them guessing,' said the President.

'How about Horn's plan of sailing a task force up there as a show of solidarity.'

'We could do that. But frankly I really don't care. American citizens don't give a damn about Taiwan. What they give a damn about is their trains and planes aren't moving, they can't fill up the car with gas, the power is out across half the country, they can't eat meat and we got a nuclear power station ready to blow. And they don't even know about the dirty nuke attack yet.'

The President walked over to the window and watched a gardener cutting edges on the White House lawn. The gardener set down his sheers and lit up a cigarette. Job apparently done. If only the President's own work could be accomplished in similar methodical, uncomplicated fashion.

'How did we lose control of this, Martha? We're supposed to be the most technologically advanced nation on earth and we're getting picked apart by a bunch of cyber terrorists.'

'I don't fully understand either,' said Martha. 'My problem is I'm not really of the cyber generation.'

'The problem is none of us are. Calvara, Asimov, Flood. We're all too old to understand this cyber stuff.'

'Cresta's young.'

'Not young enough. How about that FBI cyber kid? I didn't see him at the last security meeting.'

'He's in London apparently.'

'What the hell is he doing in London? We need all hands on deck. Get him back here.'

95

Mickey had been knocking on doors until his knuckles were red, but hadn't turned up a single fresh lead. But he had to keep trying. He rang another door bell.

A young woman opened an upstairs window. 'Yeah?'

'Hi. I'm Mickey. I live down the road at number seven. I don't think we've met.'

'No, we haven't.'

'I was just wondering if you were around yesterday afternoon and noticed anything strange.'

'Like what?'

'Like maybe some men hanging around. Or anything out of the ordinary.'

'Are you police?'

'No. Thing is my wife was kidnapped. I'm trying to find her.'

'Kidnapped?'

'That's right. I'm asking around to see if anybody saw anything.'

'Hang on.' The woman closed the window. A moment later she opened the front door. 'Your wife was kidnapped?'

'That's right.'

'Who's done that then?'

'That's what I'm trying to find out. Did you see anything?'

The woman screwed up her face then shook her head. 'I was at work yesterday. Sorry.'

'Never mind. Thanks anyway.'

'That's a terrible thing. I hope you find her.'

'Thanks.'

It certainly was a terrible thing.

Mickey walked on to the next house. His phone vibrated in his pocket. He snatched it out, hoping.

But it was just Frank. 'Mickey? Where are you?'

'I'm here. Where are you?'

'I was expecting you at the embassy.'

Mickey checked his watch. He'd totally forgotten. 'I can't make that. I'm looking for Helen.'

'Leave that to the police.'

'Well they ain't doing a lot about it are they?'

'Peterson has issued a missing persons report and circulated her photo. There isn't anything more he can do.'

'Well I've got to do something, Frank. I'm going crazy just sitting around doing nothing.'

'The best use of your time would be to come and help us crack the insider-trading investigation. That should hopefully lead to Helen.'

Mickey sighed. He knew Frank was right. 'I'm on my way.'

96

'The big thing we are missing,' said Declin, 'Is how Crispin gets his inside information.'

'Actually I might have an idea,' Mickey said, remembering

Crispin's startled look as he turned from the fax machine. 'Are your boys monitoring incoming fax messages?'

'Fax?' Declin slapped his forehead. 'Faxes are analogue, not digital, so nobody monitored them. Shit! We forgot about the fax.'

'That could be your carrier pigeon,' said Mickey. 'Communicate the inside information by fax and shred the paper. There's no evidence.'

'Is the fax an MFD?' asked Declin.

'Speak English.'

'A multi-functional device that can do copying and email and printing as well. Or was it a stand-alone simple fax?'

'I'm pretty sure it was a stand-alone fax and it looked years old.'

'Pity. Was it connected to a network server?'

'I said speak English.'

'Was it plugged into a network point or a traditional telephone socket?'

'I'm sorry, I must pay more attention next time.'

'It doesn't matter,' said Declin. 'We can find out from their service support. There's just a chance.'

Declin rang someone in America. Mickey recognized the words he used: analogue device, fax server, audit trail. But not for the first time, he didn't know what the young geek was talking about.

A few minutes later Declin printed out a stack of papers and clipped them together. 'We've managed to check the fax machine. All it ever receives is this same thing each day from a broker in Dubai.'

Mickey looked at the top print out. 'It's just a low quality report on Middle Eastern markets. About as far as you can get from value-added inside information.'

'It doesn't look suspicious,' Declin agreed. 'Would be grateful for a second opinion, though.'

Mickey walked over to an easy chair to read through the papers. He was glad to have something to take his mind off Helen. Out of habit he set about the pile back to front, the same way he tackled financial reports. The faxes contained daily closing values for eight main equity markets in the Middle East, and lists of the best and worst performers. This was accompanied by a market report and some fairly banal commentary. There was also a section on top long-term stock recommendations and trading strategies. It was all low-quality broking fare, but he pressed on. Soon he started to get tired of the repetition.

He glanced at the clock and was about to give up when he noticed the top-performing stock on one sheet was called Nebu. Two problems with that, he thought. First Nebu was a Canadian mining stock listed in Toronto. Second it hadn't been the top performing stock for years. He knew because he'd stuffed a few clients in and they'd never let him forget it.

He presumed there was also a Middle Eastern stock with the same name. But after Googling around for a few minutes he could find no quoted company in the Middle East named Nebu or anything that could be shortened to that. It might just be a typo. Then again it might not. He regrouped with a fresh coffee and worked back through the faxes. He came across Nebu again and set aside that paper. He carried on and came across six fax sheets where Nebu had been the best performing stock. Although the share prices varied wildly. Strange.

'There is something odd here,' he declared.

Declin and Frank hurried over.

'It's just that occasionally, whoever is compiling this tip sheet puts in that the top performing stock is Nebu. Except Nebu is a Canadian stock. And also the share price is always different. It's probably just a computer glitch but …'

'Show me,' said Declin, straining his head to read upside down. He turned the six pages the right way round. 'This is interesting.'

'It is?' said Mickey doubtfully.

Declin smacked Mickey on the back. 'I think you've cracked it.'

'I have?'

'I don't think Nebu is a company. It's short-hand for Nebuchadnezzar.'

'Who's he when he's at home?'

'That is the *nom de guerre* of the man coordinating the cyber attacks. And those numbers are the identifiers for the malware used in each attack.' Declin wrote down some dates on each fax. 'He's sent them to the Quadra just a matter of days before each attack.'

'So you already know about these numbers then,' said Mickey.

'We guessed they are a code to identify each attack somehow. But we can't figure how. We tried matching them with phone numbers, ISP addresses, physical addresses, dates of birth, bank account numbers, tax numbers, Sudoku and scrabble scores. You name it, we've tried it.'

'Maybe we don't need to crack the code,' said Frank. 'Crispin understands it. And probably so too does the Dubai broker. Now we've got hard evidence of a connection we can bring them both in.'

'Whoa!' Declin said. 'Let's not go crashing in just yet. That's the mistake we've been making all along. Neither Crispin or the broker know we've found out about the fax, so they'll keep on using this. That gives us a heads-up on the next cyber attack.'

'But we don't understand the code. So how does it help?'

'We can add any new code into the malware filters. So for example this one here I don't recognise.' Declin pulled out one paper. 'We haven't seen this code on any malware yet. So this is an attack that has yet to happen.'

'And we know the Quadra Fund is still betting on an oil price rise,' said Mickey. 'So it has something to do with that.'

'Maybe they plan to blow up an oil terminal or another pipeline,' suggested Declin. 'Whatever, we can now add these numbers to the malware filters in the energy sector. For the first time we will actually be ahead of the curve.'

'So what else do we do?' asked Frank.

'We discretely investigate this Dubai broker,' Declin said. 'Find out who is passing the malware codes into it. That person is either Nebuchadnezzar or at least one step closer to him.'

97

Hue looked up above the gate of the Forbidden City and studied the sprinkling of world leaders that had ignored the American-led boycott of the parade. Russia, Brazil, South Africa, Cambodia and Korea he could identify. But he was pleased to confirm for himself the rumors that almost the rest of Asia and every country in Europe were absent. General Wing sniffed the cold, acrid air nonchalantly, but Hue suspected his father would have been angered by their absence.

Hue's attention turned to huge LED displays around the square showing footage of the retaking of the South and East China Sea Islands, which drew genuine applause from the crowds in the square. Live footage appeared of an invasion fleet being readied to cross the Taiwan Straits. This drew some cautious applause from Party stalwarts, but as Hue studied the people around him he saw great anxiety. The ordinary citizen wanted Taiwan back, of course, but they did not want to go to war with their Chinese brothers and sisters.

Only one person in the square would have no qualms about killing. Hue looked back up at the leaders over the gate. His father had of course risen to fame because of his violence. As a Red Guard during the cultural revolution he had enthusiastically followed Mao's exhortations to rise up against bourgeois elements, subjecting his teachers at Beijing University to beatings and torture. Most infamously, his gang had captured the Vice Principal, shaved his head, stabbed it with scissors and beaten him to death. Far from being punished for his crime, his father was publicly praised by Mao himself.

But the crime which Hue could never forgive or forget had been the drowning of his baby daughter. Murdering his own flesh and blood. Simply because he already had one child. He already had Hue.

Hue could never understand how he had done that. He often wondered whether his father ever felt any guilt for such a monstrous act. He looked back up at the screens showing an impressive display of military hardware. It would be murder again to unleash that on Taiwan. The only thing that could stop Wing now was the Americans.

But where were they?

98

Declin handed Frank and Mickey a two-sided print out. 'The first page lists all the named investors. As Frank has already said, they all check out.'

Mickey recognized most of the names, all recognizable institutional investors. He turned over. 'So what's on this second page?'

'Those are all the offshore accounts invested in the Quadra Fund,' Declin explained. 'If you want to hide your investment, from the tax man or from us, that's how you do it.'

Mickey looked down the list and recognized the three names he had turned up when he had looked for himself. But Declin had the full list. Mickey quickly realized that at least half of the fund was owned by dozens of companies incorporated in far-flung tax havens such as Belize, the Seychelles, the Cook Islands. But he knew that the real ownership of those was masked by nominee directors and further layers of holding companies. 'But we don't know who really owns any of these companies.'

'Yes we do,' Declin said with a smile. 'The financial team have been digging around. The ultimate owner of half of these offshore companies, accounting for about one third of the Quadra Fund, is a holding company in Delaware.'

'As in Delaware in the States,' said Mickey. 'Not exactly a hot bed of terrorism.'

'It's a legitimate-sounding jurisdiction,' agreed Declin. 'But in fact it has some of the lightest corporate reporting standards in the world. Anyone can set up a company there.'

'So who owns it?' asked Frank.

'The team traced ownership through more holding layers to a bank account in the British Virgin Islands. That is owned by another anonymous holding company in Kuwait. That in turn is owned by an unknown beneficiary in the Dubai stock-broking firm that has been sending the faxes through to the Quadra Fund.'

'Bingo!' Mickey high-fived Declin.

'It gets better,' Declin said. 'We screened all communications in and out of the Dubai broker for the names Nebu and Nebuchadnezzar, and for the code numbers. They found incriminating text messages coming into the phone of one of the brokers.'

'The guy who writes the stock market report,' said Mickey.

'We can assume so. Although the source had used a different pay-as-you-go phone each time, we traced back the digital fingerprints on the phones and we've now established to about ninety-five percent certainty that a man named Saifuddin Azizi sent at least two of the messages.'

'So that's our man,' said Frank.

'This is our man,' said Declin showing them both a photograph of a dark, good-looking man in robes, long beard and white cap. 'Born August 4, 1975, in Urumqi, Xinjiang, China, he studied computer science at Urumqi university. More recently, he has taken to photographing for posterity the Middle Eastern religious architecture that was in danger of being lost in war. Perfect cover for travelling around jihadist areas. He was also in New York the date the malware was posted to the Earth Defence.'

'Definitely sounds like our man,' Frank said. 'Let's go get him.'

'It's not as easy as that,' said Declin. 'Take a look at what happens when I try to find out more about him on the NSA server.'

Declin logged into his computer and opened some form of internal search engine. He typed in the name of Saifuddin Azizi. Blood red letters jumped out of the screen: NSA Top Secret – Sensitive Compartmented Information.

Declin opened his hands. 'It's a no go.'

'Can't you get clearance?'

Declin shrugged. 'Only by asking Connelly. He doesn't know I'm looking into this. And he told Chuck and his team not to.'

'Maybe you should open up,' said Frank. 'Tell him what we know.'

'I'm not so sure,' Declin said. 'I think someone, somewhere within American intelligence is protecting Azizi. That's why our investigation has been derailed so many times. If we ask for an SCI clearance to search for him we might tip him off and lose him. Then we lose our only lead to the cyber attacks. We need to tread carefully.'

'We have to do something.'

'We keep watching the fund. That is our only window.'

Declin turned to the screens showing the trading programs at the Quadra Fund.

'There's actually been a lot of activity today,' said Frank.

'The fund's been selling positions to realize cash,' said Mickey.

'Because they are worried about a crash?' asked Declin.

'It looks more like they are expecting to meet redemptions.'

'Redemptions?'

'People wanting to sell up their stakes in the fund.'

Declin flicked through the email traffic into the Quadra Fund that morning. 'Here it is. The Dubai broker has instructed the fund to sell a string of its Delaware accounts.' He checked the names against the master list. 'It's about half of Azizi's entire holdings.'

'Why is he selling now?' asked Frank.

'He knows we're on to him,' said Declin. 'He's taking his money out before we freeze the Quadra Fund assets.'

'So let's freeze them.'

'Not yet. He's left half his holdings in the fund. So he may still use the Nebu codes to tip Crispin off about another trade. Let's leave them all in play a little longer.'

'You can't let Crispin send a billion pounds to a jihadist crazy like Azizi.'

'It's a risk worth taking,' said Declin.

'That money will be spent on weapons.'

'America is under cyber siege and nuclear threat. We don't know where we are going to get hit next. Keeping this window open might give us a clue. If we can prevent just one cyber attack it will be worth it.'

'I understand,' said Frank. 'But it sticks in my craw to let this Azizi get away with it.'

'Who said we're going to let him get away with it?' Declin winked. 'There is one trick I still have up my sleeve.'

* * *

Using his new CIA clearance, Declin booked a secure communications room in the embassy with a terminal hooked up direct into the Langley server. On his phone he pulled up the log-in details he'd seen JC McCaw use in Islamabad, and logged in.

'Are you hacking in to the CIA?' asked Frank, looking over Declin's shoulder.

'Not for the first time.'

'You've done it before?'

'Sure.'

Mickey let out a low whistle. 'Lucky you didn't get caught.'

'I did,' said Declin. 'That's how I got the job in cyber crime. Langley said I could do twenty years in prison or work for them. I wasn't going to work for the people who killed my brother, so we compromised on working in cyber crime for the FBI.'

'The CIA killed your brother!?' asked Mickey.

'As good as,' said Declin. He turned back to the terminal, clicked and tapped his way to the intranet search engine and entered the name of Saifuddin Azizi. Up came a rather different profile of the cyber expert turned academic historian. Azizi was a known jihadist. He had joined the movement for greater religious autonomy for the Muslims in Xinjiang. Increasingly radicalized, he was suspected of plotting a bomb attack on the Beijing underground. In his travels as a historian around the Middle East he had made extensive contact with various groups including al-Nusra, Islamic State and the Free Syrian Army. Surprisingly, Azizi had also worked for the CIA. It seemed he flipped from one side to the other, depending on who was offering most favorable terms.

'I don't get it,' said Frank. 'You've been busting a gut trying to identify Nebuchadnezzar and it turns out he's already known to the CIA.'

Declin said nothing as he was stopped in his tracks by something that took him back in time and place. 'Azizi's handler is Robert Biggerstaff.'

'And who is he?'

'He was one of the CIA guys who sexed up the case for war in Iraq.'

Declin took a screen shot of the page on his phone, scrolled down and took another. He was about to take a third when the screen went blank. 'We're blown.'

He jumped to his feet and ran to the door. Frank and Mickey sprinted after him. They'd taken two steps into the corridor when a security detail appeared, guns drawn.

'Hands in the air!'

Mickey smiled at the guards. 'You have to say: Simon says hands in the air.'

The guard ignored him, patted them all down and removed their cell phones. After an unclear exchange on his headset he marched them quickly down a series of turns in the embassy corridors to an elevator marked 'Restricted Access'.

The other guard opened the elevator with a fingerprint read on the entry pad. They'd been on the ninth floor and yet Declin noted that they descended fourteen. On arriving they were marched down another twisting corridor into a detention block.

They deposited Frank and Mickey in empty cells.

Declin was marched on another fifty yards and locked into his own. He remembered Connelly's words that whatever he thought of the CIA they were still on the same side. He was about to find out if that was true.

99

The dark web was a virtual coffee house for political activists such as Hue. On it he could talk fairly openly against the regime knowing that while State Security might have infiltrated the site they had little idea of the real identities of those on it. However, things were more complicated when it came to organizing demonstrations. He had found a forum planning a massive pro-democracy demonstration in Tiananmen square. Thousands of people had already committed to go, so there would be some safety in numbers. But Hue was worried it was a trap. Perhaps the organizers were really State Security and when the demonstrators unfurled their banners in the great square they would suddenly find it full of Wujing.

There was no way of knowing, but Hue had to be there and so he signed up. He went onto the dating website and told the journalist he'd like to meet again. If the Wujing did attack, he wanted to make sure someone he could trust in the press was watching this time.

100

Declin couldn't tell how long he'd been left in the dark. Long enough to sleep and feel hungry and be grateful to be let out again, even if it was obvious from the way the guards mishandled him that he was in big trouble. They led him back into the embassy maze and on to the office 'Commercial Relations'.

Declin was pretty sure the man behind the desk, who introduced himself as Director Stotton, had nothing to do with commerce. He motioned for Declin to sit and fixed him with a hard stare. 'Are you a friend, Special Agent Lehane? A friend of your country.'

'I'm a patriot,' confirmed Declin with conviction.

'That's good. Because I've been asked by people state-side to turn a blind eye to your transgression, but I need certain assurances before I do that.'

Declin presumed it was Connelly who'd been rooting for him. 'What assurances?'

'First. Keep your focus on fighting cyber crime. No more moonlighting as an intelligence analyst.'

'That moonlighting led me to Saifuddin Azizi.'

'Who the intelligence community already know.'

'Why is the information on Saifuddin Azizi highly classified?'

'I can't tell you that of course. Highly classified means it's on a need to know basis. And you don't need to know.'

'But he is Nebuchadnezzar, the man we've all been looking for. And yet he is a CIA asset.'

'Was a CIA asset. He's gone native.'

'So let's take him out.'

'We certainly don't want to do that.'

Declin was confused. 'Why are you protecting him?'

'Azizi is, shall we say, unreliable.' Stotton smiled. 'But when he is onside he's our most credible asset in the Islamic world. He's plugged into ISIS, Al Queda, Nusfra Front, Hezbolla, Iran. Sunni or Shia, it doesn't matter. You name it and he's got an in to each of those organizations.'

'So can we make contact with Azizi?'

'Not without compromising him.'

'But he must know about the dirty nuke. He can surely tell us where it is? How it's coming to hit us?'

'I suspect he is doing his best to tell us that. It was probably Azizi that left behind the Uranium pellet you found.'

Declin sat in silence a moment, recalibrating. His mind flashed back to an empty warehouse in Iraq. 'Did you tip him off in Basra?'

'I'm not going to discuss operational matters.'

'You did tip him off, so he got away. That's how they knew we were coming.'

'Perhaps.'

'You fucking paper pusher. They booby-trapped that building. Our lives were on the line.'

Stotton stared impassively. 'You just concentrate on stopping the cyber attacks. There are a lot of people counting on you.'

'You know Azizi's handler is Robert Biggerstaff.'

'And?'

'He had links to the Black Chamber.'

'There's no such thing as the Black Chamber.'

'Let's cut the shit. Biggerstaff was suspected of being a member of it. He was found to have exaggerated the evidence for WMD.'

'So?'

'So why are we still using him if he was discredited?'

Stotton laughed. 'If we'd got rid of every person connected to the bad intelligence in Iraq we wouldn't have much of an agency left in the Middle East.' He opened a drawer and pulled out Declin's phone. 'Apologies, but we had to have it scrubbed.'

Declin took the phone and turned for the door.

'One last thing. You've got into trouble for hacking into this agency twice now. There better not be a third time.'

101

President Topps dropped the security briefing paper on the table. 'So it was Red China behind the cyber attacks all along.'

'That's right,' said Martha. 'It has all been a distraction while they did their dirty work in Asia.'

'And we fell for it!'

He desperately wanted a coffee but he didn't want to compound his headache, so he sipped the sour grapefruit juice his secretary had insisted would be good for him.

As he drained the glass his Chief of Staff called through on the intercom. 'I have Mr Wu on line one.'

'Who?'

'He is the Chinese High Commissioner in Washington.'

'Got it.'

A click and a rattle of static. 'Hello, hello. Who am I speaking to?'

'This is the President of the United States.'

'This is Fung Wu from the Chinese embassy in Washington.'

'Good afternoon High Commissioner.'

'I have been asked to arrange a phone call for President Li.'

Now there was a name he didn't need reminding of. 'What does he want to talk about?'

'He will tell you that. However in order to follow the correct verification procedure I wish to give you the number from which to expect the call. It is of course a Beijing number …'

The President made a note of the number and ran at a pace he thought he'd lost over to his secretary's desk. 'Expect this call. It has priority over anything.'

He hurried back to his office and took a deep breath to slow the pounding in his chest.

'I have President Li on line two.'

He snatched the phone. 'President William Topps.'

'How are you, Bill?'

He resented the chatty tone and didn't hide it. 'Not good at all, President Li.'

'Why is that?'

'I think you know quite a bit about why. My country has been under cyber siege for the last few weeks.'

'This is the subject I have called you about.'

I bet you have, he thought. 'I'm listening.'

'We know the man who is behind these attacks.'

Thanks for nothing, thought the President. He looked back at his security briefing paper and read the name aloud. 'Saifuddin Azizi. A Chinese man.'

'A Chinese Uigher,' replied Li. 'In fact a jihadist separatist.'

'Still a Chinese national.'

'He is wanted for terrorism against the Chinese state. He is an enemy of China as well as the United States. We may be able to help you find him.'

'Let's see if you can get him before we do.'

'We may also be in a position to help prevent further cyber attacks. It seems that Azizi stole the cyber techniques used in the attacks from the PLA.'

The President would have laughed if it didn't have the weight of the world bearing down on him. 'He *stole* them did he?'

'Of course,' replied Li. 'But we can find out precisely what Azizi stole and protect you from further cyber attacks.'

'Appreciate any help you can give us,' said Topps who was suddenly wondering whether he was being overly cynical.

'We want something in return.'

Ah! Here it comes. 'I'm listening.'

'As you know, we are in the process of re-uniting lost territories with the motherland. We appreciate that the United States had so far not become involved. We need you to continue to not interfere in these matters.'

President Topps could barely contain his anger. 'You have miscalculated, President Li. I won't succumb to blackmail. Good-bye.'

The President replaced the receiver, rubbed his forehead vigorously and called in his Chief of Staff.

'I may have just made a dreadful mistake.'

102

Declin received a text from Frank telling him he was waiting for him with Mickey Summer in the Nine Elms pub. He bought a coke from the bar and joined the other two, who were drinking dark English beer at a table overlooking the Thames.

'What happened to you two?'

'We were locked in a room for an hour,' said Frank. 'Then unceremoniously kicked out of the embassy.'

'How about you?' Mickey asked. 'We were just planning a rescue mission.'

'In the pub?'

'I needed a couple of pints before I took on a whole embassy,' said Mickey. 'So what happened?'

'I had a cozy chat with the CIA station head,' said Declin.

'And?'

'He admitted that Nebuchadnezzar or Azizi is an agency asset. That's why they've been protecting him.'

'What else did he say?'

'He said I should focus on stopping the cyber attacks and not worry about the Black Chamber.'

'What's that?'

'It's a group within Langley that sexed up the case for war with Iraq. I think it's still alive and kicking and has something to do with these cyber attacks.'

'They don't exactly need sexing up,' said Frank.

'They're real enough,' agreed Declin. 'And now we know that Nebuchadnezzar is a Chinese Uigher called Azizi we can be reasonably confident it was the Chinese that devised the malware and gave them to the jihadists.'

'To distract America while they expanded in Asia,' said Frank. 'It's all making a lot more sense now.'

'Problem is that if we now know Nebuchadnezzar is Azizi and someone in Langley is protecting him ...'

'Then he knows for sure we are onto him.'

'It's time to go bust open the Quadra Fund.'

103

President Topps explained his decision to those gathered in the White House situation room. Most agreed with his adopting the long-standing position of not giving way to blackmail.

Calvara was not so sure. 'President Li's offer of help might have been genuine. Perhaps Azizi did steal the malwares and exploits. Perhaps they genuinely want to help us and it's only fair they ask for a quid pro quo.'

'That wasn't my reading,' said the President.

'China is clearly the guilty party here,' Asimov declared. 'Whether Azizi stole the malwares or not, the Chinese devised them. They are guilty either way. Even if we give them the benefit of the doubt, after the first cyber attack against us the Chinese must have suspected someone had stolen and was using their exploits. Certainly by attack number two or three they should have figured it out. They should have told us and helped us defend against the other attacks. They are guilty by omission. And that is shining the best possible light on their position.'

The President looked around the table at the representatives from the various differing intelligence factions. Something was missing. 'Azizi has previously worked for us, right? Why did it take us so long to identify him? Shouldn't he have been top of our suspect list?'

'The last we knew he was fighting for Uigher liberation,' Calvara said. 'He wasn't really on our radar. We only managed to identify him because he got greedy. Declin Lehane discovered Azizi had been passing advance notice of the cyber attacks to a hedge fund in London. They'd made billions for themselves and for Azizi.'

'So that's why Lehane was in London,' said the President. 'That kid was ahead of the curve again. Does he have proof? Something that would stand up in the United Nations?'

'I don't know yet.'

'Even if we had it,' said Martha. 'The Russians would defend China at the UN regardless. So we have to respond unilaterally.'

The President turned to Calvara. 'Leon? Do you think China supplied the Uranium?'

Leon nodded slowly. 'I'm one hundred percent sure.'

'Previously you were sure it was Iran.'

'I never said one hundred percent for Iran.' Leon waved a fat finger.

The President shook his head. 'I can't believe that all these cyber attacks were just a distraction so the Chinese could gain some crappy real estate.'

'And Taiwan. That's what they are really after.'

'They could have had it,' said the President. 'I made it clear I was putting America first. No more global policeman. But they went and attacked us. We have to retaliate.'

'Correct,' said Asimov.

'The question is how?'

'With overwhelming force,' said Horn.

'Maybe,' said the President. He looked at his Chief of Staff. 'Get Declin Lehane patched in.'

104

The Liaoning aircraft carrier pitched and rolled through the wallowing waters of the Taiwan Straits, closely monitored by two Taiwanese Perry-class frigates sailing parallel, less than a mile away.

The navies of the China's People Liberation Army and Taiwan's Republic of China had faced off over the Taiwan Straits many times over the decades. Mostly this had been a matter of the mainland flexing muscles over the island with no real intent. However this felt more serious, like the time before Taiwan's first democratic elections when China had tried to intimidate voters by firing missiles and conducting large-scale military exercises off its coast. That time, the United States had dispatched two aircraft carrier battle groups to defend Taiwan. Now there was no American support. Taiwan's so-called ally, led by the isolationist William Topps, had left them to face off China alone.

A sortie by the Liaoning's Sukhoi Su-33 fighters flew overhead and was immediately shadowed by Taiwanese Mirage fighters.

Again each party held back, neither straying outside their own air space. And so the game of cat and mouse continued through the day and into the night.

105

The President looked around the situation room until his eyes settled on General Horn. 'So what are our response options?'

'If we want to hit China where it hurts most we should defend Taiwan.' Horn sat forward in his seat. 'We take every piece of hardware that floats and make a defensive ring around Taiwan.'

'What about the carrier killers,' asked the President, referring to the Chinese missile that could be launched into orbit before returning to its target at incredible speed.

'The Dongfengs are a known unknown,' said Horn, producing a few raised eyebrows around the table. 'We think we can intercept a missile travelling at Mach ten but we don't yet know for sure.'

'Do you want to risk losing a carrier?' asked the President.

'Do we want to risk a full scale, possibly nuclear war with China?' asked Hank Hoffmann. He turned his chair to face the President. 'You were against this a few days ago. You were worried about the Chinese carrier busters. You didn't want to risk your fleet for the safety of Taiwan. What's changed?'

'What's changed is we now know that China has been screwing us around,' said the President. 'What other options do we have?'

'Militarily?'

'I'm thinking cyber. Let's hit them back like for like.'

'Do we have time to develop cyber offensive capabilities?' asked Martha. 'Can Taiwan wait?'

'We've already developed an entire suite of offensive cyber weapons,' said Cresta. 'Operation Olympic Games, or Stuxnet as it's commonly known, was the first, but we've been plenty busy since.'

'Really? said the President. 'I don't remember agreeing to that or seeing any previous Presidential authority?'

She hesitated and looked at Asimov.

'We did it without any presidential approval,' said Asimov. 'It was done under preparation of the battlefield, Mr President. So it didn't require approval.'

The President shrugged. 'So what can you do?'

'We can scramble the PLA Navy signals,' Cresta explained. 'Hamper their fleet manoeuvres and disrupt any planned amphibious landing on Taiwan.'

'I like it,' said the President. 'That sounds like a smarter approach than sending in a carrier group. What else?'

'We can generally mess with PLA communications. Without them they can't win a war.'

'I like that also.' The President rubbed his hands together. 'But I also want to hit their industry the way they hit ours. That's what I mean by like for like.'

'We could turn the lights out in China like that,' Cresta clicked her fingers.

'Do it. What else?'

'Open dams and flood the rice fields. Close their internet. Shut their transport systems down …'

'Flesh out these ideas. I want real, actionable cyber offensive plans, good to go as soon as I give the okay.' The President looked around the room. 'Where is that Declin Lehane kid?'

'I couldn't reach him,' said the Chief of Staff. 'But we know he's in London busting this insider-trading ring.'

'Forget insider trading. We're in cyber war. That's his bailiwick. I want him in the loop.'

106

Mickey, Frank and Declin sat in the back seat of a marked police Range Rover, at the head of a convoy of silent flashing blue lights that sped through the increasingly busy London streets. The car broke hard into a disabled parking spot outside the Quadra Fund offices. Other cars and vans discharged police into a wet Berkeley Square as onlookers were ushered back inside buildings or away down side streets. Armed officers ran into the entrance and disappeared up the steps.

'What the hell is going on?' shouted the security guard.

Frank waved some paperwork in the guard's face. 'We're conducting a search of the Quadra Fund offices.'

'What's with all the guns?'

'Just a precaution. Don't be alarmed.'

A stream of unarmed officers marched quickly up the stairs. Mickey stayed in the foyer with the enforcement team from the Financial Conduct Authority. Everyone braced for gunfire that never came.

Frank got a signal in his ear piece. 'Okay everyone. We can go up now.'

Mickey was swept along in a flotsam of bodies and empty evidence boxes. On the trading floor the frightened Quadra employees were all cautioned and led away for questioning. Mickey realized someone was missing. He stopped Crispin as he passed. 'Where's Cindy?'

'She must be running late.'

Mickey checked his watch. 'Two hours late?'

'Is she expected in?' asked Frank, who had picked up on the conversation.

'She didn't book the day off.'

Frank flicked through his notebook and called over a uniformed officer. 'Send a patrol to pick up Cindy Hamilton of two Walbrook Avenue, EC2 4BH. If she isn't there put out an all-points bulletin and alert airports and ports.'

'You think she knew we were coming?'

'We'll know soon enough.'

* * *

Mickey waited anxiously for Frank to return from the interviews. 'Any news about Helen?'

Frank shook his head. 'Sorry. Nobody knows anything about it.'

'Well, what do we do now? How do I find her?'

'DS Peterson has now had a kick up the arse and the Met is pulling out all the stops now. We'll find her.'

'Did you make any progress on the insider trading?' Declin

195

asked.

'Some,' said Frank. 'Do you want the good news or the bad news first?'

'Give us some good news. We could do with it.'

'The Quadra Fund staff are all cooperating. Their stories corroborate.'

'And the bad news?'

'Although they all guessed there was insider trading going on none of them knew how the fund was getting the information. They knew nothing about the fax. Crispin never looked at it. He just gave it to Cindy Hamilton. It transpires that Crispin hasn't actually made any investment decisions for a couple of years. Cindy took all the decisions.'

'That's not what I understood,' Mickey said.

'They presented it that way because that worked better for marketing. But actually Cindy brought in a ton of new money when she joined the firm...'

'Azizi's money,' said Declin.

'We haven't checked, but we can assume so. She steadily took over control of investing and as her performance had been so good Crispin left her to it.'

'Do we know where she is?'

'She flew out of Heathrow nine o'clock last night. Destination Turkey.'

'And she's not going on holiday,' Declin said. 'Probably going to meet Azizi. We need to find her. She understands the code.'

'How about the broker who sent the fax?' asked Mickey, remembering that while they had been at Berkeley Square the Dubai authorities had raided the premises.

'That's also blank. The employee who produced the daily fax was an ignorant conduit. He got paid for his service but he had no idea what he was doing. He just received the Nebu numbers by text every now and again and incorporated them into the daily fax.'

'So we've hit another dead end,' Declin said.

Mickey's phone vibrated silently in his pocket. He pulled it out and glanced to see if it was important.

'It's Helen!'

107

Hue had started to wonder, given how ineffective she had been, if the journalist really was connected to American intelligence, as she claimed, or whether she was just a dreamer or wannabe spy on whom he had wasted many months. He was also worried about the increasingly aggressive crackdown on all pro-democracy activity. Party eyes were reporting anything suspicious. And a private chat with an American journalist was bound to attract attention.

But eventually he did go to meet her at the gallery again. This time the exhibition was of vintage nature paintings, and while he waited for the journalist he wandered among the mountains, pines, and rivers. That was the China that had been here before the Party and that would be here when communism was just another chapter in the history books.

'This is my favorite,' a familiar voice announced over his shoulder.

'Bamboos under rain,' said Hue, reading the title.

They talked about the picture while they waited for an old lady to move out of hearing.

'I have been asked to make you an offer,' the journalist said.

'What offer?'

'My superiors believe another cyber attack is coming. Bigger than any previous. Involving a nuclear bomb.'

'I don't know about a nuclear bomb, only about the cyber attacks.'

'The nuclear bomb is also a cyber attack,' she said.

'I still don't know about it. But what is this offer?'

'My superiors want to pay you five million dollars for the information.'

'Up to now I've been giving the information for free.'

'The money is to reward you for giving us your name so we can validate you. Five million dollars in a Swiss bank account and a visa to go to America, if you want it.'

Hue turned to look in her eyes. She struggled to meet his gaze. 'Funny. For all this time I trusted you but you didn't trust me. Now it's the other way round. Goodbye. We will not meet again.'

108

Helen Summer didn't look a lot like the photos that Declin had studied. Her hair was a mess, her eyes were bloodshot and she looked to be dressed in the clothes she'd been wearing when she was taken.

'Are you all right?' Mickey asked as he hugged her. 'Did they hurt you?'

'No. No they didn't. But who were they?'

'We don't know,' Declin answered. 'But you're safe now. That's what matters.'

'But why did they take me? What's this all about?'

Mickey puffed out his cheeks. 'I'm not sure where to start.'

'Start at the beginning.'

'Big bang? Or do you want the Bible version.'

'I could do without the jokes, Mickey. I've just been kidnapped.'

Mickey nodded. 'You remember DI Brighouse?'

Helen nodded an acknowledgement to Frank.

'He asked me to help investigate a dodgy hedge fund,' Mickey continued. 'I agreed. But someone kidnapped you to stop me talking.'

'Why didn't you tell me about this?'

'I'm sorry. I'm really sorry. I never imagined there would be any danger for you.'

'Special agent Declin Lehane with the FBI.' Declin shook her hand gently. 'Can you describe the people who kidnapped you?'

'They had masks on the whole time.'

'Did you hear them talk?'

'One had a West Country accent. The other might have been Scottish.'

'Did they have names?'

'They seemed to have pirate names. Bluebeard and Flint, and they talked to a Hook on the phone.'

It sounded like they'd had military training to Declin, but she didn't need to know. 'Do you know why they let you go?'

'I just heard Bluebeard say: Hook says she's no longer currency. Let her go.'

'Then what?' asked Declin.

'They drove me into Epping Forest and let me go. I walked until I met a lady with a phone and I rang Mickey, and she gave me a lift here to the police station.'

'Did they say anything else that may be helpful?'

'They kept assuring me that I wouldn't come to any harm. They almost seemed apologetic. Who do you think they were?'

'I don't know,' said Declin. 'But everything seems to have been done by the book. I suspect you were never really in danger. They simply wanted to slow Mickey down. Once they realized that hadn't worked they let you go.'

'We'll arrange police protection officers to look after you now, just to be on the safe side,' said Frank. He looked down at a message on his phone. He showed it to Declin.

'SIS has a marker on missing woman. Meeting her friend in Istanbul.'

'That's perfect,' said Declin. 'When they meet we'll need a snatch squad to pick them both up.'

'You mean you're going to kidnap people as well!?' shouted Helen. 'What's happening here?'

'We're going to arrest them,' explained Frank. He turned back to Declin. 'Unless you want to pick this up from your side and make it an American operation.'

Declin gave it some thought then shook his head. 'Right now I have more faith in Vauxhall Cross. Obviously keep us in the loop, but let's play this as a British intelligence operation.'

109

In the London embassy's secure communications room, Declin was patched in to the White House Security Council meeting. He listened with increasing concern at Cyber Command's lack of progress on its cyber offensive.

'We tried to scramble the PLA Navy's signals,' Cresta explained to the President. 'But they managed to successfully defend against us. So we tried further afield. We tried interrupting and corrupting PLA signals large and small, local and long distance, top commanders and infantrymen, chains of command, provision and munitions suppliers. We've tried sensors, networks, launches, weapons, missiles, command and control centers. But the Chinese military cyber defences held tight.'

'You assured me that our cyber offensive capability was proven,' said the President.

'Our probes and forages were successful,' replied Cresta. 'That suggested that full scale attacks would work.'

'An old Indian trick,' said the President. 'Lull the enemy into complacency with a false weak spot and draw them in. And you fell for it.'

'It seems so.'

'What about turning the lights out like that!' The President clicked his fingers.

'We haven't had any more success with our attacks against their industrial infrastructure.'

'And I guess you didn't flood the rice fields?'

'I'm afraid not.'

'Or take down their internet.'

'Not yet. But I'm confident we'll overcome these defences with more time. We just need to crack the encryption they're using.'

'How long?'

'It's difficult to put a timeframe on it,' said Cresta. 'Weeks. Maybe months.'

'We don't have time on our side,' said the President.

'There is something else we could try,' said Declin, forgetting the protocol that he was only to liaise through Connelly. 'Sorry for butting in, this is Declin Lehane.'

The President turned to look at Declin via the video link. 'Welcome back on the team, Declin. Let's hear what you're thinking.'

'Psyber with a PS. That is Cyber Psyops.'

'Can you pad that out for me?' the President asked.

'We manipulate Chinese public opinion using the internet. That would only require us to attack the public domain network which, like our own, is way more open than the military or their critical industries because, like us, they need it open to monitor the people.'

'But where does that get us?'

'The Party is already troubled by the pro-democracy movement,' Declin explained. 'If we raise the protest level it puts them under greater pressure. They may be so worried about matters in house that they abandon plans to attack Taiwan.'

'They also may be more likely to attack,' pointed out Hoffmann.

'If we play it right they might not be in a position to,' replied Declin. 'They might not be in power.'

There was a second or two of silence in the room while everyone realized what Declin was proposing.

'The key assumption here,' said the President, 'is that the Chinese people want freedom from communism. How confident are we on that?'

'Hopeful but not confident,' said Hank. 'We might draw a parallel with the collapse of the Soviet Union. But the Soviet Union was an empire in decline with mass unemployment and poverty. China, on the other hand, is the Twenty First Century economic success story.'

'Was a success story,' Sandy corrected. 'Its debt bubble has burst and the economy is in recession. That was the deal with the Communist Party. You can keep power so long as we all get rich. But they haven't all. There is serious inequality of wealth coupled with massive corruption. There is impetus for change.'

'What do you think, Leon?' asked the President. 'Is the Chinese Communist Party vulnerable?'

'This is a good time to find out,' said Calvara, avoiding expressing an opinion.

'Face facts,' General Horn growled. 'We're not going to manage regime change with cyber operations when we can't even dim a light bulb. We need to go Kinetic. I'd like to put forward the recommendation from the Joint Chiefs of Staff.'

'Let's hear it,' agreed the President.

Horn cleared his throat and took to his feet while his assistant pulled up a busy slide showing a map of the straits filled with arrows, ships and planes. White for Taiwan, yellow for Japan, blue for America and, of course, red for China.

'The Japanese are boxing the PLA in the East China Sea from their position on the Ryukyu Islands chain,' said Horn. 'The Taiwanese Navy is facing them off in the Straits. We can move our fleet up from the South China Sea and catch the Chinese in a pincer.'

'What if the Chinese cyber offensive capabilities succeed where we failed?' asked the President. 'What if they scramble our signals, get us firing on our own ships, compromise our command and control network?'

Horn shook his head and waved a hand for good measure. 'That's just not going to happen. Our military cyber defences are one hundred percent secure.'

'We used to say the same about our critical infrastructure.' The President closed his eyes and rubbed his forehead. 'I don't feel sure about your capabilities anymore.'

'I can assure you we still have superiority in conventional military,' said Horn.

'And this is the time to use it,' said Asimov. 'Because if we let the Chinese go unchallenged they will become the dominant power in Asia.'

'I don't buy the Thucydides Trap argument,' said the President. 'But we've got plenty of good reasons to hit back at China without it. The question is what's the smartest way to do it. I'm not convinced facing down the PLA in the Straits of Taiwan is the smartest way. I'd like to hear more along the lines of Declin Lehane's thinking. I want a fleshed out actionable plan by tomorrow.' The President looked up at the screen. 'And next time I want you here in the room, Declin.'

* * *

Declin was so busy packing that he didn't at first notice the secretary flapping a piece of paper in his face.

'A fax for you,' she said.

'Let me see.'

'We hardly ever get faxes anymore, so I only check it …'

202

'Thanks.' Declin snatched the fax from her.

To- Declin Lehane only. Highly Confidential.

We need to communicate urgently. Do not discuss with colleagues or superiors. I need to confirm that I am speaking to Declin Lehane.

Security question 1. What is your favorite color?

Fax your reply to +86 10 5129 6656

'It's some sort of scam,' said Declin, screwing the paper into a ball and throwing it into the bin. He returned to packing files and papers. Though most of what he needed was in the secure cloud or in his head he wanted to make sure he didn't leave anything behind. Most importantly, he wanted to make sure he didn't leave behind any notes he'd made on the Black Chamber.

He was all ready to go when the secretary returned.

'It's another fax,' she said, tossing it unceremoniously onto his desk.

'Thanks,' Declin said, realizing he'd done something to upset her but unsure what it was. He picked up the fax.

To- Declin Lehane only. Highly Confidential.

We need to communicate urgently. Do not discuss with colleagues or superiors. I need to confirm that I am speaking to Declin Lehane.

Security question 1. What is your favorite color?

Answer 1- I give you. Answer Pink.

Security question 2. What is the name of your favorite school teacher?

Fax your reply to +86 10 5129 6656

Whoever it was at the other end had aroused Declin's curiosity. He entered the number into a telephone search engine. The fax was located in Beijing. The obvious danger was that it had come from China's Ministry of Security. But what harm could come from replying? His curiosity made him take it further. He faxed back the name of Mr Gilbert, who had been the most memorable teacher for his Star Wars quotes and impersonations. It was also the name he used in security questions.

A minute later another fax came through.

To- Declin Lehane only. Highly Confidential.

Answer 2. Correct.

Security question 3. What is your mother's maiden name?

Answer 3 - I will give you. Answer is Lemmon.
Security question 4. What is your memorable date?
Fax your reply to +86 10 5129 6656

Somebody had clearly done their homework. But they could have said correct to any answer he'd given for his favorite school teacher and it wouldn't have been too tricky to find his favorite color and his mother's maiden name, with a little enthusiastic hacking. He decided not to give his memorable date but instead faxed back his date of birth.

To- Declin Lehane only. Highly Confidential.
Answer 4. Incorrect. Not your DOB. Your memorable date. Try again.
Fax your reply to +86 10 5129 6656

Declin faxed back the correct date October 30th, 2006. A minute later came the reply.

To- Declin Lehane only. Highly Confidential.
Answer 4. Correct. The date your brother died.
I will send you login password and address of a website where we can talk freely.

Now this person had Declin's full attention. He logged into a website on the dark net where they would be able to exchange messages more quickly.

Messenger- *I have a package to help with your cyber investigations. It is waiting for collection in Beijing. Send a courier. Must not be from CIA, FBI, police, army or government. All identities known to Ministry of State Security.*

Declin – *Do you work for them?*

Messenger – *No.*

Declin – *Who are you?*

Messenger – *I cannot answer that.*

Declin – *What is your motive for helping America?*

Messenger – *I want freedom for the people of China. Send a courier.*
Do not inform CIA in Beijing. This is compromised. Courier must buy a local China phone on arrival and text 010 5569 7867.

Declin – *Please explain. How is CIA Beijing compromised?*

Messenger – *I tried to give this information about cyber investigations before but they stopped me. Do not know why. Then they try to bribe me to give away my name. I think they want to kill me. That is why I have come to you.*

Are you going to send someone?

Declin knew he had to send somebody. But who? There was only one person he could think of.

110

Mickey checked all the windows were shut, the gas and electrics turned off and the back door locked. He zipped up his raincoat and swung the rucksack onto his back. He was heading for the front door when the bell rang. Outside, sheltering from the rain under a folded newspaper, stood Frank. Beside him, his punk hair getting a useful free wash, Declin.

'Evening ladies. I'm a Jehovah's Witness myself so I suggest you try next door.'

'Looks like we got you just in time,' said Frank, pointing at the rucksack.

'I'm on my way to meet Helen. So come on then. What are you two after now?'

Frank and Declin exchanged a glance as if they were wondering which of them was going to talk.

'Look, I'm in a rush.'

'Can we come in?' asked Declin. 'It's kinda wet out here.'

Mickey sighed, ushered them inside and closed the door.

'I need to ask you a question,' said Declin.

'Too late.' Mickey shrugged sympathetically. 'Already married.'

'I need you to pick up a packet for me.'

'Have you tried Parcel Force?'

'It needs to be you,' said Declin. 'It has to be someone who knows about the cyber investigation but isn't in the CIA, the army, police or FBI.'

Mickey sighed. 'I've really had enough of all this. I need to spend time with Helen. She's still shook up.'

'I understand,' said Declin. 'But this really is important.'

'If I get this packet for you I'm all done. You leave me on my Jack Jones.'

'Alone?'

'Got it in one.'

Declin nodded. 'Promise.'

'Okay. So what's the address?'

'Someone will make contact with you. First you have to go to Beijing.'

'Beijing!?'

'That's right,' said Declin.

'And you're not talking about the restaurant on the high street. You mean the capital of China, on the other side of the planet.'

'I'm afraid so.'

'This is crazy.'

'Like I say, it's important.'

'So I go to Beijing and pick up this packet from someone and come home. Simple as that?'

Declin shifted his weight from one foot to the other. 'It may not be as simple as that. We think the packet will contain state secrets. If the Chinese Secret Service find out, things could get difficult.'

'For difficult read dangerous?'

'Potentially.'

'Great,' said Mickey, with a heavy sigh.

'You're really the only person that fits the spec,' said Frank.

'That's what you said to get me to go to the Quadra Fund. I must be even more special than I realized.'

111

President Li's guards ushered him into the Riviera Restaurant via a back door, along a staff corridor and out onto a terrace that had been reserved that evening for just two. As protocol dictated, his dinner partner was already waiting at the table. Jiao stood and performed an acceptably deferential bow. 'Leader. I am so pleased you could come.'

Li pointed to a bird dropping that had been deposited on his chair. The attendant hurriedly wiped it clean and helped Li take his seat.

'Beautiful view,' said Jiao, turning to a panorama of Shanghai.

Li glanced at the huge purple Tianjin eye looking down on the countless new buildings that outnumbered, but in his mind did not outshine, the pretty old colonial style. He turned back to his guest and asked: 'How do you think the conference is going?'

'Excellent.'

Li shook his head. 'I value your company, Jiao, because you are one of the few people who is strong enough to tell me the truth.'

'It has been overshadowed by the Freedom Movement.'

Jiao hesitated. He waited for the leader's response. 'Go on.'

'Even our own delegates are talking about it.'

'Do people really believe the Freedom Movement can win?'

Again Jiao hesitated.

'Speak your mind.'

'The movement has been gathering strength. And people have seen the collapse of communism in Cuba and Vietnam. They are worried China will be next.'

Li had of course heard as much from his security briefings. But it meant more to hear it from a party stalwart such as Jiao. 'What will it take to stop these calls for freedom?'

'I'm not sure anything can stop them. We just need to ignore them.'

Jiao held up a hand. 'Let's eat.'

They ordered a local meat dish. A sommelier appeared and recommended a vintage burgundy. But although both he and the waiters had been screened for loyalty to the party they were not as discreet as those in restaurants in Beijing, and so Li ordered fruit juice. Jiao skilfully kept the conversation on small talk about the conference until the meal was finished.

Li dismissed the waiters and asked the bodyguards to give them space.

'Why do people listen to these agitators? Why are people dissatisfied? The Party has delivered so much.'

'Too much.'

'Too much?'

'The peoples' needs used to be simple,' Jiao explained. 'They wanted food, a warm home, time with their family. They didn't care if the government was Communist, Democratic or Ming

Dynasty. So long as it delivered a better life for their children, they did not care about ideology.'

'So why is this a problem now? The economy has fallen back but the country is still richer than ten years ago.'

'Nobody likes to go backwards. Man is restless. This is why there is growing support for the Freedom Movement.'

'But what will democracy give them? Really, I don't understand. What will it change?'

'The people are not so bothered about democracy. They simply want to overturn the establishment. It is the same urge for change that has swept America and Europe.'

'But if they get change, then what? They want freedom to do what?'

'Freedom of speech, freedom from censorship, freedom from corruption, freedom for minority opinions and groups. Freedom from fear. Freedom from the State. Freedom ...'

'Enough,' Li interrupted. 'You are too well-versed, my friend.'

Jiao shook his head. 'I am of the elite. I already enjoy those freedoms. I do not want change.'

'What about the new territories? The people cheered when we reclaimed the South China Sea. They came out on the streets when we took Diaoyu back from the Japanese.'

'The action in Taiwan is not so popular.'

'The people want Taiwan back. They have always wanted it back.'

'They want reunification,' agreed Jiao. 'But they don't want war.'

Li folded his hands on the table. 'We have waited a long time for the return of Taiwan. America with this new President is at its most isolationist. The time for reunification is now.'

'The people do not want reunification by force.'

Li knew Jiao was right. He'd known it all along. 'Wing is determined to press ahead.'

'You must stop him.'

Yes. He knew it of course. But how? 'I cannot stop him without triggering a leadership challenge. One that I fear I would lose.'

'But where will his madness end? What after Taiwan?'

Li studied Jiao, wondering whether to confide what he knew. But he needed to tell someone who understood. 'Next he wants to occupy Southern Tibet.'

'That will pit us against India. We'll be economically and politically isolated from the whole world.'

'I understand. But I'm not sure I can stop him.'

'You are the President!'

'Yes. I am the President. But Wing controls the military.'

112

Beijing airport had a disorientating mix of futuristic white steel architecture and classic Chinese displays of wooden pagodas and pot ornaments. The arrivals hall was full of bright brown eyes searching for friends and family. Mickey looked expectantly for a certain Yu Fung who had been sent to meet him. He had idly imagined that, coming as she did from Heavenly Tours, she would be a delicate, angelic figure. And so he was a little surprised that the board with his name scrawled in blue was held by a woman who looked about as delicate as a section of the Great Wall.

He walked up and extended a hand.

'Welcome to China, Mr Summer. My name is Yu Fung.'

'Yes, I was expecting Yu!' Mickey grinned.

'Thank you,' she said, not getting his joke. 'How was your flight?'

'Easy. I let the pilot do most of the work.'

They exchanged small talk as she walked him out to a waiting black Audi. He was surprised at how gracefully she moved for her size, like a fridge on casters.

'Your passport please.'

She made a note of the number and handed it back. After struggling through traffic congestion, no doubt worsened by heavy rain, pro-democracy protests and police checkpoints, they arrived downtown and pulled up at the Grand Hyatt.

The receptionist in the golden foyer was having trouble explaining to some American businessmen that she could not check them in, as all Americans, other than consular staff, had been ordered to leave the country in retaliation for American 'aggressive actions'.

Mickey was grateful to escape to the sanctuary of his room where he slept off the jet lag for a couple of hours before Yu picked him up again for a tour of Beijing. Not that Mickey wanted to go sightseeing. He just wanted to pick up the package for Declin and jump on the next plane out of the country. But he'd been told to play the typical tourist. Yu talked like a DJ, finding something to say about every building and street corner. Mickey didn't do buildings. He did people. He wanted to hear what she thought about politics but whenever he moved the conversation in that direction she feigned ignorance or disinterest. As they approached Tiananmen Square, Yu warned Mickey.

'Be careful what you say here. Don't talk about politics.'

'Why not?'

'A forbidden subject, especially in Tiananmen square.'

'Because of the protests?' asked Mickey.

'We don't talk about that. The police are watching and listening to everything.'

As they walked slowly around the enormous square with its high-profile police presence, Mickey spotted hundreds, perhaps thousands, of cameras. He tried to imagine the square during the student uprising.

'Is this where that lone student faced down a column of tanks?' he asked Yu.

'That never happened,' she said with a forced smile. 'That is western propaganda.'

Mickey had seen it live on CNN in the day. But he let it drop.

Leaving the square, still on foot, though Mickey was getting tired, they came upon a crowd waving banners and blowing horns and whistles.

'What's that all about?' asked Mickey.

'They want freedom,' she explained. 'From One Party rule.'

'And the police let them?'

'It's difficult to stop. There are so many rallies now, all over the country. So long as they are peaceful, the police leave them alone.'

'And what does Yu think about democracy? '

'Democracy is just a voting system.'

'So you're happy with your government? You don't want change.'

Yu covered her mouth, with her hand. 'The government is another matter. Many, many people are not happy with the government.'

Mickey realized that she was one of them, but she was too frightened to say it openly. She seemed paranoid that the police were listening to her every word. Maybe they were. Yu walked him back to his hotel and left him with detailed recommendations on various restaurants nearby.

'I will see you in the morning.'

'No,' said Mickey, unable to stop himself. 'I will see Yu.'

She turned away, still not getting the joke. Mickey was still chuckling to himself as he checked reception for messages. There was still nothing from Declin's illusive contact.

He took a walk into a park to kill time before dinner. Arriving at a fountain he sat down on a bench. A hoody on blades rolled up the path, bending one knee as he turned. He straightened up, drained the last of his coke and tossed the can into the bushes. Mickey half expected to see him arrested, but the park was surprisingly empty. Mickey stepped over, picked the can off the ground and put it in the bin. He retreated to the bench as the hoody turned around further up the path and rolled slowly back.

'Thank you for picking up my litter, Mr Summer.'

'And you are?'

'The man you have come to meet.'

Mickey hadn't known what to expect, but it hadn't been a hoody on blades. 'What's with the litter routine?'

'That was to flush out any party members that might otherwise have noticed our meeting.'

Mickey looked around the park. A mother with a baby in a papoose hurrying one way, an old man hobbling, a gaggle of students arguing animatedly.

'But as you see,' continued Hoody, 'nobody has shown interest. Because in this oppressed society they have more important things to care about than litter. But the oppressors, the party members, they worry about things such as litter. They would have shouted out.' He nodded to the fountain. 'Would you like me to take a photo of you by the fountain?'

'No thanks, mate. I just want to get out of here as soon as possible.'

But Hoody insisted, shaping his hands as if to take a picture. 'Give me your phone.'

Mickey hesitated, wondering now if this was an elaborate scam to steal it. But if it was, no matter. His own phone was back in the hotel. This was the cheap one he'd been instructed to buy on arrival and had been using for tourist photos. He handed it over. Hoody took a photo, handed back the phone and returned to the bench.

'Tell Declin that I offered to give this package to CIA Beijing, but they didn't take it.'

'Why not?'

'That's for you to work out. It was nice to meet you, Mickey.'

'Wait. Where's the package?'

'It's on your phone,' said the man as he walked away. 'Don't look at it here. Get it to Declin.'

Mickey put his hand in his pocket and touched the phone. He wondered what Hoody had managed to get on it in those few seconds. As Hoody rolled off Mickey walked quickly the other way out of the park. He had to force himself not to run.

As agreed with Declin, he jumped straight into a taxi and went to the British Embassy. The chargé d'affaires had been primed to expect him, but still wanted to know why he wanted to send a secure package to an FBI agent in Washington.

Mickey had been given clear instructions to reveal as little as possible. Which worked fine because he didn't actually know what the package was.

'It's just a phone. I bought it local and took a few photos.'

'Show me.'

Mickey showed him. But oddly all the photos other than the one of him by the fountain had been scrubbed. He checked sent messages. That was empty. Mickey realized that Hoody had switched phones when he took the photo.

The diplomat satisfied himself that everything was in order and the phone was bagged and sent off to Washington. Job done. Mickey returned to the hotel bar, concluding that the spying game wasn't really all that difficult. On the second glass of wine he remembered how scared he'd been and changed his mind. It was actually very stressful and difficult. He was just naturally brilliant at it.

113

A secretary met Declin at Fort Meade reception and whisked him off to a room marked 'Restricted Access'.

'Please take a seat,' she said. 'Director Patton will be along presently.'

'Thanks,' said Declin. Everything was altogether more friendly than on his first visit to NSA headquarters.

Cresta arrived with a couple of guys who didn't introduce themselves. But one was the bodyguard she took everywhere and the other was a tech guy Declin had seen around the place.

'Morning,' Cresta said curtly.

'Good morning. How's it going?'

'This package arrived for you.' She handed him an opened white diplomatic bag.

Inside Declin found a cell phone and an envelope addressed to him, also opened.

'I took the liberty,' said Cresta.

Declin shrugged. 'So does it explain how the source code worked?'

'Unfortunately not. The codes on this phone are identical to the ones we found already, except they do not have the number identifiers. It looks like they were added by Azizi.'

'As a way to identify them for insider trading.'

'It would seem that way. The numbers are otherwise superfluous.'

'So our best chance of cracking them is still to pick up Cindy or Azizi. How is that shaping up?'

'British Intelligence is following Cindy. When she makes contact with Azizi a snatch squad will be ready.'

Declin was relieved. The nuclear cyber attack was still the thing that troubled him most. Although a war between Taiwan and China was a close run second. 'So back to the phone. What have we got?'

'The phone has details of all the cyber attacks. The source code for all the malwares and mappings of the exploits.'

'That is dynamite.'

'It also has the same for several attacks that may yet be coming to hit us.'

'Such as?'

'Well, without being able to crack the number code we still don't know precisely what is planned. But we've got the unique identifier numbers for all the devices targeted in the malware. So we know what make and model of device they were targeting even if we don't know where.'

'Good work. So what were they going to hit?'

'One attack was going to feed fake data to the traffic sensors of smart traffic signals. Possibly via drones.'

'That would be chaos,' Declin said, quietly impressed with the Chinese ingenuity. 'What else?'

'Another simple but effective hack would target air-conditioning systems such as those used in the Telco Hotels. We assume the plan was to cause the servers to overheat and break down.'

'So banks and ecommerce get hit. Wall Street and Main Street crash together. What else?'

'Another malware targets the software used in some shipping navigation. We think maybe they plan to hijack the controls of a ship, perhaps an oil tanker, and crash it into Manhattan, say, or an offshore oil port.'

'The oil port would produce more upward pressure on the oil price, which is what the fund was betting on,' Declin pointed out. 'What about the dirty nuclear material? Where does that come in?'

'We don't know. Your Chinese friend makes no mention of it.'

'I guess he can't know.'

'Or he doesn't want to tell us.'

'Maybe. But you need to add these codes onto the malware filters.'

'Already done. I do know my job, Special Agent Lehane. The question is - do you know yours?'

Declin frowned. 'I don't get you?'

'Read the letter.'

Inside the envelope was a handwritten note from Mickey Summer.

'Hi Declin, hope this phone contains stuff you can use. The guy who gave me this told me to tell you that he offered this information to CIA Beijing repeatedly over the last few months. But they ignored him. More evidence to support your theory. Mickey.'

'What exactly is your theory?' asked Cresta.

Declin didn't have to tell her, but he wanted to see her reaction. 'I think someone in Langley knew about these cyber attacks but they kept a lid on it for some reason.'

She folded her arms. 'You don't need a conspiracy theory to explain why CIA Beijing ignored your source.'

'Why did they then?'

'Because they believe he worked for the PLA cyber unit and was going to give us misinformation.'

'Well, they were wrong,' said Declin. 'You just admitted he's given us dynamite.'

'You called it dynamite, not me. The information on the historic attacks is no use to us. The information on future attacks may or may not be good. It could well be a distraction.'

'I trust him.'

'That's why you don't work in intelligence, Special Agent Lehane. You stick to cyber crime. Leave the spy games to Langley. And get your friend Mickey Summer out of Beijing on the next flight.'

114

Saifuddin Azizi felt as if a new chapter in his life was about to open. Once he was reunited with Cindy they would escape to a new life together. She would take a Muslim first name and they would both live under his own family name. The *nom de guerre* of Nebuchadnezzar had served its purpose while he was mixing with the middle eastern jihadists struggling for their homeland. His future lay back in Xinjiang, freeing his own homeland from a much greater enemy of Islam than America; the religious-nihilist communist Chinese occupiers. And for that task he would be better served using the name of his illustrious forefather, the first Chairman of the autonomous region.

But for now he was still travelling incognito as he wandered admiringly around the Ottoman and Baroque architecture of Topkapi Palace. He arrived at the Palace Kitchens and smiled as he saw Chinese tourists admiring the display of blue-and-white porcelain that had arrived centuries ago along the silk route. The group was perhaps fifty strong and would provide perfect cover.

He joined the tour and mingled, hating the Mandarin he had to speak in as the party meandered around the lush green courtyards. He discovered that the next stop on the tour would be the Galata Tower. He knew this to be a better rendezvous point because it was nestled in amongst a busy neighborhood with backstreets that he knew well. If anyone was following Cindy he could lose them in those streets.

As the group stopped to admire the mighty sparkling Bosphorus Strait, he texted Cindy: 'Galata Tower. Walk around the base outside.'

* * *

Frank took a seat in the operation room in Vauxhall Cross to watch the show. The Secret Intelligence Service were tracking Cindy. A team of agents were ready to snatch her and Azizi as soon as they met and hand them over to the regular Turkish police.

He read the live exchanges between the agents on the ground in Istanbul and Control in London:

ONE. Snow White is moving over bridge. Direction Galata Peninsular. Suggest proceed alone.

TWO. On bike with FOUR. Green.

THREE. In position at Tower. Still no visual on A. Amber.

CONTROL–FOUR. Proceed on foot with ONE. Follow Snow White. THREE proceed to tower.

* * *

Saifuddin spotted Cindy as the bus pulled up to park beside the tower. She was walking slowly anti-clockwise around the base. He had no reason to think the Americans had made a connection between him and Cindy but he had to assume they had. He looked for evidence of a surveillance team following her, turning when she turned, pausing when she did, like a murmuration of starlings. But he saw nothing.

Perhaps Biggerstaff was telling the truth when he said they were no longer interested in him. Though he still did not understand why Biggerstaff had not taken up his offer of information to stop the cyber attacks. The hundred-million dollars he had demanded was a pittance compared to the damage to the American economy. Still, that was not his problem.

He pulled his baseball cap lower as he descended the steps of the coach and flicked up his coat collar against the winter cold. He kept his eyes averted as he passed Cindy and walked up the steps to the entrance foyer. He texted her again. 'Come inside.'

* * *

THREE. SW has entered the tower.
CONTROL. Do we have a visual on A.
THREE. Negative.
ONE. Party of Chinese just entered.
CONTROL. ONE and FOUR stay outside. THREE enter tower.

* * *

Cindy stood to one side of the spiral wooden staircase to allow the party to pass. Her eyes lit at the sight of Saifuddin.

'Come with me,' he whispered in her ear, as he put an arm around her and pulled her into the crowd. 'Put on this hat and coat.' He took her old coat and hat and stuffed them into a carrier bag.

'Nobody has followed me,' she said. 'I was very …'

'Shh. Don't talk to me or look at me. Just stay in the middle of this crowd. Get on the bus with them after the tour.'

They continued the tour of the tower, although Saifuddin was soon bored of the talk from a guide who could not speak Mandarin well and constantly had to look up words in a dictionary. He was pleased when they finally returned to ground level and walked out into the street.

* * *

ONE. SW has switched to a red hat and black top. She is in the middle of the Chinese group. Moving to exit now.
CONTROL. Visual on A?
ONE. Possible. Short hair, baseball cap.
TWO. That's him. I have him too.
CONTROL. Please confirm. You have visual on both SW and A.
ONE. Affirmative.
TWO. Affirmative.
CONTROL. ONE and THREE. Position to intercept SW when exits. TWO and FOUR position to intercept A when exits. Extraction team. You are good to go.

* * *

Azizi saw the move for his hand too late. By the time he pulled it his other was also caught and he was pushed up against a wall. His face pressed into the crumbling medieval brickwork as he was roughly cuffed behind. His abductors wore balaclavas. Special forces. Turkish? Hopefully American, and then there would be a chance that Biggerstaff could get him out of this.

They pushed him towards a van where Turkish police, uni-formed and undercover, were waiting.

'Don't hurt her,' he shouted at the men who were dragging Cindy to a separate van.

She turned to look at him and smiled with those beautiful hazel eyes. 'Everything will be all right,' he called out.

She opened her mouth to reply but jumped as a hole burst open in her chest. Another through the top teeth.

In freeze-frame he turned to face the direction in which the sniper lay. He was clearly a professional. Make it as painless as …

* * *

ONE. Problem.
CONTROL. Are SW and A both apprehended?
ONE. Negative.
CONTROL. Sit rep?
ONE. Sniper attack.
CONTROL. Say again.
ONE. Snow White and A shot. Two down.
CONTROL. Say again.
ONE. SW and A both shot. Two down. Shall I approach?
CONTROL. Negative. Emergency egress.

115

'They're both dead?' Declin said, still not really believing what he was hearing down the phone. 'How?'

'Professional sniper is what the guys here in Vauxhall tell me. One bullet through the heart, a second through the brain.'

'Hell!' Declin threw the receiver onto his desk and kicked a waste basket as hard as he could. It flew through the air and landed on Cresta's desk, scattering pens and papers onto the floor.

'What's going on!?' she demanded.

'Sorry. Lost control.' Declin picked the receiver back up. 'So who do they think it was?'

'Suspicion is that it was ISIS.'

'Why would they do that?'

'He had two tickets to Kuwait. The thinking is he was going to pick up his money and escape. So ISIS took him out.'

'I don't buy that. Look, Frank, I've got to go. I'll get back to you.'

'What on earth is going on?' Cresta asked again.

'Azizi and Cindy Hamilton were arrested by British Intelligence and the Turkish Police. We had our hands on them. And then they were both shot dead.'

'In custody?'

'Just as they were being arrested.'

'Are you sure they're both dead?'

'Well without going over and checking the body bags myself I can't be certain, but it certainly looks that way. Both had a bullet through the heart and another through the head.'

'Who shot them?'

'You tell me.'

Cresta screwed up her face. 'I have no idea. Why would I know?'

'I think they were assassinated by Langley. To stop them talking.'

'Talking about what?'

Declin wasn't really sure of the answer to that. 'I don't know yet. But I do know that we are back running blind on the cyber nuclear threat.'

'We're hardly running blind,' Cresta replied, handing him back his waste basket. 'We've identified the threats, thanks to your friend in Beijing, and we are screening for the malwares he told us about.'

'We've worked out the cyber threats but we still don't understand how they're co-ordinated with the dirty nuke.'

'How many times do we need to go over this?' Cresta said, struggling to keep her voice down. 'So it's possible the plan is to leave the uranium in the hotel telcos when they overheat. Then the fire crews can't go near. Or they planned to drop pellets from the drones as they go over the traffic signals to add to the confusion. Or maybe they cyber hack the navigation of an oil tanker and drive it into Manhattan. They would all create mass disruption and panic. That's why we've added the malware filters to the tankers, to the hotel telcos and to the traffic signals. That's also why we're trying to stop the nuclear material arriving here in the first place. What else can we do?'

'We can crack Azizi's code,' said Declin.

'We've tried.'

'We can try again.'

'Go right ahead.' Cresta turned and walked out of the room.

Declin knew the code numbers off by heart and wrote them out on a piece of paper. He stared at them a while, then wrote them on a fresh sheet in a different order, each with its own color. As he had done many times before.

But he was slowly coming to the conclusion that this was one puzzle he was never going to crack. He screwed up the papers and threw them into the waste bin. If only he had caught Azizi. He had suspected someone had been protecting Azizi. He should have realized that once he had served his useful function that same person would want him eliminated. He should never have left it to Frank and British Intelligence to pick him up in Istanbul. He should have been there. Someone in Langley was always one step ahead of him. But who?

He looked at the wall clock and calculated that it would be early morning in Pakistan. He was fairly certain his own line was being monitored so he left the room and found an empty office down the corridor to make the call.

JC did not sound pleased to hear from him.

'How's tricks?' Declin asked, to lighten the tone.

'Not so great since you used my username and password to hack into Langley's main server.'

'Sorry about that. I wouldn't have done it if it wasn't important.'

'I hope it was.'

'Look, JC, I need an answer to a question.'

'Feels like I should be asking the favors after the stunt you pulled.'

'I was wondering,' Declin pressed on, 'whether we might have done things differently out in Pakistan if left to our own devices.'

'How do you mean?' asked JC, his voice distancing quickly.

'Well, we were pushed into the drone strike when we might have learned a whole lot more by listening in for a while.'

'Look, I'm real busy, Declin.'

'And your interrogation of the prisoner might …'

'Our interrogation,' interrupted JC. 'You were there too.'

Declin didn't want to get distracted, so let it pass. 'I think we pushed the prisoner too hard too soon.'

'Don't ask me to start feeling sorry for a T-man.'

'That's not what concerns me. I just want to know if you pushed him deliberately.'

'That would be murder, Declin.'

'I need to know if someone above you wanted him dead. Or at least let it be known that it might not be such a bad thing if the prisoner stopped talking.'

'You're over-thinking this.'

'When I pulled you from the line of fire in that village, you did say you owed me one.'

There was a long pause, followed by JC clearing his throat. 'It was nice talking to you again, Declin.'

'Don't go, JC. You don't need to say anything. Just give me a name.'

Another long pause. 'You alone where you are?'

'Just me.'

'Nobody listening in on the call.'

'Nobody.'

'You didn't get this from me. And I'm not implying anything by telling you this. But it's not unusual to get a call from above on an operation.'

'I understand. Who from?'

'No names.'

'Does it go all the way to the top?' Declin asked.

'Got to go.'

The line went dead.

* * *

Declin jumped in a cab and told the driver to forget the speed limits and get him as quickly as possible to the Intelligence Community Campus at Bethesda. Asimov met him in his agreeable top-floor office with a view out over the Chesapeake & Ohio park.

'Great work,' he said before Declin had even taken a seat. 'The information you recovered from Beijing is like a present from God. Question now is: can we trust it?'

'Why not?'

'It was all a bit too easy. I'm worried that the information is a decoy. While we're defending against those malwares something else could be coming down the wire.'

'The exploits are real enough,' Declin replied. 'We need to fix them anyway.'

'You're right.' Asimov nodded. 'Tell me about the source.'

'Best guess is a disaffected cyber soldier in the PLA.'

'Langley hasn't verified its source?'

'This didn't come through Langley. I sourced it after the asset contacted me direct. He had previously been in contact with an agency case officer in Beijing but because she couldn't verify him she was told to drop him. That's why he came to me.'

'But you kept Langley in the loop?'

'The asset requested I didn't.'

Asimov sat forward. 'So who is running your asset?'

'Goes by the name of Mickey Summer. He was working at the Quadra Fund. Turned snitch to help the British police when they were looking into insider trading.'

'So let me get this straight. We have an FBI agent running an unknown Chinese asset via an English banker. And all this without the knowledge of the CIA.'

'That's about it,' agreed Declin.

'Well now that we have the information, I think it's time to let Langley know.'

'Two reasons why not. First off, we haven't finished with the asset. He says if we do what he wants he has another package that will be even more useful to us.'

'So what does he want?'

'Freedom.'

Asimov shrugged. 'He wants out, we'll get him ex-filtrated, no problem.'

'Not personal freedom. He wants regime change.'

'Well I'm on the same page.' Asimov ran his fingers through his thinning hair. 'So we keep your asset in play using your English case officer, but we can still keep Langley in the loop.'

'I don't know who we can trust at Langley.'

'Leave that to Calvara.'

'Can we trust him?'

'Whoa! You're talking about the Director of the Central Intelligence Agency. Of course I trust him.'

Declin raised his hands in submission. 'Something isn't right with our reading of this cyber threat. We had Azizi, who was an agency asset, and we didn't spot him and make the link that the malware came from China.'

'We got there eventually.'

'I got there,' Declin pointed out. 'And I had to ignore a stop sign that had been given to the Financial Crime boys. A stop sign put up probably by the same person who rushed us into action in Waziristan, tipped off Azizi in Basra, and then once he was about to be apprehended had him assassinated.'

'You got evidence to back up these claims?'

'The evidence is that these things happened,' Declin said. 'Someone on the inside had to have been behind it all.'

Asimov removed his spectacles, sprayed them with aerosol and cleaned them with a micro-fibre cloth. He put them back on and turned back to Declin. 'Any other feelings I should be aware of?'

Declin could tell Asimov thought he was a conspiracy nut, but he figured he may as well lay it all out on the table. 'I'd like access to the Black Chamber files.'

'The investigation concluded that it never even existed.'

'I think it did. I think it's still active. I'd like access to the files.'

'You don't have time to indulge in conspiracy theories, Special Agent Lehane. The country remains under cyber siege and we have a dirty nuke heading our way. Concentrate on stopping those real and present dangers.'

116

The President had called a full meeting of the National Security Council and the White House Cabinet Room bristled with ministers and military brass accompanied by their deputies, special protection officers, assorted aides and advisors. Declin stood against the wall behind Director Connelly's seat. Connelly had reminded Declin that protocol dictated only those seated could talk. If Declin had something to say he had to pass a note to Connelly.

The President opened the meeting. 'I was elected on the premise that America would no longer play the role of world policeman. But I never said I would ignore a direct threat to our country. It is clear that Red China is responsible for the cyber attacks on our country. Yes, it was jihadist terrorists who actually pressed the buttons on the keyboards. But China devised the exploits and supplied the malware. We can be fairly confident they also supplied the Uranium that is heading for our shores. So we are going to hit them back. But in a smart way. Where it hurts.' The President signalled to the Secretary of Defence to take over.

Pawel Syzmanski cleared his throat. 'We now have a fully worked out battle plan to bring down China's Communist Party. It's based on a similar narrative agenda to the one we used to collapse the Soviet Union. Then we had agents and agencies feeding propaganda about Polish unionists, East German nationalists, Romanian democracy activists and others. Now we will use the internet to spread the story that the time has come for an end to one-party rule in China.'

Pawel passed over to Cresta.

'Critical to this plan,' she said, 'is our ability to bring down the Great Firewall of China. The primary purpose of this firewall, as you know, is to censor political dissent. That dissent is now widespread. Without this censorship the Party cannot survive. The Great Firewall is China's Berlin wall. If we bring it down, the people will do the rest and the regime will fall.'

Cresta explained that Cyber Command would also support the pro-democracy movement with propaganda initiatives of its own. Many of these were real stories that had not yet been told.

'How long will it take?' the President asked.

'Impossible to call,' Cresta replied. 'The speed of collapse of the Soviet Union took everyone by surprise and that was before the internet.'

'How long?' the President pressed. 'Central estimate.'

'Weeks?'

'Taiwan doesn't have weeks,' said General Horn who, Declin

understood, was still pushing for military action.

'Once the wall starts cracking the Politburo will be fighting for its own life,' said Cresta. 'They'll be too busy to attack Taiwan.'

'On the contrary,' said Horn. 'They could attack Taiwan to shore up popular support. We're not in a position to defend it right now.'

'The Chinese threat to Taiwan is just a symptom.' The President took a deep breath. 'We're going to cure the disease.'

* * *

Declin sat in the waiting room outside the oval office and worked through a back-log of email traffic as various top brass and politicians pulled rank and jumped ahead of him in the queue for an audience with the President. It was late into the evening and through the windows a full moon was flooding the White House rose garden by the time Declin's turn arrived.

President Topps looked like he'd had a long day but he still managed a warm smile as Declin entered the room.

'I'm sorry to keep you waiting, Declin. Can I get you a drink? It's late. What's your tipple?'

'No thanks. I don't drink.'

'Me neither. Life is too short. So what can I do for you?'

'Have you heard of the Black Chamber, Mr President?'

'The Black Chamber is something to do with Iraq, right? A bunch of guys who sexed up the case for war.'

'That's it. I'd like your approval to access any files at Langley relating to the Black Chamber.'

'Why are you interested?'

'I think the Black Chamber is still operating. And it has some involvement in this cyber war.'

The President sat back in his chair. 'What does Leon Calvara think?'

'I haven't asked him. I asked Asimov. He said no.'

'As a general rule I don't like people going over the heads of their direct reports. And you're jumping over more than one, Declin.'

'What harm can it do?'

'That's a good question. You tell me.'

Declin thought about it a moment. 'If I'm right then there is a group in Langley that has been manipulating intelligence to press the case for war with China. If that comes out, you won't look too clever, Mr President.'

'I appreciate your candor. You have my authorization.'

117

The White House
Office of the Press Secretary
For Immediate Release
Statement by the President of the United States

12:58 P.M. EST
THE PRESIDENT: As President and Commander in Chief, my highest priority is the security of the American people. As you know, we have been facing an unprecedented level of cyber attack against our critical industrial infrastructure. Attacks that have cost the lives of innocent Americans as well causing great economic damage for millions of others. We have known for some time that these attacks were executed by cyber jihadists but I promised that we would leave no stone unturned to find out who was ultimately behind these attacks. We now know that the attackers were aided and abetted by the Communist Government in China. with the aim of distracting us from their territorial aggression in Asia.

China's seizures of disputed islands in the South and East China Seas are a flagrant violation of the rulings of the International Arbitration court in The Hague. China's leadership has shown contempt for international law, for the principles of freedom of navigation and over flight, and disregard for peaceful resolution of these land disputes. It is now threatening to invade the sovereign state of Taiwan. This is yet another destabilizing and provocative action and is a flagrant violation of multiple United Nations Security Council resolutions. China's aggression represents a serious threat to our interests – including the security of some of our closest allies

– and undermines peace and security in the broader region. The United States is fully committed to the security of our allies in the region, and we will take all necessary steps to defend ourselves and our allies and respond to China's provocations.

We condemn the Communist Party's actions and determination to prioritize its overseas expansion over the well-being of its people, whose struggles only intensify with China's diversion of scarce resources to such destabilizing activities. The people of China have been gravely let down by a leadership that spends under three percent of its GDP on healthcare, allows unfettered official corruption and levels of pollution beyond anything anywhere else in the world. Sixty million people are illiterate and three hundred million people have no access to clean water, while the thousand most privileged red capitalists own a trillion dollars.

Further, the United States has repeatedly raised concerns about human rights developments in China and especially its censorship of the media and the continued persecution of those citizens expressing their desire to see peaceful political change in China. The United States wants the ordinary citizens of China to know that we understand and share their desire to be free to choose their own government and to speak openly.

Only when its citizens are free from the burden of war and only after a peaceful transition to democracy will China be allowed back into the international community, enabling its banks to be recapitalized, new investment to flood into the economy for the benefit of the most populous people on earth.

The United States calls upon the international community to stand together and demonstrate to the Communist Party of China that it can no longer bully its people and its neighbors. We call on the Chinese Leadership to set a date for free elections.

* * *

Declin had just finished reading the President's press release when he received another fax.

To- Declin Lehane. Highly Confidential.
Question 1: What is letter 5,6 and 11 from your favorite song?

Fax your reply to +86 10 5139 6787

He checked the number. Again it was Beijing, although different from the previous one. He faxed back letters 'T, A and N'. He didn't actually have a favorite song but he used The Star Spangled Banner in security questions because the song originated in his birthplace of Baltimore. Another fax came through in reply.

Answer 4. Correct. The Star Spangled Banner.

Message as follows – I like President Topps's message. This support is what our Freedom movement needs. As a reward I will try to get you something that will help. But it will be very dangerous for me. Tell your courier to stay in Beijing two days more. If I do not contact him I will have failed and you will not hear from me again.

At once Declin sent a WhatsApp message to Mickey:

'Keep enjoying your holiday. No need to come back yet.'

After receiving an OK in return and then satisfying himself that the Psyber strategy was nicely on track, he decided to get a third plate spinning. He took the President's authorization letter from the drawer and headed for Langley.

* * *

The winter sun was setting reluctantly as Declin's cab pulled off the George Washington Memorial Highway and passed through clearance at security, before continuing down the private road to CIA headquarters.

He jogged through reception and on to the elevator up to Calvara's office. The Director dispensed with any formalities and motioned for Declin to take a seat. He studied Declin in silence for several long seconds. He cleared his throat, cracked his knuckles and growled: 'Remind me of the mission statement of your employer, the FBI?'

'Our mission,' replied Declin, 'is to protect and defend the United States against terrorist and foreign intelligence threats, to uphold and enforce the criminal laws of the United States, and to provide leadership and criminal justice services to federal, state, municipal, and international agencies and partners.'

Calvara nodded. 'And what would you say is the FBI's primary function?'

'First and foremost, we are a law enforcement agency.'

'Very good. And now can I tell you about the agency that *I* run?'

'Shoot.'

'The CIA is an international intelligence agency whose primary mission is to collect, evaluate, and disseminate foreign intelligence to assist the president and senior US government policymakers in making decisions relating to national security.'

Declin said nothing.

'You understand the difference between the two organizations?'

'Sure.'

'So what the hell is an FBI agent doing running an unauthorized Chinese asset without the involvement of this agency?'

'The asset instructed us not to use the CIA. He didn't trust it.'

'And who the hell is Mickey Summer?'

'He's a British banker who ...'

'Has precisely zero training, experience or knowledge in intelligence tradecraft.'

'The asset instructed us to use a clean skin. Mickey Summer was already working with me. He is friendly and outgoing, which is of course a prerequisite for working in the Directorate of Operations. I'm comfortable with the decision.'

'Well I am not. But as he is now in play we will have to continue to use him. But with Beijing station kept fully in the loop. Understood.'

'I understand what you're saying,' Declin replied evasively. 'Can I ask you a question?'

'Shoot.'

'What do you know about the Black Chamber?'

'The Black Chamber,' repeated Calvara. 'Why is a problem long since forgotten about troubling you?'

'Because Azizi's handler, Biggerstaff, was part of the conspiracy.'

'That is total crap. There was no conspiracy. There was just an intelligence failure.'

'Well, if it was an intelligence failure, why do you still employ them?'

'So they mistakenly concluded that Saddam Hussein had weapons of mass destruction. So did plenty of others, including Deputy Director Operations Ladyman. We can't hold that against them forever.'

'That mistake led this country to invade Iraq.'

'We'd have gone in anyway. The invasion was in the interests of this country.'

'Four thousand five hundred American soldiers, one of them my brother, might not have died.'

Calvara pulled at an ear lobe and stopped himself saying something. 'I'm sorry about your brother. I'm sorry about all of those heroes. But the Black Chamber has been chewed over and over. There's nothing there. It's a closed book.'

'I want to look at it.'

'You just stick to …'

'And here,' interrupted Declin, laying a paper on the desk in front of Calvara, 'is a letter from President Topps granting me unrestricted access to all information concerning the Black Chamber.'

Calvara put on his reading glasses and studied the paperwork before looking back to Declin. 'You sure this isn't some personal vendetta you have against this agency because of your brother?'

'I'll let you know after I've read the files.'

Calvara shrugged. 'Go ahead. Better people than you have been over those files and found nothing.'

118

Big, bold lies. That was the approach that old Xian believed in, and it had served Hue well before. But as he went to work that morning he knew he was about to try the biggest, boldest lie imaginable. He figured he had a fifty percent chance of making it out without being arrested. And if he did get out he would never be going back in. One way or another his life was about to undergo a dramatic change.

Familiar yet unfriendly eyes stared as he passed the concrete guardhouse. In reception he emptied his pockets into a grey plastic tray and passed it and his bag through the metal detectors. A guard swept him with a wand while another searched the bag. He walked on to the Department of Internal Security. Another bag search and wand sweep before he proceeded to his desk where he logged on to his computer with a thumb scan.

He worked as diligently as possible until eleven o'clock, when he knew the Politburo were meeting and its members would be out of contact. Using his own password he logged into the PLA Cyber brigade network and found the database containing the names and ISP addresses of all the pro-party cyber mamas that were used to positively troll the web in favor of the Party. He copied this onto a memory drive and worked his way into the Cyber brigade operating system. As he began making a copy of that, an alarm went off.

His supervisor came hurrying over. 'What's happening?'

'Nothing to worry about,' said Hue calmly.

The supervisor pointed a finger at Hue's screen. 'What are you doing?'

'I'm making a copy of the operating system for General Wing.'

Hue handed over a letter, written on military headed paper, giving him authorization. The supervisor read it carefully. Hue never talked about his father and had never used the relationship for special privilege. Until now. But he knew that everyone was aware of who his father was. And it was not inconceivable that the General would ask his son to carry out such a task.

'Why does he want this?'

'You ask him.'

'Why does he use you?'

'Because there is a traitor amongst us who has been passing details of the cyber attacks to the Americans. I'm the only person General Wing can trust. Now do you understand why he asked me?'

'Of course.' The supervisor hesitated a while longer before hurrying back to his office. Out of the corner of his eye, Hue could see him making a frantic phone call to his superior. No doubt the superior would in turn call up the line of command until eventually someone would check with General Wing.

Hue copied for another twenty minutes. Each minute felt like an hour. Finally he could take no more. He removed the memory stick, popped it in his mouth when nobody was looking and swallowed it with a cup of water. He left his jacket on his chair and his computer switched on as if he had just stepped away from his desk.

His supervisor made a half-hearted attempt to stop him leaving the room but Hue showed his empty pockets and explained that he was popping out to the canteen for some food. He did go straight to the canteen but directly out the other door. He hurried to the main entrance. Another body search and a wand did not detect his little secret. As he walked down the steps to the street he expected at any moment to be pulled up by a shout to stop. Or the shot from a gun. But nothing.

He breathed again. Five minutes later he was flying on the subway, desperate to get into hiding because he knew that very soon he would be the most wanted man in Beijing.

119

Calvara had clearly let it filter down that the FBI agent sniffing around in the Langley library was to be tolerated but not welcomed. He wasn't even offered a glass of water, let alone a coffee. But Declin hadn't come to make friends. He also didn't have time on his side. He was increasingly worried that Asimov and Calvara were right and he was wasting his time indulging in conspiracy theories while the country was under cyber siege, nuclear threat and facing war with China if the Psyber strategy did not go well. He gave himself one hour.

He zipped through countless Department of Defence briefings and intelligence reports on the situation in Iraq prior to the invasion, including a number from Iraqi intelligence. He made a note of some familiar names included on the circulation list.

He skimmed over the transcripts of interviews with Ahmad Chalabi, the exiled Iraqi opposition leader, who some blamed for feeding inaccurate and alarming information to decision makers in the White House and Pentagon. He came across the evidence given to Lawson Ladyman by an engineer named al-Haderi who had been working on weapon storage and development, and interviews with the defector Harith who gave evidence about mobile weapons labs. Finally he came to Biggerstaff, who said he'd seen a memorandum of understanding between the governments of Niger and Iraq concerning the sale of uranium. No such memorandum was ever discovered, let alone evidence of any uranium shipments to Iraq.

Most interestingly, Declin found revelations from the interrogation of Saddam Hussein himself, and the fact that the warlord had dismantled Iraq's WMD program in the face of international pressure.

Declin had filled in gaps in his knowledge about the sexing up of the case for invading Iraq, but it had done little to change the overall picture. The Black Chamber proved to be as elusive as the weapons of mass destruction. There was no hard evidence that a group of this name existed. It had simply been referred to so often that it had become a code name for the possible collaborative efforts of those who wanted to push America into war with Iraq. But nobody had ever made a clear case for its existence, and certainly not for its continuation.

He was about to leave when he came across an appendix that appeared to have no connection to the Black Chamber. It was a hard copy power-point presentation given by Asimov on the P2OG, Proactive, Pre-emptive Operations Group. Declin recalled it had been set up by Donald Rumsfeld in the nineties to bring together CIA and military covert action. As Declin leafed through he noted certain lines on various pages had been highlighted: Psyops. Managed Information Dissemination. Influence Warfare. Cover & Deception. Signal to states that their sovereignty will be at risk. Network attack.

It seemed that whoever had put together the Black Chamber files had identified a possible relationship between it and P20G.

Declin's alarm sounded. His time was up and he was satisfied it had been a useful hour. He had some names and leads and the kernel of an idea that he could hand over to Vin to explore. Meantime, Declin was needed back at Cyber Command.

120

Operation Dragon Slay was swinging into action with an avalanche of 'full spectre cyber missions', the euphemism for Cyber offence. Declin looked on in quiet admiration at the array of screens and terminals, and the army of cyber warriors; geeks in T-shirts and jeans sitting alongside officers in crisp uniforms. Most of those wore Cyber Command's dappled grey, but many wore the colors of the service components for whom they were liaising.

Declin knew there were also hundreds more technicians off site, including the British Brigade Seventy Seven and the Israeli Cyber unit 8200. All were working on their own missions and sending the fruits of their labour into the Joint Operations Center for assessment. Those that were approved were then forwarded for execution by the Tailored Access team in the Remote Operations Center.

They were certainly throwing plenty of resources into Dragon Slay. Altogether ten thousand cyber warriors were ready for battle. But would it be enough?

Declin knew the key to it all was what happened to the Great Firewall. Ideally it needed to be dismantled. At the very least it needed to be severely compromised. He asked control for a status report.

'We've run a botnet attack on the servers used by the state-run search engines,' he explained. 'We are also ready to corrupt Weibo, Renren and Baidu's own censorship teams by destroying the algorithms they use to search and delete key words and posts.'

'Will it work?' Declin asked.

'We can't bring the Firewall down entirely. But we sure can knock some holes in it. The Chinese will get work around solutions eventually, but at least for a time the party will be unable to censor dissent.'

'The billion-person puzzle is whether that time will be sufficient.' Declin returned to his desk to watch events unfold. His monitor could switch to any in the room, while the main screen on the wall showed mission control's selected highlights.

First up on screen was a fake release by the Supreme People's

Procurator stating that an investigation had revealed that General Wing had used his position to garner profits for himself.

Next was something to destabilize the Politburo's credibility in Chinese Financial markets. A team from Air Force Cyber Command had managed to hack into the People's Daily. Not only had they hacked the online version of this communist party mouthpiece, they had also managed to hack into the hard copy print between editorial and printing. They inserted a statement from the Ministry of Finance saying that it planned a 'Patriotic' tax on domestic retail cash balances held in Chinese banks. This was to pay for the costs of war against Taiwan.

The online corruption went out after the hard copy had been circulated. And Operation Dragon Slay had a thousand fingers ready to talk about it on every website and chat room.

Cyber Command also managed to hack into the Department for Administration of Industry and Commerce. Here they were able to alter the records for a number of major state-owned companies to suggest that they had gone into receivership. Within a matter of hours suppliers were calling the companies to terminate orders and credit facilities were drawn down. The protestations from management that the financial positions were sound were not believed, and soon the problem became self-fulfilling. Credit agencies downgraded their debt to junk, and soon the companies really were heading for liquidation. The Chinese stock and currency markets went into freefall.

Cyber Command also posted rumors about China's designs on Himalayan territories. This brought a furious diplomatic response from India, who scrambled its armed forces. The Japanese were quick to declare their support for India and denounce China again. Markets across Asia went into free-fall, as commentators discussed the very real prospect of a truly Pan-Asian war with China fighting against Taiwan, Japan and India, and perhaps the Americans.

Other cyber attacks used real evidence gathered by agents over the years but not previously released, showing corruption among members of the nine-man Standing Party. On Weibo they leaked a flood of gossip about various politburo officials;

marital indiscretions, dining out on the critically endangered giant salamander, secret religious beliefs, personal hygiene problems, drunken outbursts against the common people, and various other anti-social activities.

121

The scene outside the Beijing branch of Henzen Bank was similar to that being played out at every bank across China. A queue had formed before first light but it quickly morphed into a crowd that spilled off the pavement and into the road. Ordinarily this would have stopped the early morning rush-hour traffic. But there was none that day. The country had gone to the bank to stop its savings being stolen by the Party.

Following directions from Head Office, the branch manager had tried in vain to line up extra security. But only two had posted for duty. The others were in the crowd. Anxious staff watched from behind the glass doors as the manager briefed them to remain calm and advise customers that their savings were safe.

He opened the doors, but whatever he tried to say was drowned out as the crowd pushed aside the security guards and flooded to the cashier desks.

The manager climbed onto a table. 'I am the manager. I have just received a personal call from the Chairman of Henzen Bank. He wants me to tell you that the rumors are false and there is no need for you to withdraw your money from the bank.'

'I don't care if you got a call from President Li,' said a man. 'I want my money.'

'The Chairman has spoken to President Li, and he has given his personal guarantee that there is no plan for a loyalty tax. It is American propaganda.'

'He's a liar,' called a woman down the line. 'The President is a liar.'

Worried eyes flashed at the woman's brazen dissent.

'She's right.'

'We don't trust you.'

'We don't trust the Party.'

'We want our money.'

'So don't try and stop us.'

Those at the front of the crowd began banging on the security glass at the cashier desks. The manager was under orders not to allow withdrawals, but he knew there was going to be a riot if he tried to stop it. He motioned his staff to let them have the money. He guessed they would run out of cash by mid morning. By which time he planned to be long gone.

122

Mickey met Yu again in the hotel lobby and they took the subway to Tiananmen Square. It was a surprisingly clear day as they emerged above ground to find huge crowds protesting about the loyalty tax, the financial crisis and the Party. Police were monitoring and allowing the protests, but the tension was palpable.

'We should not stay here long,' said Yu. 'Normally you would see children and adults flying kites here. But today is a different atmosphere.'

They walked the length of the square, keeping well away from the protests and moved on to the Forbidden City. Mickey let Yu do her tour piece without interruption. At the Memorial Hall of Chairman Mao she began checking her phone repeatedly.

'It's time to go shopping,' she suddenly announced.

Ten minutes later they were on a street lined with ancient building fronts hiding modern shops behind. Keeping out of the way of the old-style trams, they passed little shops selling clothes, shoes and tourist paraphernalia. Yu took a detour into a side lane to show Mickey traditional Beijing foods such as stir-fried liver and boiled lamb tripe.

'And my favorite, sugar-coated haws.' She handed him a stick of sliced fruits. 'Try it.'

Mickey took the stick with its yams, bananas and oranges and something he didn't recognise. 'Is that the haw?'

'That is a chufa,' she laughed. 'When I was a child these were made from hawthorn. That is why it is called a sugar-coated haw.'

Mickey had never really had a sweet tooth, but he gave it a go. It was at first sickly sweet and then he shivered at a tangy surprise.

'Sweet and sour,' said Yu studying her phone intently. 'To remind us of the ups and downs of life.' She seemed hooked on her phone, constantly checking it like a little girl checking for social media approvals. Her expression turned very serious. 'We need to go. Quickly.'

She pulled Mickey back into Qianmen Street with a sense of purpose and urgency, in stark contrast to the slow touring that had filled the afternoon. A blacked-out car pulled up sharply in the street ahead and Yu pushed Mickey into a clothes shop.

'You wanted a new coat, didn't you,' she said, grabbing a leather number off a stand.

'Right.' Mickey realized she was up to something and he best just go along with it.

'And a new hat,' she said pulling a ridiculously large rimmed black Fedora off a stand. 'Go try them on.'

Mickey let an assistant lead him to a changing room as two charity fund raisers entered the shop. One of them, dressed as Sergeant Black Cat, waved a toy gun around and demanded money while a tall girl in a robot outfit held a blue-and-white space helmet upside down for the collection. Mickey was grateful to get out of the way. But when he got to the changing room, hanging on the peg was another Sergeant Black Cat outfit.

'Take your clothes off and put that outfit on, quickly,' said the shop assistant, pointing at the suit. She pulled the curtain closed behind her.

Mickey hesitated. He had no idea what was going on but he did as instructed. Suddenly the curtain opened and the other Sergeant Black Cat appeared, shoved his gun into Mickey's hands and pushed him out of the cubicle. The shop assistant pulled him back into the shop.

'Out,' she said. 'You can't go in the changing rooms. Out you go now.'

The robot now took Mickey's arm and lead him into the street. He passed the blacked-out car and a beefy guy stood beside it who looked in no mood for charity fun.

The robot took him down a lane where a motorbike was waiting, engine running. 'Get on.'

Again Mickey did as instructed. He just hoped these were the good guys.

123

The bike zipped along Beijing's wet streets at speed. Mickey gripped the driver tight around the waist, closed his eyes and tried to pretend it was just a fairground ride. They arrived eventually at a theatre side entrance and he was led through the stage door and down a dimly lit corridor to a dressing room. The girl in the robot outfit reappeared and handed him a bag of clothes.

'You can get out of the outfit.'

He had been as hot as a docker's armpit while wearing the Sergeant Black Cat suit, and was relieved to climb out. 'What was all that fancy dress routine about?'

'You were being followed,' she explained. 'My friend in the Sergeant Black Cat suit changed into your clothes in the changing rooms and led the followers back to your hotel.'

'Who was following me?'

'We're not sure. Perhaps Ministry. Perhaps CIA. Perhaps both.'

'So what happens now?' asked Mickey, looking around what appeared to be a theatre dressing room. As if on cue the door opened and in came the edgy hoody that he had first met in the park. Mickey extended a hand. 'We must stop meeting like this.'

'This will be the last time. You need to take a package and hand it personally to Declin.'

'Last time I went to the British embassy and sent it from there.'

'That won't be possible now. State Security are on high alert. You would be stopped from going in.'

'Why would they stop me?'

'The information in the package will bring down the Party. The Ministry know it has gone missing. They know I took it so they are looking for me and they will probably soon find you because there will be CCTV pictures of our meeting in the park. Your face will be on the top of every police wanted list.'

'I've always been a popular chap,' said Mickey, feeling suddenly ice cold in spite of the heat.

'Please sit down.'

Mickey sat on a stool in front of a makeup table littered with cosmetics and tea cups. The girl switched on the lights surrounding the large mirror. She pulled at some curls on the top of his head. 'There is not much I can do with this.'

'Me neither, darling.'

'I think I will shave it all off.'

Before Mickey could protest she produced some clippers and attacked the back of his hair. Five minutes later Mickey was staring at a strange skinhead.

The girl produced a lotion which she rubbed into his face, neck and hands, to darken his skin. She applied a little eyeliner and finally she selected a pair of thick black spectacles and a heavy cotton jacket and trouser combo. Mickey figured his own mum wouldn't recognise him.

An older man came in, took a photograph and left again.

'Here is the present for Declin,' said Hoody, handing Mickey a thumb drive coated in a rubbery film. 'If you need to swallow it to hide it you can. It is coated to survive passing through your body. I have tested it.'

Mickey realized the implication. 'Sweet.'

'Here is a travel permit and a plane ticket to Llasa, Tibet. You will be met by a tour guide there who will take you overland into Nepal. From there you can fly to Washington.'

The dressing room door opened again and the old man returned with a British passport under the name of Edward Short but using the photograph he had just taken.

'Don't use your real passport or your credit cards until you get to Nepal.'

'What do I say if I'm caught?' asked Mickey.

'Do exactly as I've said and you won't be.'

124

The man at airport arrivals holding a sign for 'Edward Short' had dark leathery skin, a barrel chest and muscular arms and legs. Introducing himself as Lalit he took Mickey's luggage and led the way out of the airport building to a white jeep. Mickey could feel the altitude bleeding his lungs of oxygen. Llasa was living up to its name as the City of Sunlight as they left the capital under clear blue skies and drove fast along the Friendship Highway.

Mickey noted the speed limit was a snail's pace of seventy kilometers an hour. Lalit was doing double that. An ex-Gurkha solider who now ferried tourists between Nepal and Tibet, he clearly knew the road and his steely concentration left Mickey feeling safe, but he was worried about attracting the attention of the police.

'Is it a good idea to go so fast?'

'I've been told to get you out of the country as quickly as possible.'

'But what if you get stopped for speeding?'

'No problem. I just pay the fine. That is all they want.'

It took the best part of the night to reach the Himalayan foothills. Lalit dropped down the gears and kept his foot on the floor, overtaking the slower moving traffic. A couple of hours winding up to the five kilometer high Lalung La Pass produced sunrise views of the mountains and the stunning descent off the Tibetan plateau. With the jeep gamely avoiding the sheer drops off the side of the road and upcoming trucks in its middle, they wound down, the engine screaming as it over-revved in low gear. Soon the mountain scrub gave way to lush vegetation and the temperature rose sharply.

The border crossing came into view and Lalit pulled over in a passing place.

'Stay here,' he insisted, as he climbed out of the car.

Mickey watched Lalit disappear into the tour groups and traders bustling around the bridge. He returned minutes later wearing a worried frown. 'They're looking for you.'

'How do you know?'

'Your picture is on the walls in the border control.'

'But I'm wearing a disguise.'

'It might fool the guards, but they will have face recognition cameras. Too risky. I have checked out another route that we should be able to do.' Lalit looked Mickey up and down. 'Can you climb?'

'I can climb into a cab. Climb aboard a ship. Climbed the promotion ladder quite successfully.'

'What about real climbing?'

Mickey shook his head. 'Scared of heights.'

'No need to be scared.'

'I'm serious. I get wobbly on a bar stool.'

'No problem. You won't be able to see anything. We'll be climbing in the dark.'

'Oh great.'

125

Cyber Command's initial success in spreading dissent among the Chinese people had stalled, as the Ministry of Security recovered more quickly than anyone had expected.

'The Firewall is back up,' Declin said to Cresta. 'Any post against the party is spotted by the censors, immediately deleted and countered with state propaganda.'

'That's online,' said Cresta. 'On the streets it's different. We're seeing more and more demonstrations.'

'They were organized when the Firewall was broken,' said Declin. 'They'll peter out now that its fixed.'

'Well we just have to hope the guys working on the encryption get lucky.'

'Or Mickey Summer brings back something useful,' said Declin.

'Any news from him?'

'Nothing.'

* * *

Lalit had dropped the driver's seat flat and was snoring like a walrus. Mickey was too scared to sleep. He wasn't sure what frightened him most: getting caught by the Chinese smuggling state secrets out of the country or climbing in the dark.

He watched the traders and tourists slowly advancing to the border posts until, as a purple sun set over the mountains, Lalit's alarm rang and he sat up and rubbed his eyes. He walked round to the back of the jeep and lifted out a heavy holdall.

'Come.'

Mickey followed Lalit to the edge of the town and along a footpath that ran down the side of the gorge before petering out at a cliff face. To his left Mickey suspected there was a sheer drop. He was glad he couldn't see it.

Lalit knocked two metal anchors into the ledge about a metre apart. He secured two ropes to these and tied them together into a Y shape. He fastened a third rope to the anchor and threw the long coil into the darkness. Mickey waited for the plop of the rope landing, but heard nothing.

'I can't do this,' he said. 'I'll take my chances back at the border crossing.'

'My decision, not yours,' Lalit said, with an uncompromising stare.

'I told you, I can't climb.'

'Abseiling is easier than climbing. We will go together. I do the work. You just relax.'

'Relax?' Mickey felt sick as he was fitted into a helmet and harness. Lalit attached them both, let out the rope and backed to the edge.

Mickey couldn't move.

'Turn round,' said Lalit.

Mickey turned around slowly and Lalit pulled him firmly backwards over the edge. Suspended in the dark by a rope he grit his teeth to stop himself screaming. They made steady progress as Lalit walked down the cliff with Mickey knocking alternately against him and the rock face.

Suddenly the beam of a torch swept by. Mickey saw a flashlight pointing down at them.

A voice shouted.

Lalit shouted back.

'What's going on?' asked Mickey.

'Border guards. They say: stop or we shoot.'

'What did you shout?'

'I told them we are coming back up.'

Mickey didn't argue. He didn't fancy being target practice for some Chinese soldiers. But when they found him with the memory stick they might shoot him anyway. He unzipped his pocket and took hold of the stick, wondering whether he should throw it into the water roaring below. Instead he made a split-second decision to pop it into his mouth. He swallowed just as Lalit pushed off from the wall in a huge leap that also dropped them sharply. Then another. And again as the shouting resumed above them.

One last huge drop and they landed on solid ground. Lalit pulled frantically at the rope and threw it away. A gunshot rent the darkness, reverberating deafeningly around the canyon.

Lalit dragged Mickey by the arm. 'We swim now. Just keep swimming across the current. Not against it. Not with it. Sideways.'

Before he could say anything Mickey had been pushed waist deep into freezing-cold water. He couldn't see a thing. Another gunshot and a ricochet close by launched him into the river. He swam hard, aware he was also being carried downstream and daring not to think of the waterfall he had seen near the bridge. His hand hit a rock. It hurt, but he was on the other side. He scrambled out of the water. Heard grunting behind. Lalit appeared, grabbed his arm and pulled him quickly along a path and behind a rock.

They lay down flat, breathing heavily in odd synchronicity.

'We are safe now,' said Lalit. 'We are in Nepal.'

'Won't they come after us?'

'They won't do anything or tell anyone. They would be punished for letting us get over the border.'

'What next?'

'We get you to the airport. Then to America.'

126

Hue needed to join the protestors in Tiananmen square. It was foolhardy. It was dangerous. But he could not stay away. He knew that his photo would have been circulated to all police and neighborhood watchers and uploaded into the facial recognition software on surveillance cameras. And so he called in at the theatre. After an hour of his friend's creative endeavour Hue didn't recognise the face in the mirror with its mop of unruly hair, boxer's nose, protruding teeth.

He was still nervous of the cameras and so avoided the subway and instead walked to the square where the protest was in full swing. His spirits were raised by the forest of umbrellas. A year ago people could only dream of such a protest. But the Party had lost the people.

There were also rumors that the Party had lost itself in vicious infighting between the two rival factions of his father and President Li. This realization that change was within their grasp added to the tension. It could be felt by the hesitant lines of police watching from the sidelines and the foreign film crews dotted among the crowd.

The girl in the yellow dress climbed up on the podium. He waved at her but she didn't recognise him in his disguise.

'We have been here before,' she spoke calmly into a microphone. 'In nineteen eighty nine the Party ignored the people and broke up the demonstrations. But we will not be driven away. Not even by the tanks. This time they must listen to us.'

She waited for the cheering to subside.

'Our demands are being made across the country. You may not know this because the censors have blocked the news, but protests such as this are happening in Hainan, Guangdong, Sichuan, Shanghai, and Hong Kong. This is about freedom for all of China.'

Hue clapped as she climbed back down. She still didn't recognise him as he patted her encouragingly on her back, but he was afraid to remove his disguise. A ping sounded an incoming message on WhatsApp. It was from Lalit.

'Package is on a plane to Washington.'

He punched the air. He had done all he could. Now he needed Declin to come good.

127

Mickey's already high heart rate rose again at the sight of the two police officers waiting with a name card for him in the airport arrivals hall.

'Michael Summer?'

'Mickey.'

'We're to escort you to Declin Lehane at Fort Meade, Sir.'

They led him to a car parked on the hatched lines protecting a disability parking spot. Soon they were speeding away under a flashing blue light and racing down the highway, cars peeling out of their path like the Red Sea before Moses.

The two huge black cuboids of Fort Meade came into view. At reception the police officers passed Mickey onto a guard who marched him off into the building. A sudden stirring in the bowels told Mickey the moment he had been waiting for had arrived.

'I need to go to the little boy's room.'

'Go right ahead,' said the guard, walking over to a toilet and taking a position outside the door.

Mickey went into a cubicle, closed the toilet seat and pulled out the plastic bag he'd been carrying since Kathmandu airport. He kicked off his shoes, removed his trousers and underpants and spread his legs over the bag. He hesitated while he tried to think of a better way to go about it. But he couldn't.

He groaned and grimaced. Up came a right old stink. He cleaned his bum and then, keeping his nose high and as far away as possible, he broke up the dark brown turd. The memory stick emerged and he cleaned it as well as he could in the toilet, flushed the rest away, cleaned himself up again and got dressed. He was glad nobody was at the sinks as he washed the stick and his hands thoroughly with soap and water.

The guard opened the door. 'Sorry to rush you, Mr Summer

but I got a call from Special Agent Lehane and he is real keen to see you.'

'I'm done.'

They set off again at a trot. Down corridors. Up an elevator. Down another. Finally they came to a room where Declin was waiting at a computer terminal.

'You got the package?' asked Declin, without any preliminaries.

'Here.' Mickey held it up.

'Great,' said Declin, holding out his hand.

Mickey was oddly reluctant to hand it over. Like the 'one ring' he'd gone to a lot of trouble to carry it this far. But it was of no use to him. He dropped it in Declin's palm and decided to spare him the knowledge of its little side trip.

'This is a non-networked computer, in case this is just a trick,' explained Declin.

'It better not be a trick,' said Mickey. 'I almost got killed for that.'

Declin opened up the stick and studied a long list of filenames. He worked through them in what looked liked random order though Mickey suspected Declin didn't do random. From the occasional grunt and murmuring approval Mickey sensed Declin liked what he was seeing.

'This is going to be useful, then?'

'If it's for real, it's dynamite,' replied Declin.

'Worth me nearly getting killed?'

'Worth it if you'd actually been killed,' said Declin, keeping his eyes firmly on the screen. 'You've brought back the command structure for PLA Cyber brigade and details of the operating system they use, so we can find exploits and vulnerabilities.'

'Translation please.'

'We'll be able to basically neutralise China's Cyber brigade. You also brought back details of the root kits and cloaked surveillance packages that allow PLA Cyber to hack into every phone in China. We can dismantle the spyware and blind the Ministry of State Security. We can also use it ourselves and turn the Party propaganda machine on itself.'

'Nice irony.'

'There's more. We've got the names and ISP addresses of all the pro-party hackers and cyber mamas and neighborhood surveillance teams. So we can disable them.'

'So in a nutshell, you can bring down the Great Firewall of China?'

Declin looked impressed. 'We'll make a cyber expert out of you yet, Mickey.'

128

Wao Chu gripped the leather arm rests as his Cessna bounced onto the runway at Beijing International Airport and its engines roared into reverse. He breathed again as the plane decelerated and taxied over to a quiet corner of the airport, where it was met by a waiting limousine.

The limo carried him swiftly out of the airport and south towards the capital. The towers of the Financial District came into view, and finally he arrived at the stumpy block that housed the China Banking Regulatory Commission.

He regrouped on the steps with his coterie of advisers and deputies. In the foyer he recognized the Chief Executive of a competitor bank and so hung back discreetly to allow his party to clear reception.

Wao's sense of occasion was heightened when he entered a meeting room packed with representations from the ten largest banks in China. Everyone exchanged pleasantries then sat in silence, waiting for the arrival of the Chairman of the regulatory body. He entered and took his seat at the top of the table, looking around the faces as if expecting someone to speak first. 'So what do you want to speak to me about?' he asked eventually.

Wao exchanged confused glances with the other Chief Execs.

'We are here because you called us,' said one.

It was the Chair's turn to look confused. 'I did not call anyone. I was asked to come because you wanted to see me.'

Wao pulled the letter from his inside jacket pocket and slipped it in front of the Chairman. 'This is your letter asking us to come to discuss the financial regime that will be in place after Communism.'

The Chair read the letter hurriedly. 'This is nonsense.'

Others waved their own versions of the letter.

The Chair frowned as he read it again. 'I know nothing about this. This is a hoax.'

'It came from your own personal email account,' continued Wao. 'And your reception desk was expecting us.'

'This is madness!' he shouted. 'If people find out that you are all here together they will believe this. You must all leave. Go!'

He turned on his heel and marched out. The room descended into chaos. A general consensus emerged that the Chair had called the meeting then decided it was too dangerous. And if it was dangerous for the Chair, it was dangerous for all.

Quickly they made their way down to the lobby again, handed in their passes and returned to a waiting line of limousines. And a press reception committee.

'What was your meeting about?' asked one reporter as cameras flashed and rolled.

'We have not had a meeting,' said someone, ducking into his car.

'We have heard that the regulator called all the banks together to discuss the financial regime after Communism.' The journalist waved a letter in his hand. 'I have a copy of the invitation here.'

'That is not true!' Wao was about to protest further when his Head of Legal pushed him into the car and shut the door behind him. As the car pulled away Wao looked at a news headline on his phone and realized that events were taking on an unstoppable momentum of their own.

Chinese markets rally as banking Chiefs meet to discuss post-communist financial regime.

129

In the airless control center, Declin monitored the progress of Operation Dragon Slay on the banks of monitors showing work in progress and selected displays from news channels and social media. 'The Great Firewall is down again,' he declared.

'Check out that online petition calling for free elections,' Cresta said, pointing at one of the monitors.

'And Falun Gong are back,' said Declin, looking at a forum for the spiritual movement that had been closed by the censors but was now discussing the systematic organ harvesting of thousands of Falun Gong prisoners over the years.

'The Hong Kong Umbrella Movement is also up again,' said Cresta, 'demanding full democracy in Hong Kong. Same thing with the Shanghai Freedom Party who have openly denounced the Politburo's corruption.'

'Punchy,' said Declin. 'Check out that Twitter call for a new Jasmine Revolution. It's already got a hundred-million followers.'

Across Chinese cyber space, websites and forums were screaming for democracy. The little that remained of the crumbling state propaganda apparatus tried a counter-offensive: denying the stories of corruption, denouncing the radicals who were undermining the Party and relaying stories of the great works done by the Party and the freedoms and happiness enjoyed by Chinese citizens.

But now the battle was between the small number of state propagandists that Cyber Command had not managed to silence, along with a few million diehard Communist Party members, on one side, while on the other there were now a billion people finally allowed to say exactly what they thought. The Chinese public had never seen anything like it.

130

Hue had not been born when the pro-democracy movement had come so close to removing the Party at Tiananmen Square. But he had seen the banned video footage of the showdown between peaceful protesters and the authorities; of the tanks rolling into the square from every approach; the troops firing indiscriminately at the trapped demonstrators. Hundreds, perhaps thousands, had been killed, and the democracy movement had fled underground and abroad.

Now the story had come full circle. The students were here again. But this time they were supported by just as many ordinary citizens. They filled Tiananmen square and the overflow ran into Zhongshan Park and right up to the gates of the Forbidden City. He climbed a lamppost to look out over the crowd. The army were standing back. Waiting for orders. Would they be sent in again?

He threw away his disguise. It was do or die now.

The girl in the yellow dress appeared. She smiled as she recognized him. 'My name is Yida.'

'I am Hue.'

He didn't know why, perhaps he was simply swept up in the general euphoria of optimism, but he kissed her gently on the cheek. She held his hand. He felt as if he had known her forever.

* * *

Cocooned inside the Imperial Garden complex of Zhongnanhai, President Li knew he needed to talk to General Wing. But he in turn was holed up in the imposing Ministry of National Defence compound in West Beijing, and insisted on meeting in neutral territory.

Li suggested the Summer Palace, and Wing's security detail selected the Heralding Spring Pavilion, which was built on a small open island near Kunming Lake's east bank. An advance party secured and cleared the site of citizens and tourists. Protocol dictated that the General Secretary of the Party and President should arrive last and so Li waited in his blacked-out sedan until informed of Wing's arrival.

He waited another fifteen minutes for good measure and walked onto the island. Both sets of guards satisfied themselves as to the security of their charges and left the two men to talk.

They sat in silence for a few moments facing the beautiful view of Longevity Hill and the lake.

'Challenging times,' said Li eventually.

'Requiring strong leadership,' Wing replied. 'Which you are lacking.'

Li glanced at Wing. 'Open your eyes. The Party has lost control of the people.'

'You have lost control,' snapped Wing. 'I will wrest it back by uniting Taiwan with the motherland.'

'You are destroying the Party. Your cyber war diversion on America has backfired. They are wreaking their revenge on the Party.'

'The Party will survive.'

'I don't share your confidence.'

'We must close our borders. To people, to financial speculation and to the internet.'

'The problem is not outside our borders. It is inside!'

'We must crush the pro-democracy movement.'

'How many are you prepared to kill?'

'However many it takes.'

'There are hundreds of millions now calling for democracy.'

'They will soon be quiet. Especially once the fighting begins in Taiwan.'

'The people do not want war with Taiwan. This will only make the Party's position more vulnerable.'

'Anyone proposing democracy once we are at war with Taiwan will be equated with the nationalists in Taiwan. They will be undermining our soldiers. They will be seen as traitors to China.'

'We must leave Taiwan alone and focus all our resources on preserving the Party.'

'I already have the mandate to attack Taiwan. I am Chairman of the Central Military Commission. You can't stop me.'

'Don't be so sure of that,' said Li. 'Your warmongering is making you enemies.'

'Only among weak-minded pacifists like yourself. The soft underbelly that has grown like a cancer through our years of peace. I am returning the country to the revolution.'

'The revolution was internal. You are taking us to war with our neighbors.'

'The first revolution was internal,' said Wing. 'Now we must bring the revolution to the whole of Asia. Expand and grow or retreat and die. There is no middle way. The Islamists understand this. Soon they will occupy the whole of the Middle East. The

Americans rule Europe. We must rule Asia.'

'You will never get the Party to vote for war with India.'

'When I am Paramount Leader the party will bend to my will.'

Li laughed at Wing's brazen declaration of ambition. 'Don't be so sure.'

131

Operation Dragon Slay was progressing well and the threat of the nuclear cyber attack appeared to have receded. Either the death of Azizi or the increased security measures, or both, seemed to have derailed whatever had been planned.

But Declin didn't want to leave anything to chance. He arranged a brain-storming session for a group that included people from Cyber Command, Chuck from the FBI financial team, Frank by video link from London. He purposely did not include a rep from Langley.

'Let's start from the top. Review everything we know.'

Declin wrote it all on a whiteboard, drawing links from one cyber attack to another. After two hours the board was full, but Declin was empty of ideas. The disappointment must have shown on his face.

'We can't give up now,' said Vin.

'But we're just not getting anywhere,' said Declin throwing his pen onto the table.

'Do not be discouraged,' Frank called through on the video link. 'Be strong and courageous. Joshua, ten twenty five, in case you're interested.'

'What did you say?' asked Declin, turning to look at Frank.

'Do not be …'

'Not the words. The verse. The numbers.'

'It's a quote from the book of Joshua, in the Old Testament.'

'The verse. The numbers,' repeated Declin.

'Verse ten, line twenty five.'

'Now that is interesting.'

'Thanks.'

Declin took out his phone and pulled up an online copy of the Koran. 'It's just possible …'

'What's going on?' asked Frank struggling to see from the other side of the Atlantic.

'Has anyone here ever read the Koran?'

All heads in the room shook side to side.

Declin snatched up a pen and a wipe and cleared a space on the whiteboard. He scribbled down the first malware identifier, forty four, forty five. 'The Koran is like the Bible. Laid out in chapters and verses. Suras.'

'And?'

'It's maybe nothing, but bear with me.' Declin scrolled through the book. 'Interesting.'

'What is it?' asked Vin.

'Give me a moment.' Declin scribbled more malware identifiers on the board and looked them up in the Koran. After a few minutes he punched the air. 'Yes!'

'What is it?' asked Vin again.

'This is it. Alleluia!'

'I think Declin just got religion,' Frank called through on the link.

'What the hell is going on, Declin?' Vin demanded.

'I've cracked the code,' said Declin pointing to the board. 'Take Forty four, forty five. That is a direction to Sura number forty four and line forty five: Like drops of oil it shall boil in their bellies. That was the code hidden as a price for Nebu stock in the fax, a few days ahead of the Earth Defence cyber attacks on Ryan Oil.'

'So that would give Cindy at the Quadra Fund the heads-up on the right timing to short Ryan Oil and start buying oil futures,' said Chuck.

'Seventy two twelve,' Declin pointed at the next number on the board, 'was the code on the fax a few days before the airline attack. So we turn to Sura seventy two and line twelve. This is the verse: 'And that we know we cannot escape Allah in the earth nor can we escape him by flight.'

'How about Plum Island?' asked Vin, edging closer to look at Declin's phone.

255

'The Plum Island malware identifier was two and sixty nine,' said Declin as he pulled up the second Sura and line sixty nine. 'He said surely she is a yellow cow, her color is intensely yellow.'

'I think maybe you are onto something.'

'The railway attack code was eighteen and ninety six,' said Declin, his heart racing as he found the relevant verse. 'Bring me iron to fill the space between the mountains. Blow until when he had made it as fire.'

'You have cracked it,' said Frank.

'Two and seventeen,' continued Declin. 'Allah took away their light and left them in utter darkness! That was the tip off for the power outage.'

'What about the nuclear attack?' asked Vin.

Declin found Sura eight and read out line fifty three. 'The Angels cause the infidels to die! Taste ye the torture of the burning.'

'That could be the attack,' Vin agreed. 'But it doesn't really help us.'

'Wait,' said Declin. 'This one is a two-part code. The second part is eighteen, fifty nine.' He found the relevant line. 'Moses said to his servant: I will not stop till I reach the confluence of the two seas.'

'What is the confluence of the two seas?' asked Vin.

'That,' Declin said, 'is the detonation site.'

132

As the *Amelia Riviera* approached the strait of Hormuz, the pilot considered relying on the auto navigation. But he was old school at heart and decided it was safer to navigate manually through such a crowded shipping lane.

However, when he tried to manoeuvre the ship, she failed to respond. She remained stuck on auto. Again and again he tried, but there was no change in path. With rising panic, he realized that the ship was going to cut right across one of the busiest shipping lanes in the world.

'Holy Fuji!' He buzzed the Captain.

'Yes,' answered a sleepy voice.

'You better get up here, Captain. We're on a collision course.'

'Change course!'

'I can't. The controls are not responding.'

'I'm on my way up.'

A minute later the captain appeared on the bridge, tucking his vest into his trousers. 'What's happening?'

'We can't control the ship,' replied the pilot. 'If I steer to port the auto-pilot over rides and steers to starboard.'

'That's not possible.' The Captain hurried over to the steering position. 'Show me.'

The pilot turned the wheel to starboard but the auto-pilot overrode him and steered the ship back to port. The Captain grabbed the auxiliary steering wheel. He tried to alter course but again the ship did not respond. 'Kill the auto-pilot.'

'I can't.'

'Well for God's sake slow her down while I think what to do.'

'I've tried that as well. I can't slow her down.'

'Use the emergency override,' ordered the Captain. 'Cut all engines.'

'I can't do that either.'

They stared at the line of vessels tailing each other in the shipping lane ahead.

'Well what the hell can we do?'

133

Declin, Chuck and Vin ran to the office of the NSA's top Islamic expert. Declin's heart was pounding and he felt damp under his shirt. Panting for breath he explained how Nebuchadnezzar's code worked using lines of the Koran.

He showed him Sura eighteen, line fifty nine. 'So tell me where exactly is this confluence of the two seas.'

'Ah!' The expert bridged the tips of his fingers and placed them under his chin. 'The literal translation of 'Majma' al-bahrayn' is 'the place where two waters meet'.'

'So we might be talking about where two rivers meet,' said Declin, and thinking of Manhattan he added, 'or a river and the sea.'

'Possibly. Scholars have debated this location for years.' He sat back in his chair and smiled as if enjoying a parlour game. 'There have been thousands of studies and books and …'

'I don't have time for a history lesson,' interrupted Declin. 'Where do you think it is?'

'Let me first say where I think it is not. I don't agree with Ibn 'Atiyyah who says it is a place near Azerbaijan.'

'So where the hell is it?'

'I think it is more likely to be near land that the Prophet walked upon.'

'That's good news,' said Vin. 'Muhammad never went to America.'

'Correct.'

'Somewhere in the Middle East then,' suggested Declin.

'Undoubtedly. Which is why I do not really trust those scholars who say it is the Cape of Good Hope, where the Atlantic meets the Pacific. Or the straits of Gibraltar. Or …'

'I don't give a shit where it isn't!' shouted Declin. 'Just tell me where it is.'

'According to Qatadah it is the meeting of the seas of Faris and Rum.'

'So where is that?'

'Nobody knows for sure.'

'But where do you think?' asked Vin, before Declin could blow his top.

'In my opinion the meeting of the two seas is where the Persian Gulf meets the Sea of Oman.'

'Map,' said Vin, looking round the room. 'Do you have a map?'

Declin pulled up a map on his phone. 'Holy shit! It's the Strait of Hormuz.'

'Correct,' said the expert. 'At least …'

'Thanks,' said Declin raising a hand to shut him up. He needed head space. Suddenly all the pieces fit together. He turned to Chuck. 'What is the life blood of the American economy?'

'Food?'

'Oil. Something like half the oil America consumes passes through the Strait of Hormuz.'

'So they're going to blow up the Strait of Hormuz,' said Chuck. 'That's why the Quadra fund was buying oil. The oil price will go through the roof.'

'It's more than that,' said Declin. 'The line talks about poisoning the blood of the Great Satan.'

'The dirty nuke. That would produce a burning radioactive oil slick that no fire crew is going to go near. The Strait would be closed for weeks, months even. With no oil, the world economy will crash.'

'It's worse even than that.'

'How bad can it get?' asked Vin.

Declin was slowly coming to terms with that question. 'If they blow up the enriched uranium with an oil tanker that could be a sufficient thermal explosion to cause the uranium to go critical. This will be the jihadists first nuclear bomb.'

134

Captain Hirohito stood weak-legged and helpless on the bridge of the *Amelia*. For once the pain in his back was forgotten. The ship had not careered into the outbound shipping lane as they had feared. In fact it had settled nicely into line on the inbound lane through the strait. All well and good, except he, the Captain, couldn't control any aspect of the ship. He couldn't even stop it.

Yet all seemed calm. Visibility was perfect, with a flat sea broken only by the smallest white ringlets from a faint breeze. In the distance the sandy islands of Qeshm and Larak baked under the high sun, while to starboard the Iranian mountains rose majestically. Several hundred yards behind the Amelia sailed a multi-speckled container ship, while perhaps a kilometer in front was a white cruise ship.

'What are we going to do?' asked the pilot, in an unusually high pitched voice.

'Stay calm,' the Captain croaked through his dry mouth.

The engines suddenly groaned and the ship veered to port. He checked the radar. She was making a new course for the outward lane some two miles away.

'We are on collision course again,' said the pilot.

'I know. I know.'

They passed a red buoy that signalled the edge of their inbound lane. He hoped for the autopilot to correct and bring them back in, but the ship sailed steadfastly forward.

'We are still on collision course,' said the pilot.

'Cut the engines.'

'I already tried.'

'Try again.'

The pilot tried and failed to cut the engines. 'I can't. What are we going to do?'

135

Declin stood at the back of the White House Situation Room, staring over the shoulders of various top brass at a screen showing a view from the *USS Ashley*. It had been sent to patrol the Strait of Hormuz and was currently racing to intercept the *Amelia Riviera*, an LPG carrier that had left Kuwaiti City Port and was now crossing between the outbound and inbound lanes.

Declin had mixed feelings. He didn't want another disaster, but he wanted to prove his theory. He hadn't convinced all those present that he'd cracked Nebuchadnezzar's code and some clearly thought the *Ashley* had been sent on a wild goose chase.

But all faces were growing ever graver as it became clear that the *Amelia* was on collision course with an ultra-large crude oil carrier.

'A nuclear technician checked the math,' said Declin to the backs of most people's heads. 'Back of the envelope she reckons the combined explosive power of the LPG ship and crude oil carrier would be a sufficient thermal explosion to turn the uranium critical.'

'So we are staring at a nuclear bomb in the making,' said President Topps.

'Unless the *Ashley* stops it,' said Declin.

Hirohito trained his binoculars on the ultra-large crude carrier. He read the name of the tanker and searched its specifications on the ship's computer. The *Caulisian* had over half a million tons displacement. 'Fully loaded that can carry six-hundred cubic meters of crude oil.'

'If we hit that with our own cargo of gas …' the pilot didn't bother to finish his sentence. They both knew such an explosion would be cataclysmic.

'Signal from the *Caulisian*,' called the radio operator.

He put the signal on speaker. 'This is the *Caulisian*. Change course immediately, *Amelia Riviera*. You are on a collision course and you are the give-way vessel. Please acknowledge.'

'Tell them we cannot comply. We do not have control of the ship.'

The operator signalled the message.

The same voice came over the radio, more urgently now. 'Cut your engines. You are still on a collision course. Acknowledge.'

The *Caulisian* let off a short blast of its horn, followed by four more. Another voice came on the radio.

'This is the *USS Ashley*. *Amelia Riviera* stop your vessel immediately. Repeat signal Lima. Stop your vessel immediately.'

Through his binoculars Hirohito could now see the *USS Ashley*, cutting rapidly through the water like a great white shark. On its signal deck a black-and-yellow checkered flag instructed them to stop.

But the *Amelia* sailed on, drawing inexorably closer to the giant *Caulisian*, which sounded another five blasts of its horn. On the impossibly high deck, her crew wrestled their lifeboats.

Hirohito realized he had forgotten about the safety of his own charges. 'Abandon ship! Get our crew overboard.'

The crew of the *Amelia* dashed for the lifeboats while Hirohito remained on the bridge.

'*Amelia Riviera*, stop your vessel immediately,' the *Ashley* called again. 'Or we will open fire.'

'I do not have control of the ship,' replied Hirohito. 'I cannot stop her or steer her.'

136

Declin listened to the exchange between the two Captains with increasing alarm. 'Can I talk to the *Amelia* captain?' he called from the back of the situation room.

'You can communicate through the *Ashley* captain.' The communications officer flicked a switch and motioned Declin to approach the microphone.

Declin pushed past the various top brass cluttering his path. There was no time for introductions. 'Tell the *Amelia* captain to disable his WIFI.'

'Roger that,' replied the *Ashley* captain. 'Captain Hirohito. Disable your WIFI.'

'Disable my what?'

'Disable your WIFI.'

'Explain he's been hacked by cyber terrorists,' said Declin. 'So he needs to disable the WIFI.'

The *Ashley* captain relayed the message.

'I don't know how.'

Declin smacked a hand on his forehead. 'Tell him to throw the uranium he is carrying overboard.'

'Roger that. Captain Hirohito, we believe you are carrying uranium on board your vessel.'

'Uranium? No.'

'Our intelligence believes the cyber terrorists smuggled uranium on board.'

'I know nothing about this. Wait. The elephant.'

'What about the elephant?'

Declin exchanged puzzled glances with the President.

'Some men asked me to transport an ornamental elephant,' Hirohito explained.

'That's it,' said Declin. 'Tell him to throw it overboard.'

'You must throw the elephant into the sea,' the Ashley captain ordered.

'I can't!' Hirohito shouted. 'It is below decks and I am on my own. It is too heavy.'

'You have to stop those ships from colliding,' Declin called out in desperation.

'I'm going to disable your ship,' the *Ashley* captain said.

On the screen a red flare spouted from the *Ashley's* gun deck followed almost instantly by an explosion and spray over the *Amelia's* bow. 'That was a warning shot. If you do not stop your vessel immediately, I will cripple your engines.'

'Go ahead,' called Hirohito.

'Clear your engine room.'

'It is clear. Go ahead.'

'No!' shouted Declin. 'It's too risky. The uranium might be in the engine room. And you are too close to the tanker. If you trigger a nuclear explosion, you'll be vaporized.'

'Roger. So what do we do. It's getting critical here.'

'Board the ship and bring her to,' shouted General Horn, grabbing hold of the microphone.

'Roger that. Captain Hirohito we are coming aboard.'

137

The *Ashley* drew alongside, rocking a bandy-legged boarding party in a figure of eight, until the crew had secured her to the larger vessel. The boarding party clambered aboard and split. Some secured lines from the ship to the *Ashley*, others disappeared below deck while another group ran up to the bridge.

The *Ashley* captain was the first through the door. 'Where is your WIFI router?'

'What is a WIFI router?' Hirohito asked. He knew about ships, not technology.

As Hirohito watched the American sailors search frantically over the bridge, the *Caulisian* appeared to be within touching distance.

'We are going to collide! We should abandon ship.'

'Got it!' shouted someone. 'WIFI disabled.'

'Reverse engines!'

Hirohito slammed the *Amelia's* engines full astern. With an explosion of wild foaming water, the *Amelia* started to slow. But it was still closing on the *Caulisian.*

'We are too late!'

'Fifty meters,' someone called.

The *Ashley* was also pulling back and the *Amelia* shuddered and groaned under the competing forces.

'Twenty meters.'

'Ten.'

The grinding continued as the *Caulisian's* huge hull towered over the bow of the *Amelia.*

'Twenty meters.'

'Thirty!'

'Forty.'

Cheers rose from the crew.

The Captain of the *Ashley* called back to his ship. 'Collision averted. *Amelia* secured.'

* * *

High fives and hugs circulated round the situation room.

'That was close,' said General Horn.

'Well done, Declin Lehane,' said the President, smacking Declin on his back with a strength that belied his years. 'Good work, everyone. The cyber threat is I think under control. Now let's get back to work hitting the people who started this cyber war. The Chinese Communist Party is hanging by a thread. Let's go cut it.'

138

As Declin and Cresta had anticipated, China had, as a last resort, shut internet access with the outside world.

'We need to use the agents on the ground in China now,' said Declin. 'Nothing much more we can do from here.'

On a signal from Cyber Command, agents secreted around China uploaded various cyber mischief. Soon the country was reading a fake interview with the Minister of Trade saying that following free political elections it would be time for great economic freedoms. Another piece that looked to have come from the Secretary of the Political and Legislative Affairs Committee instructed the police and all involved in public security that they must no longer arrest anyone for making political statements against the Party. All peaceful protest was acceptable.

'I think this is the time for the *piece de resistance*,' said Declin, referring to the secret weapon that they had been keeping until last. Cyber Command had pushed a Trojan app onto Chinese computers and cell phones, which were now primed to accept a broadcast from Cyber Command of President Li addressing the nation. It had been created using real footage and recordings of Li's voice and was utterly believable, even to Declin who knew it was fake.

Cyber Command operatives in Shanghai overrode the broadcast onto local TV signals. The clip soon went viral and was carried throughout the six-hundred-million smartphone users in the country. Local operatives also hacked into the China Central TV news channel, waited for a suitable pause in the program, cut the transmission and replaced it with the clip.

'The strong one-party state was vital in securing the economic progress of China in recent times. But today our country stands at the edge of a new era. It is time for more discussion about the best way to govern this greatest country in the world. This will not be western-style, corrupt, capitalist democracy that has been shown to fail. But the time is right for a Chinese-style of socialist democracy. Strong central political leadership running the state as well as local level leadership working for the local interests in our differing zones such as Shanghai, Hong Kong, and our soon to be peacefully reunited brothers and sisters in Taiwan. One country but many systems. And the people will have free elections to choose their leaders. It is time for change.'

139

Hue was once more on the top of his lamppost from where he could look over the crowd at the Wujing standing beside their armored vehicles.

They looked somehow less threatening than usual and he realized that their riot shields and batons were hanging loosely by their sides. Suddenly they turned round and walked away, with their armored vehicles following behind like pet trolls.

The crowd began cheering.

Hue climbed down from the lamppost and Yida hugged him as he returned to the ground.

'We have won,' she said. 'The Wujing are moving away!'

'It could just be a tactical retreat,' Hue warned. 'They may come back in more force later.'

Hue checked other reports on his phone. It soon became clear that the Wujing were heading away from the crowds, west down Xichang'an Jie and Qianmen. However it was also reported that a part of the force had peeled off and arrived at Xinhua Gate to re-enforce those units already protecting the party leadership in Zhongnanhai.

'It doesn't matter what they do now,' she said. 'The people want change. It is happening.'

'But will President Li allow it?' asked Hue. He was very afraid, and it must have shown in his face.

She took his hand. 'Whatever happens, we must remain strong.'

140

Declin was head down at his desk, reading opinions on what would be the Communist Party's next move, when he felt a hand on his shoulder.

He turned to see Vin.

'Let's go get a coffee.'

'I'm too busy,' said Declin.

'Not too busy for what I'm going to show you.'

They grabbed coffee from a machine and found an empty room. 'This better be good.'

'I've joined some dots on your Black Chamber puzzle.' Vin opened an encrypted file on his laptop.

Declin stared with alarm at the names of the top brass Vin had been monitoring. 'Before you start, run me through the protocols you used.'

Vin smiled disarmingly. 'So we used section two-fifteen to collect the calls made and received by Azizi who, even though he is of course dead, remains a relevant person to an authorized investigation.'

'We already had those calls.'

'You had them for the cyber terrorism investigation. We started a fresh insider-trading investigation. Cast the net wider. We got a court order to monitor text messages over one-hundred-eighty days, and that's where we found the messages to his handler.'

'We already knew about Biggerstaff.'

'You did, and you couldn't investigate a CIA agent. But how were us simple Feebs to know Biggerstaff was a CIA operative?' Vin smiled again. 'It was just a name to us. So we managed to get a court order to monitor his texts.'

'Oh boy,' said Declin. 'We've been doing surveillance on a CIA agent. Calvara will just love that. Go on.'

'We used location tracking on every number on Biggerstaff's phone, ostensibly to see if he was part of an insider-trading ring. We then looked for patterns to find out who he's been meeting.'

Vin started to scroll down through pages of overlapping colored circles. 'Take a look at this,' he said, pulling up a chart. 'It shows us the times that Biggerstaff is at the Holiday Inn near Langley. And the overlap shows how often he is there at the same time as Jennifer Lawrence.'

'Who's she?'

'An intern.'

'So what's the relevance?'

'He's having an affair. He's got a wife and two kids. You can use that as leverage.'

'That's the sort of trick Langley gets up to,' said Declin. 'But it's not my style.'

Vin shrugged.

'Then the table you want is this one showing Biggerstaff regularly meeting offsite with the people on this list.'

Declin looked down at the list. Deputy Director Operations, Lawson Ladyman. Deputy Director Analysis, John Charles. There was also a subsidiary list showing the names of others who had on occasion met with them there. The China Controller, Director Stotton from London and Karl Asimov.

Declin let out a long whistle. 'That's a real who's-who of the intelligence community.'

'They meet at the Washington Golf and Country club,' explained Vin. 'Membership there is a who's-who of the great and powerful in Washington. They could be meeting other contacts that Biggerstaff doesn't have on his cell phone. But I'd need another court approval to start looking into that.'

'You'd need probable cause before a judge would let you near those guys. No crime in meeting up with colleagues at a country club. Besides, these guys are pros. None of them are going to say anything incriminating on a cell phone.'

'In that case I'm not sure where we can go from here.'

Declin studied the list of names again. 'Who would you say is the strongest link on this list? The most likely to feel invulnerable.'

After a few seconds Vin replied: 'Ladyman. I'd guess Ladyman.'

'I'd guess Ladyman too. So let's shake him down.'

'You can't shake down the Deputy Director Operations of the CIA. He's just not going to be worried by an FBI special agent.'

'I can't. But I have a friend who can.'

* * *

Dear Deputy Director Ladyman,

Pursuant to enquiries following the publication of the Chilcot report, I would be grateful if you could spare some of your valuable time to talk to me, strictly off the record, about the Black Chamber.

It is clear now that the Black Chamber includes members of MI6 and I would be interested to know whether you have identified these individuals. In return for your help I will be able to give you some useful insights that I have recently unearthed. In particular I have discovered that the Black Chamber has been manufacturing a case for regime change in China. I have identified at least six of its members who are currently serving within your organization. I can tell you more when we meet.

I look forward to meeting you at your earliest convenience.

Detective Inspector Frank Brighouse, City of London Police.

Frank hit send and smiled as he imagined the reaction when Deputy Director Ladyman received the email. If Declin was right about the Black Chamber, Ladyman would be reaching for the panic button.

141

President Li ruffled through his papers as they waited for the last two members of the Standing Committee to arrive. Li knew of course that they would not be doing so. He had arranged for their planes to be diverted to Kunming in the far south. But he frowned disapprovingly and checked the wall clock for the benefit of General Wing, who was behaving in similar fashion.

Though in Wing's case the anxiety was genuine. Li knew that Wing would not be able to make his putsch without the backing of the two missing members.

'We have waited long enough for Qishan and Zhengsheng,' said Li eventually. 'They are already half-an-hour late. I propose we proceed.'

'We must not start until everyone is present,' Wing insisted.

'We have a quorum,' said Li. 'And we have important business to attend to. Let's put it to the vote. A show of hands if you support going ahead with the meeting without Qishan and Zhengsheng.'

The motion was carried by four votes to three.

'We must now make two historic decisions. First, do we press ahead with the invasion of Taiwan, or stand down our armies. Second, do we allow free elections with the Party standing on its past record, or do we crack down on the pro-democracy movement.'

'It is not a movement,' said Wing. 'Only a handful of radicals.'

Li turned to the Secretary of Central Commission for Discipline Inspection. 'What do you think? Are we facing demands from a handful of radicals as Wing said. Or is this now, as I believe, a full-blown revolution of the majority.'

The Secretary gave an unambiguous analysis showing that there were hundreds of millions of citizens actively calling for free elections.

'They are like sheep,' said Wing. 'Led by a handful of radicals. Once we arrest the ring leaders they will go back to grazing in the grass. And when we take back Taiwan they will all believe in the Party again. We are only where we are because of inaction and weak leadership.'

An aide standing on a back wall coughed to get Wing's attention and handed him a slip of paper with a handwritten message.

Li suspected the message informed Wing that his two allies would not be arriving anytime soon. When Wing looked up from the note and stared at him, he knew that Wing understood what was about to happen.

Li signalled an aide to open the door. Four guards marched in and stood around Wing, hands crossed in front of their bodies.

'You are under arrest, General Zhang Wing,' President Li announced. 'Your warmongering has turned the Chinese people against the Party. You are charged with counter-revolutionary crimes.'

Wing looked desperately around the group. 'If I go this will be the end. The end of the Party. The end of the Motherland. Do you want that?'

Li's supporters stared impassively. Wing's own two men averted their eyes. They knew he had lost. They were looking after themselves now.

The guards gently lifted Wing to his feet and lead him out of the room. Li walked to the window and looked down at the ten identical, unmarked black sedans waiting below. Wing was secreted into the middle car before they all pulled away in random order to confuse any attempted rescuers. Once outside, the cars would break up and head for different locations. Even Li did not know where the Secret Police would take Wing. He did know that he would never be seen again.

142

Connelly was watching the news on China when Declin and Vin called on him to present the evidence for the Black Chamber. He hit mute. 'Okay guys. What have you got?'

Vin deferred to Declin.

'We believe that a group of senior executives in the CIA have colluded and manipulated intelligence and ignored intelligence that warned of the attacks, all with the purpose of forcing the country to take action against the Chinese state and push for regime change.'

'Doesn't seem like a problem to me. We want regime change.'

'They deliberately mislead the President,' Declin explained. 'That's not just a problem. That is criminal.'

Connelly offered his large palms up to the ceiling. 'So where's the evidence?'

'First off, Langley knew all about the cyber attacks months before they occurred. It could have stopped them, but it allowed them to go ahead in order to turn opinion, in particular the opinion of the President, against China.'

'Who says?'

'The Chinese cyber contact who has been helping us says he told his contact in Beijing about the cyber attacks months ago. China control claim they didn't act because they couldn't verify the source.'

'Maybe they couldn't.'

'Once the attacks started coming in as predicted you'd think they'd let Cyber Command know.'

'Maybe.' Connelly shrugged. 'I hope you've got more to offer than that.'

'We think Biggerstaff knew what Azizi was up to, but didn't pass that on because he didn't want the attacks stopped. Then when Financial Crime came across Azizi via the insider trading route they were told by you to stand down the investigation.'

Connelly raised an eyebrow. 'You suggesting I'm tied up in this conspiracy?'

'No,' said Declin, with conviction. 'But Ladyman is. He told you to stand down Chuck. He also told the British to stop their investigations.'

'He was protecting Azizi, who is an agency asset.'

'He was protecting him while he wanted to keep him in play. But then when the British were ready to capture him, Ladyman had him shot so he didn't spill the beans.'

'Again. Any evidence for that?'

'Not yet,' Declin admitted. 'And Asimov is tied up in this as well.'

'How do you figure that?'

'He has slowed down the cyber enquiry at every turn. He pushed for us to move on Earth Defence before we had gathered evidence. He ordered a drone strike in Waziristan and the raid in Latakia, both of which stopped us from gathering real-time intelligence. Plus someone senior at Langley let JC know he didn't want the prisoner in Islamabad to live. At every turn they were hindering the investigation so that the attacks kept coming.'

Connelly ran his fingers through his hair and sat back in his chair. 'Even if you're right. And I'm not saying you are. That's all circumstantial. You can't do anything with it.'

'We also have this.' Declin opened up the file of phone records. 'We've been monitoring the phone records of certain people we think are members of the Black Chamber.'

Connelly's eyes widened as he read the names. 'Did you get authorization?'

'Of course.'

'How? You've got a Senator, the Deputy Director of Operations of the CIA, and the Director of National Intelligence.'

'We were investigating the insider trading, and we didn't use their full titles.'

'Plus I know a judge on a quiet circuit who'll sign off anything that might hit the establishment,' explained Vin.

'Oh boy,' muttered Connelly.

'So you can see a group of them regularly go to the Washington Golf and Country club at the same times,' continued Declin.

'No crime in that.'

'We also sent in this email to Ladyman.' Declin showed him Frank's email. 'Right after Ladyman received that email from Frank he made a series of short calls to the other members of the Black Chamber. The next day they all met at the club.'

'What do you guys expect me to do?' asked Connelly.

'Give us your backing to make arrests.'

Connelly chewed his lower lip.

'This one has come straight from the Too Hard Box. These guys are the establishment. They'll have the best legal defence money can buy. If you prosecute them and fail, and in all probability you will fail, then it's career over.'

Declin exchanged a glance with Vin. 'We'll take that risk.'

143

The pro-democracy strikes had shut most of Beijing's manufacturing and dramatically curtailed transport, so for a change the air was clear enough for Hue to see right across Tiananmen Square to the huge screens on all four sides.

Ordinarily these would be displaying propaganda shows of military prowess, commercial success, and the smiling, happy masses. But surprisingly, Hue hoped portentously, the screens were full of the natural beauty of China: the snaking Great Wall; the muddy-green Yellow River; the limestone rock spires of Guilin.

Suddenly the members of the Standing Committee appeared on the ramparts above the Forbidden City. Rumors of a coup had been raging and Hue studied the composition of the committee.

'General Wing is missing,' said Yida.

Hue had not told her that the General was his father. Some instinct told him he was dead and he felt strangely at peace with that thought. 'Wing's supporters Qishan and Zhengsheng are also missing.'

'So there has been a coup.'

President Li moved to the microphone as spontaneous, hopeful cheering erupted from some in the crowd. 'The nation of China is the greatest nation on earth. This has been achieved through the hard work of the people of China; the greatest people on earth.'

He paused to accept the customary polite applause.

'And by the wise leadership of the Party from the earliest days of the revolution up until the present.'

This claim was met with silence.

'Today the Party has removed an unwise member from office. General Wing wanted to lead us into war with Taiwan. But we will not fight our brothers and sisters. I have instructed the armed forces to stand down. There will be no war. We still want reunification with our lost family in Taiwan. But this will be done through peaceful means.'

As cheering broke out through the square Yida and Hue hugged.

'So what of these calls for democracy?' President Li asked. 'What shall your wise and glorious leadership do about this?'

'Give us freedom! Freedom!'

Chanting and shouting continued for almost five minutes before President Li put up his hand to call for quiet.

'You already have freedom! A man can walk from Beijing to Kunming without needing to ask the permission of Imperialist rulers, as happened in the past. He can be a doctor or a soldier if he wishes, unlike our forefathers, who were only allowed to be farmers or opium cows. He can have greater prosperity than any man ever achieved in our long history. All this has come about because we had the stability of the Party. And so we could plan and build for the future. For your future. Nobody can deny this.'

'This is just the same old party lines,' said Yida as the crowd grew restless.

'However. Now is the right time for a new style of government.'

Stunned silence gave way to cautious clapping around the square. Yida took hold of Hue's hand.

'The people's Communist Party of China is proud of its track record in government,' President Li continued. 'I am confident that when the people have the choice to vote for their leaders they will not go down the route of other new democracies and vote in chaos. Look at history: Russia, Yugoslavia, The Middle East. They voted out the ruling party that had made them strong. They voted for change and saw their countries descend into chaos. I am confident you will not make the same mistake. I am confident you will vote for your Communist Party; the people's party. But you will decide. You will have your free elections.'

144

A wedding reception was taking advantage of the first warm day of spring and serving cocktails on the veranda at the Washington Golf and Country Club. As the guests mingled over iced teas with lemonade and bourbon, the conversation bounced between the wedding and the news of the collapse of communism in China.

Declin could have done with a shot to steady his nerves. Instead he drank from a water fountain to relieve his bone-dry mouth and wiped his hands dry on his trouser knees. He looked around at the small army of bureau agents he had gathered. They looked equally nervous.

'Okay guys. Let's be polite but firm. No matter how senior the people we arrest today they are not above the law of the land. So let's be confident in our work.'

With that he lead the way to the Woodrow Wilson room. The security detail walked a few paces down the corridor to meet them.

'Where do you think you're all going?'

'I have a warrant to search that room,' said Declin, showing the guard the warrant.

The guard gave it a cursory glance and handed it back. 'And you are?'

'Special Agent Declin Lehane,' he announced, showing his badge.

'Well Special Agent Lehane, you're aware of who is in that room. I'm not going to let a bunch of armed feebs go busting in.'

'You want us to leave our weapons with you?'

'I want you to go back wherever you came from.'

'Leave your weapons here,' Declin ordered his men.

'Why?' asked Vin. 'Just because this knuckle head says so.'

'Because I said so.'

Reluctantly, the agents dropped their guns on a table. Declin pushed passed the security detail, opened the door and entered the room. Inside, people were gathered into couples and small groups. Ladyman and Asimov sipped fizz by the white marble fireplace. Biggerstaff and the Chinese controller picked at hors d'oeuvres in leather armchairs. By a window offering a view of the first tee, Senator Martin was holding court.

One by one, as they became aware of the intrusion, they stopped their conversation and turned to look at Declin.

'Special Agent Declin Lehane of the FBI,' he announced holding up his badge. 'I have a warrant to search these premises.'

'For what?' asked Ladyman.

'For evidence of insider trading.'

Astonished gasps of disbelief and then laughter broke out.

'Go right ahead,' said Ladyman.

Senator Martin smirked as he made some joke that was clearly at Declin's expense.

'Each of you will now be searched by one of my agents,' Declin called out loudly. 'You will be relieved of your cell phone and any other evidence as seen fit. Anyone resisting this will be placed under immediate arrest.'

To emphasise the point, Declin uncoupled his cuffs and marched over to Senator Martin. 'Empty your pockets, please senator.'

The senator hesitated, shrugged and did as he was told. Declin bagged and recorded the evidence and the rest of his team took that as the cue to do the same around the room.

'You know there is no insider trading ring here,' said the senator. 'You are simply taking a shot in the dark.'

'We'll see,' replied Declin, surprised that the senator was talking without a lawyer present. 'What's the celebration?'

'We're celebrating the collapse of communist China. Would you care to join us?'

'I guess we should toast the success of the Black Chamber,' said Declin. 'Tell me, did you have a similar celebration party after you managed regime change in Iraq?'

But the senator didn't flinch. He wasn't falling for that. 'You won't find anything that contravenes our rights under the first amendment to freedom of expression and association.'

'We'll see about that too,' said Declin.

145

Hue's mother invited him round for a celebratory dinner of bean curd with a peasant's portion of shredded pork, for which she had overcompensated with chilli sauce.

Hue sucked in his cheeks at the first sting.

'Too hot?' his mother asked. 'But you like it hot.'

'It's fine Mama. It's just right.' He ate another spoonful as proof, and they finished the meal in silence.

Hue took the plates to the sink and washed them by hand.

They moved into the sitting room. He noticed that the picture of his father was no longer on the mantelpiece.

'You know that General Wing has been removed.'

'Yes. I saw on the news.'

'He is probably dead.'

She nodded, but made no comment.

'I have met a girl,' he announced, surprising himself. 'Her name is Yida and we are in love.'

'Now that is a cause for celebration,' she said producing some rice wine from a cupboard.

She poured them both a drink. 'Ganbei!'

'Ganbei!' Hue replied, before taking a drink.

'You will be getting married?'

It was early days and Hue hadn't really thought about that. 'I hope so, yes.'

'Soon I will have a daughter,' she said quietly.

She smiled as her eyes filled with tears.

146

Mickey raised his glass. 'To my health and your good fortune.'

Frank chinked his own against it. 'Last time I seem to remember you said it the other way round.'

'I did, but I figure I'm in a lot worse shape than you and you're the one without a job.'

'Actually they offered me the job back,' Frank replied. 'Though I'm not sure I'll take it. Might try pastures new.'

'What would you do instead? Banking!?'

'No. And not trading veg either.'

'What about the tribunal you were facing for carrying on with the Quadra investigation?'

'The charge has been dropped. Apparently President Topps put in a call to the Prime Minister.'

'Really?' Mickey wiped some froth off his top lip. 'You do move in high circles.'

'Declin moves in high circles,' Frank corrected him. 'So what next for Mickey Summer?'

'Back to selling veg on the market. I'm happy with it, I guess.'

'Really?' Frank looked about as convinced as Mickey was himself. 'I'm sorry about the money, Mickey. That we never managed to get you a reward. But without a prosecution we just can't do it.'

'I played a small part in freeing a billion people from a totalitarian regime. As did you. That's reward enough, I reckon.'

Frank raised his glass. 'I'll drink to that as well. And at least you didn't get prosecuted yourself for insider trading. To be honest, Mickey, you got away with murder. I had to fight like hell to stop DI Stone from going after you.'

'After all I've done.'

'I know.'

'Just don't tell him about my China trade.'

Frank put his glass down on the table. 'What China trade?'

Mickey winked but said nothing.

'What China trade?' Frank asked again.

'Well I did deliver Declin the means to bring down China's Communist Party. What do you expect a trader like me to do with that information?'

'You didn't?'

'Course I did. Everything I had I put on contracts for differences on the Shanghai Index. Made out like a bandit. House all paid for now.'

'Now that,' Frank pushed a finger in front of Mickey's eyes, 'really is trading on inside information.'

'But who's to know?'

147

Declin waited outside Calvara's office for thirty minutes. When he was finally shown in he realized Calvara was moving out. The walls were bare of paintings. The telescope was gone. Three dark-plastic storage boxes were piled one on top of the other on the floor in front of the cleared desk.

'Thanks for coming.'

'No problem,' said Declin, still uncertain why Calvara had asked to see him.

'I just wanted to say thank you.'

Declin certainly hadn't expected that. 'For what?'

'For cracking the cyber threat, heading off the nuke, finding the Chinese Cyber Brigade exploits.' He laughed. 'You've had a busy time of it.'

'We all have.'

'And most of all, thank you for uncovering the Black Chamber.'

'I'm sorry if that's causing you trouble.'

'Don't be sorry. You may not manage to prosecute them in any meaningful manner but at least you've exposed the network and cleaned up what was a stain on the agency. I also want you to know that despite the Black Chamber I firmly believe that the Central

Intelligence Agency is the finest intelligence service in the world.'

Declin said nothing, just returned Calvara's stare.

'And I hope that someday you'll feel the same.'

The door opened and the secretary called in. 'It's time for you to go, Leon.'

Calvara picked an envelope off the table and put it in his pocket. He looked around the room one last time, sniffed and walked to the door. 'Mustn't keep the President waiting.'

JoshLehane@us.army.mil sun, October 22 2006 @ 18:46
To: PJD21@Lehane.com

Dear Mom and Declin,

I'm writing this letter because I couldn't say what I wanted to over the phone. Words got stuck. Easier to write. I want to say I love you both so much. You were both always there for me even when I was a jerk.

Anyhow. We are flushing out Ramadi (second time round!). Lot of red on red doing the job for us. But Hajis hit us with Chlorine bombs yesterday. This is a big battle. We already sustained 10 casualties and one KIA.

I don't want you to worry about me. I'm not afraid to die. We all gotta go sometime. Maybe this isn't the greatest war. We all know a lot of armchair experts back in Fort Living Room are saying we shouldn't be here at all. Sometimes I wonder as well. But hey – Shut up and Color.

But if I don't come home for any reason I want you both to be proud of me and to know I will always be with you. And don't go beating up on the guys who sent us to war. They're doing the best job they can just like I am. I have to believe that.

Your loving son and big bro,

Josh

About the Author

Michael Crawshaw grew up in Leeds. He studied Chemistry at Manchester University and passed up the opportunity to spend his life researching metal benzoate compounds in favour of a spell in the City. He decided to give it two years. Sixteen years later he got out, having worked for several of the world's leading investment banks.

His first novel *To Make a Killing* was published in 2012. When he's not writing, Mike devotes his time to the charity *Hands Together – Tiplyang Project,* **www.handstogether.org.uk**

Acknowledgements

Thanks to the inspirational Lynne McCallister for ruthlessly attacking the first draft. To the meticulous Helen Judge, who cut the word count by thousands, plus Helen Wilkinson, Barbara Gibbs, Richard Hewittson, Louise Pugh, John Newsome, Frank Crawshaw and Dave Stacey. Also Joelle White, whose translation into French revealed a number of mistakes that the rest of us had all missed, Deyan Audio for Americanizing the English text, and Michael Roscoe at Broadpen Books.

34810031R00167

Printed in Great Britain
by Amazon